THE
BOOKS OF
RACHEL

THE BOOKS OF RACHEL

JOEL GROSS

AN AUTHORS GUILD BACKINPRINT.COM EDITION

The Books of Rachel

AN AUTHORS GUILD BACKINPRINT.COM EDITION
Published by iUniverse, Inc.

For information address:
iUniverse, Inc.
2021 Pine Lake Road, Suite 100
Lincoln, NE 68512
www.iuniverse.com

Originally published by Seaview

ISBN-13: 978-0-595-12820-4
ISBN-10: 0-595-12820-3

Printed in the United States of America

FOR *Linda Rachel*

We shall hear the angels, we shall see the whole sky all diamonds, we shall see how all earthly evil, all our sufferings are drowned in the mercy that will fill the whole world. And our life will grow peaceful, tender, sweet as a caress.

ANTON PAVLOVICH CHEKHOV

THE
BOOKS OF
RACHEL

PROLOGUE: JUNE 1979

Ninety miles north of New York City a family gathered to celebrate a marriage. Relatives greeted each other in German, in French, in Spanish, in the English of London's Mayfair district, in the Yiddish English of New York's Lower East Side. A wedding canopy had been erected on the great lawn at the rear of the Kane house, allowing the wedding party a vista of pine trees, a shining pond, and the blue, endlessly broad waters of a distant lake.

The groom, a tall young man in a white suit, walked about the beautiful lawn with grave steps, allowing a cousin of the bride's to introduce him to members of the family. The bride, Rachel Kane, waited for the start of the ceremony that would release her from the surveillance of brothers and mother and aunts and cousins. Rachel sat on a couch in a front room of the house, so that she would catch no glimpse of her groom.

About an hour before the ceremony was scheduled to begin, this room began to empty. Cousins squeezed her wrists, her brothers kissed her cheeks, her mother cried over the fact of impending joy. Rachel knew that this was the time reserved for her to be alone with her father, to accept the gift that was her birthright. He stood in a corner of the room, sober and self-absorbed, waiting for the last relative to leave. In his hand he held a black jewel case.

"I'm sorry to be so dramatic," said her father, when they were alone.

"It is dramatic, Daddy," said Rachel. "I can't wait to see it."

Suddenly, she saw that her father's eyes were filled with tears. The bride got to her feet and went over to comfort him. "I'm all right," said her father.

"You were thinking about your sister?"

"My sister," he admitted. "But not just her. More. It's incredible, you know. This." He indicated the black case in his hands. "It's not just my sister you were named for."

"I know," said Rachel. "It was my favorite story when I was little."

"Think of it. She was named for a Rachel, *that* Rachel was named for a Rachel, all the way back. Longer than we can imagine."

"Do you really think we came from Spain?" said Rachel suddenly.

"I don't know. The name of the stone is Spanish. That is the legend, isn't it? But if we did, it hardly matters. We've been all over Europe, moving around for five hundred years. And always, there was a Rachel. For as long as the family has been in the diamond trade, for longer than we have records, there must have been a Rachel. This stone was always for Rachel, and now it's for you."

Her father opened the jewel case, and Rachel looked into the heart of a flawless, table-cut, sixty-carat white diamond. It was her wedding day. She was nervous, exhilarated, enervated; her mind ran with a thousand thoughts. But the stark beauty of this perfect stone cut through every fragment of her brain, clamoring for attention. Of course she had seen larger diamonds, diamonds more brilliant, more finely cut; she was a Kane, and she'd looked at the fire reflecting from South African brilliants before they'd been passed on to Cartier's or Harry Winston to sell to a sheik or a movie star or a king. But this stone was old. Its brilliance lay fettered behind an old cut, the old-fashioned table-cut of museum-piece diamonds, brought from India to the Renaissance courts of European kings. Its beauty was in its color, the rarest of whites; but much more than this, its beauty was in its age, in its story. It was as if Rachel had been presented with something from out of her own past, something her subconscious had always known existed, something that she had only to look out to to realize that it was hers by birthright.

Rachel reached out and touched the stone in the jewel case. All her senses rioted at the touch. Some part of her brain seemed to reach back, to search time and space, to search the unknown reaches of ancestral memory for the story of this stone, her stone, the stone of the Rachel and all the Rachels for whom she was named.

Her father's voice ran, and she tried to concentrate on his narration of the stone's history, but the touch of her diamond, already warmed by the contact of her flesh, continued to twist and roil the unknown, ineluctable past in an unreachable part of her mind.

"The Spanish name," she said finally, speaking in a whisper. "Tell me again. What is the name of the stone? The old name?"

"Cuheno," said her father, and the forgotten syllables penetrated her consciousness like a sharp retort.

"Cuheno," said Rachel, giving the name a Spanish lilt.

Her father looked at her oddly. "Are you all right?" he said.

"Cuheno," she said, feeling her heart race. All her muscles tensed, as if to be ready for a shock. A tremor of knowledge, a trembling of pain, stood on the verge of consciousness.

Jewish folklore tells of an angel who comes to whisper every last detail of the Torah to the baby in its mother's womb, only to reappear in the split second before birth and awareness, to erase all the knowledge so easily won. Rachel felt as if a flood of knowledge were upon her, held back by a flimsy barrier, a barrier that shuddered at the sound of this name.

Rachel's father kept talking. "That's probably the main reason a lot of the family think we come from Spain. It's just as possible as anything else. The Cuheno diamond is definitely a pre–sixteenth-century cut. Maybe Cuheno was the name of the man who cut the stone. Or maybe it was the family name five hundred years ago."

"Cuheno," said Rachel again, and her father rushed toward her because she seemed about to fall to the floor. He took hold of the young bride and helped her to the couch, and looked in wonder at her green, awestruck eyes. "Cuheno," said Rachel for the last time, clutching the stone, and then the barrier broke, and all she had time to say was, "I remember," and then she collapsed. Knowledge rushed through her like the wind of a spirit, like an ineffable, fast-receding dream. She remembered, she dreamed, she wandered through half a millennium holding her diamond— and she awoke moments later with no more knowledge of her ancestors than that of the newborn baby, screaming of its loss of wisdom and home to the world.

PART ONE

SPAIN, 1484

CHAPTER ONE

The Cuheno diamond was discovered by a slave, one of twenty thousand men, women, and children beating the earth at the mine of Kollur, in the kingdom of Golconda in central India, in 1475. The slave was seventeen, illiterate, exhausted from eight hours in the sun, weak from lack of food and the festering sores on his bare back where the overseer had whipped him two days before. The diamond was embedded in a large, gray stone, much too big to swallow or conceal under his loincloth. He picked up his heavy wooden stick and smashed it into the stone, but the diamond remained in place and the stone didn't shatter.

Dropping his stick, the slave picked up the stone and began to run. Other slaves looked up from their work of beating the earth with sticks, winnowing it with baskets, looking for rough diamonds on their hands and knees in the sun-dried sand, but none called out to him. This was not the first time a slave had gone berserk. An overseer shouted at him to stop, and when this command went unheeded, gave chase. The slave ran well, skirting the deep pits dug in the earth, ignoring the harsh rocks cutting at his calloused feet, running toward the setting sun. He had been working on the periphery of the great mining area, but, even so, there were hundreds of overseers ringing the area through which he would have to pass to freedom.

One of these overseers was a young man from a family of gem merchants. When the slave was finally brought down by the pursuing overseer, this second overseer helped in killing the runaway. That done, he looked at the diamond embedded in the stone and told the other overseer that they had better keep it for themselves. The first overseer agreed, and a week later they set out on the long journey to Goa, on the west coast of India. Both were waylaid by bandits, and killed.

The diamond, though it had been carefully chiseled free of its stone, was still encased in a dull covering. Even in the brightest sunshine, the gem hardly shone. The bandits sold it for a pittance in Bassein, to a merchant who had no idea of its worth. Calling it a rare opaque diamond, he sold it along with a score of other gems to a wandering Chinese jeweler, who had a suspicion of its true worth. The Chinese took passage with a group of his countrymen on a junk that had deposited cloves, mace, and nutmeg from the East Indies in Goa and Bassein and was now returning to Malacca. There, the jeweler waited five weeks for passage back to the Chinese mainland, and finally took a chance with a Muslim trader. The Muslim ship captain threw the Chinese overboard after five hours at sea, and tossed the jewels into an old sack.

The Muslim traded horses from Mesopotamia and copper from Arabia for jade and spices, and returned to Malacca more than a year later. A Hindu dealer in jade and emeralds in Malacca convinced him that the diamond in his possession was practically worthless, and the captain included it in a large sale of jade as a gesture of goodwill. The Hindu took the diamond across the Bay of Bengal to Calicut and sold it to an Arab for very little, but the payment was in gold.

The diamond, still in its dull covering, was sold by the Arab to an East African merchant aboard the dhow that took them across the Arabian Sea to Oman. The East African was afraid to try the route to Baghdad up the Persian Gulf, and instead shipped out with another East African going round the coast of Arabia to the Red Sea. The East African ship was attacked by pirates near the approach to Aden, and all aboard were slain.

An Egyptian bought the diamond in Aden, and took it up the Red Sea to Alexandria. Here, at the temporary marketplace of the Venetian traders, the diamond was sold to an old jeweler from Ferrara. Another European then in Alexandria, a young Spanish Jew named Judah Cuheno, bought the diamond from this old Italian for five times what he had paid only days before. Even so, the price was ridiculously cheap. Beneath the dull skin of the enormous stone was a perfect white diamond; of this the young man was certain. If he could return safely to Zaragoza, to the freedom of his workshop, he would remove every last bit of ugliness that prevented the fire and beauty of this diamond from revealing itself to the world.

Judah Cuheno bought passage on a galley ship returning to Venice. He had no trouble with the ship's crew, or the merchants and pilgrims returning from the Holy Land, because he always traveled in the guise of a Catholic. There was a Jew on board with whom he would have liked to speak—a religious man from Provence, returning, like the Catholics, from Jerusalem—but Judah reasoned that it was not worth the risk. The Jew would not like the fact that he was posing as a Gentile, that he ate of the Gentile's food, and that he had risked his life to cross the world not for religious but for commercial gains. It would be difficult enough for Judah, a wellborn Spanish gentleman, to bear the insults of Jew-baiting inferiors; it would be intolerable to be revealed as a Jew and be reviled by both Gentiles and the only other Jew aboard.

Judah had spent nearly eight months at Alexandria before buying the diamond. He had spent six months getting to Alexandria from his native city of Zaragoza, and on the return trip, he had to put up with an interminable delay in booking passage to Barcelona from Genoa, so that when he had finally completed the journey from Barcelona to Zaragoza, riding with a company of government archers, he had been absent from his family for nearly two years.

It was an hour before sunrise when he arrived at the Cuheno house, but he hesitated not at all about waking every last member of his family, no matter what the hour. The servants who came to the door carried torches and swords. Even through the dark and his thick beard, they knew him at once.

"Master Judah," they said, and he had to order them to rise. They were Moors, and they wanted to remove his boots and wash his feet in the long-honored welcoming custom of their people, but Judah had no time for this.

"Wake my father," he said. "Bring wine to his study." And then he washed his face and hands, muttering the blessing: "Blessed are you, Lord, our God, King of the Universe, who bestows favor upon the undeserving just as you have bestowed favor upon me." Judah didn't think about the words he uttered. He was back home, in the house of his father, and this was the prayer one said after a safe journey home. It was as automatic to him, even after two years, as washing away the dust of his travels.

A moment later his father appeared, green eyes flashing in his pallid face. "My son," he said, and they kissed, and Master Abraham Cuheno, the great doctor of Aragon, body physician to King Ferdinand, began to cry.

"Father, I'm all right," said Judah, and he laughed out loud, kissed his father again, sat him down in a chair, and poured them both great quantities of wine in the enormous silver goblets brought by the servants.

"I have not heard from you in eight months," said his father.

"That is not unusual."

"Perhaps, but these have not been easy times. Thank God you're alive."

"Of course I'm alive—what else would you expect?" said Judah. "I couldn't very well bring these back if I weren't still breathing." Judah removed the leather pouch from under his doublet and spread out the wealth of gems—rubies, emeralds, and a score of diamonds—before his father. It was a mark of Master Cuheno's concern that he did not yet look at the result of his son's two years of dangerous travel.

"The king sent a message to Venice, more than six months ago, and no one had heard of you. No one had heard of your arrival or departure, not in Genoa either."

"But you did get mail from Venice before I left."

"Judah, we didn't know what to think. You're a Jew carrying precious stones. When they said no one had heard of you, I was afraid they'd murdered you and forgotten your name."

"My name is Rodrigo de Montoro," said Judah.

"What?"

"I don't travel as a Jew, Father," said Judah. "I travel as a Spanish nobleman. What religion I carry in my heart is my business. If I'm more apt to live with a different name, then I'm more than happy to use it."

Master Cuheno said nothing to this. He lived in an age where half his blood relations had formally adopted Christianity to escape persecution and allow themselves the advantages denied to Moors and Jews in Spain. If his own immediate family had been able to remain Jewish and still retain all the advantages of aristocratic birth, it had been because of his skill as a physician and, perhaps more important, his family's skill with gems. The court was more than willing to allow their Aragonese physician the right to live outside the Jewish quarter, to shave his beard, to ride a horse, bear weapons, even possess a noble coat of arms. No matter what the Church said about preventing Jewish doctors from practicing medicine on Christians, the court and the nobles of Spain had no faith in any other doctors but Jews. Even the pope had a Jewish body physician, regardless of the Christian physicians he pretended to have on call. Still and all, in the last two years Master Cuheno, for all his prestige at court, for all the flattery afforded his physician's calling, for all the privileges given the family who provided the king and queen with jewels, had become afraid.

"What's the matter?" said Judah. "You're not angry with me, are you, Father? I'm not the first Jewish merchant to travel under a Christian name."

"Have you—" said Judah's father suddenly, "have you brought back something magnificent?"

"Yes," said Judah, smiling broadly, prepared to show his father the gems he'd spread out on the table. But his father was serious rather than excited, brooding rather than giving thanks.

"I need something magnificent for the king," he said.

"Has he so much gold left over from his campaigning in Granada?"

"I need something magnificent as a *gift* for the king," said his father.

"A gift?"

"A gift, a bribe—whatever you want to call it. Something magnificent, something unique. I need a reason to go to Toledo and speak with him. A magnificent jewel would be a reason."

"I don't understand, Father. Why do you need to speak with the king? Why do you need to bribe him?"

"Tell me, Judah," said Master Cuheno, pouring out some more wine. "Tell me what you've heard about the condition of Jews in Italy, in Germany, in France."

"No different than it's always been."

"Have you met any Germans? I've heard that some of the communities are getting protection. A Castilian Jew with relatives in the Palatinate is moving his whole family there."

"Moving from Spain?" said Judah with an incredulous laugh. "He must be crazy. I met a merchant from Speier, in the Palatinate. A Christian. He ranted and raved about the Jews. He said they started the Great Plague of thirteen forty-eight. Can you imagine? Blaming the Jews for something that happened before his grandfather was born. He even told me how the Jews do it: We poison the wells to bring the Black Death."

"People still believe this?"

"Intelligent people believe this," said Judah. "At least they do in Germany. This man was a printer. He spoke excellent Latin. He even told me what the Jews put in their poison: bits of frogs and spiders, the heads of lizards, consecrated wafers used in the Mass, human flesh, and the hearts of young Christians."

"How can anyone believe such a thing?" said Master Cuheno. "How can anyone seriously believe such a thing in this day and age?"

"At least they don't just hate Jews, they fear Jews, too. Christian doctors fear Jewish magic, astrologers think Jews can twist around the stars. Still, there are some Christians who work side by side with Jews, and forget for a while that we have killed their God and possess black, nefarious powers. But when I tell German Jews, or Italian Jews, that there are Jews in Spain who don't have to wear the badge of shame, or who can enter the courts of kings, they can hardly believe it. In all this world there is no place as good for the Jews as Spain, and no place in Spain as good as Aragon, and no place in Aragon as good as our Zaragoza."

"I am sorry to hear you say it, Judah," said his father. "Because Spain may no longer be a place for Jews at all." He ran his fingers through the jewels on the table. "King Ferdinand has taken quite a fancy to diamonds all of a sudden. Ever since the English envoy showed up with a faceted diamond ring. We need a diamond, a wonderful diamond for you to cut so that it sparkles more than anything that even Charles the Bold has." Master

Cuheno looked up at his son and laughed. "I don't think it'll do any good, but one never knows."

"What do you mean? What is it that you want the king to do?"

"Stop the Inquisition from coming here."

"Coming where? To Zaragoza? What do you care about an Inquisition against heretics? Jews aren't heretics, we're just heathens," said Judah, encouraging his father to smile.

The first tribunal of the Spanish Inquisition had been set up in Seville in 1480. By the time Judah had left for Alexandria two years later, there were tribunals set up at Cordoba, Jaen, Ciudad Real, and Segovia. Just a few weeks before Judah's return to Zaragoza, thirty men and women had been burned alive at the great auto-da-fé at Ciudad Real. But the targets of the Inquisition were supposed to have been Christians who were not faithful to the basic tenets of their religion, not Jews. But Judah had not yet heard of the terror of false converts, Jews who had converted to Christianity in order to pass into the mainstream of Spanish life, but who had remained faithful to Judaism in the privacy of their own homes. These converts, having undergone baptism, were guilty of heresy upon uttering the first syllable of a Hebrew prayer.

"If the Inquisition comes here," said Master Cuheno, "anyone can burn. Jew and Christian, rich man and poor man, false convert and pious priest. Anyone. Is this all you have? Isn't there a diamond among your jewels that could interest the king?"

"Father, I'm afraid I don't understand you. I can't understand what we have to be afraid of. We're jewelers to the court, and you're the king's favorite physician. We've always been Jews and can hardly be accused of heresy by a Christian tribunal. Besides, I want the diamond I've brought back."

"What diamond?" said his father, looking through the small rough diamonds on the table, intermixed with the far prettier emeralds and rubies. "You've brought back something other than these?"

"I've brought back this," said Judah, and he removed the enormous rough diamond from the bottom of his pouch and placed it before his father. "I've brought back this diamond for Rachel."

"Oh, praise God!" said a young girl's voice, before Master Cuheno could react to the diamond. And as Judah turned to the source of sound, his sister, Rachel, crossed the room and flung herself upon him. "Judah," she said, "Judah, you're home, you're home, Judah."

"Of course I'm home," said Judah, but his sister wouldn't leave off kissing him, and shaking him by the shoulders, and crying into his face.

"Judah, do you know what today is?" she finally said. "There's a fair today!"

"Rachel, don't bother your brother with such nonsense," said Master Cuheno.

"Oh, it's not nonsense, it's not nonsense at all. I couldn't possibly go to the fair without Judah, and now we can go, we can go right away, we can go before it gets light!"

"Only bandits and murderers wander around in the dark," said her father severely. "And your brother is tired."

"I'm ready to go at once," said Judah. He made a grave bow in his father's direction. "With your permission, Father, of course."

"You're both just like your mother," he said with a sigh. Under his breath, he added the obligatory: "She of blessed memory."

"Father!" said Judah. "May we go?"

"Of course. Of course you may. But not until you've eaten something. Not until you've eaten, had your beard shaved off, and put on some decent clothing."

"I'm sorry, Father," said Judah. "I'm sorry, but that's quite impossible. You heard Rachel. We simply have to go before it gets light."

"Judah—" protested Master Cuheno, but his son interrupted him.

"And when we return from the fair, you can give Rachel the gift you asked me to find for her."

"I didn't ask you—" began Master Cuheno, but then he lowered his hands over the great diamond and smiled at his son. For a moment, the doctor couldn't believe in all the horrors of the world around him; not with a son so casually sure of his perfect right to be happy. "All right," said Master Cuheno. "I shall select an emerald for Queen Isabella while you two are enjoying the other early-morning vagabonds."

"What gift?" said Rachel. "Did you bring me a gift?"

"I thought you wanted to go to the fair," said Judah.

"But what did you bring for me?"

"I know what I *should* have brought for you," said Judah, taking her by the arm and leading her out of the study. "I should have brought you home a husband."

"Oh, stop that!" Rachel broke away from Judah and ran back to her father, who was sitting in his chair. "You're not angry with us for going?"

"Have a good time, children," said Master Cuheno, his beautiful hands covering the enormous rough diamond before him. Rachel kissed him, and she and Judah walked quickly out of the study and through the dark corridors of the great house.

Outside, the dawn was already threatening to break through the remnants of night. Arm in arm they walked toward the main square of the town, Rachel chattering away about their hundred cousins, both Jewish and New Christian converts, and their thousand marriage alliances, court appearances, new appointments, horses, suits of armor, necklaces of pearls, Italian headdresses, silken skirts, fashionable mistresses, dangerous duels.

"I still say I should have brought you home a husband."

"Thank you very much, but I'm not in any hurry. And besides, when I want a husband, a hundred men will be asking Father for my hand."

"Naturally, because you've got a rich father."

"You don't think I'm pretty?"

"You, pretty?" laughed Judah. "We'll be lucky if they don't send you back after the wedding. Once they've got your dowry, these men won't be so full of praises. What you need is an ugly husband."

"I want to marry a knight."

"A knight? I hope you're making a joke, Rachel. Father and I have discussed this seriously, and often. We're going to find you an ugly husband, old and very pious—the kind of Jew who never lifts his eyes up from the Bible. That's what you need. We may have to send away to the Holy Land for one old and ugly enough. And there aren't too many pious Jews in all of Spain anyway."

"I shall get someone tall and handsome, a knight and a scholar, a doctor and a banker, a courtier and a warrior," said Rachel.

"And a Jew?"

"Of course a Jew."

"What Jew with all those wonderful qualities is going to marry a girl like you?" said Judah.

"Only a lucky one, only the most fortunate man in the world," said Rachel.

Judah allowed her the little conversational victory. She was, after all, only approaching her seventeenth birthday, and there were many girls of that age still unmarried in Zaragoza, at least among the wellborn Jews. What was unusual was not to be spoken for at all. No marriage contract had been signed, no prospective husband offered by the wealthiest Jews of Spain had been found worthy enough for Abraham Cuheno's daughter. She had pale skin, glossy black hair, eyes as green as her father's. She wasn't shy with young men, and she wasn't afraid to show them that she knew more than they about geography, astrology, or Latin. Like her mother, who had died with her last, stillborn child ten years before, Rachel knew the names of flowers. Rachel also knew many folktales, tales she had been told by her mother in their walks about the garden. Though Rachel's father was a doctor, her mother had died quite swiftly, following the stillborn baby by a few hours. She'd died on a Monday. Rachel had been told that Tuesday was a good-luck day for Jews; that was one of her mother's teachings. Perhaps if her mother had lived long enough to reach Tuesday, she'd have bested her fever and been alive today.

Her mother had also told her many stories about King David, the great leader of the ancient Jews. He was the handsomest man who ever lived, and he sang songs, wrote poetry, and fought with the strength of a dozen men. Her mother had said that King David's descendants came to Spain when the First Temple of the Jews was still standing in Jerusalem, that they brought with them gems and books and medicines, and that even today their descendants were jewelers and scholars and doctors.

Rachel's mother had wanted to impress upon her the legend of a descent from kings and queens, of a lineage separate and distinct from, and superior to, that of the splendid Christians who came to call upon her father. But what Rachel had gleaned from that part of her childhood inhabited by her mother's memory had nothing to do with religion or race: She remembered a woman impossibly kind, impossibly lovely, whose stories were of a heavenly world. If Rachel was not anxious to forge a marriage alliance, it was because she had aspirations to a world of romance that existed nowhere on earth.

The town square, already transformed into a bustling miniature city by the mob of traders, awaited the morning. Judah had known that a fair had come to town when he approached the walls of Zaragoza hours before. Ordinarily he would have had to wait for morning for the gates of the city to open, but the players from France, jugglers from Italy, singers and astrologers and conjurers and strong men, the merchants of silk and brocades and velvet and spices and wine, all these fairgoers had to be let in to set up their booths and stalls. The two small inns outside the city gates could hardly accommodate more than a few of the travelers, and the leaders of Zaragoza, who looked forward to these fairs as much as their fellow citizens, preferred to let them enter the city after dark rather than riot outside the walls till morning.

There were merchants from France, England, Italy, Germany, Russia, Poland—merchants so far from home, so long gone from wives and kinsmen, that they owed a greater allegiance to the towns and cities throughout Europe where they brought their wares. The polyglot muddle of outlandish dialects that buzzed through the makeshift streets of the fair had more meaning for them than the sharp syllables of their native languages. Judah had often, during the course of his travels, taken up with such travelers—Gentiles and Jews, men of many nations and men of no nations, men who carried Venetian ducats, papal carlini, Spanish maravedis, Florentine grossi, men who'd been to Pskov to buy silver; who'd sold slaves to the Turk in Salonica; who'd walked among the sheep of Yorkshire; who'd sent cotton from Sicily to the states of the Palatinate; who'd bought Spain's merino wool and sold it in Naples. These men had seen each other at fairs in Brugge and Lyons, in Champagne and Brie, in Stourbridge, Smithfield, Leipzig, and Nijni Novgorod. If this fair in Zaragoza was less important than the one next month in Seville, it was still immense and varied and cacophonous: It was wild with a life more secular than religious, more international than national, more dedicated to passion than to the simple selling of wares.

"Look," said Judah. "A printer."

"Judah, that man is staring at me—the one with the yellow hair."

Judah laughed at the impertinence of the vendor and pulled

his sister to the printer's booth. "In this early light," he said, "he must mistake you for a beautiful girl."

"What did you bring me from Egypt?" said Rachel. "Tell me, Judah. Tell me everywhere you went, tell me the names of all the girls you met, tell me how long the trip across the sea was, tell me everything."

"First you tell me," said Judah. "Tell me if you've really not fallen in love with anyone in all of Zaragoza."

"Of course I haven't."

"What about Thomas?"

"Thomas?" said Rachel. "You're not talking about our cousin?"

"Who else would I be talking about?" he said. "Cousin Thomas whom you were in love with when I left Zaragoza two years ago."

"He's not even a Jew," said Rachel, trying to cover her embarrassment with anger. "How am I to fall in love with someone who's not even of our religion?"

Judah smiled carelessly. "What do you mean he's not a Jew, silly girl? Just because he's got a Christian name, and his father took him twice to Mass—"

"Judah!" said Rachel, interrupting him fiercely. Then, looking into his startled face, she said in a loud, clear voice, "Judah, tell me, have you seen such printing work in your travels?" Rachel held a packet of loose printed sheets from the printer's booth up to the light. "Here, feel the quality of the paper."

"Rachel," said Judah. "What's the matter?"

"Nothing," she said. "Can you imagine how many scribes would be needed to cover all these pages? Father says that this machine is more important than any other invention in history. He says it will one day make all men brothers." Suddenly, something seemed to catch her eye across the way, and she pulled her brother away from the printer's booth.

"Rachel, what's got into you?" he said.

"What's got into *you* would be a better question," Rachel whispered harshly. Pulling her brother into a dark corner, she said, "You can't talk like that about Thomas."

"I can't tease my own sister?" said Judah incredulously.

"Judah," said Rachel, speaking with grave deliberation, "you can't talk about New Christians. Not unless you want them to be burned alive."

"Rachel, everyone knows that the New Christians in Zaragoza are good Jews."

"*Judah*," she said, with real anger. But then her face seemed to reflect an incredible, instantly calming thought. "Oh, my God. You don't know, do you?"

"Know what?"

"The Inquisition. Didn't Father tell you?"

"He began to, but I don't see what that's got to do with us."

"You've been gone so long, Judah. I didn't realize. I mean, it seems as if it's always been near us. It makes me very afraid." She shook her head. "I'm surprised you didn't feel it. Even before you got to Spain. And certainly when you arrived in Barcelona."

"What is it that I'm supposed to feel? I told Father I didn't understand what he's got to be afraid of. And I can't imagine why anyone would want to bother the New Christians of Zaragoza. Everyone knows they're Jewish. The king knows they're Jewish, and he doesn't care."

The fear had come back to her face. "No," she said. "You're not to say that. You're not even to think that."

"I'll think what I like, thank you."

"No you won't," said Rachel. "Not when it can kill your entire family." She paused to look over his shoulder to the quickly growing crowds. "Listen, our New Christian cousins are Christians, not Jews. Your knowing anything else about them can bring you and them to the Inquisitional prison. And when one member of a family goes, the rest usually follow. Don't ask questions now. It's not safe to stand in the dark and talk in whispers. Let's see the fair."

She took his hand and pulled him into the morning light. They passed a silk merchant, a vendor of sheets of songs, an ironmonger with a red beard. Judah tried to absorb his sister's words, but couldn't. How could he be afraid of anything in Zaragoza? The Chief Justice of the city was his father's first cousin, the police officers recognized Judah—at least without his traveler's beard—on sight, and gave him the honor due his class. He had been at court in Toledo. He had attended lectures at Salamanca, and the only instance of discrimination he'd met with there had ended in his having thrashed the Catalonian who'd insulted his Jewish name. The sight of a jeweler's booth broke his reverie. "Come on," he said to Rachel. "Let's see what he's got."

The booth was run by a man and a woman, apparently husband

and wife. The woman spoke a more comprehensible mixture of Castilian and Aragonese than the man, and they spoke Wendish to each other. They had very inferior pearls, rubies, and topazes, but the woman smiled a great deal and seemed to defer to Rachel, as if that were the way to make a sale; perhaps Rachel's beautiful clothing, contrasted with Judah's travel-worn costume, gave her greater prominence in the vendor's eyes.

The woman extended a bit of topaz to Rachel and placed it in her hand. She pointed to the sun, and then moved the topaz about in Rachel's palm so that it caught the morning light. "*Adamas*," she said with a smile, using the Greek word for "unconquerable." Her accent was so bad that only the falseness of her smile gave Judah the clue that she was attempting to pass the topaz off as a diamond.

"Diamond?" said Judah, and the woman smiled and nodded her head with vigor.

"Diamond," she said. "The hardest thing in all the world. If you wear it close to your heart, you will always be brave and can never break a bone."

In Hebrew, Judah asked Rachel: "What do you think? Do you think this is much of a diamond?"

In rapid-fire Aragonese, Rachel answered: "I don't understand Latin, sir. You know that it's not fair to use it in front of me."

Still speaking Hebrew, Judah said, "Do you mean to say that we're not even allowed to speak our native language?"

In Hebrew, and under her breath, Rachel answered: "Not when you're dressed like a New Christian." She squeezed her brother's hand. "Don't be angry with me, Judah. You don't understand what's happening here. We're being left alone, as Jews, only if we don't incite others. We can't give anyone an excuse for finding fault with our conduct. Speaking Hebrew in a public place might lead to our being denounced. Really. Someone might think we're trying to pass a secret to a New Christian. I don't want to burn, Judah. I'm afraid of what I might say if I'm denounced. I'm not very brave. Please don't think badly of me."

"How do I know this is a diamond?" said Judah suddenly to the woman behind the counter of the jewel booth.

"Just a minute," said the woman to Judah, and she began to chatter with her husband in their native tongue.

Judah took the topaz from Rachel's hand. "It glitters," he said to her in Hebrew, "but it doesn't have the fire of a diamond.

Look, so you'll learn the difference." Judah rapped the topaz on the counter of the booth, so that husband and wife ceased their talk and watched him with fear. Slowly, he turned round the leather bracelet he wore on his right wrist, and revealed the five-carat diamond clasped to it, covered by a leather tongue.

"Diamond," he said in loud Aragonese, removing his own diamond from its clasp and letting it dazzle them with its fire. "Not diamond," he said, holding up the topaz next to the diamond, so that the topaz's formerly glittering surface now looked as dull as sunshine glancing off mud. Judah shook off the man's loud protests in Wendish, and kept his hand on the topaz. "Look," he said. He took the topaz and drove it hard against the surface of his diamond; but the topaz didn't scratch the harder stone. "Only a diamond can scratch a diamond," said Judah. A crowd had begun to gather round the jeweler's booth, and as Judah raised his diamond against the topaz's surface, he spoke into a respectful hush. "But a diamond can scratch anything, because anything is inferior to a diamond." With a sharp thrust, Judah scratched a line across the topaz, and then, with a contemptuous look, returned the stone to the terrified couple.

"Throw them out!" said a neighboring vendor, and all the merchants who had assembled during the demonstration took up the cry to exclude the charlatans from the fair. In cases of fraud, all the merchants who had participated in any fair had to make up losses suffered by duped townspeople. Honesty was enforced both by the pressure of religious teachings and the fear of physical violence.

"Why did you have to do that?" said Rachel to Judah. But her brother was already remorseful, and he quieted the crowd.

"It's all right," he said. "They're not cheats. They just made an honest mistake. These people are simple jewelers and should not be allowed to trade in diamonds. Their rubies are real and their pearls are beautiful, and not very expensive."

"You want us to stay?" said the woman to Judah in her bad Aragonese.

"You can stay. Just don't try to sell topaz as diamonds," said Judah quietly, "or the other merchants might tear you apart." To the crowd still about them, he said, "Okay, go back to your booths. There's a big day ahead. We've settled our differences, and no one has been hurt. Go on. Get back to work."

And then Judah took hold of his sister and walked her toward the opposite end of the square. "A Jew in Zaragoza doesn't have to be afraid of anything," he said. "I'll speak Hebrew, and so will you, if that's what we want. If someone cheats us, we'll complain to the authorities, and if the mob threatens us, we'll beat them back like dogs. Who taught you all this crazy fear? Can you imagine mother being afraid? Afraid of people who can't read, or add numbers past ten, who can hardly speak their own language?"

"I am afraid," said Rachel. "I'm not afraid just for me. I'm afraid for people like you. You don't understand what's happening here, and I'm afraid for what that's going to mean for all of us."

As they came round the corner of the money changer's booth, run by a local, religious Jew, Rachel and Judah both caught sight of the sun-blackened face of a man in the town pillory. And both recognized him at once: Isaac the shoemaker.

It was so astounding to see a Jew in the pillory that neither of them spoke for a moment. Several old pairs of shoes hung about the shoemaker's trammeled neck, marking him as a seller of defective merchandise, with the evidence of his crimes—the defective shoes—framing his shut eyes. And yet Isaac was the most popular shoemaker in the city. Everyone from the archbishop to the Chief Justice had him make up their shoes, and if he could have been party to any crime, it could only be the crime of stealing away all the other shoemakers' customers.

In a daze, Judah went right up to the man, ignoring the police officer who stood guard nearby, and spoke to him. "Isaac," he said. "Isaac, what's happened to you?"

The sun-blackened face seemed to stir in its wooden vise. There were bruises about the nose and mouth, and dried blood all along the jawline. After dark, or even during the heat of the day, any ruffian could make sport with the prisoner; it had come to be part of the punishment of being pilloried. Those who had been cheated by an unscrupulous merchant, or been robbed by a penniless thief, could vent their fury once the culprit was imprisoned in the pillory. But it had never happened to a Jew, not in Rachel's or Judah's experience. Jews were exiled, Jews were set upon by drunken peasants and beaten; sometimes, even in Zaragoza, Jews were chosen at random by self-appointed avengers of the Christian god, and murdered. But Jews were never put in the pillory. A merchant had to sell rancid grain, a money changer had to pass false gold, a miller had to steal more than his share of the peasants' flour to end up in the exposed main square of the town, victim of the rage of the elements and the people he cheated. It was inconceivable that Isaac was guilty of selling inferior work; and it was inconceivable, too, that the famous justice of Aragon would condemn a man on the false testimony of his enemies and competitors. The judges of Zaragoza had never before descended to the level of peasants, condemning a man only on the basis of his faith.

"Get away from there, you two," said the police officer. Even before Judah could turn to face the insolent man, he heard him say, "Get away from that cheating Jew."

"We have every right to be here," said Judah, watching the police officer advance. "But you have no right to speak to my sister and to me in that fashion."

"If you were a man, instead of a Jew, I'd show you what right I have to say anything I want to you or to your whore of a sister."

Rachel shrank from the officer, trying to retain her balance under the incredible insult of his words. She was not used to going out in public, and when she did, it was invariably with her father, a man respected and recognized in Zaragoza. She did not recognize this police officer, but, by the very fact that he had called them Jews, she was certain that he knew they were of the Cuheno family, that he knew the name and station of their father. The police officer's contempt in the light of this knowledge was impossible to understand; he had spoken openly, he had said a terrible thing about the daughter of Master Abraham Cuheno, and yet he had shown no fear of the consequences of such action. For much of her life Rachel had been aware of the precarious status of Jews in Spain; but along with this, she had always been conscious of the special status granted her family, a status which gave them honor, privileges, authority. Her father had ministered to the health of the king, had brought him jewels from distant kingdoms; her ancestors had been jewelers and confidants to the crown of Aragon for two hundred years.

No matter what fears she'd communicated to Judah that day, it was as if a favorite child, spoiled by parents and friends all her life, had been suddenly slapped across the face by the household's lowliest servant. It didn't occur to her to fall upon her brother and beg him to refrain from rash action. In the light of the insult, Judah had no choice but to act, and Rachel no choice but to approve.

"I'm going to kill you," said Judah, and he drove his fist across the police officer's face. The officer raised his hands to strike back, but something prevented him from actually hitting the son of Master Cuheno. Judah hit the man again, striking him behind the ear, and then, grabbing his long hair, slowly forced him to the ground. "I'm going to kill you," he said again, but a burly young merchant threw himself at Judah, and then a minstrel joined the merchant, and by the time three police officers had arrived, Judah was held in check by four strong men.

Rachel watched the whole thing as if it were a dream. She heard Judah scream at her to go home, and she heard the police officer accuse her brother of attacking without provocation, and she heard the crowd call him a *Marrano*, a swine, a false Jew.

"Go home," Judah yelled at her one last time, and then the police officers took him with them, away from the square.

Rachel watched them disappear in the direction of the House of Justice, and then, without hesitation, she turned the other way and walked the fifteen paces to the water well in the square. A young woman in an ancient kirtle, her soiled linen shift showing through at the waist and shoulders, drew water for Rachel, slowly, methodically. Rachel took a cup from her hands and returned to the man in the pillory. She called the shoemaker's name, she raised the cup of water to his blackened lips, she begged him to open his mouth and take a drink. Oblivious to the stares from the milling crowd, she remained rooted to her place beside the pillory, until a kindly old man, a seller of secondhand clothes, came up to her and softly told her that Isaac the shoemaker was dead.

It was only then that Rachel could put down the cup, and return home to tell her father of Judah's arrest.

CHAPTER TWO

Rachel walked home swiftly, her eyes on the ground before her. She had no thought of the shame of walking unescorted; rather, the horror of having touched a dead man was giving way to the terrible fear of what would happen to Judah while he was under arrest. Somehow, her father would be able to set matters right. She had only to arrive home, maintain her composure, and tell her father everything that had happened in a clear, unexcited fashion.

But when she finally reached her destination, and found her father in his study, she could say nothing at all. She burst into tears, and when he demanded to know what was wrong, where was her brother, why was she crying, she was unable to get her thoughts in order. "Isaac the shoemaker is dead, and now they've got Judah," she said.

"What are you talking about? Who has Judah?"

"They put him in the pillory, and a soldier insulted me, and Judah hit him, and the police arrested him, and he doesn't know about the Inquisition, he doesn't understand anything at all."

Abraham Cuheno was a physician, and he knew precisely what

to do with a hysterical patient. With a single easy motion, he tossed a glass of wine into Rachel's face. "Stop," he said.

She stopped crying, shocked at her father's action, and began wiping her eyes with her hands. "Father," she said, beginning to tell him everything he wanted to know, all at once, as before, but he broke in.

"Stop," he said again. "Listen, Rachel. Answer only what I ask. No, child. Listen." Master Cuheno waited, and then he said, very slowly, very definitely, "Was Judah arrested?"

"Yes," she said, and her father put up his hand to prevent her from continuing.

"Was he arrested by the regular city police?"

"I think so."

"Did the police wear the blue uniforms of Zaragoza?"

"Yes. But he didn't do anything. I mean anything that was wrong. He had to hit the man—the man called me something horrible. He knew who I was, but he insulted me, and he said if Judah was a man instead of a Jew, he would fight him, and then Judah hit him, and then the others came and took him away."

"Sit down," said her father, and he moved her toward a chair and left the room. Rachel quieted down. Her father was going to make matters right. Judah would be safe. She would not be made responsible for any harm coming to her brother.

Master Cuheno returned a few minutes later, dressed in his austere black doctor's robes. "I want you to come with me," he said. Rachel got up at once and they left the house, entered the closed carriage built for the doctor by a grateful patient, a Catalonian nobleman, and were driven with speed the short distance to the home of Diego de Santangel.

In the carriage, Rachel told her father about Isaac the shoemaker, about how she had brought water to his lips, until she'd been told that he was dead. "Listen," said her father. "Diego is our cousin, but he is also a judge, and impartial before the law. You must tell him everything that happened, so that he can have Judah released from prison at once."

Diego de Santangel was a Christian, and the son of Christians. His father had been born a Jew, and converted to Christianity not for material advantage, or to save his life, but for love; his wife was a Christian, a member of the Mendoza family, and to marry her, he had to accept baptism. A year after the marriage, she died with her stillborn child, giving the hatemongers a good example of the evil fruits of intermarriage. Diego's father, never a sincere Christian, could not convert back to Judaism; to do so would have been a heretical act, punishable by death. He married another insincere convert from Judaism, a lovely blond-haired girl from Seville, and Diego was their child.

Born a Christian, and socially well connected from his rich Jewish relations, Diego was treated to the special advantages of his class. He was a hunter and a swordsman, and he had fought the Moors in the South on three separate occasions. Twenty-two years ago, when he was twenty-five, he'd unhorsed eight men in a row in a tournament in France, and the glory he'd achieved for Aragon had been rewarded with a judgeship. But the same violent temperament that won him glory as a knight prevented him from rising into the confidence of the king, and into important national affairs. He became the Chief Justice of Zaragoza simply by outliving so many others.

Master Cuheno and his daughter were ushered at once into the great reception room, and served wine by scarlet-liveried servants. Because of the impossibility of getting a daily supply of fresh water in any city of their time, people drank wine or ale in enormous quantities. Rachel herself drank a half-gallon of wine a day, and now, in her nervousness, she quickly consumed two great cups. Just as she feared, they were greeted not by Diego de Santangel but by his son, her cousin Thomas. Even as he spoke his respectful greeting to her father, his eyes were reaching out for hers.

"Thomas, this is terribly urgent," said Master Cuheno. "Is your father in the house?"

"Yes, sir," said Thomas. "I'll run and get him." And he ran past the attending servants, exhibiting his powerfully muscled legs in their tight hose, and nearly collided with his father at the room's threshold. Diego de Santangel, a handsome, straight-backed man, bypassed the formalities of greeting and asked his cousin what was wrong.

"Judah's been arrested," said Master Cuheno.

"Judah!" said Thomas. "I didn't even know he was home."

"When, and on what charge?" said Diego de Santangel.

"He attacked a police officer who had insulted him and Rachel."

"Who insulted Rachel?" said Thomas. "What was his name?"

"Thomas, be quiet," said the Chief Justice. He turned to Rachel. "You were there?"

"Yes, sir."

"What was the nature of the insult?"

"He called me a terrible thing," said Rachel.

"What thing?"

Thomas, seeing Rachel's embarrassment, interjected: "What difference does it make what he called her? It's enough that he insulted her. He'll answer to me for that, of that you can all be sure."

"The difference," said the Chief Justice, "is that I must know if the attack was motivated by an insult to the Jewish religion."

"Why on earth—" Thomas began, but his father gave him an angry look and moved closer to Rachel.

"You know how the times are, Rachel," he said. "We'll take care of Judah, of course we will. But I must know if the police officer insulted you and him personally, or simply insulted your religion."

Everyone suddenly understood the import of the Chief Justice's statement. For a moment, even Thomas was silent, unable to speak out the dreaded word.

Master Cuheno spoke for all of them. "The Inquisition," he said. "You are implying that we are to be threatened by the Inquisition?"

"Yes," said Diego de Santangel.

"It is definite?"

"Yes."

"How soon?"

"Almost immediately," said Diego de Santangel. He went on, if only to break the fearful hush in the room. "The news came last night. Now it's the turn of Zaragoza. The Grand Inquisitor is to be Ramirez del Pulgar. He will head the tribunal. I'm not a coward, Abraham, but I'm not about to discipline a police officer who called your son a Jewish swine days before del Ramirez comes to take charge of the city."

"He did insult Judah for being Jewish," said Rachel. "He said that he would fight him if Judah were a man instead of a Jew."

"Fight him for what reason?" said Thomas.

"Isaac the shoemaker was in the pillory. We went up to him. The police officer ordered us to go away. He was disrespectful.

Judah talked back to him. That's when he said what he did about Judah, but Judah didn't hit him only for that. He hit him for the insult he gave to me."

"What insult?" said the Chief Justice.

"He called me a whore," said Rachel.

"Let's go," said Thomas, his face white. "What are we standing here for? Aren't we going to get Judah out of prison?"

"Thomas," said the Chief Justice.

"I am going to kill him," said Thomas. "Please do not ask me to do otherwise. You are my father, and I love and obey you, and now I am begging you, please—do not tell me to do otherwise than kill this man."

The Chief Justice looked at his eighteen-year-old son, remembering himself at the same age, remembering his own prowess with a sword and his own violent sense of honor. Slowly he said, "Rachel is not to go with us to the prison. You will do her the service of escorting her safely to her home."

"Yes, sir," said Thomas. His father had not forbidden him to duel the police officer. He had only to learn the fool's name, and there was ample time for that. The Chief Justice left with Master Cuheno in the latter's carriage, and Thomas had the distinct pleasure of watching his cousin's profile as they walked with a mutual grave shyness to the Cuheno house.

"Do you think that it'll be all right?" said Rachel.

"Do you mean with Judah? Of course. My father will have him released at once." Thomas reached out to touch her arm. "Rachel, do you remember what he looked like?"

"Who?"

"The man who insulted you."

"Why do you want to know?"

"You know why I want to know," said Thomas. "I'm going to kill him."

"Don't be ridiculous. You're not going to kill him. What Judah did was enough. Judah's my brother, and he answered him enough for me."

"Judah's in prison."

"He'll be out."

"I don't think an insult is answered by letting yourself get thrown into prison."

"Judah didn't let himself," said Rachel. "He could hardly fight all the police officers in Zaragoza."

"I would."

"Perhaps."

"Rachel, what did the man look like?"

"I don't know. You don't look long at such a man."

"It doesn't matter," said Thomas. "If you don't want to help me, I'll still find him out. I'm going to kill him, Rachel."

"You can't duel a man who's beneath your own dignity."

"I can. I can when he's insulted you."

"To kill someone for stupid words directed at a cousin—"

"I won't kill him because you're my cousin, Rachel."

"Then why else? Why is it your concern at all?"

"Rachel," said Thomas. "Does it matter so very much to you that I'm not a Jew?"

"You are my cousin, Thomas. I regard you the way I would regard any blood relation."

"We're not such very close cousins," he said. "If you were a Christian, cousins like you and me could marry."

"I am not a Christian, Thomas," said Rachel. "And even if I were, or if you were a Jew, this would hardly be proper conversation for the two of us."

"I love you," he said.

"You're not to say that," she said, turning her face from his.

"It's all right to say it. People say it to each other. It's only in Spain that people are afraid to say what they feel."

"Thomas, are you going to take me home or aren't you?" They had stopped walking, and now both of them turned to look at an ancient peasant leading his empty cart toward the city walls.

"Come on," Thomas said finally, and again he touched her arm, and drew it away quickly. They walked in silence till the enormous Cuheno home, one of the few Jewish homes to be allowed outside the Jewish quarter, was before them. "My blood is as Jewish as yours," he said. "My mother's parents were Jewish, my father's parents were Jewish. My father's father was a Cuheno. Couldn't you tell me how it would be, how you would feel if I were the same as a Jew in your eyes?"

"I can't tell you."

"Why?"

"Because I don't want to speak about such things."

"Does that mean that you feel the same way I do?" said Thomas.

"No."

"I don't believe you," said Thomas, suddenly exultant. "I know you feel something, or you would be able to say more than that you just don't want to talk about it."

"I don't love you," said Rachel.

"Yes you do," said Thomas, laughing now. "I love you, we love each other, and anything you say to the contrary is simply a lie."

"That's not very gallant of you, calling me a liar."

"You're worse than a liar. You're a liar and a coward. But I forgive you."

"I'm going in," said Rachel, but he reached for her hand and brought it to his lips. "No, please don't do that," she said. Thomas kissed her hand, not releasing it for a long while.

"We could go to France, Rachel."

"This is our city. Spain is our country."

"If we had to, we could go to France. There are Jews in Provence. If you became a Christian, we could go almost anywhere."

"I will never become a Christian," she said. "And I will never leave Spain."

"But you will marry me."

"No."

"And you do love me?"

"I don't."

"Then I shall become a Jew, and be burned at the stake for my heresy," said Thomas gaily. "I shall go at once to the archbishop and tell him of my decision."

"I don't think it's right to joke about such things. Not when Judah is in prison. Not when a Jew died in the pillory for a crime he didn't commit. Not when the Inquisition is coming to Zaragoza."

"You're right," said Thomas, and now he stepped beyond the boundaries of everything decent; he pulled Rachel's beautiful face close and kissed her lips, refusing to let go his embrace, ignoring her shut mouth, her fighting arms, her straining neck. They were alone on the narrow street flanking the great house's west side, and he didn't let her go until he was satisfied. When he did, Rachel slapped him across the face, stared at him with perfect hatred, then slapped him again and ran toward the back of the house. Thomas laughed out loud, and began the walk back to the de Santangel home. He would soon know the name of the

man who had insulted Rachel in the public square, and he already
felt the glory of his certain triumph.

The man's name was Hernando, and he was the twenty-year-
old bastard son of a priest, who had gotten him this job with the
city police. Diego de Santangel had the man brought before him
together with Judah in the examination room of the city's prison.

"Do you know this man's name?" asked the Chief Justice.

"No," said Hernando. "No, sir, only that he is a Jew."

"How do you know that he is a Jew?"

"By his beard."

"Not only Jews wear beards." ·

"I saw him with the girl. I know the girl is a Jewess."

"How do you know that?"

"That man there." Hernando pointed to Master Cuheno, sitting
silently in a corner of the room. "That man there is her father."

"You know that man?"

"Sir, yes, everyone knows that man. He's the doctor. He's
famous. Master Cuheno. He's the one who cured the duke of his
blindness, and let a child grow in the barren womb of the queen
of Granada. Everyone knows of his Jewish magic. I've seen him
in Zaragoza, and I've seen the girl with him. They say that his
daughter is the wisest person in the city, and that she knows more
magic even than her father."

"Do you know that Master Cuheno is under the protection of
the royal court?"

"No, sir."

"Do you know that he has ministered to the health of King
Ferdinand?"

"No, sir. But I don't doubt it. My father was a priest, so I don't
go for that Jewish superstition. I go to a Christian doctor, or I
don't go at all. But I know that kings and dukes and even bishops
like to have their Jewish doctors. I was just brought up to think
differently. I don't believe in running after magic. I'm more concerned with my soul."

"But you knew that Master Cuheno was an important, honored
citizen of Zaragoza."

"With all respect, sir, I was taught not to honor any Jew. No
matter what they do, they can't help but come from the seed of
the men who killed our Lord. That's what they're here in the

world for—everyone who goes to church knows that. They're here to remind us of their crime, and of our Lord's sacrifice. How can I honor a man like that?"

"Do you honor the king?"

"Yes, sir."

"Do you honor the laws of the city of Zaragoza, and the state of Aragon?"

"Yes, sir."

"Then you must honor the family of Cuheno, their esteemed position in our city, their noble rank, and their noble privileges. Do you understand what I am saying, Hernando?"

"Yes, sir."

"Take him away," said the Chief Justice, and Hernando was escorted from the room by two of his fellow officers. "Give him ten lashes and release him," said Diego de Santangel. The scribe looked up in surprise from where he had been recording the proceedings. It was a very light punishment for such a disrespectful man. Fifty lashes would have been much more appropriate, and, depending on the zeal of the man inflicting the punishment, could have killed or crippled the man, as an example to all those who would attack the fabric of the city's social order. The Chief Justice dismissed the scribe, and then he and his two kinsmen left the prison.

In the closed carriage, the talk thundered back and forth without pause.

"How can you be sure that the Inquisitor is coming?"

"If you need any proof, just look at the way Hernando behaved in front of me. It's the people like him who know that the Inquisition is coming. It's been to half the cities in Spain. It's never been stopped. Hernando knows that he can speak with impunity, so long as he speaks from a point of view that sounds like it's church-inspired. A year ago I would have smashed him across the face for his smart answers today. Today I had to swallow it, as if he were teaching me religion."

"But why did you sentence him at all then?" said Judah. "I don't want you to get in trouble on my account."

"I didn't do it for you, Judah," said Diego. "I can bend a little bit in the interest of myself and my family, but I can't let a low-born fool like that walk over me. Lecturing *me* about Jewish magic. The bastard was born to be whipped. I'd like to do it myself."

"I've brought you a present, cousin," said Judah.

"Yes," said Master Cuheno. "Something beautiful and small and valuable and easy to carry in the lining of your coat."

"I don't think it's going to be that bad, Abraham," said the Chief Justice. Still, he didn't directly contradict his cousin's hint. There were many Christians of Jewish descent who'd left Seville under cover of darkness, their clothing lined with gems. The Inquisition had frightened them from their city, fueling its power on the wealth of its victims. Anyone accused of heresy stood the risk of losing his life; but long before the examination of the accused's soul took place before the dread Inquisitor, all of the alleged heretic's worldly property was confiscated by the holy men of the Inquisition, for use in their holy work.

Most men and women brought before the Inquisitor confessed their sins, or begged to be told what their sins were, so that they could then confess more properly. The reports of torture and terror preceded the Inquisitional Tribunal into the cities in which they were held, so that most of the accused heretics caught up in their net were quick to comply with any and all wishes. Few thought they could withstand torture and be cleared of all accusations. Since Christians of Jewish descent were often rich, and particularly susceptible to heretical crimes—the crimes of practicing Jewish customs—they were often the first to be informed upon. Anyone with a Jewish ancestor was liable to dislike pork, or change his linen on Friday evenings, or bathe on Saturday, and these were heretical actions, as they were solidly linked to the practices of their forefathers.

Diego de Santangel knew all this, of course. His family had never served pork in the house, though it was a staple in the meals of the rich. (The poor, Jew or Gentile, could hardly afford any meat, except three or four times a year.) And he hadn't been raised to honor the Christian god either. From an early age, he understood that his family was Jewish, and that their Christian name and social standing was merely a convenience, a mark of the difficult times. If he knew almost no Hebrew, he did know one or two memorized prayers. And like most *conversos*, he always tried to observe one Jewish holiday with his still-Jewish kinsmen. Not the somber Day of Atonement, or joyous celebration of the New Year; the de Santangel family celebrated Passover, the joyous feast celebrating the exodus from slavery in the land of Egypt.

"What have you heard about this Ramirez del Pulgar?" asked Master Cuheno. "Is he a sincere zealot, or someone after land and money?"

"He's sincere," said the Chief Justice. "They're all sincere, and why shouldn't they be? How can you bribe people who can take all you own simply by accusing you of heresy?"

"Then you are in more danger than we," said Judah, thinking of the risk his cousin had just taken in freeing a Jew, and punishing a Christian.

"We are all in exactly the same amount of danger," said Master Cuheno. "Jews and Christians of Jewish descent are burned alike. If a Jew is accused of spreading his religious teachings, he is guilty of a crime that the Inquisition can punish. And we're all guilty of such crimes. We've even celebrated the Passover together."

"And will continue to do so," said Diego de Santangel with sudden ferocity. Then he paused, looking at his cousin with serious eyes. "That is, if you will continue to invite me, Cousin."

"Of course," said Master Cuheno, and at that moment he believed intensely in the courage of his cousin, he believed that no torture would ever lead the Chief Justice to betray himself, or anyone close to him. "We are already bound together with blood. We will remain bound together with the secrets we share."

"I shall tell you another secret, Cousin," said Diego de Santangel. "I don't think it's going to be as bad as it was in Seville. There are too many powerful Christians of Jewish descent for the Inquisitor to act the way he did in Seville. Men were singled out there by their business competitors, by jealous servants, by anyone who knew them in the slightest way. The Inquisitor made it his business to arrest all those who were of Jewish descent, and who had sizable fortunes for the Inquisitional Tribunal to confiscate. If we are attacked here in Zaragoza, if all Christians of Jewish descent are arrested, or charged, or frightened into fleeing, we will not do what they did in Seville. We shall make it our business to kill the Inquisitor, and any members of his tribunal who don't leave the city."

"You'd murder the Inquisitor?" said Master Cuheno.

"To prevent the murder of my family—yes, of course I would."

"And so would I, Father," said Judah.

"Judah," said Master Cuheno. He didn't want his son talking

so openly, talking without thinking or planning. "You'd do well to speak to your father before agreeing to a murder."

"You don't agree?" said Diego de Santangel. "If your Rachel was accused of proselytizing Thomas, my own son, her cousin—just for this, she could be imprisoned, tortured, burned alive at the stake."

"I would kill anyone who would harm Rachel," said Master Cuheno.

"So there you have it," said Diego de Santangel. "Even a physician is ready to kill for the sake of family and honor."

"But I don't think it will have to come to that," said Master Cuheno. "Before committing myself to murder, I would prefer to flee."

"Flee to where?" said the Chief Justice.

"Flee to what?" said Judah.

"There's more to this world than just Spain," said the doctor. "Especially with diamonds in your pocket."

In reality, however, it was inconceivable to him that his life in Zaragoza, in the state of Aragon, could end so completely. He was not an immigrant to Spain, nor was he the child or grandchild of immigrants. His family's sojourn in Spain stretched back to time immemorial.

Jews had lived among the Moors, had served the Moslem kings since the eighth century. Family legend claimed Hasdai ibn Shaprut—the tenth-century Jewish physician who'd become the chief adviser to Caliph Abd-ur-Rahman III—as an ancestor. As a child, Abraham Cuheno had heard of Samuel ibn Nagdela, the poet and vizier to the King of Granada five hundred years before; he'd heard of Abraham ibn Ezra, the Jew from Toledo who wandered around the known boundaries of the world in the twelfth century; he'd heard of Judah Ha-Levi, who died in Jerusalem in 1141 after a life of poetry and passion. These men weren't ancestors, but they were Jews, and he was told their stories to remind him of his place in his own land: Spain.

Jews were there before the Christians; and when the Christians came, they were able to aid the transfer of power and transfusion of culture from the Arabs to their conquerors, as the Jews spoke both the languages of the West and the Arabic that had prevailed in Spain since the followers of Mohammed ousted the Visigoths in 715. Master Cuheno's people had been there too long to believe in the possibility of deserting Spain forever. The history of a hundred riots, of massacres by Moors or Christians against the Jews, were counterbalanced by their sheer flourishing presence. Even the conversion to Christianity of hundreds of thousands of Jews over the past century wasn't threatening in light of the common knowledge that these conversions were mostly insincere, that these New Christians were still Jews, living among their own people in the Spain of their ancestors. King Ferdinand himself was rumored to be of Jewish descent, on his mother's side, and his very marriage to Isabella had been made possible by the help of Jews and their New Christian kinsmen. How could the king possibly betray them? He had promised more than once that the Inquisition would never cross into the state of Aragon.

Even as Master Cuheno spoke of flight, of making a life in another country with the aid of gems and foreign Jews and noblemen in search of a man who could cut their old diamonds to a new brilliance, his mind reached out for a complacent refusal to think of any other future than a future in his city, in his state, in his united country.

When they arrived at the Cuheno house, Master Cuheno was the last out of the carriage, and thus the last to see the dozen armed men wearing the colors of the archbishop of Zaragoza waiting for him. One of the men approached the doctor and made a cursory bow.

"Your Honor, the archbishop requires your attendance at once upon a most important visitor to his palace," he said. The man stole a glance at the Chief Justice, but made no bow in his direction. His authority was of a spiritual source, and he had no need to defer to this secular source, who frequented the home of a Jew.

"I'll go alone, Judah," said Master Cuheno. "Please take our guest into our home."

"You," said the Chief Justice to the servant of the archbishop. "Who is this visitor?"

"A poor friar, sir," said the servant with a smile. "But a famous one. Perhaps you've heard of Friar Ramirez del Pulgar?"

The Inquisitor had come to Zaragoza, and all the talk of flight and murder now paled in the face of reality.

The doctor restrained his cousin from saying something dangerous to the archbishop's servant. It was obvious that the man had spoken with peremptory disregard for the Chief Justice's position; but it was obvious, too, that there was a reason for that disregard. The Inquisition's presence in the city would mean a realignment of power and position, a rush to befriend new men, to avoid old acquaintances. This was not the time to say something cross to a servant who would later rush to testify before the Inquisitional Tribunal that one was a Judaizer, a heretic, a blasphemer.

"Go with Judah, Diego," said Master Cuheno, speaking with perfect authority, absolute calm. This was no longer a time for conjecture and flights of the imagination. A man was ill and needed medical attention. He was a doctor, a good doctor, and would take his medical bag and ride off with these men to treat a patient.

CHAPTER THREE

After the Chief Justice had accepted his gift from Judah and left the Cuheno house, Judah sent a servant to search out his sister and bring her to the study where he sat contemplating the gems he'd brought back from the other side of the world.

"You're not hurt?" said Rachel, when she found him.

"No, of course not."

"Where's Father? Didn't he return with you?"

"He was called to a patient."

"What patient?"

"Rachel, you're asking too many questions. I've been home all these hours and you still haven't seen the gift I've brought you from across all those miles."

"No," she said, freezing a smile on her face. How could one think of gifts at a time like this? "I don't need a gift, Judah, though I thank you for whatever it is you've brought. But it's not right. Not with Isaac the shoemaker dead."

"I didn't know he was dead."

"Well, he is. He died in the pillory. I don't know how anybody could have wished it on him. I don't know how our cousin could have allowed such a thing—"

"Diego just had me released from prison. And the man who insulted you is being flogged at his command."

"That's because we're rich. He could have done something for Isaac. He wasn't guilty of anything, that poor Isaac. He was such a nice man, and they let him die out in the sun for no reason, no reason at all."

"Rachel, we don't know that Diego had anything to do with it. He's not the only judge in Zaragoza. A shoemaker selling defective shoes is not the sort of case that Diego would try."

"He knew about it," said Rachel.

"We don't know that."

"Don't be stupid!" said Rachel. "Of course he knew about it. The city isn't so big that its Chief Justice won't hear about a man being sentenced to the town square's pillory. Especially when that man is innocent. Especially when that man is a Jew. Don't you know that? Can't you see that?" Suddenly, this inexplicable outburst against Diego de Santangel was capped with an explosion of tears. Judah said nothing. She would react to the silence and explain herself. "I'm sorry," she said, after a long pause. "Maybe you're right. Maybe Diego didn't know about Isaac." She looked up at her brother and shook her head slowly. "Thomas tried to kiss me."

"Thomas," said Judah. He laughed once, then screwed his face into a more serious set of lines. "And did he succeed?"

"This isn't funny."

"I know. He's your cousin and he's not Jewish, and he's not even handsome."

"Not handsome!" said Rachel. "He's the handsomest man I've ever seen!"

"So he succeeded," said Judah.

"I never want to see him again," said Rachel.

Judah decided to let this statement go unchallenged. He asked her to sit next to him, before the glittering gems, and when she had, he took the enormous rough diamond from its pouch and placed it in the center of the pile of much brighter stones.

"This is for you," he said.

Rachel looked at the stone with wonder. It didn't catch the light the way others did; neither did it have any fiery colors within. It was white, massive, strong. Its beauty lay in something she could sense, but not understand. Perhaps it was that its beauty was all potential, all anticipation. She could feel her brother's excitement, and realized at once that he would share in the creation of beauty—that his talent would do more than shape this raw material, it would merge with it; this stone would be hers only as it passed through his hands, his genius. It would be Rachel's stone only by the testament of her brother's love.

She reached out to touch it, and as her fingers lent their warmth to the stone, her brother began to speak: He had been studying the stone for weeks, for months, having time on his hands and no facilities for cutting. He knew where the grain was, and this was the great secret to unlocking the beauty of the diamond. "In India," he said, "they simply polish these, and men love them because of what they know them to be—the hardest substance in the world. But it's a crime to leave so much beauty hidden, so much beauty for no one to see." Judah showed her where he had inked a tiny mark on the face of the stone: This is where he had planned the first cleavage. He told her that the stone weighed nearly two hundred carats, a carat being the weight of a seed of the carob tree; and that he hoped to end up with a stone of perhaps eighty carats.

The latest fashion in the diamond world—the daring cutting of diamonds to one-third their original weight, or less, to bring fire and light to the previously dull surface of the stone—was only fifteen or twenty years old and was sweeping the courts of Europe. It was this cutting that Judah had studied in Venice. Later he had spent two months with an old Indian in Alexandria, who showed him, and watched him perform, the intricate cutting of one enormous Panna diamond. That great diamond had been table-cut; that is, without greatly altering the original shape of the stone, the cutter had flattened one end into a wide table, the opposite end into a smaller table, and then ground out facets on the upper and lower parts of the diamond. The Panna diamond had retained more than half of its original weight, and had greatly increased its brilliance. What Judah planned with Rachel's diamond was far more adventurous: He'd follow the table cut, but increase the number of facets, and cut away as much as was necessary to show the diamond's fire and its rare white color.

"Come," he said. "We'll make the first cut together." As they walked to the cool, dark room at the rear of the house, where Judah had his workshop, the fact that his father was then waiting on the Inquisitor of Zaragoza was repelled from his consciousness. There was nothing that he could do but hope that the world would go on. If his father, and then his whole family, were to be arrested on the morrow, he would at least have had this time with Rachel, this perfect time of sharing her gift, of exhibiting the family's craft. His mother had learned to cut diamonds, and had been remarkably adept at the skill in the short time she practiced it before her death. Perhaps Rachel would learn the craft, too, as a remembrance of her mother.

Neither woman, of course, had had need of learning a trade; but this was more art than commerce, and one of the few nonhomely actions open to women in their time—simply because anyone, man or woman, who could learn this esoteric skill, and do it well, would be in demand, regardless of age or sex or race. In any case, he would try to draw her into the mystery of the diamond, to let her understand its meaning for their family as more than just a means of entry to royal courts, or a passport to riches.

A diamond, like faith, could be shattered by a misplaced blow; and like faith, too, it could resist any impulse, any force. Because the only thing as hard as diamond is diamond, the only thing as lasting as faith is faith. He had faith at that moment in his father's fate, and thus in their own, and began to light the many lamps in the dark workshop to make ready for the first cutting of Rachel's diamond.

Master Cuheno was at that moment in the palace of the archbishop of Zaragoza. The archbishop was a friend, and had been since the two of them had been students at Salamanca. When Cuheno had gone off to Padua to study medicine, and his friend to Paris to study theology, they had corresponded as diligently as the schedule of traders who carried letters allowed. In Zaragoza, they saw each other over chess at least once every two months. And the archbishop had been a patient of the doctor's for twenty years. Still, it did not surprise Master Cuheno that when the archbishop introduced him to Friar Ramirez del Pulgar, his manner was distant, though correct; it was obvious that the archbishop would not want to flaunt his friendship with a Jew in front of the new Inquisitor.

The Dominican friar, Ramirez del Pulgar, lay fully clothed on an enormous bed at the opposite end of the palace from the archbishop's own bedroom. He had black eyes, a fat, oily face marked with pimples and the scars of a childhood case of smallpox. He was obese, and he was filthy enough to give off a stench detectable from ten paces. Before the archbishop had completed his introduction, the friar, trying to disguise his peasantlike fear of medicine, pretended anger: "How are we to know this beardless face belongs to a Jew, Your Excellency?" Only Jews of high social status were allowed to ignore the law prohibiting them the right to shave their faces.

Perhaps to compensate for his lack of cordiality thus far to an old friend, the archbishop now hissed out his words, incensed at the lowborn friar's treatment of a respected citizen. "This Jew is Master Abraham Cuheno," he said. "He has served as body physician to our sovereign, King Ferdinand. His father was Master Mordecai Cuheno, who served as financial minister to two kings. His grandfather, Master Jonathan Cuheno, fortified the walls of Zaragoza out of the gems accumulated in a lifetime of trading, thus saving the cathedral and the people from an enormous army of Moors."

"All that makes him no less a Jew, Your Excellency."

Cuheno was less amazed at the insolence shown to himself than by that shown by a friar to an archbishop. It frightened him, for it was another mark of the power of the Inquisition over all the old hierarchies of the country.

"He's right, Your Excellency," said Master Cuheno. "All that makes me no less a Jew."

At this the friar began to laugh, but the laugh was just another disguise, another attempt to stall off the examination and its aftermath. As the laughter pulled the ugly face forward, the doctor could see enormous boils at the base of the friar's neck. Perhaps to hide these boils from him, the friar placed both hands about the back of his neck, laughing and flapping his bent arms like a madman.

"Are you sick, Friar Ramirez?" said the doctor suddenly, fixing the Inquisitor with an omnipotent stare. Master Cuheno knew better than anyone how little power over the sick he possessed; and how much of what power he did possess was allied to the patient's belief in the doctor's omnipotence.

The friar stopped his laughing, and looked with terrified eyes at the archbishop. "You say this Jew is the best doctor in Aragon?"

"Yes," said the archbishop.

"I suggest, Your Excellency," said Master Cuheno, "that you

leave the friar with me for the present. It is sometimes more comfortable for a patient to talk to his doctor in private."

The archbishop left at once, nodding gravely to both men.

"Do you know what's wrong with me?" said the friar.

"No," said the doctor. "Not yet."

"Why not? I thought a good Jewish doctor could tell in a second, just by looking at a man. You should know how long I'm going to live. You should be able to tell me what month I was born in, and what time of day."

"I can't do any of those things," said the doctor. "But I can examine you, search for the cause of whatever it is that ails you, and give you the best advice that I can."

The friar suddenly looked fearful again, but he stoppered his fear and blurted out, "Do you know who I am?"

"Yes," said Master Cuheno.

"Do you know why I have come to Zaragoza?"

"No," said Master Cuheno. "Not precisely."

"I've come to weed out the heretics and their accomplices from the Holy Catholic Church," said the friar. "I am to be the Grand Inquisitor of Zaragoza. And I will tell you now that I am not afraid of Jews, nor their friends in high places, nor their money, nor their magic. I burned thirty-five Jews in Ciudad Real, less than a month ago. They go up in fire and smoke, just like anyone else."

Abraham Cuheno could not restrain himself. This man was his patient, and he knew that the Inquisitor was simply trying to express his power before relinquishing it to the doctor.

"Why do you say 'Jews'?" said Master Cuheno.

"Only the sinful need be afraid, Doctor," said the Inquisitor. "Tell me, are you so sinful that you need fear the just arm of the Holy Inquisition?"

"I am a Jew, Friar Ramirez. I answer to the authority of my church, not to yours."

"The Jews I burned were those who had led Christians astray, or those who had themselves converted to Christianity, but remained faithful to your unholy church. Everyone I burn is a Jew, either by descent, or by practice, or by heresy." The Inquisitor straightened himself majestically on the bed. "In Castile they say that every bishop in Aragon has got Jewish blood in him, and that the archbishops are all secret Jews. I hear that the Chief

Justice of this city, Diego de Santangel, had a Jewish father. I hear that the archbishop who's just left us is one-eighth Jewish, and that half his friends are of Jewish descent."

"Friar Ramirez," said Master Cuheno, "how long have you had those boils on the back of your neck?"

"The boils?" said the friar fearfully, forgetting his diatribe. "What do the boils signify to you?"

"Please, Friar Ramirez. I'd like you to help me, so that I can help you. I want to examine you carefully, I want you to answer whatever questions I ask you."

"I'll ask *you* a question, Doctor," said the friar. "What's the most delicate thing in the world?"

Master Cuheno shook his head at the friar's attempt at humor, but he answered anyway: "A doctor's shoulder," said Cuheno. "You have only to touch it and his hand shoots out for money."

The doctor's familiarity with the proverb put a sudden chill into the friar. Instead of laughing at the joke that he had himself begun, he became suddenly gloomy, pessimistic, resigned to his fear. "Doctor," he said, "I'm afraid I might go blind."

Master Cuheno took a step closer to the bed, and watched as the black, hateful eyes began to glimmer with a horror of the unknown.

"I'm afraid I might go blind," the Inquisitor said again, and then all his fears came out in a rush. "I know that too much lying down with women can give you dyspepsia, and even gout, and sometimes—I think it happens a lot—it can thin out your blood, make it weak like water. Doctor, in Seville, and later on in Toledo, I was with this woman, and she was like a devil. She never had enough, she kept me at it, again and again, and I was afraid of the gout like some people get from too much of it, and then I got these boils, just like you asked me about, that's what I got them from, and now I feel weak, it hurts me all over, and mostly I can't help but think that the next thing—this is what everyone says—after the weak blood and the boils and the gout and the dyspepsia—after that you can go blind, and I'd rather just cut my throat than that. I have to know, Doctor. I have to know right away if I'm going blind—because if I don't know, I'm going to go crazy first, I'm going to go crazy first from the fear."

Master Cuheno waited for the rush of words to cease, and then he placed a hand on the friar's greasy head and pushed it forward for a look at the boils on his neck. "What makes you think you might be going blind?" he said.

"I told you, I have all the signs. This woman devoured all my strength, and I've got all the signs except the blindness, and I'm afraid that's next."

"You're dyspeptic?"

"Yes, and when the doctors bled me in Ciudad Real, they found my blood as thin as water, so weak that my phlegm remains dominant past midnight and my choler overwhelms my blood-dominance much before dawn."

"You seem to know a good deal about medicine."

"When we question the heretics in our dungeons, a doctor is always at our sides. As we know from the ancients, four humors rule our bodies according to times of the day. We've found that the best time to question our reluctant heretics is from noon to dusk, when melancholy is dominant."

"What did the doctors tell you in Ciudad Real?"

"To stay away from my woman."

"And did you?"

"Yes." The friar smiled here for a moment, remembering how he had rid himself of the she-devil. "She eventually confessed to having practiced witchcraft, as well as to being a secret Jewess."

The doctor started at this. This man who was to affect the lives of everyone in their city had arranged for the public burning of his own lover. "But you felt no better," said Cuheno. "With or without your woman, you felt weak, developed these boils, and remained dyspeptic."

"Yes."

"When did you last have a bath?"

"A bath?" The question surprised the friar: What did a bath have to do with his problems? "I don't know. Why? What does it matter?"

"Since you've been here at the palace?"

"I've only been here a day!" said the friar, but then he smiled, a smile of recognition, and said with considerable asperity: "I know why you're asking me that! Why don't you ask me if I bathe on Friday afternoons?"

"Have you had a bath within the last month?"

"I know about your Jewish customs," said the Inquisitor. "This obsession with bathing. That's one way we have of finding out which New Christians are secret Jews. They can hide a lot of things, these converts, but they can't hide a bath on Friday afternoon from a houseful of servants."

"You're filthy," said the doctor.

"What?" said the Inquisitor, not insulted, simply surprised that the doctor was continuing in this vein.

"You're filthy. You need a bath. You need a long bath in a tub of hot water. You need to be scrubbed clean with a heavy brush and good olive oil. After that, I can do something for you to help your pain."

"I don't understand. What will you do?"

"I will cure you," said the doctor. "I will take away your pain, I will remove your boils, and you shall not become blind." It did not make sense to Cuheno to disabuse the friar of a lifetime of wrong notions about medicine. He was not the only doctor in Aragon, or even in Zaragoza, who thought contemporary notions about the devouring power of women's sexuality to be absurd; but among doctors, his views were the views of the minority, and doctors like himself had long since learned to ignore, rather than try to reform, superstition. The doctor ordered the hot bath to be prepared, and drew about himself the mantle of arcane knowledge, the air of being privy to vast stores of ancient wisdom, to ward off further questions from the worried friar. His patient would be best served by believing implicity in a man accomplished in black arts, arts that encompassed astrology and medicine and philosophy, arts that were the natural province of the Jew.

The Inquisitor showed the doctor the mulberry twigs he kept under his bed, to ward off fleas in the night. The twigs were a gift from a friend who had studied medicine with a Jew at Salamanca, and who had been taught that Jews were less prone to disease because frequent bathing made their bodies less agreeable to fleas.

"What will you do to me after I bathe?" said the friar, but the doctor ignored the question, continued to consult a thick book, bound in old, cracked leather, mulling over the tiny handwritten letters. The friar allowed himself to be stripped, placed in the steaming water of a great wooden tub brought by four servants. He ignored the pain of the heat and the scrubbing; it was sufficient to know that the doctor had promised a cure, and that he now consulted secret books. Friar Ramirez could not know that the doctor was passing the time with an anthology of quotations from Plato and Aristotle, Virgil, Cicero, and Ovid, compiled in Italy by an unknown monk more than a century before; the Grand Inquisitor of Zaragoza was completely illiterate.

An hour later, the doctor had four servants hold down the dread man, and then he tore into the ugly bubbles about his neck with a lancet, bought in Padua during his student days. Blood and pus poured onto the bed, over the friar's screams. Master Cuheno worked diligently, swiftly, his only care the health of his patient. It was not the first time that he had helped an enemy of his people, but he was of the ancient opinion that a doctor could not make discriminatory judgments on the amount and quality of care to be given to any one person: All patients must needs be equal, at least when under the doctor's knife.

Later, when the friar had been bandaged and made comfortable and clean in the great bed, he expressed his thanks to the doctor. "I'll remember this, Doctor," he said. "You're one Jew who won't have to worry, as long as I remain healthy."

The doctor thought it beneath his dignity to answer this. He suggested to the friar that he sleep for twelve hours, and stay in bed for two more days, and then Master Cuheno returned to his home.

Perhaps a moment before he entered his own study, a joyous shout rang out from across the other side of the house. Rachel, having imbibed most of the joyous terror of the moment, had watched as Judah had set up the diamond in a little wooden cup, and made a little cut in the stone—using a small diamond for the task—along the grain he had marked before. The wooden cup was then set firmly into the surface of his workbench, and Judah placed a thin knife blade, made of the finest Toledo steel, into the little gash, and held it there.

"Now," he said, his breath racing, "all I've got to do is hit the knife blade with this stick, and we shall have begun to make your diamond beautiful."

"What if the diamond shatters to bits?"

"Then I'll have made the biggest mistake of my life," he said. "But don't worry—it won't happen." And without waiting for further comment or fears, Judah turned back to the diamond, straightened the knife blade, and hit it sharply with his wooden stick.

The diamond split along the grain, seemingly without effort or strain, beginning to reveal its beautiful symmetry. Rachel let out her shout of joy, and then brother and sister embraced and began to laugh and scream.

"What are you doing, children?" It was the voice of their father. And when they turned to see him at the door to the workshop, their faces alive with joy, he tried to hide the fear and loathing still in his face. Abraham Cuheno walked up to where the newly cleaved diamond caught the light. "It's beautiful," he said. "Congratulations."

But his heart was not in his words. Even as the stone glittered, he received a premonition more powerful than hope: This diamond would not be finished before his daughter would die.

CHAPTER FOUR

It was two days before Thomas de Santangel found Hernando, the man who had insulted Rachel Cuheno, and the two days had done much to diminish his zeal in wanting to kill the man. Hernando had been whipped, dismissed from his job, and had quarreled with his mistress. His back no longer ached from the light whipping—his fellow police officer tried to do no more than mark his skin—but his head ached from drinking, and from contemplating the awful power of the Jews. He had already been in two brawls, in two different taverns, when Thomas found him in the little ale room of the inn just outside the city walls. Hernando heard the young gentleman asking for him by name, and heard Thomas refer to him as a "just dismissed police officer."

"I'm Hernando," he said, pushing aside the only other patron in the small room. Hernando was twenty-two to Thomas's eighteen, but Thomas was taller, and had the added advantage of not having been drinking to the point of exhaustion and delirium for the past forty-eight hours. "What do you want with Hernando?" he said, his awful breath blaring out his belligerence.

Thomas looked at the man, and then, with a movement so fast that it surprised Thomas as much as Hernando, he slapped him across the face. Hernando recoiled in shock, but then stood up very straight, his eyes twisting back from drunkenness. He understood that he had been challenged, and now he waited to understand why.

"Are you the dog who insulted Rachel Cuheno in the town square?"

"What?" said Hernando, trying to comprehend the reason for the violence that was about to take place. "The town square?"

"The town square," said Thomas, advancing on the man. "The pillory. The girl you insulted that led to your being whipped."

Hernando's face went white with rage. This man came from the Jews, to wreak further vengeance on him. He reached out to grab Thomas by the throat, but the young man slapped away Hernando's arm. Thomas remembered that he had come here to kill this man; but perhaps, seeing how lowly and disreputable the creature was, it would be more honorable to simply demand an obsequious apology, and beat him with his fists.

"Jew!" said Hernando, the word rising from deep in his throat. "You filthy Jew!"

Thomas stopped his advance. He had never before been called a Jew, certainly not as an insult. For a moment the young man thought he should explain, explain to the keeper of the ale room, to the other drunken peasant who was buying drink, to the dismissed police officer, explain to all of them that the insult was absurd—he was Thomas de Santangel, and he was not a Jew but a Christian of aristocratic birth. But Hernando, fired by his own epithet, repeated it: "Jew!" he said, and he said it again, and he drove his large right fist into the side of the young gentleman's face.

Thomas no longer thought of dueling, nor of Rachel, but only of himself at that moment. He had been called a Jew and he had been struck across the face, and now he ducked his head and drove it into the drunken man's chest, sending both of them crashing into a table, and then onto the floor. Thomas kicked away a chair, threw himself over Hernando's body, and punched the furious man's face. Hernando tried to beat Thomas away, but the younger man now straddled his chest and, in his anger, continued to punch into Hernando's eyes and mouth and nose, until the face was bloody and still.

The keeper of the ale room finally came over to Thomas and touched him lightly on the shoulder. Thomas got up and walked over to a chair, while the keeper of the ale room splashed water in Hernando's face. The drunken peasant came over to Thomas and said, "Why'd you beat him, sir?"

"He called me a Jew," said Thomas, without thinking. Realizing that he had explained nothing, he started to explain about the insult to his cousin, but then he looked at the idiotic face confronting his, and got up from the rickety chair. "Get out of my way," said Thomas de Santangel to the peasant, and pushed past the keeper of the ale house and went outside.

The peasant was drunk, but not too drunk to recognize the son of the Chief Justice of Zaragoza, who had often hunted with the peasant's former overlord on land that the peasant had planted with vegetables for his own family. That same day Hernando went to the Inquisitional Tribunal, newly set up in the prison where he had so recently been tried and flogged. The Grand Inquisitor saw him a day later, and Hernando denounced Thomas de Santangel by name as a Jew and a defender of the Jewish religion.

When the special officers of the Inquisition came to arrest Thomas de Santangel, his initial reaction was neither fear nor surprise. It was wonderment. He wondered if he felt like a Jew, if he felt himself guilty of betraying the Christian church. His father, Diego de Santangel, the Chief Justice of Zaragoza—whose offices and prison had been temporarily commandeered by authority of the two crowns of Aragon and Castile—did not have any such feeling. He had a moment alone with his son, while the servants held the Inquisitional officers at bay.

"You are a Christian," he told his son. "You have never observed Jewish rites. You almost never visit with your Jewish kinsmen. You have never participated in the Passover feast. No Jew has ever given you instruction in the religion of your ancestors. You are a Christian, body and soul, and you respect the Church and its greatest protector, the Holy Inquisition. Do not waver on any of these points, or you, and your mother, and your little sister, and your Jewish kinsmen, are all doomed. I need not tell you more than that. I know you are brave." And the Chief

Justice of the city kissed his son, and then watched in despair as the armed men marched him away.

He was the first man to be denounced to and arrested by the Inquisitional Tribunal of Zaragoza. The Chief Justice sent off letters to his friends at court, and Master Cuheno sent an emerald to Queen Isabella in Toledo with a letter begging the royal couple for their protection over the frightened citizens of the city. Rachel, upon hearing the news, let out a scream, and then another, and couldn't be quieted for hours. Her father gave her a sleeping draft, and she slept for more than a day, waking to a quiet, profound depression, and a plan that she shared with nobody, not even her brother.

A guard was placed about the home of the Chief Justice, a guard responsible only to the Inquisitor; while no one other than Thomas was under suspicion, or arrest, the movements of the family of a suspected heretic were always under surveillance, particularly if they were rich. Everyone expected another arrest —either of a de Santangel or a Cuheno—but the only news from the Inquisitional prison was a request for maravedis to pay for the meals given to their single prisoner.

The maravedis would have payed for a king's banquet, but all Thomas got in his cell was brackish water and a thin soup, with a bit of stale bread floating on its surface. His cell was tiny and dark, but he was not chained to the wall, and he wore his own clothes. On his fourth day of incarceration, the door to his cell was flung open and he was led by five men down a dark, steep flight of steps to the enormous underground chamber where Friar Ramirez del Pulgar was to conduct all examinations into the faith of the men and women of Zaragoza.

"I demand to know what precisely are the crimes for which I am now being held in this filthy place," said Thomas. He held himself back from saying more, and looked instead to the Inquisitor, sitting in a great chair, his black eyes firmly on his prisoner. Thomas felt strong, and clearheaded; if he had spoken too quickly, he told himself, it was simply because he had spoken to no one at all for so long a time. Four days in which to think about the nature of his crime had been an eternity.

He had thought often of telling the Inquisitor at once that he was a Jew, and proud of it, like his father and his sister and his mother, and that the Inquisitor could kill them all if he liked, but that he, Thomas, would go down fighting. He had thought more about saying nothing, refusing to answer any questions asked of him by an ill-born, fanatic friar. He had thought of swallowing all the rocks in his cell, so that he would die without having the chance of incriminating anyone. He had thought about the fact that the truth would kill him and his family, that the refusal to speak would do the same; that the most difficult thing to do would be to lie, and continue lying, until he had resisted all impulses to incriminate anyone he loved. But a hundred resolutions now whirled within him as he caught the scent of the friar's hate. How much simpler to break away from these men and die by his own hand with a blade in his belly, having first choked the life out of the Inquisitor of Zaragoza.

"Is it true that you're a Jew?" said the Inquisitor.

Thomas heard himself answer without anger, in an absurd, matter-of-fact tone: "No, it is not true." He hoped that his words carried no hint of slavery, or fear. If he was to lie, he must retain his dignity before this lowborn friar.

Two of the guards who had brought him to the examination room now held him from either side, their strong hands locked on his elbows. Still, they were more than a little afraid of Thomas, and not simply because he was the son of the Chief Justice of their city; they were afraid he might be guilty of some supernatural crime, of some witchery outside their ken. Even burning such a creature did not insure them against his coming back from the dead to poison their children or lead them through endless nights of howling dreams.

"Is it true that you have been instructed in the Laws of Moses by your cousin Rachel Cuheno, including the special blessings for the dead?"

"No!" said Thomas, and then he gave in to his temper and added: "I am not used to being held in place by louts while a lowly friar stares at me from his throne."

The Inquisitor smiled, even as the guards stiffened their hold on Thomas's elbows. "Chain him," said the Inquisitor.

Thomas tore his arm away from one of the guards, and the others all came at him. "I want a chair!" he screamed. "I want a chair to sit in! I'm not going to stand while he sits! I want to know what crime I'm charged with! I want to see the archbishop! I want to see my father! I want to know what authority allows you to treat me like a slave!"

The guards took hold of his flailing limbs and pulled him across the room. There were staples set high in a stone wall, and even a man as tall as Thomas had to rise up nearly on his toes when they chained his strong wrists to the staples. As the blood drained out of his raised arms, he felt the will drain out of him. For the first time, Thomas noticed a little humpbacked scribe, his bad eyes an inch from the paper on which he wrote every word uttered in the cavernous room.

"Have you ever fucked your cousin, the Jewess Rachel Cuheno?" said the friar.

The word uttered from that filthy face, the name blackened by the horrible question, drove strength into Thomas's tired limbs. He pulled on the chains and screamed at the friar to let him go, to let him go so that he could kill him.

As Thomas ranted and raved, the Inquisitor quietly shut his eyes and waited. Experience had taught him to allow his prisoners a good deal of free play, especially when they were as eager to exhaust themselves as this young man. Indeed it was not more than three minutes before Thomas, his voice already hoarse, quieted. His arms felt devoid of any strength, and seemed to be fast losing all signs of life as well.

"Do you ever eat pork?" said the Inquisitor finally.

Thomas looked at the man and tried to comprehend the question being thrown his way. The friar raised his voice, and repeated: *"Do you ever eat pork?"*

"Of course I eat pork," said Thomas. He felt his head grow clearer as the rage subsided, and the pain in his chained, raised arms took on a steady, stabbing rhythm. He would be asked questions designed to incriminate himself and Rachel and his family; he would answer them at once, intelligently, without fear.

"Are you certain you eat the flesh of the pig? After all, it is well known that your family never eats anything but meat sanctioned by your own butchers, your own rabbis."

"I am a Christian, and the son of Christians."

"Your father is a *Marrano*, a secret Jew," said the Inquisitor. "A secret Jew who married another secret Jew."

"My father is a good Christian. We go to Mass every Sunday. My mother is a saintly, religious woman."

"Your mother and your father are both the children of secret Jews. I don't call secret Jews, who masquerade as Christians, good Christians. I call them heretics. Your parents are heretics, and the children of heretics. They taught you the secrets of the Jewish priests, and you learned your secrets very well."

"All that is a lie."

"So you eat pork?"

"Yes."

"And you change your linen on Saturdays?"

"No!" said Thomas, not allowing himself to fall into the examiner's trap. "My arms are weak, but I'm not about to lie the way you want me to."

"I only want the truth," said the Inquisitor. "If you are not a heretic, which I doubt, then you must continue to have faith in your answers, and in the Holy Church."

The pain was beginning to rise from the arms to the shoulders to the neck; a wave was beginning to touch his temples and the region behind his own eyes. "Listen, sir," said Thomas. "I will tell you what you want to know. I will hide nothing. But if my arms remain like this, it shall be difficult for me to think."

"Now you call me 'sir'?" said the Inquisitor, vastly pleased. "Before I was a lowly friar, and my guards louts, but now I see that I am worthy of your *hidalgo* blood."

"I am a good Christian, wrongly accused," said Thomas. "Please ask me what you want to know."

"First, I shall tell you what I already know," said the Inquisitor. "You are first of all a heretic, a baptized Christian with no belief in our Lord. You are secondly a liar, for it is a proven fact that you, like the rest of your family, abominate pork, change your linen on Saturday, bathe Friday nights to prepare for your Jewish sabbath; that you gather around your mother as she lights candles on Friday nights; that you pray in the Jewish manner, swaying back and forth and sighing; that you give money for the oil in the lamps of the synagogue; that you take religious training from your kinsmen the Cuhenos; that you have killed one Christian male servant; that you have killed a dog and a cat and have beaten a Christian maidservant—"

"Wait," said Thomas. "Please, listen to me. I've never killed anyone. That's ridiculous. I've never killed a man, or a dog or a cat. I certainly don't beat my servants. I've never touched a maidservant—"

"No, of course not," said the Inquisitor. The fat, oily-faced man got out of his thronelike chair and walked slowly to his captive. "You've killed no one, and by the loud and certain way in which you protect your innocence on that point, I am more certain than ever that you are guilty on every other."

"I am guilty of nothing but hatred for your ugly face," said Thomas. "Let me out of these chains!"

Again, the Inquisitor smiled, and allowed Thomas his tantrum. It took even less time than before for the young man to exhaust himself. When the screaming and the chain-rattling had subsided, Friar Ramirez del Pulgar stood up and walked slowly to Thomas. He smiled into his prisoner's face, and then calmly, without the hurry or worry that runs through a street fight, swung his right fist into the pit of the young man's stomach, putting all his considerable weight into the punch. The hump-backed scribe looked up at this, but not in surprise; he had seen worse, much worse, and committed against men and women venerable with age and greater aristocratic lineage. Ramirez del Pulgar watched the young man finish his spasmodic shaking, and then turned his back to him and walked slowly back to his seat. The Inquisitor stared at Thomas, and when he had decided that the young man had accepted the steady, terrible pain in the arms, the shoulders, the small of the back, and had begun to know fear, he said:

"I am doing God's work, Jew, as you shall very soon be able to see. Some Jews die before they get a chance to go to the stake. I shall personally see to it that you are not so lucky. I will tell you now that your only chance for salvation is a full and open confession of your sins, and the sins you have observed in your fellow secret Jews, and the sins committed by the Jews who led you into the path of heresy. Only then shall you be granted the grace of a speedy garroting before the terrible fire you must face. Only then shall the Lord take mercy on your eternal soul and not sentence you to hellfire. Only a full and sincere and open confession of all your sins will allow you an easy death and a free spirit. If you choose to be recalcitrant, Thomas de Santangel, you shall be starved in your cell, and then handed over to the torturers. Everything you know will be known to us one way or the other. Even your little sister would tell everything she knows about you in a minute if confronted with one-tenth of what you must face."

Thomas shut his eyes and tried to slow the pace of his rapidly deteriorating will. The pain running through his body seemed to awake a hunger that he thought he had learned to ignore; both conditions reminded him of his mortal state, his potential for weakness. It was maddening to realize how fast he had come from pride to beggary. He tried to shut his mind to the inescapable message: All he could hope for was a quick death; minutes before he had been planning vengeance, violence on the Inquisitor. With shut eyes, he heard the Inquisitor speak; and Thomas was shaken and full of self-loathing, accepting the fact of his fear.

"Answer me."

"What?"

"Answer me," repeated the Inquisitor. "Who are the Jews who have taught you the way of heresy?"

"No one," he said, and then he realized that he was speaking stupidly, without conviction or purpose. A sudden fear at the power he possessed over the lives of his family—and Rachel—took hold of him: It was sin enough to long for one's own death; it was unthinkable to be the agent of torture and destruction for his own loved ones.

"Listen, sir," said Thomas. "Listen, please. I have lied, and I won't lie anymore. I shall tell you what you want to know. I shall tell you everything. I am a secret Jew. Not my parents, not my sister, but only I. A rabbi from Toledo, a tall man with a great nose, he came and taught me everything about the way of the Jews. Even on the day I was baptized, this rabbi came to the house of my parents and, without them knowing, washed off the holy water and cast a spell over my body, to ward off anything Christian. This rabbi taught me the Hebrew prayer for the dead, and when he died I recited it for eleven months, as he had told me to do. But it is five years since he has died, and I have forgotten much. I try not to eat pork in my house and to keep all my Jewish practices secret from my parents. For the same reason, I keep the knowledge of my Jewish rites secret from my Jewish kinsmen, for fear that they will tell my parents. I alone am guilty of being a secret Jew, and I implore you now to accept my confession and decide on my punishment."

"What did you practice?" said the Inquisitor, his question coming as fast as the crack of a whip.

"What?" said Thomas, not comprehending. What else did this man want? Hadn't he confessed to everything that the friar could possibly want?

"What did you practice, boy?" said the Inquisitor. "You're a

Jew, you practiced Jewish rites. What rites? Black magic? Desecration of the Host? What?"

"No, no, not that," said Thomas. He tried to remember something of his Jewish heritage, but the fact was he knew practically nothing. He knew far more about the Church. What he remembered most was the beautiful Pesach feast, and Rachel reciting the four questions in her clear, confident Hebrew. But his father had specifically warned him against mention of the Pesach, or Passover, feast. "I tried to remember a few holidays, to think about them, because there really wasn't much I could do to observe them."

"With your mythical rabbi gone and buried?"

"He died, yes."

"He never existed, boy. What holidays did you celebrate with your parents and your sister, and your kinsmen, the Cuhenos?"

"They never celebrated anything."

"What holidays did *you* celebrate then?"

"I don't remember," said Thomas. "My arms are so uncomfortable—"

"The Passover feast? Did you perform the Jewish rites on the Passover, the time of our Saviour's murder?"

"No, never."

"And Yom Kippur—the Day of Atonement? I suppose you and your family didn't remember to fast?"

"I fasted! That's right! I'm sorry, I'd forgotten. But I'm guilty of that. I fasted on Yom Kippur, every year."

"When is it?"

"I'm sorry?"

"Yom Kippur. What day of the year is it?"

"I don't know."

"What? You just said that you fast on Yom Kippur every year."

"There are so many fasts."

"Are there? I didn't realize. I thought you Jews were more apt to feast than to fast. Do you perhaps know when the Pesach feast comes?"

"I'm not sure," said Thomas, remembering his father's injunction.

"It's at Easter time, Jew," thundered the Inquisitor. "As you very well know. It is at Easter time that you meet with your kinsmen and perform the sacrilege of the Pesach feast, the sacrilege

that is a deliberate desecration of Holy Week, a deliberate celebration of the Jewish Judas, à deliberate mockery of the Last
Supper. It is about the Pesach feast that I want to know. It is
about the Pesach feast that you must tell me. Every Jew at the
Pesach feast with a New Christian comes under my jurisdiction
as an enemy of the Faith. Every New Christian celebrating the
treachery of Judas is a heretic. You are already doomed, Thomas
de Santangel. Save your soul by telling me all you know, by
hiding nothing."

"I have told you all I know. I have never attended a Pesach
feast. I have never consorted with Jews during their festivals. All
my immediate family are good, sincere Christians."

"Your sister, Isabelle, for example?"

"Of course," said Thomas, a terrible fear beginning to rise up
in his throat.

"Does she know that you're a secret Jew?"

"No!"

"And if she did, of course, she would never report the crime.
Or so you think."

"She has nothing to do with this! Why do you mention Isabelle? Please, sir, I have told you everything—I have told you
all I know!"

"Bring in the girl," said the Inquisitor, and Thomas thought
he would go mad with fury. Isabelle de Santangel was fourteen,
and had never attended a Pesach feast. Her Jewish instruction
had been minimal, consisting mostly of stories told her by her
mother's very old aunt, still a professing Jew. She had not been
told that Thomas had been arrested; and when, a day after the
arrest, her father decided to follow his letter to the court at
Toledo with a personal appearance before the king, her mother
told her that father and brother had gone to a tournament outside
of Toledo. She had been arrested only an hour before, and when
she first understood that the men, in their beautiful uniforms, had
to come to arrest *her*, she had been afraid, but not hysterical.
Her mother had become hysterical. Isabelle had gone away with
the officers calmly, but her mother had to be restrained by half a
dozen men.

Waiting outside the door to the Inquisitor's examining chambers, Isabelle tried to review her sins, in the way the nuns had
taught her. But in a moment the door was opened and she was
thrust, rather than led, inside. The Inquisitor, an ugly little man,

smiled at her across the great space of the room, and the smile cut right through her. Immediately she heard a cry. As she turned to the source of sound, she saw the absolutely incredible sight of her brother chained to the wall, like a felon. A man standing on a stool was shoving a rag into her brother's open mouth to gag his outbursts; Thomas's face was red with rage. Everything about the image was so out of place with the reality of her life that the young girl felt as if the earth had swallowed her up and she was witnessing some mad scene from out of hell.

"Look here, girl," said the Inquisitor to Isabelle, but she could not take her eyes from her brother on the wall. "Look at me and answer my questions."

"Why is Thomas like that? Why is he chained?"

"You are not to speak, girl," said the Inquisitor, with stately calm. "You are not to speak unless I ask you to answer a question. If you do not do as you're told, you'll be stripped naked, tied to that table, and whipped. Do you understand what I'm saying, girl?"

"What did Thomas do?" she said.

"Did you hear what I said, girl?"

"Why is he like that? Let him go!"

"Hold her still," said the Inquisitor, and the guards clutched her tighter now, so that she could not turn any way at all, save in the direction of the Inquisitor. "Are you a Christian girl?" he said, and when she didn't answer, he said again, "Are you a Christian? Answer me, girl! Answer me, or you shall be stripped down and whipped like a slave."

"Yes," Isabelle said finally, the fear constricting her throat. The question, the few terrible things that she'd heard about the Inquisition, the pointed remarks of her schoolmates and her teachers, the nuns, all led to a terrifying conclusion about why she was here, and why Thomas was chained to the wall: They were not true Christians because they came from Jews, and now they must be punished.

"Are you a good Christian?"

"Yes, sir."

"Is your brother a good Christian?"

"Yes, sir."

"He is not a *Marrano?*"

"What?"

"A *Marrano*—a secret Jew."

"No, sir. Thomas is a good Christian. As are my mother and father."

"Your father is dead, girl—and you are a liar." And because she was screaming and writhing, the Inquisitor said again: "Hold her still."

Slowly, he got out of his chair, and turned to look at the weak, struggling eyes of Thomas, eyes wild with sorrow. Then, facing Isabelle, Friar Ramirez said in distinct, level tones : "Your father is dead. He was a *Marrano*, a secret Jew. He was told not to leave the city until the Inquisitional Tribunal here decided whether or not he was to be questioned. He was shot down by archers shortly after he left the city, on the way to Toledo to plead with the king for his son, and himself. I didn't want him to die like that, but the archers had no choice. He was a fugitive from the justice and mercy of the Church, and thus died without a chance to save his soul. Your father is in hell now. He'll be in hell forever. You have to tell me now whether you and your brother are secret Jews, so I can save your souls. Do you understand?"

"My father isn't dead!" screamed Isabelle.

"Is your brother a secret Jew?"

"He's not dead!" she screamed again. "How can you say my father is dead and gone to hell when you know that he's the best man in the city, the Chief Justice, the kindest man, and a good Christian?"

The Inquisitor could see that she was listening to nothing now, other than the agonized screaming of her father's soul. "Strip her," he said to the guards.

For a moment it seemed that Thomas de Santangel might strangle himself on the gag in his mouth. His chains rattled, propelled by bloodless arms; the whites of his eyes became red with tiny lines of blood; his legs shook and danced uselessly. But he finally relaxed. His chains stilled, his linen gag grew wet with spit and mucus, his eyes absorbed his sister before him with an equanimity born of despair.

Thomas had never seen his sister's naked body. He could not help but stare at her now as she struggled and screamed. Quickly, her body grew tired of fighting the men who held her arms and legs, who tore off her beautiful clothes, whose hands roughed the smooth surface of her pale skin. Her screams intensified. They found their high point, and this dreadful monotone grew steadily in volume until it seemed that it must shatter the girl. But Isabelle didn't shatter. Her voice broke, and she tried to catch her breath in great gasping sobs, and all she could think of was that the humiliation of being naked before these men was far worse than dying.

"Hold her still," said the Inquisitor, and the guards forced her to stand erect, one at each arm. The Inquisitor spoke again, ordering them to pinion the arms behind her back, and as the strong men held her in that fashion, her humiliation began to give way to pain, and her fear of its increase.

"How old are you, girl?" said the Inquisitor. When she didn't answer, he nodded at the guards, who increased the pressure on her twisted arms so that she cried out in pain. "How old are you, girl?" he repeated.

"Fourteen," she said, so softly that he had to come very close to her, placing his oily head near her terrified face and asking her to repeat her answer. "Fourteen," she said, and she started with perfect horror as the Inquisitor's hand touched the tips of her little breasts.

"Bring her to her knees," said the Inquisitor, and as the guards forced the girl to the floor in this further indignity, he looked up at Thomas de Santangel. "You shall see how easy it is to betray the ones you love," he said. "You shall soon see everything."

The Inquisitor looked down at Isabelle, grabbed her lowered head in his evil-smelling hand, and turned her blue eyes upward. "Do you want to be whipped, girl?"

"No," she said.

"I can't hear you."

"No, sir, please."

"Beg," said the Inquisitor, and the girl didn't know what he wanted, she only knew that she was falling, deeper and deeper into some vague territory of weakness and terror. She didn't want to be hurt, and she had never felt so desperately afraid in all her life.

"How am I to beg, sir? I am begging you, please—please let me get dressed—please, señor."

"Stay on your knees, girl."

"Yes, sir."

"You will answer my questions?"

"Yes, sir. Whatever you ask."

"Are you a secret Jewess?"

"No, sir."

"Do you eat pork?"

"No, sir. I never eat pork."

"Why is it that you don't eat pork?"

"I don't know, sir. My parents don't like it. They say it's not healthy to eat."

"Do you fast on the Day of Atonement?"

"What?"

"Yom Kippur. The Day of Atonement."

"I don't understand."

"Do you go to the Pesach feast?"

"No, not yet."

"What do you mean, 'not yet'?"

"Maybe this year I'll go." But then she let out a scream, remembering that her father was dead. "I can't go!" she said. "I can't go without my father. I have not yet gone, but how can I ever go without my father?"

The Inquisitor looked at her for a moment, not showing his rage at her innocence, and then brought his open palm crashing across her upraised face. As she cried out in terror and pain, he said, "You are to answer questions, not ask them. Who told you that you are to attend a Pesach feast? Was it a Jew or a Christian?"

"I don't remember, sir."

"Bring her to the table," said the Inquisitor.

"No!" said Isabelle. "I am answering your questions. What do you want of me? I'll tell you everything."

But they had already dragged her to her feet and begun to pull her taut, protesting body to the ornate table in the center of the great room. The guards lifted the light young body and sat her down on the edge of the table, then pulled her backward, flattening her back to the hard wood surface, pressing her shoulders down so that the girl could only look up at the high, impassive ceiling of the dreadful, oppressive space.

There were men all about her now, one at each arm, one at each leg, and they were holding her flat for the Inquisitor; she could feel their eyes and his devouring every inch of her soft skin. She moved her head slightly forward, and immediately the ugly face of her tormentor blew up in her line of vision. He was leaning over her, his sweaty hand on her little belly, grabbing the sparse pubic hair, touching her thigh, touching her neck, and she was shouting at him, demanding to be let alone, demanding to be allowed to do his bidding, demanding to do anything other than submit to his touch. Through the protective fog she'd thrown about her violated senses, she heard a question, but it didn't register. Nothing could register as long as his face hovered over hers, as long as his hand met the surface of her skin.

Then a sudden, incredible pain erupted in her left thigh—incredible because she didn't understand its source. But the pain repeated itself, and the fog lifted. She heard the whistle of a whip through still air; she heard the crack of its lash on her bare skin; she saw the wild friar swing the whip over his head, out of her line of vision, and watched his face as he brought the whip out of space, from behind his head to the flat surface of her belly and breasts.

Isabelle understood now what was happening. She was being whipped by the Inquisitor because she had not answered his questions. What *were* his questions? He wanted to know who had told her that she'd be able to attend the Pesach feast. He wanted her to admit that Thomas was a secret Jew. He wanted her to say that she had seen her cousin Rachel teach her brother Thomas the Jewish prayer for the dead. But Isabelle didn't even know what this prayer was. She was a Christian girl, educated by devout nuns. They had Jewish ancestors, and this year she would learn more about them and their practices; this year she would be old enough. A little girl could blurt out a dangerous phrase, a phrase that could kill an entire family.

"Thomas, Thomas, Thomas!"

The girl felt her head being raised by a great force, and with speed; the ugly friar's face seemed to lurch at her, and as she tried to catch her racing breath, a silence descended from the ceiling to the table. She was not being whipped, the far ceiling was gone from her sight, and she blinked to clear her eyes of tears. Isabelle was sitting up straight on the great table, facing the Inquisitor. Two men held her arms behind her back, two other men secured her ankles to the tabletop; the blood scattered about her thin white thighs was her own. She was whispering, and the Inquisitor was listening to what she said, but Isabelle couldn't make sense of her own words; all she could concentrate on was the blood on her thighs, the marks on her belly, the exhausted beating of her heart.

She made an effort to understand the words of the Inquisitor, because she felt that understanding them might allow her to be cleaned up, soothed, and sent home in her own clothes. But the pain racking her body was too great. The pain had been too severe for so short a time; it had need of catching up with her. She remembered the whipping, the sense of horror at being spread flat and open to the men in the room, to the terrible friar's eyes and hands. And she was still open. Still naked. No, she couldn't move her hands; she couldn't edge her stretched-out legs together; she couldn't avoid the friar's face.

"Thomas," she said again, understanding that by saying this name there would be an end to her pain.

"It was Thomas, your brother," said the Inquisitor. "He told you that this year you'd attend the Pesach feast?"

"Yes, sir."

"So then you are now giving witness that your brother, Thomas de Santangel, is a secret Jew?"

"Yes, sir, *yes*," said Isabelle, nodding her head as much as she could with a powerful hand gripping her long hair, keeping her eyes level with those of the Inquisitor. The part of her that was responding to pain and fear tried desperately hard to understand the part of her that was speaking, the part of her that was answering the question of the terrible man before her. But she couldn't make sense of what was happening. It seemed as if her hair were being pulled out of her scalp, that her heart was trying to burst out of her breast, that the stinging sensation in her thighs and belly was reprimanding her for some unfathomable childish sin. The part of her that spoke could speak only one phrase, could answer only one question; and this part of her was in another world from the part of her that drifted madly through pain, humiliation, and utter confusion. "Thomas, yes," she said. "It was Thomas."

"Put her in a cell," said the Inquisitor.

As two guards rushed to obey the command, the friar resumed his thronelike chair. Without looking at the young man chained to the wall, he began to speak.

"You see how many minutes it takes to wring the truth out of your own loving sister, Thomas de Santangel?" he said. "You are a confessed secret Jew, and condemned now by your own sister. Either you can start answering my questions, and thereby hope for a speedy death and the chance of eternal salvation, or you can continue with your lies. Your sister is very young and very pretty. It will not be amusing for you to watch her tortured for not being able to give me information that her own brother possesses."

The friar rose abruptly. "Remove his gag," he said, and he walked over to the humpbacked scribe and looked down at the record. As a guard got up on the stool to remove the gag that had been forced into Thomas's mouth, the Inquisitor spoke again.

"I want to know about the diamonds," he said. "You are Rachel Cuheno's lover, and her student in all things related to the practice of Jewish rites. To this you will confess very soon. But even sooner than that, you shall tell me about the diamonds. Everyone in Spain knows of the Cuheno fortune, hidden in diamonds and rubies and emeralds and pearls. It is with diamonds that they have bribed the poor Christians who surround the king and queen, and have kept the Inquisition from coming to Zaragoza—until now. It is no use trying to confiscate what these Jews have hidden—Jews care more about their gems than they do about their lives. You must tell me where the Cuhenos hide their stones, so that the Holy Inquisition can claim what is rightfully its own property. That is, once you formally accuse Rachel Cuheno of her crimes."

The friar picked up his whip from the table and turned to face Thomas de Santangel. "I am waiting," he said. "We will begin with your confession of Rachel Cuheno's crimes." But as he cracked his whip impatiently against the leg of the scribe's chair, he could see that the guard standing erect next to where the young man hung limply from his chained wrists was waiting for a chance to speak.

"I'm sorry, sir," said the guard. "I'm afraid there's been an accident. I'm afraid he's swallowed half the gag. I'm sorry, sir, but he's choked, sir. I'm sorry, sir, but he's dead."

CHAPTER FIVE

A week after the death of Thomas de Santangel, Rachel decided that she was in love with him. She did not know that Thomas was dead. The only death that had been bruited about was the death of Thomas's father, Diego de Santangel, the Chief Justice of Zaragoza. The death had terrified the city. The Chief Justice had been shot down by a score of archers, though he rode in the company of only half a dozen men, none of whom offered any resistance; these men had been allowed to continue on their way. If anyone had doubted the power or the severity of the Inquisition Tribunal, this murder had ended all doubts.

Many Christians of Jewish descent left the city on various pretexts, never to return. The shipmasters in Barcelona asked whatever price they liked of New Christians eager to begin a new life in Italy or France. Caravans of poor Jews, terrified of new outbreaks of violence against them, set out for Portugal, or Granada, often meeting death at the hands of Ferdinand's undisciplined troops, on their way to battle the Moors. But most of the city stayed put; the Jews hoping that the Inquisitor would concern himself only with Christian heretics; the New Christian converts hoping that they'd be saved by the evidence of their conversion; the Old Christian families hoping that their names and lineages would put them above suspicion of the dreaded tribunal.

Abraham Cuheno prepared a small bag of gems, a small collection of medical texts, and a large wallet of maravedis, so that they would be ready to flee at a moment's notice. Meanwhile, he continued his medical duties in the city and tried to maintain calm among his coreligionists. As Judah's travels had underlined, there was nowhere better for Jews to run to. As for Judah, he continued to work on Rachel's diamond, cutting away its weight in the quest for a purer form. Rachel spent little time with Judah, or her father, or anyone else. She asked for news of Thomas, she appeared at family meals, but she spoke little and kept to herself.

The decision she finally came to, she told herself, had nothing to do with the fact that she loved him, that she remembered the insolent way he had kissed her, that she liked the long athletic steps he took as he crossed a room to greet her. No, she told herself, she would do as much for anyone wrongly imprisoned. His life was in danger, and only she could rectify the error.

Rachel left a note for her father and brother. She wrote it in Aragonese, with a postscript in Hebrew—an emotional postscript reminding them of her mother, asking them to imagine what she would have done under similar circumstances. Leaving the note in her father's study, she left the house and began the long walk to the Inquisitional prison. She walked slowly, fighting back her fear, and it took her nearly two hours to reach her goal. The guards at the gates of the prison were given her name, and her request, and in a matter of moments she was ushered inside the prison and led by a group of five guards along a dark, twisting corridor.

"Are you taking me to the Inquisitor?" she said. "Is he going to see me right away?"

But the guards didn't answer her. They walked her to the end of the massive building, and then down a flight of steps, and then along a horrible, fetid corridor, the backbone of a hundred tiny cells.

"I'm Rachel Cuheno," she said. "I came here to see the Inquisitor. Why did you take me down here?"

The guards still didn't answer her, and in a few more moments they were, incredibly, opening the door to a dark cell and motioning for her to enter.

Rachel let out an incredulous laugh. "No," she said. "You don't understand. I wasn't arrested. I came here to see the Inquisitor. I have information for him. It's only to see him that I came here. He wouldn't want to put me in a cell for only wanting to speak with him. Please, just tell him that Rachel Cuheno, the daughter of Abraham Cuheno, has come to see him. *Please.*"

"He knows," said a guard, and then two of the guards pushed her very hard into the black depths of the cell, and one of them ran his hand across her breasts and laughed, his filthy breath blowing in her face.

Master Cuheno rode out with Judah and two of the jurists from the Chief Justice's—the *late* Chief Justice's—office, and approached the gates of the Inquisitional prison. Rachel's note had been well written, succinct: Thomas de Santangel had been accused of Judaizing simply because he had defended the honor of his cousin, a Jewess. Only this same Jewess could provide testimony to the contrary.

The note was monstrous in its simplicity, its utter innocence. How could Rachel not see that Thomas was imprisoned simply because evil existed in the world? How could Rachel not see that offering herself as victim would never release another victim? Abraham Cuheno was so overcome with grief, instantaneous grief, that upon first reading the note he prostrated himself on the floor and intoned the Kaddish, the prayer affirming faith in God, recited in the moment of a mourner's remembrance and sorrow. Cuheno needed the words of the prayer, needed to recite them again and again, because, in any absence of praying, inescapable thoughts of Rachel's fate flooded his mind.

When he had stopped praying, he had taken the note to Judah, and the two men had armed themselves and ridden to the late Chief Justice's office, where they procured the aid of two Old Christian jurists. But when all four men rode to the gates of the Inquisitional prison, they were turned away by a force of archers. Master Cuheno returned home and wrote to the king and queen, reminding them of his services on their behalf, speaking of the purity of his daughter's soul, begging them for the favor of their protection in this time of need.

Every day, father and brother rode to the prison to ask for

news, and offer money for Rachel's sustenance. Every day, they were turned away rudely, with no information. Every day, Master Cuheno felt himself closer to the precipice of madness and death; he began to feel that his sanity would break apart in the moment that Rachel's soul left her body.

Judah, too, had a mystical feeling about the approach of Rachel's death. He felt himself compelled to work on her diamond, cutting and polishing the facets, creating a flawless table reflecting pure white light; but he never felt that the work was finished. Every day he returned to the diamond, Rachel's diamond, and every day he discovered something new to be re-cut, refinished, repolished, until finally he began to believe that her diamond would not be completely ready for the world until Rachel had gone to the world-to-come.

Still, he couldn't stop work. It was not he who was hastening her death by his work; her death was coming, and it would be a release for her from something worse than death. Her death was hastening, and his only thought was to finish this gift for his sister in her lifetime.

Rachel's seventeenth birthday was at Passover time, and when she had been imprisoned for two weeks, she began to imagine that Passover had come and gone. The four questions must have been recited by Judah, and her father must have cried, remembering her mother. Of course the de Santangel family could not have been there: the Chief Justice was dead, and poor Thomas was lying in a cell, just as mad and miserable as she. She tried to remember some parts of the Passover service.

> This is the bread of affliction that our fathers ate in the land of Egypt. All who are hungry, let them come and eat; all who are needy, let them come and celebrate the Pesach. Now we are here. Next year we shall be in the land of Israel. Now we are slaves. Next year we shall be free men.

The words she remembered were Aramaic, the vernacular of the Jews in the land of Israel fifteen hundred years before. Rachel didn't understand this language very well, but she remembered its meaning from the many times she'd heard it explained in Hebrew and in Spanish. The prayer began with the words *Ha Lahmah*, meaning "Here is the bread." In Hebrew, the Hebrew of her time, it would be *Henay Halehem*. The next word, *Anyah*, meaning "affliction," was a word she didn't know in Hebrew at all.

Rachel began to intone the works of the prayer, speaking the Aramaic with a Hebrew pronunciation, accented by the Spanish of Aragon. The words assembled themselves into a tune, dipping and rising along an ancient melodic line; a lugubrious memory from the time of the Jewish enslavement in the Egypt of the pharaohs. She was not praying to God. Not at all. Rachel was remembering the Passover service, remembering her birthday, remembering her father reclining on his pillowed seat, remembering her brother Judah's interruptions of the seder with his irrelevant, charming stories. Rachel was remembering, not praying. Lying flat on her back on the stone floor, she could see the brilliant blue sky through the tiny breathing hole in her cell. She had prayed when she'd first gotten here: Prayed for her father to appear, prayed for Thomas to arrive and avenge her for the insults hurled at her by her jailers, prayed for the door to the cell to open—to let in air, light, a sense of space—prayed for a man to come in and take away the vile presence of her bodily wastes, prayed for food that she could eat, prayed for water, prayed for the Inquisitor to enter her cell and tell her exactly what sins she had committed against the Church in Zaragoza.

But she was through praying.

She seemed to sleep an hour at a time, sleeping half the day, three-quarters of the day, but always fitfully, always waking with shuddering suddenness, always shocked by the realization that her nightmares were in perfect consonance with her waking hours. The terrible odors, the dark fetid air that drifted through her dreams, greeted her with yet fuller force upon waking. Always, she jerked her head erect, her eyes reaching for the sky through the tiny chimney hole that prevented her from suffocating. She was always exhausted, always hungry, always carrying a dull headache that beat through her sleep, through her memories, through her shut-eyed visions of the world-to-come.

But the memories of the Passover had a calming effect on her. She recited the prayer, she sang the prayer, she remembered the prayer as a familial rhythm—and slowly, slowly, the brilliant blue of the sky faded, a whisper of the northwest wind penetrated her cell, a blackness dropped from the heavens; and when she next opened her eyes, it was daylight, and the excrement had been removed from her cell, and a short, heavy jailer stooped over her with a bowl of cold soup.

"Eat," he said.

Rachel took the bowl from his thick hands and poured the thin stuff into her mouth. She drank so fast that the taste didn't reach her senses; but she gagged anyway, choking on a lump of old bread, coughing up soup, and vomiting up air out of her famished belly.

"Stupid bitch," said the jailer. "Don't you even know how to eat soup?" She had spilled perhaps half the bowl, and he took the now empty container out of her white hands.

"I'm hungry," she said.

"Take off your clothes."

"Please," said Rachel. "I want to eat something."

"I said take off your clothes," said the jailer, and now he didn't wait for her to comply, but began ripping at her flimsy, high-waisted gown.

"What are you doing?" said Rachel, too tired to understand. "You're not allowed to do that. Sir!" She slapped the man across the face, still not understanding what he was doing to her gown—so wet and filthy with soup and dirt and blood.

Rachel's slap incensed the jailer. He pulled at the square neckline of the linen kirtle underneath her gown and wrenched the girl up from the floor to her knees. Rachel felt the anger and confusion drain out of her body, like a foreign substance leaving a purer realm. She had been on her back so long—on her back, and on her side, trying to find a comfortable way in which to pass the endless minutes in the terrible space—that the sudden rush to her knees, and now to her feet, drove her away from her body, away to a purity of purpose: If she could not help Thomas, she must not harm him; and more, she could not harm her father and brother.

Forgetting the jailer, letting him play with her body as if it were no longer hers, she realized that she had begun to long for death. She had grown so weak that she no longer succored herself on the knowledge that she'd have to be brave when the time of her questioning came. No one was interested in her testimony in support of Thomas. The only testimony they wanted from her was damning testimony. She'd have to remain silent, and not send innocent people to their deaths.

The jailer finished ripping away the girl's gown, and then

proceeded to the kirtle she wore beneath it. He was laughing, and he was touching her, slapping at her chin to raise her face, calling her names of mock-endearment, squeezing her breasts, pinching her belly. But it was nothing physical that drove Rachel to speak, and to an awareness of what the man was doing; it was a sudden overwhelming fear that perhaps, in her abandonment of her bodily presence, she had spoken.

"What did I say?" she said, so suddenly that the jailer laughed out loud. "What did I say? Tell me what I said!" she demanded, and then Rachel realized she was naked, that her body was being touched, that an iron ring had been placed round her neck, that she was chained to the wall, that she was shouting: "I don't know anything, you can't keep me here, you can't touch me, I'm a Jewess, you can't touch me!"

The thickset jailer pushed her back against the wall, laughing into her frenzied face. He shut up her screaming by pressing his mouth to hers. Rachel felt the full weight of his body pushing her naked back into the stone wall, felt his teeth ripping into her lips and tongue like some monstrous beast; and hungry and tired as she was, no fog lifted her from terror and pain. She couldn't retreat into memory, she couldn't abandon this moment. Every bit of her was alive with violent repulsion, perfect hate.

The man held her shoulders pressed to the wall and drove his knee into her groin. He ceased laughing, and his breath came fast with lust. The jailer spoke to her softly, harshly, whispering through the heaving rhythm of his laboring heart: "You slut, you Jew-bitch, you filthy whore, I'm going to fuck you good, you lousy cunt, I'm going to fuck you like you deserve, bitch, I'm going to fuck you like the cunt that you are."

Rachel was fighting, fighting as hard as she could; but her shoulders didn't move from the stone wall, the terrible words wouldn't stop coming from the gasping mouth, the knee in her groin could not be fought away. Every moment, Rachel's head grew clearer. She had been in her cell not a year, but two weeks—not more than three weeks. She was hungry, but not nearly starved to death. She was crazed, but not nearly crazy. She wanted to live. She wanted to kill this man who was trying to violate her. She wanted to live to see Thomas, her father, and her brother. She wanted to live to show them that she was a Jewess and not afraid.

At the auto-da-fé in Seville, women had gone to the stake

pregnant—women who'd been in the prisons of the Inquisition for months, women who'd left their families virgins, and left the world concubines to their jailers.

Rachel tried to move a shoulder, release a hand. The man had stripped away his doublet and now pulled her with the chain about her neck to the floor of stone. Rachel saw his raging face, answered his screams with her own. He tried to mount her, and she plunged three fingers into his right eye.

The jailer fell back, shutting his eye, recoiling from her, and Rachel saw the man's fully erect, already dribbling penis. In a second, he was back for her, one eye shut, his teeth clenched, growling like a wild beast. He leaped on her, clutching her neck ring and shaking her head while his legs tried to spread wide her own.

If she had not been so fully alive, she'd have missed the soft words that blew into the tiny room. But Rachel missed nothing now; an energy had taken hold of her spirit, giving her strength. If she had no food in her, it didn't prevent her from being as strong and as sharp and as fully awake as she had ever been. The words were "Leave us," and they were spoken by an ugly little man at the just-opened door to her cell. And when the jailer continued his vile actions, the same ugly little man stepped aside and allowed a guard to enter.

The guard was tall and thin, and for a moment, for all her new clarity, Rachel thought that it was Thomas de Santangel—for who else would do what this man did? The guard grabbed the jailer's hair, ripped him off the girl's tortured body, and sent him sprawling against the opposite wall of the cell.

"Leave us," repeated the ugly little man, and the jailer looked in terror at the man and the guard, and, mumbling some phrase of contrition under his breath, scurried through the low door. "And you," said the man to the guard. The guard bowed respectfully, and left them.

Rachel, naked, badly bruised, starved, had just been saved from being raped. But the eyes she turned on the Inquisitor of Zaragoza were not glazed with gratitude. She tried to stop up her crying, to catch her breath, to cover her breasts or her loins. This was the man she had been warned against, and she must not look at him with tears or fear but with brazen intellect, and contempt. She spoke too soon. Her words came out like a string of pleas, when she had wanted them to be majestic demands.

"I want my clothes. I want to eat. I am Rachel Cuheno, daughter of Abraham Cuheno of Zaragoza, and I am a Jewess, and I have committed no crime."

"Silence," said the Inquisitor. He was looking into her eyes, not at her naked body, but she felt more exposed, more accessible to violation than when the jailer was pressing her to the ground. "I will know what crimes you have committed, Jewess. You don't have to tell me that you have committed no crime. I'm sure your God wouldn't send you to this place if you were as pure and as innocent as you like to pretend."

"Sir," said Rachel Cuheno, "I came here of my own volition. I was not arrested. I came only to speak with you. I am a Jewess and the daughter of Master Abraham Cuheno, and I demand to know by what authority I have been treated in this way."

"Silence," said the Inquisitor.

"I will not be silent until I know why I am treated this way," she said, remembering to be brave and brazen, trying to recover her station in life in the face of this dreadful man.

The Inquisitor moved so fast, it seemed to Rachel that he had pulled his whip out of the air. In a second he had lashed her twice across the forearms raised to cover her breasts. As he advanced on her, she turned to the wall, exposing her naked back and buttocks, and these he whipped until she sank exhausted to her knees, resting her forehead on the rough stone of the wall. The Inquisitor grabbed the chain connecting her neck ring to the wall and pulled her around to face him. She had stopped crying, and she had stopped thinking about anything except the rising and falling of pain where welts were now forming along her pale skin.

"Do you know what the greatest crime in history was?" said the Inquisitor.

Rachel tried to answer him, but she was still trying to catch her breath. Besides, she didn't know the answer to his question. The brazenness had already been beaten out of her eyes, and she tried to remember her resolve to be courageous, to say or do nothing that would hurt her family or her people.

"Do you know what the greatest crime in history was?" said the Inquisitor again, his face inches from Rachel's. He shook her head by the chain, and Rachel tried to clear away enough pain to give him an answer.

"No," she said, so softly that she was afraid he hadn't heard.

"No!" he thundered. "You don't know! I don't doubt it, Jewess! You know how to desecrate the Host, but you don't know what the greatest crime in the history of the world was! Have you never gone to a conversionist sermon?"

Rachel tried hard to understand this next question, and to prepare an answer before he would again shake her head by the chain. Of course—the conversionist sermons—she knew what they were! Traveling friars would be allowed to harangue Jewish congregations about the refusal of Jews to accept the true Messiah, about the certainty of their burning eternally in hell. The Jews of Zaragoza had to submit to the indignity of these tirades three or more times a year; had to watch these fiery madmen stand before the Holy Ark with giant crosses; had to try and arrive home safely after the service, when Christian ruffians would wait outside the synagogue to add their touch to the arguments of the friars to abandon Judaism.

"No," said Rachel.

"You've never gone to a conversionist sermon?" screamed Friar Pulgar del Ramirez. He himself had preached in a hundred synagogues in Castile, had preached and converted—with the mob at his side—hundreds of terrified Jews.

"No," said Rachel. "The Cuhenos did not have to attend."

"No!" said the Inquisitor, pulling at her neck ring. "And who allowed this dispensation? What Christian? What heretic allowed your family this terrible privilege?"

Rachel was so momentarily confused that she didn't know whether or not to answer the man truthfully. After all, she had resolved to be brave, and not to incriminate anyone. But it seemed unlikely that this answer, truthfully given, could lead to trouble.

"I'm asking you," screamed the Inquisitor. "Why did you not have to attend the conversionist sermons? Who permitted your family this dispensation?"

"The king," said Rachel.

"What?"

"King Ferdinand, sir," said Rachel. "He was in Zaragoza, and my father cured him of some illness, and later my father went with him to Toledo. King Ferdinand said that the Cuhenos did not have to go to the conversionist sermons. It's well known among the Jews of Zaragoza." Rachel took a deep breath, satisfied with the throttled fury in the friar's face.

The friar let go of her chain and stepped away from her. He took so long to speak that the girl began again to have time to dwell on her pain, on her nakedness, on the hopelessness of her situation. But she didn't speak.

The Inquisitor said, very slowly, "The greatest crime in the history of the world was the murder of our Lord Jesus Christ by the Jews. That is the greatest crime in the history of the world, and it is a crime that is yet to be properly avenged. The world is teeming with Jews, Jews are everywhere, Jews have money and power—enough power to talk to the king. And who are these Jews? Murderers, traitors, the lowest form of life, lower than Moors, lower than savage Negroes. They killed our Lord Jesus Christ, and every one of them must be punished, every one of them must pay for their terrible crime." The friar stopped talking, and walked slowly back to where Rachel huddled, trying to cover her nakedness. "Do you know who Jesus Christ was, girl?"

"Yes, sir."

"But you do not accept him as the Messiah?"

"No, sir."

"No," said the Inquisitor, very softly, echoing Rachel's obstinate denial. But he was suddenly calm, resolved. It seemed as if he had spent his physical violence, or knew that physical violence would lend no benefit to him or to his victim's confession at this moment. "No," repeated the Inquisitor. "Our Lord appeared on this earth to die for our sins. He appeared, and he rejected the Jewish religion. Jesus Christ himself rejected your outmoded religion, and you, a girl who knows nothing, think you know more than our Lord. You accept what he rejected once and for all time. Don't you Jews understand that you insult our Lord by refusing to abandon the religion that he himself abandoned, that he himself rejected? Don't you Jews realize that your refusal to convert is an insult to Jesus Christ?"

"I am a Jewess," said Rachel. "I am not a New Christian, sir. I cannot be a heretic, because I was never baptized, I was never a Christian. I am a Jewess, and I came here of my own free will to testify in the case of Thomas de Santangel, and no one has the right to keep me here, and to beat me and to starve me and to keep me naked."

"I know your father."

"What, sir?"

"I know your father, girl. He treated me once, not long ago. He is a Jew, but he is a good doctor. Even so, I shall have no mercy on him or his family. Even if King Ferdinand tries to protect him, I shall have him—and every Jew in Zaragoza who subverts the authority of the Church—before me. I shall do what has to be done. And what has to be done is the defeat of heresy, and the end of the influence of the Jews." The Inquisitor paused to examine the effect of his words on the young girl. She was looking at him with fear, but with the special fear one had of the deranged. "I know more than you imagine," said the friar, and once again he looked at her silently, for a long minute, until finally the girl was forced to speak.

"Can't I have my clothes, sir? Can't I at least be dressed?"

"Listen, Jewess," said the Inquisitor, ignoring her request. "Listen, so that you will understand what you face here. I know more than you imagine. I know that your father performs the Black Mass. I know that he is the one who circumcises Christian children of Jewish descent, marking them as heretics for life. I know this and more about your father, who bribes even the richest men with his diamonds. But even with all his friends and all his power, he cannot free you from a just fate at our hands. And even with all his power and friends, no one will be able to save him when his own daughter testifies against him."

"I shall never testify against my father," said Rachel. "I have come here only to tell the truth about Thomas de Santangel. That is all I shall have to tell you."

"Thomas de Santangel, the poor Christian boy you seduced and polluted with your Jewish rites, is dead."

"What?"

"He's dead, Jewess," said the Inquisitor, enjoying the horror in her face. It was easy to see that someone so easily moved by another's misfortune would soon be moved by her own fate; terrified at the ravages perpetrated upon her body, she would tell him anything he wished to know. The girl, naked and beaten, seemed to retreat from him in her sudden overwhelming sadness, a sadness that was beyond his own comprehension or control. He spoke to her, but it was clear that she didn't hear what he had to say. "You shall have a bath in any case, girl. After all, your unholy father did the same for me."

In a moment, a guard appeared at the door with a small basin of water and a rag. The Inquisitor himself picked up her ragged gown and kirtle from where they lay on the stone floor, across from where Rachel was chained. Incensed at her perfect, self-absorbed sorrow, the Inquisitor flung the clothes in her face.

"Wash and dress," he said. "And think about what I have said. You shall tell me the truth, if not tomorrow, then the next day. But tomorrow, the torture begins."

CHAPTER SIX

Thomas was dead, and had passed to a world that she didn't know. She cried for him, but the young girl's mind didn't rest long with the man who might have become her lover, her husband. Imprisoned, terrified for herself and for what she might do to her father and brother, she retreated to memories of childhood, to dreams of Judah and father and mother and the world-to-come. Judah told wonderful stories about the afterlife, but Rachel had adopted her father's attitude toward these tales. "They're all nonsense," she'd tell Judah in her father's tone of voice. "Superstitious legends you've stolen from the Gentiles."

Judah had told her of a vision of heaven he'd heard of in Germany: Scholars rise up to the world-to-come in the bodies of ten-year-old boys. They are healthy, and full of spirit, but have not yet learned lust, or the cares of the pecuniary world. Though their bodies are young, their minds retain all the knowledge accumulated in the course of their lives—but only that knowledge pertaining to the study of Torah and Talmud; all extraneous knowledge—the price of wine, the Christian name of the count's firstborn son, the image of the badge of shame worn by the Jews in the village—all such knowledge is obliterated. Heaven is an endlessly long table where good men reap their rewards, sitting about and discussing increasingly complex talmudic questions with their fellow scholars.

"Where do the women go?" Rachel had asked.

"I suppose they're somewhere up there cooking," Judah had said.

"I think I'd rather cook than spend eternity sitting with a bunch of boy-scholars going over the Torah."

"That's practically blasphemy," Judah had said, with a smile.

"Father says that most of what the Jews of Spain do would be considered sacrilege by the Jews of Germany."

"Father's wrong," Judah had said. "I met Jews like that, of course. But there are Jews in Germany who ride in tournaments, make fortunes in the slave trade, and set up their own printing presses. Their idea of heaven isn't fit to disclose to young maidens."

"What's your idea of heaven?"

"Seriously?"

"Yes."

"The world. Here and now," Judah had said. "Everything just the same, except that there'll be peace, no persecutions, and an endless supply of diamonds, so that I can cut them up to my heart's content."

"Where do you think Mother is?" Rachel had asked suddenly.

"I don't know," Judah had said. But he had held up his hand and thought about the question for a few moments more. "In heaven, of course," he'd said. "That's where she is. I don't know what it's like exactly, but that's where the good souls go."

Rachel had never asked her father where he thought Mother had gone. She had been afraid of his answer; Master Cuheno didn't run away from direct questions.

Alone in her cell, her torn clothes adhering in spots to the welts and bruises left by her beating, Rachel tried to imagine heaven. She tried to picture it in the black patch of sky floating above the tiny breathing hole. Her father believed in the existence of the immortal soul, but he said that the Torah provided no illumination on the fate of that soul; that Judaism provided a path to follow in this world, and not in the world-to-come. The world-to-come was in God's hands, and her father was content not to question the unknowable.

But Rachel had need of questioning the unknowable, because

what she faced in the morning would be a thousand times worse without centering her energy on a fundamental belief. She had always believed in God, and in her religion, because she believed in her family, and in the beliefs they all shared. But tomorrow she was to approach the limits of hell, and not in the world-to-come but in the world of the earth. And if Judaism provided a path for her to follow in this world, she wanted to discern its outlines clearly.

After all, if she were to die tomorrow, what would it mean? Where would she go? Would she see her mother? Would she see Thomas? Would Judah and her father follow her there on the wings of violent death? If death was better than life, a reward for suffering life's fate, why struggle? Why not submit to the friar at once, tell him that her father was indeed guilty of high crimes? Master Cuheno had always presided over the Passover seder, the Pesach feast, the festive holiday that the Inquisitor would think of as a desecration of the Easter—and it was at Passover that Master Cuheno brought to his home as much of the *Marrano* community as he could, to teach and to talk and to dream about the future of the Jews in Spain. Why not tell the Inquisitor all this at once? Why not confess, and receive the grace of garroting prior to being burned at the stake? Why not make it swift and easy for Father to die, so he could join his daughter and his wife and his son and all his kinsmen in heaven? So what if she didn't know what heaven looked like? It had to exist. The immortal soul had to go somewhere. Even if the world-to-come was unknowable, it had to be better than the world that was now.

Rachel didn't fall asleep till morning. All night she tried to imagine her soul, a slender bird with white wings, twisting through space. How could souls communicate? How would she be able to explain to her father why she had thought it best for them all to die? Surely, if this matter of souls were as simple as she had at first supposed, it would be common knowledge. . . . Rachel could not close her eyes until the light reassured her that they would soon come for her. She thought that when they came for her, she would know what to do.

When she awoke, it was still light, the harsh light of midday. No one had come for her, not even the jailer. She was hungry, but the sensation of hunger was so familiar that she didn't dwell on it; there was something else to trouble her, some residue of her dreams. Rachel was frightened, and she tried to examine her fear, to remember its source.

She had dreamed of her mother.

Of course. She sat up so fast that the chain rattled hideously and the taut skin of her back stretched the cuts and bruises, setting the welts throbbing. Not a dream, perhaps. Something between a dream and a visit. What her father would call superstitious nonsense. But still, she had been there, Rachel's mother, Leah Cuheno, wan-faced, black-haired, her eyes glowing in the smooth, dark surface of the dream. Rachel had seen her hair—yes, she remembered the hair, the eyes, the skin, the lips opening and closing to form words and phrases. So she had not been a bird with white wings; that was not the sort of soul her mother had become. Her mother was the same, in body and in spirit. Beautiful, young, proud. Why then was Rachel's body chilled with a preternatural fear? Why was she shaking?

Indeed, Rachel was suddenly so afraid that she felt her throat twist down to the size of a nut. No air could be squeezed past, and blood shot out of her nostrils. She began to scream, not knowing why, other than that she carried the image of her mother in her terrified heart. No one came to interrupt her screaming, to quiet her with a kick or a bowl of cold soup. After a while she sank exhausted to the ground. She calmed herself, resolved to examine her soul. What had happened during the time she slept? What had her mother's image demanded of her that left her now with such fright?

The Legend of the Brave Rachel.

The story that her mother had told her when Rachel was five years old and liked her cousin's name, Sarah, better than her own. "Do you know why you're called Rachel?" her mother had asked. Rachel was too angry even to answer, but she could see a story was forthcoming, and so she settled down to hear it told out. "Jewish girls and boys are named after members of their family who have lived before them. We never name someone after a man or woman who is still alive. When a Jewish girl or boy is born, we celebrate the birth by remembering someone who has passed away, someone whom we wish to honor with our memories."

"Who was I named after?"

"Your grandmother," Leah Cuheno had said, but she smiled.

There was much more to it than *that*. "Your father's mother. I never knew her. She died before I ever met your father. But her name has always been special in the Cuheno family. They say that the carriers of the name have always been stubborn, courageous women, particularly when they had to come face-to-face with persecution."

"What's that?"

"Persecution? When bad people try to hurt you because they don't like something about you."

"What?"

"Your religion, your opinions, your beliefs."

"I don't understand."

"Let me finish, Rachel. This is what your grandfather told me. All about the Cuheno Rachels. You know that before Spain, a thousand years and more before we came here, the Jews lived in the land of Judea. Your grandfather, Mordecai Cuheno, Rachel Cuheno's husband, told me that everyone in his family knew The Legend of the Brave Rachel. That was a Rachel that came from the Cuheno family in Judea, only at that time they were called Ha-Cohen, and she had married a Maccabee. This is more than fifteen centuries ago. Do you know what a century is?"

"No."

"It's a hundred years. Fifteen hundred years ago, this is how the story goes, a girl with your name married a Maccabee. The Maccabees were the Jews who fought for freedom under the Syrian persecution. Just listen—you don't have to understand every word of a story, darling. The important thing is to understand the story, and you *will* understand it very soon."

"Was I named for the Brave Rachel, too?"

"Yes, that's it. Of course you were. All the Rachels in the family were named after her, one after the other. I'll tell you why she was called the Brave Rachel, all right? You see, her husband was hiding outside a small village, and only she knew where he was. Rachel was captured by the Syrians, and they tried everything they could to make her tell them where the Maccabee was."

"What did they do?"

"Terrible things. They scared her and they hit her."

"But she wouldn't tell them."

"No, Rachel," her mother said. "She would never betray her husband. Just as you would never betray your father."

In her cell, Rachel sat up straight and moved the ring about her neck, searching for a more comfortable position. The memory had faded into the stuff of the dream, or the visitation, or the realization of guilt. If she remembered correctly, her mother had told her that story in the year of her own death. Of course it was possible that she remembered nothing from her mother's story; that what she recalled was one of Judah's stories, told in the name of their dead mother.

But it made no difference. She had awakened to fear because she had realized that she could never betray her father. She had awakened to fear because cowardice had tried to invent a reason for her to give in to the Inquisitor; to give in to this devil on earth, in the name of her misunderstanding of the immortal soul.

"Just as you would never betray your father." Her mother had never said that. Not to the little girl she had been. If her mother had said those words, it had been last night, or this morning, while Rachel's eyes were shut and she had slept under the light from the breathing hole. All her puerile theology had led her back to her parents. Her religion was their religion. She was Jewish back through the centuries, Rachel named after Rachel named after Rachel; a series of dead women of her family and her people living in her, living through her—

The door to her cell was flung open and two tall guards entered the tiny space.

"I haven't eaten," said Rachel, but neither of them answered her, and Rachel could feel herself growing hysterical. "I haven't eaten! I want to eat! I can't go until I have eaten! I have a right to eat, even if it's only your filthy soup! I want to eat!"

They removed her neck ring and pulled her to her feet. Rachel didn't want to fail her father, or her dead mother, or the ancestors clamoring for courage in her earthly frame. She was afraid of being weak, and she had fixed on the idea of eating as a way of avoiding weakness. As the guards pulled her along the long, cool corridors, she begged for a bowl of soup, she imagined drinking it down, imbibing fortitude and courage. She was afraid that, without soup, weakness would take over her soul and send out pleas, confessions, words that the Inquisitor would want to hear.

The guards dragged her to a deep flight of steps, leading down into blackness. Rachel shut her eyes, and her bare feet scratched along the stone steps, her body supported by the power of the two silent men. She felt herself descending into a cold, terrible region, a region of blackness and ice, but when she opened her eyes she saw first of all—fire.

"What have you decided, Rachel Cuheno?" said the Inquisitor. The friar approached her as he spoke, and she turned her eyes from the fire and wondered if she should tell him of her hunger, of her intense desire to eat a bowl of soup.

"I am a Jewess who has committed no crime, sir," said Rachel.

"Have you decided to tell us what you know about your father's criminal acts, or have you decided to submit to the torture?"

"I am a Jewess who has committed no crime, sir," said Rachel again.

The friar's face remained calm. He looked about the high-vaulted room, lit by many candles and the light of the fire. There were open slits high in the walls that may have let in air from outside; they let in no daylight. The Inquisitor's eyes rested on a slight man with an enormous nose, standing before a stool at the side of a curious rectangular table with a rough log running across its center. "This is the daughter of the great doctor," said the Inquisitor to the big-nosed man. The friar turned to Rachel. "This is your doctor, Jewess. Not as renowned as your father, but he knows his business. He will know when to tell them to stop. We are not going to kill you here today. You are not going to die in this room, or in this prison."

A humpbacked scribe sat in a corner of the room, taking down every word. Rachel's hunger left her. She felt strangely strong, ready to confront her fate. She could not yet conceive of a pain that could increase without limit; of a pain that could increase without letting her die.

The tall guards who had brought her to the place of torture had left. Other than the Inquisitor, the doctor, and the scribe, the huge room contained two powerfully built peasants, their faces devoid of human expression. These were to be her torturers, and, at a word from the Inquisitor, they took hold of her and stripped away her clothes.

Rachel tried to drive her spirit out of her body. She thought if she could concentrate on floating away to some familiar time, or place, she could forget about her body during what was about to occur. But she couldn't get her spirit to move. She remained steadfastly aware of everything said and done about her.

The Inquisitor came close to her, and the two torturers held her naked body still for his thick hands. She heard him say that she had a lovely body, that she could grow up to be a beautiful young woman, a Christian convert respected at court. She saw him breathe deeply as he plunged his hands between her legs, taking hold of her most intimate parts as if this were the way he would bring her to at once telling him everything he wanted to hear. Rachel heard him talk about a sincere wish for her to convert, for her to repent by punishing the evil Jews for their crimes, for her to have a chance to enter the kingdom of heaven. She heard him ask the doctor if she heard everything, and the doctor said: "She is fully aware."

The Inquisitor stepped back from her, removing his hands from her welt-marked body, looking at her with loathing. He shouted words at her: *strappado,* which Rachel knew was the torture of the rope, and *aselli,* which she knew as the torture of the water; but she didn't understand the details of these tortures. The words alone had been enough to shut off all desire to know more.

"Tie her," said the Inquisitor, and her torturers twisted her arms behind her back, and bound her wrists together with strong rope.

"Oh, my God," she said, not thinking, reacting to the tightness of the bond. Something inside her was agitating for understanding. It was as if some part of her—her mother, Judah, perhaps one of her legendary namesakes—had something to tell her, something urgent that would give purpose to all that was about to take place. But the Inquisitor spoke again, driving away her chance for understanding.

"Think, Rachel Cuheno. You're naked. You're starved. You're bound." He placed a finger against her forehead and moved it along her nose, around her mouth, tracing it over her chin, pausing with it against her neck. "You're absolutely defenseless. Think. You possess information that it is criminal to withhold. You know that it is only a matter of time before you tell me everything." His finger moved slowly from her neck to her chest. He spoke, rubbing the finger against her right nipple until it grew erect. "Look," he said, and she followed his gaze to the high vaulted ceiling: A pulley was bolted high above the ground, perhaps forty feet in the air. "That is what's next for you, Rachel Cuheno. Look how high you're going to go, try to imagine."

"I am a Jewess, and I have committed no crime," she said. If they were to hang her in the air, at least he would not be touching her. Perhaps, in her pain, she would discover what message raced through the back of her brain.

One of the torturers grabbed her arm and pulled her to the ends of the rope hanging from the high pulley. The man's eyes held neither malice nor pity; not even interest. The second torturer joined his fellow, and swiftly they secured her to the rope, her arms bound behind her back, and waited for the nod from the Inquisitor.

Rachel began to rise through the air. She watched the torturers work the rope from below, and the higher she rose, the more she felt the wrenching pain in her twisted shoulders. At first, she was afraid of getting loose; she was only secured at the wrists, and the wrists were tied to the great pulley rope. Rachel was looking at the tops of the men's heads, and her field of vision danced and faltered, according to the way she was jerked upward. She began to scream, even though she knew this made the rope dance even more, even though this exaggerated the pain running now from her shoulders to her back, running like a red-hot fire. Suddenly, everything grew still. She was no longer being jerked upward. She had stopped up her screaming. Rachel opened her eyes and looked down through forty feet of quiet air. She couldn't believe that she was this high up, that the men below her had grown so small, that the pain in her body was growing steadily, inexorably, when she should have already reached the threshold where pain turns into the sleep of death.

The Inquisitor's voice reached her like thunder from hell. "Are you ready?" he said. "We can let you down easily if you are ready to tell us what the Church wants to know."

Rachel tried to answer, but when she opened her mouth, she had no strength to speak. A violent tremor ran through her then, her untried muscles reacting to an unprecedented stress.

Again, the voice from hell blew up at her: "Drop her."

Rachel felt the pressure at her shoulders suddenly cease, and realized that she was falling through space. The second slowed into a hundred parts, so that it seemed to Rachel as if she were falling forever. In the delicious interstice in the fabric of pain, the voices in the back of her mind grew clearer. Even as the terror of rushing down through the air broke apart her mad smile, she heard what she had been waiting for.

"*Kill him*," said the voices, and Rachel shut her eyes and listened harder, tried to recognize the source of the command. It was absurd, of course, absurd and impossible for her to kill the Inquisitor; but she wanted to know who was talking to her, who were her voices. "*Kill him*," they said, and then the second was over, and Rachel felt her whole body stop short in space, as if some macabre giant had grabbed her out of the sky.

But so suddenly that she thought she must surely die at once.

Rachel had been dropped halfway from the ceiling to the ground, and then stopped short, in midair. The sudden wrenching was often enough to dislocate shoulders, to crack brittle bones, to snap apart the neck. The torturers and the doctor looked up at the screaming young girl, twenty feet above their heads, looking with professional interest at the way her naked body thrashed about in the void.

"She's all right," said the doctor.

"Drop her," said the Inquisitor.

This time the men let go of their rope for but a moment, so that she only slipped down a foot, and the wrenching stop was much less of a shock than before.

But what difference did it make? The first drop had so ripped apart her body that she waited only for death. Anything else was a respite that she didn't want. If they let her hang, let her think about the pain that had already transpired, that would be enough to kill her anyway.

"Drop her," said the Inquisitor, and this time she fell swiftly the rest of the way down, stopping short only a foot above the ground. The pain forced a scream out of her exhausted body, a scream whose expense of energy she couldn't afford. Rachel was certain her arms must have been wrenched out their sockets. She couldn't understand why her arms had not been left up in the air, why her torso hadn't been freed to fall to the ground. She wasn't moving, but the pain came in waves, more and more, increasing every moment, so that she felt her gums bathed in sweat and blood, the previous awful throbbing in yesterday's wounds relegated to a minor sensation. They were looking at her, and the doctor pulled at her arms and she screamed again and again, so that she couldn't hear the questions of the Inquisitor. The doctor had said that it was all right to continue.

"Rachel, we will do this again," said the Inquisitor slowly. "Listen, you miserable sinner. We will do this again and again, until the devil that aids you leaves your body and you're free to answer what must be answered."

"I'm dead," said Rachel, so softly that they couldn't hear.

"Speak up, girl," said the Inquisitor, and he raised her head from where it rested on her breast. "Speak up so I can hear you, or we'll pull you up again."

"I'm dead," she said.

"You're not dead, Jewess, and you won't die today," said the Inquisitor. "Confess that your father performs the Black Mass. Admit that Master Cuheno performs the circumcision rite on Christian infants."

"*Kill him,*" said the voices, louder this time, so loud that Rachel looked up to see if the Inquisitor had heard.

"I am a Jewess," said Rachel. "And I have committed no crime."

"Take her up," said the Inquisitor, and the torturers pulled on the pulley rope, and the blazing fire in her ravaged joints grew yet hotter, so hot that she should have been consumed, she should have been dead.

"*Kill him,*" said the voices, saying nothing about her pain, or why she was yet alive. This time they dropped her two-thirds of the way down, and she felt as if she were passing through a wall of fire, on the other side of which was sleep. The pain had so taken her by surprise—the surprise being that there was so much more space left for pain to grow—that she had passed out, and they were forced to bring her to the ground to make sure she was alive.

"She is all right," said the doctor.

"This one can't die," said the Inquisitor.

"She is all right, sir," said the doctor, and he slapped his patient across the face. Rachel's nose began to gush blood, but before the Inquisitor could berate the doctor for using such force, Rachel was screaming again, pushed back from the other side of the wall of fire, feeling numbing pain in her back and her neck, feeling the pain of a thousand hot needles in her elbows and shoulders.

"*Kill him,*" said her voices, and quite clearly she heard the Inquisitor speak.

"Listen, Jewess. The next time you're up there, you're going to experience pain like you've never before felt. The third time is always the worst. I'm telling you this, because I can see you want to tell me everything. You can see that it's useless to go on like this. Tell me about your father. Tell me about your father, and you won't go back up in the air."

"My father," said Rachel. "My father—is—a good man."

"Take her up," said the Inquisitor, and the torturers returned to the pulley rope, even as the doctor spoke:

"Tell them to stop," he said.

"Is there a danger of death?"

"No," said the doctor. "But she won't feel it this time. It's time for the water. Besides, if the water doesn't work, you can have her back here in three or four days. By then her joints will be so swollen that just looking at the rope will bring her to her knees."

The Inquisitor gave his order, and Rachel was lowered down, gently and steadily. All the throbbing had gone to her back. The fire had consumed her shoulders, and she wondered how the voices could continue to demand the impossible of her, continue to expect her to wreak vengeance on this terrible man when she hadn't the strength to stand. "*Kill him,*" she heard quite clearly, even as she collapsed to the ground, and her wrists were untied, and one of the torturers picked up her naked, broken body and carried her to the curious rectangular table she'd noticed before.

They laid her on the table, her back forced to lie painfully over the log set crosswise in the table's surface. The Inquisitor was talking to her now, but she couldn't concentrate on his words; she knew that they were about what was to take place, and all she could think of was the pain in her back and the certainty of death. The doctor's head replaced the Inquisitor's in her field of vision, and he seemed to be examining her neck and her eyes. Rachel couldn't move her arms or her legs, but she was not sure if this was because she was tied to the table or because of the damage caused by the *strappado.* When the doctor pulled his head back suddenly, she could see the blurry shapes of the torturers standing on either side of her, their hands resting on her thighs. The Inquisitor asked her another question, speaking in calm, utterly incomprehensible tones. Rachel didn't even bother to open her mouth. What was there to say? She was beyond understanding questions, and she had no answers to give. If she'd had the strength to talk, she'd have asked him a question: How on earth am I supposed to fulfill my duty to kill you, sir?

Suddenly, the torturers were upon her. One clamped his hand

over her skull, pulling her head back so far that she felt her neck would snap; with his other hand he pinched shut her nostrils. Trying to breathe through her mouth, she felt the sharp stabbing of the log lying crosswise under her back. Then the second torturer shoved a great linen rag into her open mouth and, as she gagged, continued to shove the rag deep into her throat. Trying to breathe, her eyes opened on their own accord, and she could see a great blue jar poised over her head. It seemed as if the rag in her throat were being pushed past her throat, but of course this was impossible. Every part of her body clamored for attention; each part wanted to claim itself as the greatest source of pain: Throat, and back, and shoulders, and scalp; and all the while the voices continued, indefatigably, "*Kill him, kill him.*"

Then the water came.

The jar had turned in the space over her head, and a stream of water poured into her open mouth, into the all-absorbing linen funnel blocking her throat. Rachel tried to shut her mouth, but the torturer's hands prevented this; and when a superhuman effort momentarily allowed her jaws to slip out of his wet hands, she was unable to breathe at all. All she could do was open her mouth and swallow, fast as she could. Some of what she swallowed would be air; and something made her insist on living, even when it seemed as if her whole body were shouting out for death.

The water poured into her body, flooded her belly, burst at the confines of her bodily frame. The linen in her throat swelled up hideously; and as it became momentarily more impossible to breathe, a tremendous pressure crashed down upon her in every direction, so powerful that she could see nothing but red, hear nothing but a thundering in her brain. They were pressing down on her bloated belly, forcing the suddenly swelled, already starved body over the backbreaking log so that a pain so great blew up in her that Rachel screamed again and again, "Mother, Mother, Mother!" But the screaming was only in her brain, and even if they could have heard her, nothing would have induced them to stop, nothing but the freely given confession and information that the Inquisition demanded.

Then it was over, just as suddenly as it had begun. The pressure ceased, and the water jar over her head was gone. Only the horribly swollen gag remained, but she could still breathe, and her breaths came in frequent little stabs of blinding pain.

"She can hear," said the doctor.

"Rachel, are you ready?" said the Inquisitor, but Rachel wasn't sure if it was he who had spoken. Perhaps it had been her voices again, or a dead ancestor, prepared to escort her tortured soul to the world-to-come. "Go ahead," said the Inquisitor, and, in that moment, one of the torturers ripped the linen funnel out of her throat and mouth.

Rachel was brought at once to the furthest limits of pain. She had no voice, but her eyes stretched out a scream more piteous than any mere sound. Wide open, her eyes asked how such a thing could be. To be stripped and beaten and savaged in the name of religion made no sense at all. All about her was the result of the latest torture: the rag had pulled up water and blood and tissue—had pulled apart the inside of her throat. But the horrified eyes looked past the blood. Rachel's eyes looked past blood and sense and understanding; straight ahead, she saw the past, and the past was the same as the present—bloody, insane, irrational—and she was drawn into what she saw, made witness to the fabric of history, committed herself to what was impossible. It was impossible to kill the Inquisitor; but it was impossible for man to be so cruel. It was impossible to hear the voices of ancestors, it was impossible to rise up from the water-torture table and pluck out this man's heart, it was impossible to suffer so much and remain alive. Everything in her world was impossible—equally, dreadfully impossible—and this was the message she carried with her as the Inquisitor's face blew up in a smile, and some kind spirit allowed her sleep.

Rachel awoke to blackness, and because she had no pain, she assumed that she was dead. Where was her body? she wondered, and because she felt nothing, she hoped that she had become a pure spirit, invisible, incorporeal, invulnerable to pain. But she soon became aware of heat. The region behind her eyes was blazing. But if she could imagine a region behind her eyes at all, perhaps her body was yet with her. Rachel tried to move, tried to blink. In a moment, darkness fled, and Rachel was looking up at the dawn through the air hole in her cell. She was so frightened at being alive that she had stopped breathing; and when all at once her mouth opened and her spirit began to pull in the life-giving air, a great pounding began in her temples, joining the fever raging behind her eyes.

A jailer brought soup, and she tasted it, but her starved body had lost the desire to eat, and her throat was even sensitive to the passage of air. She tried to keep her mouth shut and breathe only through her nose. She moved her right hand, lifting it a few inches, trying to test the boundaries of her pain. Her limbs were stiff and her joints swollen, but the pain she was so afraid of was more than that she experienced at this moment; and she had a reason to live, if only for a little while longer.

When the guards came for her, they were gentle, handling her body as if it were composed of brittle sticks. They wrapped a thin, scratchy blanket about her nude form and lifted her gingerly. Rachel shut her eyes. The doctor had said that her limbs and joints would swell up miserably within three or four days, and that that would be the best time to continue the *strappado* torture. But Rachel didn't think she was about to be tortured. She knew more than the Inquisitor did at that moment, because her knowledge was impossible, spiritual, driven by fever and delusion.

When she opened her eyes, she recognized one of the torturers. He seemed to be examining her, the way one examined meat in the market, to see if it was without disease. Yes, she was alive; time had passed; the torture had been finished and would soon be attempted anew. Rachel almost laughed, but the voices within her overpowered any other impulse. "*Kill him,*" they said, and the crazed, broken young girl of Zaragoza believed she would do just that.

"Can she stand?" said the Inquisitor's voice, and Rachel heard every word as if it were shouted in her ear. As the doctor's voice assured the Inquisitor that she could stand, Rachel realized that she was settled in a chair, covered by the wool blanket. One of the guards dragged her to her feet and let the covering drop to the ground. She was once again naked, looking at the Inquisitor, the *strappado* hanging behind him, before her eyes.

"Jewess, you haven't died," said the Inquisitor. "You won't die today. Look up at the *strappado*, and try to imagine how you will feel hanging up there. Try to remember how it was last time, and how much worse it will be today."

Rachel smiled—not wanting to show defiance, but smiling anyway; she was not going up there, she knew.

The Inquisitor didn't hit her. This was not the first time he'd seen a smile in the torture room. If the girl was mad, her testimony might be the more easily gotten. He leaned forward, his lips moving slowly before her devouring eyes.

"*Kill him, kill him, kill him,*" she heard, and, with the words, an otherworldly strength began to filter into her wraithlike body. Through the cacophony in her mind, she still understood what he wanted. The Inquisitor was asking whether she was prepared to confess to her guilt, and to that of her father. Rachel opened her mouth, and she realized that she was about to say yes. She didn't want to say yes, but the spirits that had taken control of her body had decided for her; still, no sound ushered from her lips. Rachel nodded her head, and her smile vanished, and to the Inquisitor and his scribe, it seemed that the girl had indeed been broken, and that all that remained for her to confess was enough strength to speak.

"I will have to bleed her," said the doctor.

"What are you saying?" said the Inquisitor. "She's hardly got any blood left in her body."

"Sir, I am the doctor, not you," he said.

The Inquisitor stopped himself from striking the doctor across the face. He wanted a confession, and perhaps the doctor had to be listened to.

"The girl cannot talk," continued the doctor, "yet she is strong enough to stand. Bleeding this area here"—the doctor indicated the lower part of Rachel's throat—"will allow her voice to return from her throat to her lips."

"You are ready to confess?" said the Inquisitor, much louder than before, as if his volume would affect her speech.

Rachel nodded her head and raised her right hand to her lips. She didn't know how the spirits managed to get her hand that high, past the region of pain from her ruined shoulders, but the fever seemed to grow stronger, the fever and her strength.

"Bleed her," said the Inquisitor. "I want her to talk."

They sat her back in the wooden chair. The fever had spread past her forehead and neck and shoulder blades to every part of her body; Rachel was no longer cold in the cold room—her bare skin reacted not at all to the hard, cool wood of the chair, and as the doctor's face loomed large over her own, she saw the sharp, metal instrument in his hand descend slowly to her throat, and louder than ever was the cry: "*Kill him, kill him, kill him.*"

There was nothing brave in what happened next. Rachel was broken in this world, filled with a spirit from another. She could not utter a word, yet a sound louder than a thunderclap burst from her lips as she rose out of the chair, her wild hand on the doctor's sharp bloodletting tool, her eyes filled with the mad lust of a thousand avenging martyrs.

"*Kill him*," she heard, and the spirit moved her broken body, and the young girl's hand drove the sharp tool into the neck and cheek and eye and breast of the Inquisitor of Zaragoza, again and again, and the two brutish torturers could hardly drag her off the body of the friar, could hardly muster the strength to combat this terrible Jewess, inspirited with preternatural strength. "*Kill him*," she heard, and she heard it again and again until her strength was gone, just as suddenly as it had come, but she didn't care, for she was certain she'd killed the Inquisitor, certain she'd fulfilled her earthly fate. Even across the room, even shrouded by fever, Rachel Cuheno could sense the friar's soul fall out of its body, and begin the descent to hell.

It was her misfortune to live three months longer. But the new Inquisitor had a kinder heart than his predecessor, and allowed Rachel the grace of being garroted prior to her conflagration. When the flames rose up on her scaffold at the auto-da-fé outside her native city, the screams of the crowd could no longer reach her. Brave Rachel Cuheno, the assassin of Friar Ramirez del Pulgar, Inquisitor of Zaragoza, had joined her ancestors in accepting death's embrace.

THE CUHENO FAMILY
1484–1610

Abraham Cuheno, who had traveled to Toledo to request an audience from his great patron, King Ferdinand, was murdered by men of the Queen's Bodyguard a month before Rachel was garroted and then burned at the stake. Isabelle de Santangel died in prison; her mother died a martyr's death, refusing to accept the mercy of garroting, and was burned alive at the auto-da-fé outside Zaragoza.

Judah Cuheno fled Zaragoza the day after his sister's execution. With him was a small bag of diamonds, including the one he had intended for her. He made his way to Amsterdam, where he married a girl of Ashkenazi origin. Their first child was a girl, and she was given the name Rachel and the birthright of the diamond that Judah had cut for her namesake. For centuries, the Cuheno diamond was to be passed along in this way, from Rachel to Rachel, in honor, in memory.

One of Judah's six sons, Samuel, inherited his father's wandering spirit. Samuel carried diamonds—and his skill as a diamond cutter—to Brescia, and to the south of France, and to Fano and Rimini. He kept moving, longing to establish a connection with a great court. In 1522, Samuel and his family moved to Constantinople, where he was finally admitted to the Sublime Porte of the Sultan. Samuel's sons established a regular trade route between the diamond mines of Kollur and Panna in India, maintaining agencies in Baghdad, Cairo, Alexandria, and Tyre.

Members of the Cuheno family based in Amsterdam took passage with Venetian traders and brought the gems of the East across the Mediterranean, and then across the Alps to the German princes and to the more sophisticated French kings.

Samuel's youngest son, Judah, named after his grandfather, left the business of gems to study medicine in Cairo. There he met a fanatically religious Jewess, the daughter of Portuguese refugees. His wife's parents had remained in Portugal after the Edict of Expulsion (of all professing Jews) was proclaimed in 1497. Their frustration in living as clandestine Jews for four decades was translated into a religious zeal when they finally fled the country and were able to reveal themselves as Jews.

Four of Judah's five boys became learned rabbis; the fifth, Avi, as religious as the others, was less learned. An uncle in Alexandria put him to work as a diamond courier, and the young religious Jew traveled to Constantinople, to the ports of the Peloponnesus, to Crete, to Dalmatia, to Venice herself. Here, his head spinning amid beauty and riches, he was attacked and beaten by a crowd of citizens incensed at a foreign Jew walking about their city without his yellow hat or his yellow badge of shame. Avi left Venice that same day, and, too ashamed to go to his kinsmen in Amsterdam—he had been robbed of the diamond he carried for them—he went into the service of a Jewish merchant of Nürnberg. There he married, and had a single child, Yehezkel.

Yehezkel grew into a giant of a man, and with the disposition of an ogre. He followed all the Laws of Moses that he could keep in his head—but grudgingly; he did what he had to, but he didn't have to pretend that he liked it. His wife had been a pretty blond girl when he married her; but he didn't have to pretend that she was a beauty, or the comfort of his life. By the time he settled in Venice in 1585, she had already borne him three girls. Their fifth girl, Rachel, was born in that city five years later.

According to family legend that his father never stopped relating, they supposedly had rich relatives somewhere in the world. But Yehezkel was skeptical about legends. He had forgotten that his father used to talk about the family's descent from a noble Spanish ancestor—all he knew was that Jews were burned in Spain. He had forgotten that his father used to talk about an ancestor who had killed an oppressor of the Jews in the city of Zaragoza—all he knew was that he had been blessed with five girls and no sons. He had forgotten that he had family in Amsterdam, in Constantinople, in Alexandria. He had forgotten that he was the grandson of Judah Cuheno of Cairo, and that this Judah had been named for Judah Cuheno of Zaragoza, and that he himself was the great-great-great-grandson of Master Abraham Cuheno of Aragon. Yehezkel sold secondhand merchandise in the ghetto of Venice. This was his world, and he found no solace in dreams of a brilliant past or tales of a glorious future.

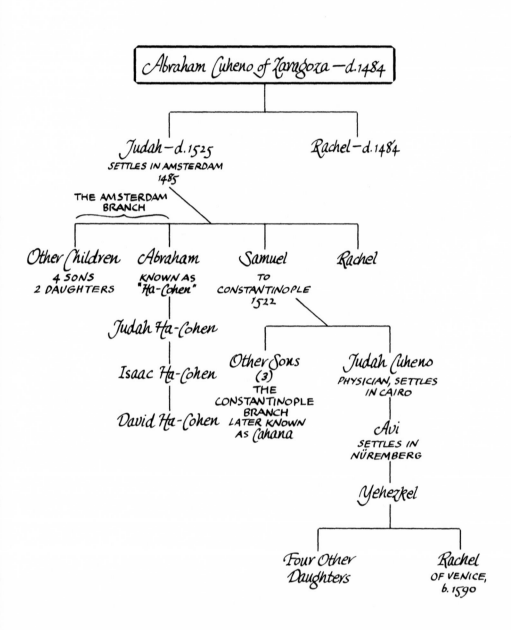

PART TWO

VENICE, 1610

CHAPTER SEVEN

Rachel woke with a start, instantly remembering her dream. An ominous rumbling, like an unnatural thunder, had quivered through her visions of dark, shaky steps, twisting round and round, higher and higher up an endless, enclosed stairwell. She had been running, chased by the dreadful sound, and could run no more. But if she could run no more, she would be beaten, bested, consumed. In the dream, she climbed, she grabbed with her hands at the endless steps, refusing to give up, to end her flight and let the thunder overtake her. Finally she could go no farther. The stairs ended, and she stepped into space, falling not into darkness but into light. She tried to wake up before the thunder would change to the tolling of bells, but the horror of her dream lay precisely in the fact that she could not wake up, she could not cease falling, she could not be ready in time for the bells.

"*Baruch Ha-Shem,*" she said, "Blessed be the Name," rushing to the tiny slice of window in the little box of a room she had shared with four sisters, until one by one they had left her—three of them for marriage, the fourth for something far different. It was still dark, and she thanked God for a multiplicity of things: that she had not overslept; that she lived on the highest floor of this very tall house—much higher than the surrounding walls of the ghetto. If she had lived on the third floor, her window would have been darkened by the incredible, contiguous structures of the ghetto: crazily built six- and seven-story tenements, one story added onto another as the Jewish population grew out of its tiny allotted space and was forced to add new floors to already decrepit, overcrowded buildings—buildings that they were forbidden by the Venetian government to own. So Rachel thanked God for being able to know whether it was morning or night, merely by looking out her window. And she thanked God for waking up healthy, in full possession of her mental faculties.

Quickly, moving as silently as possible, she washed her hands, reciting the benediction, and then washed her face, and her neck, and her underarms. As she dressed for the day, she recited the Hebrew prayer: "Blessed art thou, O Lord our God, King of the universe, who has formed man in wisdom and created in him many passages and vessels. It is well known before thy glorious throne that if but one of these be opened, or one of those be closed, it would be impossible to exist and stand before thee. Blessed art thou, O Lord, who art the wondrous healer of all flesh."

Rachel finished dressing and sat down on the edge of her bed. In another moment she would hear her father get up, hear him say something sharp to her mother, hear him grunt and sigh and bemoan his fate, hear him finally begin to leave their room and walk heavily down the rickety stairs on his way to the synagogue. She would have to wait until then before she could leave, but there would still be plenty of time. "Blessed art thou, O Lord our God, King of the universe, who hast given to the mind understanding to distinguish between day and night," she whispered; and immediately, as if in answer to an unvoiced prayer, she heard her father wake and say:

"Cards! She talks to me about cards! The madonna preserve me! My wife is going to tell me whether or not I'm allowed to play cards!"

"Please," Rachel whispered, but her mother must have answered her father back, for Rachel suddenly heard the loud crack of her father's hand, and her mother's high-pitched shout of pain.

"Jesus," said her father, and Rachel wondered if all the rabbis' injunctions to the Jews of Venice to refrain from using the endless variety of Christian references as exclamations of annoyance or outrage would ever have any effect. Once again her father hit her mother, and Rachel tried to shut out the noise of her cries and his furious words. "For the love of God, woman, I'll kill you yet," he said, and then, perhaps not even washing his hands, he ran out of their tiny apartment and down the winding flights of stairs.

She hated her father so much at that moment that she forced the words of the prayer into her mouth, to shut up any chance of sin: "These are the things of which one enjoys the fruits in this world, while the stock remains whole for the world-to-come: honoring father and mother, deeds of loving kindness—"

Rachel suddenly stopped praying. She didn't honor her father, and no amount of pious phrases would change that fact in the eyes of God. God knew how she felt. God could see right through an eternity of prayers and supplications. God knew that she loved her sister Devorah, that she hated her father, that she pitied her mother. What was the use of reciting words that were so patently untrue? God knew why she was up early, where she planned to go, whom she planned to see; God knew that she was disobeying her father's orders, breaking the laws of the Republic of Venice. God knew everything, and so he knew that she was not ashamed.

Rachel picked up her hat, the distinguishing badge of almost all Jews in the City of the Lagoons. Only a few, very privileged Jews were allowed to walk in the city without a hat identical to hers: A few doctors, a few clandestine agents, a few distinguished veterans of the war with the Turks were exempted from this dishonor. The hat, covered with shiny crimson cloth and edged with black, stood out in the eerily beautiful light of Venice, stood out against the gorgeous palaces, stood out in the beautifully dressed crowds on the Rialto Bridge, stood out on the Street of the Mercers, stood out everywhere the Jews went about their business. At day's end, the crimson hats seemed to group together, gathering into a swiftly moving stream, following the bridges and streets to the gates of the ghetto before they would be shut up for the night.

Rachel walked into the adjacent room and went over to her slight, pale mother, crying silently on a chair in the corner of the room.

"He lost everything," said her mother.

"It doesn't matter," said Rachel.

"He swore he wouldn't play cards, and then he goes and loses everything. We'd be rich if it wasn't for him. I go blind sewing in the dark, and he plays cards."

"Mother, I'm going to see Devorah."

"If we had a thousand ducats, he'd lose that. If we had ten thousand, he'd lose that, too. And all he ever says is that if it wasn't for my daughters—*my* daughters and not *his*, I suppose!— if it wasn't for my daughters and the dowries he gave them, we'd be living in ten rooms, with servants, with velvet stoles lined with silk."

"Mother, you didn't hear me," said Rachel.

"He beats me, then he goes to the synagogue. I suppose that makes it all right. He thinks that if a woman gives birth to five girls, that it was her idea, that it was just what she wanted. Well, I love you all dearly, but I don't mind telling you that it wouldn't have been bad to have had a son or two. After all, a son can do what a daughter can't. Maybe your father wouldn't be so bad then. Maybe he'd be ashamed to act this way in front of a son."

"Mother, I'm going now," said Rachel. She had seen her this way before, and it was no use trying to stopper her words and make her listen. Rachel put on her hat, and left.

There were only three gates out of the ghetto, and none of these would be opened until the sounding of the great bell in San Marco's Campanile started the day. Rachel joined the crimson-hatted Jews hurrying to the gateway to the Fondamenta della Pescaria. This was the main gateway, and she wanted to be swallowed up in a crowd, all of whom would be anxious to get their day's work under way. As she joined the front rank at the shut gates, she remembered her dream; it was this bell that she was afraid of missing.

Devorah's message had been very precise: The gondola would be coming up the Canale di Cannaregio toward the Canal Grande just after the bell tolled. The two oarsmen would not be able to pick her out from all her coreligionists; she would have to be looking for them, and she would have to be among the first out of the ghetto that morning.

When the bell finally began to toll, Rachel's heart jumped.

The Gentile guards who kept the Jews locked up at night, and were responsible for reporting any who strayed back from the city proper after the gates were closed, joked with and greeted familiar faces as they opened the gates. Most of the Jews found nothing monstrous about the idea that the guards' salaries were extorted from their victims' communty funds; most thought the guards pleasant enough, and had long since stopped thinking about the ghetto system, or the hats of shame they wore, or the innumerable restrictions put upon them by the Christians of the city. Compared to much of the world around them, Venice was a tolerant city, basking in the intellectual warmth of the nearby university in Padua and the reputation of culture and civilization that had belonged to the city for a thousand years. If the Jews were locked up at night, at least they weren't attacked in their sleep by fanatic peasants. If the Jews, even those whose ancestors had arrived there three hundred years before, were not permitted to practice law, or trade in new clothes, or deal in precious stones, at least they weren't forced to convert to Christianity, and then burned at the Inquisitional stake for heresy.

"Aren't we in a hurry to get to work!" said one of the guards to Rachel, who stopped dead in her tracks, as if she had been accused of some terrible deed.

"Good morning, sir," she said, with such stilted formality that the guard wondered if she might be joking.

"And a very good morning to you, miss," he said, with as much ceremony as he could muster.

Rachel sucked in her breath and walked slowly through the gates, and followed the crowd, in a daze, over a bridge and through the narrow alleys of the auxiliary ghetto, where Jews of Levantine and Spanish descent lived. She moved quickly, looking neither to her right nor her left, stepping agilely about knots of slower people, till with a start of recognition she saw the water of the canal, and tried at once to slow her step.

Even as she began to catch her breath, she saw the long, elegant shape of the boat, the only one on the water at this early hour, appear before the rising sun like a vision of the world-to-come. Rachel looked at the boat the way she had never looked at one before. Gondolas and other flat-bottomed boats had never been objects of interest to her; they were merely part of the Venetian backdrop as she'd made her way to the Rialto Bridge, helping her father buy or sell secondhand clothing. But this boat was for her, and she gawked at the tall, graceful pair of oarsmen in their gold and black livery as they bent forward, their lithe bodies lit from behind by the fresh ball of sun, propelling the gondola easily, bringing its otherworldly message of luxury and decadence her way.

"Over here!" she screamed, ignoring the crush of Jews at her rear. "Over here!" she cried. "I'm here, Devorah, I'm here!"

Incredibly, the gondoliers looked up, their black hair reflecting the sunlight; she had to squint to see that their eyes had found her, and that they were smiling. The gondola changed course and made straight for her, its enormous, elaborately carved prow, with its metal blade breaking the sunlight into a hundred flashing colors above the shining water of the canal, blowing up before her eyes in a silence as profound as a dream's. One of the men jumped onto the quay and took her hand, and helped her to the closed cabin. It was dark within, and smelled of musk, and her hands touched walls of embroidered silk.

"Sit," said Devorah, and Rachel sat down, her thigh touching her sister's in the small space, and she took in the colors—scarlet and gold and violet—and then she looked at her sister's face, conscious of the movement of the boat, and began to cry.

"Oh, by God's wounds!" said Devorah, "you're not going to do this to me. I'm the one who should cry, not you. You'll stop at once, or I'll have them put you into the water."

But once started, Rachel couldn't stop. She shut her eyes and let the tears run down her face, her sobs racking her body, out of love for her sister. Devorah was twenty-three, three years Rachel's senior, and for more than two years she had lived away from home, outside the ghetto, outside her religion. Her mother never spoke of her, except when someone pointed out a beautiful Jewess; and then, without thinking, she would look and say that the most beautiful girl in Venice was Devorah Cuheno. To her father, Devorah was dead. When she had left her home, leaving them a letter detailing the reasons for her conversion—a letter filled with lies—he had gone to the rabbi, and the rabbi explained why Devorah must now be dead for the family, and then mother and father both tore their clothes, covered the lone mirror in their room, and sat on the floor for seven days, in accordance with the laws of mourning after the dead.

Devorah had written in her letter that she had fallen in love with a young patrician, a distant cousin of the doge himself, who had visited the dancing class she taught to young women of

means, both Jewish and Gentile, in a house on the Calle dei
Barucchi in the ghetto. Though she was betrothed to a handsome young Jewish merchant, Leone Ha-Levi, she didn't love
him, she wrote; she loved her patrician, Pietro Bellini, and she
was going to embrace Catholicism to marry him. But none of
this was true. She didn't love Pietro Bellini, she simply found
him attractive. She had no intention of converting to Catholicism, and had no need to do so under the protection of her new
master. As for Leone Ha-Levi, she did love him, after a fashion;
it was just that she loathed her life in the ghetto, and much preferred to live as a courtesan in a palace on the Canal Grande than
to marry a young Jew whose success as a merchant might insure
her two floors in a narrow little overcrowded house, on a dark
and congested street, among people whose lives were constricted
and thwarted by the suspicion and hate of the outside world.

"Would you please take off that hat?" said Devorah.

"I'm sorry," said Rachel, trying to stop crying, not hearing
her sister's request. When Devorah snatched away the crimson
hat of shame, Rachel looked up at her in surprise. "You look very
beautiful," she said.

"You look fine, Rachel, and you'd look a lot better if you
stopped crying and sat up straight, and got that humble look off
your face. I'm sick to death of that humble Jewish look."

"I'm not humble. Not all Jews are humble."

"For the love of God, Rachel," said Devorah. "Look, look
where we are."

Through the cabin's window, Rachel could see that they had
already passed into the Canal Grande and were now gliding past
the Palazzo Vendramin-Calergi, famous for its great, round-
headed windows and circles of sun-dashed porphyry.

"I see where we are," said Rachel.

"I mean, see how beautiful it is," said Devorah. "I want you to
see how beautiful the Canal Grande is."

"I know how beautiful it is. I walk along it, I pass over it, I
see it, even if I don't have my own gondola."

"Why are you angry? I won't have you angry at me," said
Devorah.

"I'm not angry. I'm fine. I'm happy to see you. You look
beautiful." Then, for a moment, each wondered if they would
exchange kisses, for though they had exchanged letters, perhaps
a half-dozen times, this was the first time they had seen each

other face-to-face since Devorah had gone to live in sin. Rachel grabbed her sister's face with both palms and kissed her, and then Devorah almost cried, before letting out a great sigh of relief, and returning the kiss, and fussing over her sister's hair.

"I've been there," said Devorah, pointing to the Ca' d'Oro, its facade glittering with the brightest of reds and blues, surrounding gilt flowers and golden capitals, its mélange of wild colors and Oriental pinnacles throwing back the light rising up from the canal into a wild image of legendary force. And before they'd gotten to the Rialto Bridge, she'd pointed out five more palaces at which she'd visited, and Rachel wondered to whom she'd been presented, and under what name, and to what station in society she had been assigned. Devorah ran on gaily, tripping out a half-dozen patrician names, all of them unfamiliar to Rachel, and telling her that one was bald, another stupid, another preferred men to women, and so on.

Rachel looked intently at her sister, wanting so much to ask her the simplest of questions: Was she happy? Did she feel that she was living in sin? What did her master ask her to do when they were alone in his bed? But of course she could not voice any of these questions, certainly not the last; the thought of her sister's voluptuous body under the hands of an uneducated Gentile, no matter how noble his birth, revolted her.

"Do you see this? Do you know what this is?" said Devorah, pointing to a queer little yellow pattern on her damask gown. "It's a pineapple. It's a new fruit, a fruit from the New World. Look at it. It's supposed to be sweeter than sugar. Pietro tasted one and it made his ears ring, that's how sweet it was. Everyone is wearing pineapple patterns. I have another gown, in velvet, with the same pattern, only smaller. Oh, look—I brought you a present."

"I've missed you so much."

"Aren't you going to look at it? It's a book. Ariosto. You like Ariosto. You used to tell me those stories about Orlando."

"Thank you," said Rachel, taking the book of poems from her.

"I'm living very well," said Devorah. "I want you to be happy for me."

"Devorah," said Rachel, "are you never going to come back?"

"Come back to what? Are you crazy? Are you asking me about the ghetto?"

"Yes."

"First of all," said Devorah, "my name is no longer Devorah. It's Diamante."

"I've never stopped praying for you to come back."

"You can save your prayers. Why would I ever want to go back to that stinking ghetto? I'd have to have lost my mind. Do you think I enjoyed teaching those clumsy virgins how to dance, just so I'd have enough money to give to Father to lose at cards? Just so I'd be able to climb five flights of stairs to get into bed with my little sister in a room no bigger than a box? What kind of a life was that? The last day I wore that filthy crimson hat, a woman spat at me on the Rialto. Just like that. A Christian woman. Not a Venetian—she was probably from Ferrara—but all the same, she spat at me, and she thought it was her right to do just that. Her right! Let someone try and spit at me now. I'll have my servants cut their throats."

"There are people who are happy in the ghetto," said Rachel.

"I wasn't one of them. Only blind people could be happy there."

"Leone Ha-Levi isn't blind."

"Then he's not happy."

"He hasn't been happy since you ran away," said Rachel.

"I didn't run. I'm not a slave. Leone didn't own me. Father didn't buy me and he had no right to sell me."

"I'm not talking about Father right now, I'm talking about Leone," said Rachel.

"I hope that's not why you wanted to see me today."

"It is."

"I do not want to discuss Leone Ha-Levi," said Devorah. "He is from a different part of my life. The only part of that life I'm still interested in is you. I wish there were something I could do for you. It's too bad you're a girl. The only option you have is the one I took. If you were a boy, I'd send you to Padua, to the university. Pietro would arrange it. You wouldn't be the first Jew to make your mark there."

"Leone Ha-Levi has asked me to marry him," said Rachel.

For the barest slice of a moment, anger flashed across Devorah's face. But she twisted her lips into a half-smiling calm and said, "Please, I don't understand what you're saying to me."

"Leone asked *me*. He didn't ask Father."

"How could he not ask Father? What did he say to you?

What did Father say to all this? You did tell Father, didn't you?"

"No."

"What nerve to ask you! Who does he think he is? And what does he think of us, that he can just ask a girl for her hand without the consent of her parents."

"Devorah—"

"Please, my name is Diamante now, and it's been Diamante for two years."

"I can never call you that," said Rachel. "I don't care what they all call you now. You're Devorah to me."

"Oh, call me whatever you feel like!" Devorah said angrily.

"Listen to me," said Rachel. "Leone asked me before he asked Father for a very specific reason. He knows that I can be stubborn and insist on my own way, just like my sister. He didn't want the humiliation of arranging a marriage to which I would have refused."

"You refused him?"

"No."

"You didn't," said Devorah. "Of course not. I'm sorry. Even when you were a little girl, I knew you liked him."

"I didn't accept him either, Devorah. I told him I'd have to speak with you before I gave him an answer."

Devorah looked out the cabin window to the lovely marble facade of the Palazzo Dario, and then rapped sharply against the wall. At once, the gondola was turned about, and Rachel wondered if her sister would return her to the quay along the Canale di Cannaregio without saying another word to her.

Leone Ha-Levi had been coming to Yehezkel Cuheno's secondhand-merchandise stall in the ghetto since Devorah was fifteen. Since his parents were of Portuguese descent, he lived in a different part of the ghetto, and wore a yellow turban in place of a crimson hat; the Portuguese and Spanish Jews had come to Venice with more capital and skills than those of German origin, and were differentiated from these by the laws of Venice. It was particularly galling to Rachel's father that these Jews were allowed to trade in ways forbidden to the majority of the Jewish community (Leone's uncles, for example, owned five great galleys that brought the products of the Jewish silk weavers of the Peloponnesus back to Venice), especially because his own last name, Cuheno, suggested a descent from Spanish or Portuguese Jews. But Yehezkel had been born in Nürnberg, and his own father had been born in Egypt, and further back than that he considered hearsay and guesswork.

Leone himself had little need of doing business with Yehezkel; there were many secondhand-merchandise dealers with fairer prices—and easier tempers than this giant of a man from Germany. But he made it quite clear that he had fallen in love with Devorah, and he asked for her hand before her eighteenth birthday. Yehezkel immediately consented, providing that the young man would allow him time to raise a decent dowry. In view of the three dowries he'd already had to pay out for his older daughters, Leone generously offered to waive the dowry altogether, but the proud Yehezkel—despite his complaints to his wife—refused to agree.

Devorah had been impatient to get married: Leone was handsome, and he was rich—at least compared to her own family. But when she began to teach dancing to the wives and daughters of the well-to-do merchants of the ghetto, she came into contact with richer Jews, and soon with far richer Gentiles who had come to take classes with her at the suggestion of Jewish friends. It was Pietro Bellini who told her the famous legend of the origin of the gondola: that it was a crescent moon, dropped from the heavens to spirit away two secret lovers through the City of the Lagoons. He was not the only Gentile admirer who'd come to watch her teach a sister or cousin to dance, and stayed to flirt with her, and left her a gift of velvet cloth, or a carved-wood jewel box, or even a few ducats wrapped up in a silken scarf. But it was Pietro who spoke about parties and pavilions, about the all-night gambling at the country estates of the Venetian nobility, about the beautiful women from five countries who gathered in resplendent gowns and glittering jewels on the arms of their gallant lovers.

"Does he think I'm a whore? Is that what he thinks of me?" said Devorah finally.

"Of course not," said Rachel.

"What does he think then? What else could he possibly think?" When Rachel said nothing, Devorah said with great force, "Jesus Christ, you think I'm a whore, too. Don't you know what a whore is, and what a mistress is? Don't you know that I receive priests in my chambers, and that members of the Grand Council kiss my hand?"

"I don't think you're a whore. Please, don't even say that word," said Rachel. "You're what you are, you're my sister, and I've always loved you and admired you, and I always will. As for Leone, I'm sure he still loves you."

"Don't be ridiculous."

"Devorah, it's true. He does love you. And I'll tell you something else. I love him."

"Oh," said Devorah, and for the first time she stopped thinking about her own humiliation, her own pain. Rachel wasn't crying now, but there was terrible hurt in her eyes. She was pale, and she was pretty, but their mother's auburn hair and green eyes had gone to Devorah, and if the younger sister was pretty, the older one was beautiful. "Yes, of course you do," she said. "But he must love you, too, or why on earth would he want to marry you?"

"Because a Jewish man must marry," said Rachel. "The Bible says clearly that one must bring children into the world."

"The Bible doesn't tell him *whom* he has to marry."

"He doesn't love me."

"Did he tell you that?"

"No," said Rachel. "He told me that he wanted to marry me. That he always admired me, that he thought I was lovely, that he loved me. He said that, too. But it doesn't matter what he said. I know what he feels. He wants to marry me because I'm your sister and because he still loves you, and he'll always love you."

"You don't know that, Rachel. All of this—he loves me, you love him, I love Pietro—it all sounds like a chivalric romance. You'd do better to read less and study dancing."

"You don't love Pietro."

"How do you know?"

"You wrote me. You told me from the beginning why you went with Pietro, and it had nothing to do with love."

"Do you want to marry Leone?"

"I'm in love with him," said Rachel.

"Do you want to marry him?"

"No."

"All right," said Devorah. "I think maybe you're right."

"You do?"

"I have seen too many husbands who care nothing for their wives," she said. "Perhaps you're wrong about Leone, perhaps he does love you. If he does, you'll find out, and then maybe you will marry him one day. But if you're right, and he doesn't love you, you'll have a miserable life. I'm not telling you this because I love Leone for myself. I will never have Leone for myself, and I only say all this because I want you to be happy.

"I would be happy if you came home."

"Stop talking nonsense, you don't know what you're saying," said Devorah. "If I ever leave Pietro, it will not be to return to the ghetto." She paused for a moment, looking about the cabin as if there were a third party present. Then she said, softly, "Will you do me a great favor?"

"Of course."

"You're not angry with me about what I said?"

"No."

"You will love someone else one day, someone far superior to Leone."

"What is the favor you want me to do?"

"I want you to sell something for me."

"What?"

"This." Devorah removed an emerald necklace from about her throat and placed it in her sister's hand.

"But I don't understand. Why would you want to sell this?"

"For good Venetian ducats—the best currency in the world."

"But how? I mean—if this is a gift from Pietro, I don't see how you could sell it of your own accord."

"It's not a gift from Pietro. It's from someone else. It's mine. I can sell it. But I don't know what it's worth. And I know nothing about selling. All I know is that when the richest men in Europe come to Venice in search of gems, they go to the ghetto."

"Father doesn't sell gems. Even the law says Jews can't have anything to do with the gem trade."

"I don't want Father to know anything about this. This is between you and me. I want you to keep a third of whatever it fetches."

"Of course not. I wouldn't think of taking what yours."

"I want you to have a third. It's worthless to me unless you can sell it. As for Jews being forbidden to trade in gems, every patrician in Venice knows that's a joke. Jews can't buy and sell in new jewelry, but they can buy and sell anything that's second-hand. And almost every gem in the world is secondhand—including this one. Sell it for me, and keep a third for yourself, and not a word to Father."

"I don't know if I'll be able to," said Rachel. But she quickly nodded her head and put up her hands in surrender to Devorah's will, seeing that her sister was on the verge of another fit of rage. "I'll try. I'll do it for you," said Rachel.

"I need the money," said Devorah, her tone strangely level and subdued. "I need it soon, before I do something silly." Seeing her sister's incomprehension, Devorah added, "I plan to leave Venice."

"Without Pietro?" said Rachel. The thought of her sister going off without her protector, no matter how immoral he might be, terrified her. "I thought you said you were happy. What on earth can you mean? Where would you go? Who would take you?"

"I don't know," said Devorah. "Perhaps I'll know better after I see how many ducats you bring me."

"What difference will that make? What does money have to do with it?"

"With money I can do anything," said Devorah.

"Money can't do anything if you can't hold on to it. What can a woman alone do? Any man can take away whatever she possesses. Devorah, I'll do anything for you, you know that. I'll sell this emerald necklace and I'll get you a good price, but if you're not happy with Pietro, you must think carefully about what you plan to do. Even if Father and Mother don't want you home, there's a place for you in the ghetto. I'll find you a room with a good family. We don't have to tell them anything. There are so many new families who've come to the ghetto since you left—from every part of the world. Not everyone knows your story. You wouldn't have anything to fear. And perhaps, after a while, I could arrange a meeting between you and Leone. He's not a religious fanatic, you know. He's far too broad-minded for some people, you always knew that. He says the wildest things about God and religion, about keeping the sabbath, about eating unclean food. Devorah, he loves you, I'm sure he still loves you."

"Stop," said Devorah, very quietly, but with a wide-eyed stare of utter desperation. "You don't know what you're saying,

Rachel. I'm not a whore in a whorehouse, but I'm not Pietro's mistress either."

"Please, you don't have to explain any of this."

"I'm not his mistress, but I sleep with him when he wants. I'm not a whore, but I sleep with many men. I sleep with more men than I can remember. I'm not a whore in a whorehouse, I'm a courtesan in a palace. There's a difference, you see. You don't understand now, but if you had lived the way I do, you would. You'd know that there's no dishonor in being a courtesan, because you are admired by, you are lusted after, you are gifted by the greatest princes of the republic."

"Where would you go?" said Rachel. "With money I mean? Where would you go, and what would you do?"

"I would wear black, and go as a widow, traveling with half a dozen servants."

"Where?"

"Away, anywhere they don't know me, either as a Jewess or as what I am now. I don't care how I live, as long as I don't have to wear a crimson hat, or take a drunken nobleman to my bed."

"I don't see how a woman alone can survive," said Rachel, still refusing to think about the horrors of her sister's humiliation and sins.

"Of course you don't," said Devorah, and suddenly her voice was less terrible, less anxious, now that her confession was as complete as it ever would be to Rachel. "You've never been a woman alone." Devorah put her arm about her sister and drew her close. "Please, just do as I ask. Sell the emerald and keep a third for yourself. I am strong, and I know the ways of men in this world. With money, I can get along, I can find a place for myself with dignity."

There was little to be added to this. Rachel knew the worst about her sister, and any questions she could ask would lead either to angry silence or the needless elaboration of unimaginable sins. Still, Rachel loved her sister. Nothing could shake this from her—no sin, no lack of compassion for Leone, no refusal to beg forgiveness from her parents or her God. In the swift minutes of gliding in the elegant boat on its return to the quay on the Canale di Cannaregio, Rachel tried to show this love. She reached out and touched her sister's hand, her cheek. She tried to soften her shocked face with an understanding smile.

Still, in the midst of Rachel's fear and pity, there was a glimmering awareness—an awareness that gnawed at her sense of self. Her sister was a sinful woman, living outside her religion, outside her family and class; yet she spoke with authority, and with condescension: "You've never been a woman alone," she said, and the words stayed with Rachel through the remainder of the ride, through the rest of the day, and into the sleepless night.

"You've never been a woman alone." Rachel had read more books, had dreamed of ancient cities and long-forgotten kings, had taught herself chess and geometry, and read Latin, Greek, Spanish, and Hebrew. She wrote pretty rhyming couplets in Italian, she could sew up the rips in an ancient gown with such skill that its seams would be all but invisible. She was bright, she was hardworking, she was proud. But she had never been a woman alone.

Her sister's words terrified her, and they thrilled her.

Rachel had never even conceived of the possibility of taking her destiny into her own hands. Life, and its milestones, had always centered around her brooding father; and any dreams of the future had turned around the nebulous image of a husband—be it Leone Ha-Levi or anyone else—a husband who would be the ruling star of her life. That her sister could even suggest leaving Venice, on her own, going in search of a new life—these words were impossibly daring, and therefore wonderful. And Devorah hadn't said that the prerequisite for living alone was to be a fallen woman.

There was nothing inherently sinful in gathering all your courage, and capital, and leaving behind a life that was stagnant and dull. She could not marry Leone if he didn't love her—and he didn't love her, of that she was sure. So there was nothing else for Rachel in Venice. Nothing else but a mad mother, and a father who lost all their gains at cards.

"Let me know," said Rachel, "if you have word of a buyer of precious gems," and she made it a special point to add that the buyer was to speak to her, and not to her father, as she repeated her words in every nook and cranny of the teeming streets of the tiny ghetto. She had no plan, no set time when she would leave her parents or her city. All she knew was that she would like to be free, free to live as a woman alone, and that earning money would be the first step to freedom.

CHAPTER EIGHT

"Which one of you is the Jew?" said Pietro Bellini to the two gentlemen from Amsterdam. His uncle, the doge, had insisted on Pietro's housing these two guests of the state in his own palace; the Doge's Palace was occupied with visiting royalty, and even the freethinking doge would not subject a king to sleeping under the same roof with a Jew, no matter how rich or exalted.

"I am," said David Ha-Cohen, the color rising in his face.

"But I am the one who looks more Jewish," said his companion, John Clement, a tall, very handsome Englishman with curly black hair and black eyes. Ha-Cohen was still taller, with what passed in Venice for Germanic features—he was blond, broad-shouldered, and with the impassive blue eyes of a butcher.

"I was assured," said Ha-Cohen, drawing his words out to underline his displeasure, "that the doge's nephew was anxious to extend the hospitality of his house to the two of us. If you have the slightest qualms about our staying here, please say so at once."

"Do you gentlemen play cards?"

"I asked you a question," said Ha-Cohen. "If you don't answer me when I ask you a question, I am going to assume that you mean to insult me."

"I have no qualms about your staying here," said Pietro, looking first to Clement, then to Ha-Cohen. "No qualms about either of you."

In English, Clement said to Ha-Cohen: "Ignore this peacock. We're not here to smash skulls, we're here to do business."

"I'm afraid I don't understand English," said Pietro Bellini.

"What about Dutch?" said Ha-Cohen.

"No," said Bellini.

"Then we shall have two languages to employ when you are in our presence and we don't want you to know what we're saying," said Ha-Cohen. Like many big men, he had a way of moving close to the man with whom he was speaking. Intruding his dangerous body within striking distance of Bellini, he added: "I will tell you right now, I did not like the way you greeted us, I did not like that at all."

"Please, David," said Clement in English.

"I don't know what you are in this city," continued Ha-Cohen in his excellent Roman Italian, "but you look to me like the usual dandy of a courtier. You'd do well to remember that your uncle invited us to Venice, and not to listen to singers, or look at processions, or attend masked balls. We're not here to take insults from the likes of you."

"I'm terribly sorry if you feel that I've insulted you in any way," said Bellini, but his words were tinged with sarcasm. He was a dark young man with a pretty face turning to fat; the kind of face that showed inexperience with anything other than sensual pleasures.

"That's not what I want to hear," said Ha-Cohen, and suddenly his hand flew to Bellini's throat and gripped it as if it were a slender reed. "I want to hear that you're sorry for insulting me. Because you did insult me."

"I'm sorry," said Bellini, his face white, his eyes retreating from Ha-Cohen's furious face.

"You don't call me 'the Jew,'" said Ha-Cohen. "I have a name. and it's older than yours and no less noble. Do you understand that, my little host?"

"Yes," said Bellini. "I'm sorry." Finally, Ha-Cohen let go of the man's neck, and Bellini immediately stepped back from him. "I'm sorry," he said again. "I had no idea that you'd object to my question."

"Show us to our rooms," said Ha-Cohen. "After we've rested, we'll talk again."

Bellini's palace was more than a hundred years old. The first-floor-hall they walked was lit by the midday sun reflecting off the Canal Grande and through the great windows which overlooked its waters. At the distant end of the hall, another bank of windows overlooked a garden, and, as they walked in this direction, Bellini indicated paintings by Paolo Veneziano, a fresco by Guariento di Arpo, a small portrait statue of the first master of the palace by Jacobello delle Masegne, all the while smiling ingratiatingly at the Englishman, rattling off the dates of the artists, the expense of the works of art, and his great desire to insure his guests a happy stay in the palace.

Ha-Cohen shut his mind to all this. He knew that the beautiful palace was built up on wooden planks, and that these planks were supported by wood pilings sunk into the mud. All this white stone, brick and marble, all these monumental paintings and enormous halls, all these delicate riches stood on mud surrounded by water. He had no use for beauty like this. Venice had had its heyday, had had its daring warriors and explorers, its merchants who would venture anywhere in search of markets and grain. Now it was London, Amsterdam, Constantinople that were vital cities, sending out men into the world who were not afraid of battle and blood. Ha-Cohen felt himself to be such a man. He felt himself strong enough to rip through the crushed marble terrazzo flooring of the palace and strike his fist through brick and wood and drive his way straight down to the mud.

As always, he had to restrain himself. If he was furious, impatient, he had to hide this, try to smile, extend the letter of recommendation from one German prince in his family's debt to another Italian duke who loathed the sight of Jews. If he could do anything he wanted, he'd throw off his Jewish name, his constricting religion, his family ties and run off to Patagonia or the East Indies, using his fists as his only recommendation, letting the world judge him for his courage and his strength.

The hallway led to a multitude of living rooms, each with its hooded chimney, its brilliant tapestries, its gilt-framed portraits of fierce, attractive ancestors. When Bellini and the servants left them to their chambers, Ha-Cohen threw his great frame on a couch and began to eat the fruit left for them in a golden bowl.

"David," said John Clement, "that silly boy can have us killed."

"Are you criticizing me?"

"Yes," said Clement. "You're behaving like a child."

"And you're talking like my father."

"I consider it an honor to be compared to Master Ha-Cohen of Amsterdam," said Clement pleasantly. "And I wish I had one-hundredth his wealth in diamonds."

"Really? You have such a love of money, John? What on earth would you want to buy that you cannot now afford? Do you need a new cloak, a new horse? Would you like a golden scabbard? What in the world do you need that you don't now possess?"

"I would provide for my children."

"What children?" said Ha-Cohen.

"I would get married. That's what I would do if I had money. I would get married to a good woman and have a big family."

Ha-Cohen got off the couch and began to laugh. His powerful body shook with great gusts of mirth, and it was all he could do to steady himself enough to grab hold of his friend and lead him out of the room.

"Where are we going?" said Clement.

"You don't want a good woman, you want a *bad* woman," said Ha-Cohen. "And that's what I want, too, and that's what we're going to get."

Ha-Cohen's family was rich and numerous, the most important Jewish family in Amsterdam. Their business, their fortune, was based on diamonds, and legend traced their roots to Zaragoza, in the Spanish state of Aragon. At one point, their name had been Cuheno, and the family was sure of a Sephardic or Spanish origin. This new name was but one form of the original; their far-flung relations used other variations: David Ha-Cohen's family did business with cousins in Hamburg called Cahane, with other cousins in Frankfurt on the Main called Cohen. There were relatives in Turkey, but communication with them was erratic. The family that had settled in Cairo and Alexandria had scattered, and only a few Cuhenos survived in those cities as vital links in the diamond route from India. David Ha-Cohen's brother had been granted permission to settle in England, and lived there as a gentleman, with the support of the Crown, grateful for the chance to enrich the jewel boxes of the realm with the best-cut diamonds in the world.

But though his family was rich, and the recipient of honors and special dispensations, David Ha-Cohen bridled at the terrible injustice he was forced to live under. Every Christian in his class was respected for his name, his prowess at arms; he was given respect grudgingly, *in spite* of his name, *in spite* of his religion. And the respect given was secondhand; the respect given to the son of a rich man, a man whose gems could support a war, or buy a dukedom—and often did, for the royalty who patronized the Ha-Cohen family. Even now, in Venice, the city of masked balls and decadence, of pederasts and adventuresses, of artists and intrigue, he had come not as a single, strong man, eager to take a galley across the world, but as an emissary of his father, and as a Jew.

"Only a coward converts," his father had said, and David Ha-Cohen had taken this as a challenge and not as a statement of truth. He had told his father that he believed not in God but in man. He hated tales from the Bible, he hated rabbis and talmudists, he hated his relatives from Germany who shut their ears when he talked against their religion, and shook their bodies front and back in self-imposed ecstasies of fanatic prayer.

His father had six sons, and David was the youngest, so his behavior was not met with blind fury but with the patience of experience; all the sons had had moments of fury against the restrictions of their lives, but all had found solace in the study of Torah and in the love of their people. This youngest son was the biggest in size, and his temper was fierce, but his father felt that even physical strength and spontaneous raging had their place in God's world.

The increasing demand for well-cut diamonds throughout the courts of Europe had allowed the Ha-Cohen family to set up a flourishing industry for their Jewish brethren, many of them secret Jews fleeing the Inquisition in Spain and Portugal. Amsterdam had quickly become the premier diamond-cutting capital of the world. In the last decades, the demand for bright, Indian stones had accelerated enormously, as kings and princes, dukes and earls followed the example of King Charles VII of France who had gifted his beautiful mistress, Agnes Sorel, with diamonds a hundred and fifty years before. Agnes Sorel was a commoner, and where once diamonds had been worn only by the greatest aristocrats in the land, they could now be worn by anyone who could afford their extravagant cost.

David Ha-Cohen's father planned to establish a Jewish cutting industry in Venice, comparable to what the family had achieved in Amsterdam, to help meet the new demands. As the Ha-Cohen family had long used Venice and the Venetians as a link in their trade route from India to Amsterdam, Venice was a perfect candidate for a new cutting center: Rough stones would not have to be shipped to Amsterdam for finishing, then shipped back again to Venice for the profitable markets of Italy and the south of France. The only problem that the Ha-Cohen family faced in setting up an industry that would certainly profit the Venetian economy was the Venetian law against Jews trading in gems.

It was for this that David Ha-Cohen was sent to Venice, to negotiate with the doge. "Either he will allow Jews to work in the gem trade without restriction, or we will set up a cutting industry in Genova or Napoli. You tell that to the doge," said Ha-Cohen's father, "and if you bring enough force to your arguments, you will have done something courageous and good for your people."

The son, sensing some real danger in the mission, was glad to undertake it. Perhaps the doge would insult him, and he would then have to return the insult with force. These Italians would have to know that the Ha-Cohen family buried their dead with a Spanish coat of arms marking the graves. Of course David Ha-Cohen knew why his father had insisted that John Clement, the courteous Englishman who was both friend and counselor to David, accompany him on this mission. Clement had a way of forestalling riotous situations; and when this was impossible, his strong hand had helped his young friend to answer all insults, and to escape with their lives.

Sensing just such a riotous situation in the making, Clement tried to hold back Ha-Cohen in the great first-floor hallway. "Where are we going?"

"We're going to make you happy," said Ha-Cohen. "With or without my father's diamonds, we're going to make you a happy man."

"I'm tired, David."

"Stop whining, John. You're not an old woman, are you?"

"I'll soon show you who's an old woman."

"Let's hope so," said Ha-Cohen, and in a few moments a stray servant conducted them back to the master of the house. Bellini rose from his seat as the two gentlemen entered, and his face whitened, either in fear or in the expectance of some unpleasantness.

"Your rooms are comfortable, I trust?" said Bellini.

"When is the doge going to meet with us?" said Ha-Cohen.

"I don't know," said Bellini. "We assumed you'd want to rest for at least a day before you entered into any kind of discussions. I can send word to the doge if you'd like to meet earlier. I don't know if it will be possible.

"That's all right," said Ha-Cohen. He spoke with such good-fellowship that Bellini started in wonderment. "If he can't meet with us today, perhaps we can do something else."

"Something else?" said Bellini, wondering what on earth this brutish Jew could have in mind. "You mean you'd rather go out and see the city?"

"We're looking for a couple of attractive women," said Ha-Cohen.

"Women," said Bellini. "You don't mean whores?"

"We do mean whores," said Ha-Cohen.

John Clement smiled courteously for their host's benefit. "It's been a long trip from Amsterdam. A pretty woman would do wonders for my friend's temper."

"There's nothing wrong with my temper, John," said Ha-Cohen, speaking in Italian so that Bellini would understand. "I get angry only when I am provoked."

"If it's whores you want," said Bellini, "I can arrange matters for you at once, and to your great satisfaction."

"That will be greatly appreciated," said Ha-Cohen.

"Perhaps later this evening, we can further indulge ourselves in Venetian excess with some games of chance?"

"If we enjoy your women," said Ha-Cohen, "we shall return the favor by dropping some ducats at your gaming tables."

"Of course you might win," said Bellini. Ha-Cohen didn't even bother to answer this, and, after a cursory exchange of bows, Bellini left them.

What better way, he thought, to punish Diamante than to subject her to this gigantic Jew! Bellini laughed out loud, realizing that this would be the first time she'd have been made love to by one of her own race. Quickly, he made his way to her chambers and entered the anteroom. Diamante's maid stood up and made a little bow.

"How is she?" said Bellini.

"She makes no complaint, sir," said the maid.

"Naturally," said Bellini, and he thrust the maid aside and turned the key in the door to the locked room.

Devorah sat on the bed, pale and bright-eyed in her yellow silk gown. "Take off your clothes," said Bellini peremptorily.

She had been forbidden any solid food for two days, and, at Bellini's command, all she had drunk thus far that morning was a cup of wine. Her skin, always pale, now glowed with an inner radiation, as in a fever, that was pleasing to the eye. Giddy from hunger and her single cup of wine, all her movements were languid, and her lips twisted into a ill-defined smile; but the girl complied with her master's wishes.

She was being punished for her meeting with Rachel, and as she slowly removed her clothing, revealing the delicate flesh of her body to her master's jaded eyes, she wondered if Rachel would be able to sell the emerald, and, if so, how they would be able to meet again.

"Faster," said Bellini, and he began to help her pull off her gown. The gondoliers had told their master that his courtesan had picked up a Jewish girl on the quay along the Canale di Cannaregio, and when Bellini had learned this, he had her locked up in her room and denied all solid food. This was the first time he had seen her since the beginning of her punishment, and he was not about to give her the satisfaction of begging her for information. She knew perfectly well that he had forbidden her to see her sister, or for that matter any member of her family, any Jew at all. Bellini would not dignify her with a chance to deny his accusations. It was enough to know that she had disobeyed, and that she was now punished.

"I'm hungry, Pietro," she said.

"I'm not surprised," said Bellini. He spread her legs and looked at the weak, passive body before him. She was as beautiful as when he first saw her, in that awful bright green gown in the dancing school in the ghetto. But like all his conquests, she offered no novelty once he had broken her away from her family, made her dependent on his largesse, and broken her spirit to suit his whims. Pietro had never loved her, but she had once moved him. The sight of her frail frame, her green eyes, hungry for release from the drab confines of the ghetto, the lush fullness of her dark hair as it followed her sure-footed body in the dance—how clumsy all her students looked next to her! Even his cousin, the young contessa, whose beauty had made him flirt—very dangerously—with her, looked like a cow next to Diamante on the dance floor. But if she had been spirited, where was the spirit now?

"If you disobey me, you will always be hungry," he said, and he kneeled over her motionless body, waiting for her hands to excite his penis.

"I just wanted to see my sister," she said, her eyes looking to excite a kindness in his own.

"Touch me," he said. "Touch me here, Diamante."

That first night she had been his, on the day she ran away, had been so different: She had been drunk on the splendor of the palace, the looks of deference in the eyes of countless servants, the rich silks and velvets that would be hers to wear. Even the forbidden food, never before tasted—pork and pheasant and venison—had been devoured at once, so eager had she been to be his, to fit into his glorious world.

That night they had made love in a way pleasing to them both; he had raped her repeatedly, drunk from hot spiced wine, and she had learned to accept the pain, and to consider it as not so painful compared to the world she had left behind. If this was what it meant to be a mistress—the servants, the fine clothes, the rides in the gondola, the nights behind her master at the gaming tables, the attending of bawdy comedies in the pavilion of some nobleman, the crushing embraces to be accepted in the mad reaches of a ballroom peopled with gentlemen in masks and mistresses in revealing gowns—then she was glad to be a mistress, rather than a Jewess spat at upon the Rialto Bridge.

Devorah quickly learned to be grateful, thanking him for presents, acceding to his wishes when he visited her bed; but she never learned to accept what he soon demanded of her—that she share her bed with whomever else he demanded. She had accepted the life of a mistress, but could not accept the life of a courtesan.

"Touch me," he said, and he placed her hand on his penis and moved his chest over her firm little breasts. Automatically, her fingers caressed him, but her mind was flying back to the first friend he'd brought to her, and then the second, and the third. . . . Each one was the same, each one was an added humiliation, a mark of Pietro's contempt. If she had been as prized, as precious,

as he had once said, then she would not have been shared about
the palace, a receptacle for his friends' hot semen. But she was
not prized, she was merely a possession among others, a beauty
that was fine but not unique, a woman that he used to sleep with
when he so desired, but did not sanctify with a special status.
No, this palace was not a whorehouse, but she was a whore. Not
a mistress, not a courtesan—a whore.

Bellini had entered her, and had begun to breathe hard, all the
while barking commands: "Move, damn you, or you won't eat
for a week! Wrap your legs around my back—higher—that's it.
I said to move, girl. Why don't you move?"

She had been immoble, accepting in just this way—a passive
way to insure displeasing the man she was with—when she had
first begun to be loaned out to his friends. But this proved a useless tactic. If she was not agreeable to his friends, Bellini soon
found out, and rather than being pleased at her loyalty to her
master's body, he used to fly into a rage, and beat her, and lock
her up without food. She learned that it was easier to turn her
hate into sighs, her contempt into passionate movement. Bellini's
friends enjoyed her, and some even fell in love with her. If she
was a whore now, she was also loved and admired and exhibited
all about the city.

Backward and forward her mind ran on with definitions of
what she was and what she wasn't: a courtesan used like a common whore; a whore treated with the care of a mistress; a mistress
presented to the late-night revelers of the city as a lover; a lover
wooed by gems worthy of one's betrothed. As Bellini drove himself harder and harder into her nearby oblivious body, she remembered what she had decided long before the meeting with
her sister. She had decided that she was to get away, to get away
from men who called her anything—whore, courtesan, mistress,
even wife; she was to get away, and with this thought she smiled
now, smiled into Pietro's face as he came in short, ecstatic thrusts.

"Now you're smiling," he said. "All of a sudden you're smiling."

He pulled himself out of her body and fell over on his side on
the bed. Devorah allowed the smile to slowly fade on her face.
If he wanted to imagine that it was his lovemaking that made her
smile, let him; her secret would be her power over him. Perhaps
if he was pleased with himself, he'd sooner forgive her. She had
to quickly return to his favor, not merely to eat but to gain back

the use of a gondola, the freedom to move about the city. Somehow she would find a way to meet with Rachel, and then, with a few other small gems, she'd leave the palace with her lady's clothes, her lady's maid, and her counterfeit story.

"Would you like to eat then?" said Bellini, still lying on the bed.

"Yes."

"It was stupid to meet with your sister, you know that now, don't you?"

"I'm not a slave, for the love of Jesus."

"No, not a slave," said Bellini. "But you are a servant of my house, even if you don't wear livery."

"Is that supposed to be a joke?"

"No, it's not. I'm perfectly serious. If you think yourself other than a servant, you think badly."

"You never asked me to run away from the ghetto to be your servant. You never put it that way, dear Pietro, did you? You were sweet to me then, and you called me beautiful names, and you loved to fondle my hand."

"Do you want to go back to the ghetto?"

"No."

"Then stay away from the Jews, as I command you."

"I will do whatever you say, Pietro," said Devorah, and she turned her languid body toward his and ran her dead hand along his bare, hairless chest, hating him with every fiber of her being.

"You will do whatever I say?"

"Yes."

"Dress yourself, and be quick about it."

"All right. Am I going to be allowed to eat?"

"Not yet. There's someone I want you to meet, and I don't want you to be too good. This one is so gentle, he might fall in love with you. This gentleman is so soft, he could almost be a Jew."

Bellini got out of the bed, and dressed, humming a tune to himself. Devorah decided against fighting, or begging—it would be no use, not when he was in this nasty, sarcastic mood. Someone must have beaten him at cards, or otherwise irritated him, and now she had to pay the price.

"You are my master, Pietro," she said, "but you still like me a little, I know you do."

"What of it?"

"I will go with your friend, but I must eat something, or I might fall down in there and die."

Bellini moved close to her beautiful face and grabbed each of her cheeks between the thumb and forefinger of each of his hands, squeezing her pale flesh until she howled in pain. "You won't die," he said, letting go, and he laughed at her, and pushed her back against the bed. "Hurry up now, you've got a very noble gentleman anxious to see you," he said, and quickly left the room.

"Sir, I'm sorry, sir, but may we bring her some food now, sir?" said the maid outside. Bellini looked at her for a moment, then slapped her hard on the ear. "I'm sorry, sir," she said, starting in pain, bowing and bobbing her head.

"Bring her a glass of wine," said Bellini.

"Wine?" said the maid, her voice doubtful.

"I said wine, you stupid bitch, bring her a glass of wine," he said, and the maid stepped back from him in fright. "Wine," he repeated, in a soft voice, so that the maid had no choice but to pour out a glass and take it into the adjacent room.

Bellini shook his head and walked back to the other side of the palace, where Ha-Cohen and Clement waited. "I'm sorry, gentlemen," said Bellini. "But I think you'll both agree it was worth waiting for." He asked Clement to go with a servant, who would conduct him to another courtesan he kept in the house, a brown-haired beauty from Napoli who had been a prostitute ever since she was thirteen. "She is very lovely, Clement," he said, "and innocent as well. A poor girl, one of twelve children, who has experienced very few men."

Clement didn't like the idea of being separated from his hot-tempered young charge, but Ha-Cohen waved him off. Already, this hot temper was rising, but Ha-Cohen kept it beneath the surface; he was curious to see if an insult was to be attempted, or if one had already been made. If this man Bellini, no matter how wellborn, retained a quantity of prostitutes in his home, then it was obvious that the dodge's office had sent him to a whorehouse, and not the home of a respected citizen of the republic.

"And for you, Ha-Cohen," said Bellini, leading him through the corridors to Devorah's chambers, "we have the most beautiful whore in Venice. One with a great appetite for strong men."

Even his words were those of a whoremaster, but Ha-Cohen didn't allow them to sound him into a fury. He wanted a woman now, and he could allow his anger to rise after he had bedded this man's whore. All he allowed himself now was the pleasure of saying, "We are fortunate to be guests in a home where so many whores are available to us. In my part of the world, gentlemen usually have to leave their palaces to find women who sell their flesh."

"It's only the two," said Bellini, his voice genuinely innocent. "But I've saved you the best." And without further ado, he waved the Jewish merchant prince into the antechamber to Devorah's room. The maid there bobbed her head in greeting and offered him a glass of wine. "She'll take care of you," said Bellini, and he left Ha-Cohen drinking his wine in the company of the maid.

"My lady is just getting up, sir," said the maid.

"Your lady?" said Ha-Cohen, wondering at the use of the word.

The maid stared at him, fascinated by his great size. "Are you a German gentleman, sir?" said the maid.

"What's it your concern?" said Ha-Cohen. "Is that where she is? It doesn't matter if she's still in bed, she's not going to have to get out of it on my account." And the tall, powerful blond man pushed past the maid and entered Devorah's room.

"How dare you enter my room?" said Devorah. She was dressed in her yellow silk gown, sitting before an ornate mirror, brushing her dark, thick hair. She turned her eyes on him with real anger, and Ho-Cohen was struck with the strength of her beauty. He had been with many whores in many places, but this young woman looked nothing like the sad-eyed, desperate-to-please creatures he'd known.

"You needn't brush your hair, girl," said Ha-Cohen.

"I'll brush my hair if I want," said Devorah. "And I'm not a servant that you call 'girl.' My name is Diamante."

"Diamante?" said Ha-Cohen, laughing, and coming up to where she sat. He gripped her thin shoulders in his powerful hands. "So you are a diamond? We have something in common then, you and I. Diamonds are my business."

With that, Ha-Cohen turned her about in the chair and brought her forcibly to her feet. She was so light, so nonresistant, that for a moment he almost stopped to examine more gently what he was about to ravage. But Ha-Cohen was not a contemplative man. He rushed past the rare beauty of her green eyes and drew her mouth to his, crushing her thin body against his great chest.

He kissed her with his tongue and his teeth, and bore down so hard on her lips that he tasted blood in his hungry mouth. When he let her go, she fell back from him, and there was terror in her eyes.

"Please, sir, I am not as strong as all that," she said. "Please be gentle with me."

"Come here," said Ha-Cohen. And she let herself be drawn back to this great blond giant, trying to divine the origin of his accent, trying to imagine why Pietro had sent him to her—why her master had seemed to take delight in making this match. "You're a beautiful one," said Ha-Cohen. "I've never seen a whore more beautiful." And without further ado, he was undressing her, his hands pulling at the silk with so little caution that only a miracle prevented the fabric from tearing.

Devorah tried to slow down the rush of the man's lovemaking. She asked if he wanted wine, she begged him to remove his shoes, his cloak—but the blond giant wanted nothing other than her nakedness, and at once. "Let me look at you," he said, and turned her about as if she were a tiny statue, an object he could have placed in his hand. He didn't touch her at first, he simply examined her, his rough hands poised an inch from her buttocks, looming over her neck, her breasts, her hair. "Let me look at you," he said again, and then he said, "Diamante, you're wonderful, Diamante. You're much more than I would have expected."

"I'm cold," she said.

"You won't be," said Ha-Cohen. And still without touching her, he kept her at arm's length and stripped off all of his own clothes, every last stitch, in a way that was uncommon to gentlemen of that period. Devorah looked at the blond hairs on his massive chest, the powerful muscles of his neck, the arms as thick with strength as a statue of Hercules or Prometheus. "You won't be cold, but we won't hurry now. It's good not to hurry," he said, and then, with surprising softness, just as Pietro had said, the man who had kissed her hard enough to draw blood now drew her naked body softly against his, and she felt the penis begin to swell and grow against her upper belly.

She was too weak, too tired to think of giving pleasure, to try and perform the tasks of a whore with any measure of skill, but something in the substance of the moment made her press her head against his chest and softly kiss the man that had come to use her. "It'll be wonderful," he said. "Diamante, it'll be wonderful, it'll be like lovers, only because you are so beautiful and I am so hungry for your body."

He picked her up, like a princess on her wedding night, and carried her to the great bed and placed her softly on her back. As he bent over her, she caught her own reflection in his blue eyes, and saw again, for that moment, the edge of savagery there, the hint of violence that had first terrified her.

He kissed her breasts, and kissed her neck, and ran his hands along the sweet curving of her waist, about the gentle swell of her thighs, the tiny muscles in her calves.

A wave of excitement began to rise in her chest, and, with it, a sense of passion in her groin; through her hunger, a light sense of wonder began to shine. The powerful man swooped over her and kissed her thighs, her knees, her forehead, and suddenly her hands reached out for his mouth, only to caress in kind. It was extraordinary, but this man who meant nothing to her, this man who seemed a brute, was treating her with kindness, with respect, with love.

Ha-Cohen kissed the hands she'd brought to his lips, and now rested his body alongside hers, cradling his head on her shoulder. Slowly, he guided her hands to his penis, now grown fully erect, and as she stretched out her fingers to caress it, she was struck with a sensation that was altogether new and startling.

But this sense of wonder passed in an instant. She didn't have to ask. She looked at his penis for the first time, and was struck with perfect horror. Devorah drew back her hands as if she had touched fire.

"What is it?" he said, his voice suddenly angry, as if all the tenderness he'd lavished on her had vanished in a moment.

"I've never seen—" she began.

"I've no foreskin. I'm circumcised," said Ha-Cohen. Even a whore had to remind him of his Jewishness. His hatred of the world blew up in him so suddenly that it was all he could to do to restrain himself from violence.

"I know," said Devorah. It seemed to Ha-Cohen as if she were shrinking from him.

"It's still a penis—I'm just as much a man. It's cleaner this way, they say. I've been with many women, and they've all said they preferred this to the other way."

"You don't understand," said Devorah. Her body, so weak and frail, had suddenly found strength enough to twist away from him. Ha-Cohen looked at her with fury as she reached for her gown to cover her nakedness. "I've never been with a Jewish man."

"Where do you think you're going?" said Ha-Cohen, and, all the tenderness gone, he reached out and grabbed her shoulder, pulling her back to the bed and pushing her flat on her back. "I'm a Jew, but that doesn't mean that I'm not going to want to make love to you." Ha-Cohen looked down at the beauty now, wondering what she was thinking, trying to understand why what was before beginning to please was now revolting. "I'm a Jew," he said, "but I'm a man. I breathe, I eat, I sleep, I make love to a woman—and if I want, I'm going to make love to you."

"No!" said Devorah, And then, in a little voice, her words emerging in tandem with her thought: "It's a sin."

"What?" said Ha-Cohen, not understanding how a whore could reach out for religion. Even the German whores who loathed Jews never thought of mentioning the prohibitions of the Church against fornication with Jews. But even in his anger he could sense something different from hate or revulsion rising out of the terror in her eyes; it was a terror yet more fundamental than prejudicial revulsion, a terror that he didn't understand, and he let her speak, rather than drive his wild lips to hers.

"I'm a Jewess," she said.

There was no moment of disbelief. Ha-Cohen at once understood her terror and felt its force now beneath his own skin. He got out of the bed and began to dress.

CHAPTER NINE

For three days, Rachel had gone about the ghetto, looking for a man to whom she could sell her sister's emerald. Many men had been interested, but none had offered her a great sum of ducats. Emeralds were not the fashion, she had been told, and what good was a fine stone if it could not be sold to a rich patrician?

On the fourth day after her meeting with Devorah, Rachel read a secondhand volume of Tasso's poetry, by the light of a single candle in the small secondhand-merchandise shop of her father Yehezkel. The shop was tiny, dark, and without sufficient air. Reconditioned mattresses were piled in the back, where Miriam, Rachel's mother, sewed in the near-dark, humming to herself in a revery that excluded the outside world. Yehezkel sat on a stool at the front of the shop, which occupied the ground floor of the narrow tenement on whose topmost floor his family slept. Here were the secondhand jewels, mostly strands of inexpensive pearls, torn off the once-elegant gowns of great ladies whose husbands needed to pay gambling debts.

Suddenly, the lethargic Yehezkel shot to his feet, his head making a little bow. Rabbi Yakov of Modena had entered the shop, and was smiling courteously at the uneducated merchant.

"Please sit down, Yehezkel," he said.

"I'm not so old that I need to sit down in the presence of Rabbi Yakov," said Yehezkel.

"I have not come on a religious mission."

"I didn't suppose you did. Still, that is no reason to abandon respect for you and your learning. Besides, I'm afraid I have no money."

"Really?" said the rabbi, his blue eyes smiling mischievously. "Not even for a little bet?" Rabbi Yakov was famous both inside and outside the ghetto for his eloquent sermons, and his insatiable appetite for cardplaying. Learned Christians, clergy and laymen alike, visited the synagogues where he preached to listen to his powerful figures of speech, his thunderous delivery, his passion derived mostly from art. He was the only rabbi of the period who was invited to preach in the great cathedrals of the city—not, of course, on the merits of Judaism, but on moral and ethical principles that were not tied to any one religion. Princes of the Church, English dukes, members of half a dozen royal families ventured near and far to hear him speak on charity and goodness, though it was well known that the rabbi only sermonized if he was paid for it, in advance, in Venetian coin. And whatever great sums he could command for his good work he lost almost immediately to Jewish cardsharps, Venetian noblemen, or Russian merchants. He loved betting on dice, on the dates of arrival of galleys from abroad, on the number of congregants who'd come to hear him speak on any given occasion—but most of all, he loved betting on the turn of a playing card.

This was all the immensely learned rabbi had in common with Yehezkel Cuheno.

"A bet?" said Yehezkel. "What sort of bet?"

"A very simple one. The first one to pull out the Duc de Langre."

Yehezkel smiled. Rabbi Yakov was either paying him a great compliment or wanted something of his very badly. At that time, gamblers in Venice used many different kinds of playing cards, and most attached a great significance to the kind which they themselves favored. Some used a deck of seventy-eight cards, some fifty-six, some fifty-two. In Italy, most preferred four suits of swords, batons, cups, and money; in Germany, the usual preference was for hearts, bells, leaves, and acorns; in France, that great follower of Italian fashions, the preference was for the locally printed fifty-two-card deck, with suits of diamonds, clubs, hearts, and spades. Yehezkel Cuheno had often voiced his preference for the French deck, much to the amusement of his fellow cardplayers. Rabbi Yakov, in suggesting a bet on who would be the first to pull out the Duc de Langre, was referring to the King of Hearts in the French deck—the same deck in which the King of Diamonds was the Duc de Bourgogne, the King of Clubs was the Comte de Beauvais, and the King of Spades was the Duc de Reims.

"You want to gamble with the French deck?" said Yehezkel.

"Yes, if it suits you," said the rabbi.

Rachel put down her book and walked up to the front of the shop. Though she admired this rabbi, and had often sat spellbound in the women's gallery listening to him preach, she had no use for his profligate habits, especially when they involved her father.

"Good morning, Rabbi," she said.

"Ah, I see you're reading Tasso," he said.

"She's always reading, always burning up my candles, even in the daytime," said Yehezkel.

"What's a hundred candles against the light of human knowledge?" said the rabbi. Then he looked with peculiar intensity at the girl, and reached under his cloak for something wrapped in a rag.

"My father has had bad luck at gambling these last few weeks," said Rachel. "I know you wouldn't want to deprive him of a chance to earn his livelihood."

"Silence," said Yehezkel, turning from Rachel to the rabbi. "She is the last of five daughters and is afraid of missing her dowry. If her mother would have given me only one son, life would have been so much easier for all of us. But no, only daughters. And now the youngest of them complains."

"Women always complain about gambling, except when you win."

"Is that your stake?" said Yehezkel, wondering at the unseen item wrapped up in the rag in Rabbi Yakov's hand.

"Yes."

"What is it?"

"Do you know what my wife is always telling me?" said the rabbi, still glancing at Rachel. "Always she's calling me to task for gambling, as if it were some sort of terrible sin. I'm her husband and her master, I'm the man who stands and preaches to the congregation every sabbath afternoon—I'm the only preacher for whom the hourglass is removed from the pulpit, because no one cares if I run over an hour, or even two—and yet she lectures me on the nature of sin." Rabbi Yakov turned to Rachel and raised his hand to the ceiling. "Tell me, child, you who read so much, how many commandments are there in the Torah, and how many prohibitions?"

"There are two hundred and forty-eight commandments," said Rachel, proud of her knowledge. "There are three hundred and sixty-five prohibitions."

"Is it not interesting," said the learned rabbi, "that the number of commandments, two hundred and forty-eight, corresponds precisely to the number of bones in the human body?"

"Yes," said Rachel, not seeing fit to mention that she had read in the work of a Gentile anatomist that the human body had not two hundred and forty-eight but two hundred and six bones.

"And do you know, dear child," said the rabbi, "out of all the many prohibitions, three hundred and sixty-five of them—so many prohibitions for us poor Jews!—out of all those prohibitions, do you know even one that forbids the playing of cards?"

"That is not the point," said Rachel, but she stopped short, for at that moment the usually impoverished rabbi opened up his rag and revealed a small, delightfully gleaming emerald, and placed it on the counter in front of her father.

Yehezkel was flabbergasted at the value of such a bet, but before he could react to it, the rabbi continued. "And do you remember, dear child, that included among the two hundred and forty-eight commandments is that often ignored precept 'Honor thy father and thy mother, that thy days may be long upon the land which the Lord thy God giveth thee'?"

"Yes," said Rachel, her eyes unable to avoid the emerald.

"I can't match that stake," said Yehezkel Cuheno. "All I've got here are some bad pearls, taken from an old gown."

"You can match the stake," said Rabbi Yakov.

"I don't understand," said Yehezkel.

"Ask your daughter," said Rabbi Yakov.

"My daughter doesn't have enough money to buy green glass."

"Ask your daughter," repeated Rabbi Yakov. "Ask your daughter to tell you what every gem merchant in the ghetto already knows."

But Rachel didn't stand still for the question. In a moment, she had thrust her way past the rabbi and out into the crowded alleyway. A mass of humanity greeted her, Jews and Gentiles, men from all over Venice, and from all over the word as well. The roar of a thousand conversations, the haggling over goods bartered in the open air, the score of languages, the endless profusion of accents and dialects, the clash of bright clothing, children's voices, women hawking their husbands' goods, affected her not at all: This was her world, as ordinary as a morning, as predictable as the coming of night. Even the goggle-eyed tourists, pushing their way through the ghetto for the first time, looking for the beautiful Jewish women, or the incredible bargains—so they imagined—of the Jewish men, had no interest for her; they were there every day. She had seen Turks and Germans and Moslems; even the black page boys—slaves captured by the Portuguese along the West African coast for the pleasure of jaded kings and queens—were no longer a novelty to her. Rachel pushed her way through the crowd, trying not to topple any stand or booth of secondhand goods, trying not to be stopped by any of a hundred acquaintances, trying only to distance herself from her father.

There was really only one place for her to go, one man who could still help her.

Leone Ha-Levi.

She had seen him once since the meeting with her sister. His privileged yellow turban, the mark of the Portuguese Jewish community, had stood out in the crowd near the main gate to the ghetto; it struck her that he was searching the crowd, looking for a familiar face in the throngs entering and exiting. Rachel had hidden her face under her shawl and made her escape between two old women. She had not wanted him to see her, not before she had formulated a precise answer to his proposal of marriage. Of course the answer was to be no, but she had to give him more than this; particularly because she was in love with him.

Now she was not thinking of love. She was thinking of her sister's emerald, and her responsibility for its sale. Unless she could dispose of it immediately, it would pass into her father's control. This would not only be of no use to Devorah, it would certainly be of no use to the Cuheno family as a whole, as her father would simply gamble it all away. Not only that, but under her father's hands, she might confess where the emerald had come from, and then one mad beating would follow another—his love for his prettiest daughter, transmuted to rage at the only daughter left under his command.

Quickly, running through the brief interstices between the knots of people clustering about particular shops, she made her way to the more affluent Portuguese section of the ghetto. Yellow turbans began to appear with more frequency, and she let out one or two cries of recognition before realizing that the men she saw were not in fact Leone but other young men, of average height, dressed like him.

"I'm sorry," said Rachel to one of these young men. "I mistook you for someone else."

"Keep mistaking me," said the young man. "I don't mind."

"I beg your pardon, sir," said Rachel, not realizing that the young man was flirting with her—flirting with her in a way that would have had him excommunicated in the other, more orthodox part of the ghetto. She had heard that there were young Jews of the Portuguese community who refused to attend services in the synagogue, even on the High Holy Days. There was talk of Jewish men who openly ate unclean food, who denied the fact that the Torah was written with divine inspiration, who claimed that God existed but did not take much notice of men, and took no notice at all of the ways in which men prayed to him. But Rachel couldn't imagine how a Jew could believe these things and still remain Jewish. If one was an apostate, why not throw off the restrictions of the ghetto and go to live with the Gentiles?

"Don't beg me for anything other than my name," said the young man. "It's Mordecai, and I'm very pleased to meet you. What did you say your name was?"

"Excuse me," said Rachel, frightened by his audacity. She tried to remember that she was planning to learn to fend for herself in the world, but she didn't see how that could justify answering a strange man who addressed her on a public thoroughfare. "I'm not talking to you, sir. I'm looking for Leone Ha-Levi, and I made a mistake."

"What do you want with Leone Ha-Levi? That man's got nothing in his head but prayer shawls. Listen, I'm not trying to frighten you, but I am trying to get you to talk to me."

"I don't want to talk to you," said Rachel, becoming frightened. They had come to the entrance to a tiny alley, and the young Jew was apparently trying to talk her into its opening. When Rachel resisted, the young man put his hand on her arm.

"Take it easy, I'm not going to hurt you," he said. "All you German Jews are alike. All you think about is the evils of the world, and you never get a chance to enjoy any of them."

Rachel stopped short, planting her feet on the ground. The young man gripped her forearm more tightly, to assert his control. In terror, Rachel realized that there were no passersby on this tiny street. "All I want you to do is look at me, and say my name," said the young man. "Mordecai. That's a nice Jewish name. Even your Leone doesn't have such a nice Jewish name. Mordecai, that's a name you can trust. Go on. Just look at me. All you German women act like slaves. You can talk to a man. What's a man going to do to you anyway? You don't even know."

"Leone!" screamed Rachel, for again she saw another yellow-turbaned man approaching, and as Mordecai turned around to see to whom she called, she lashed out with her free hand at the young man's chest and twisted her arm free from his grip. "Leone!" she screamed again, and ran toward the approaching stranger.

"Rachel!" she heard from across the way, and there, incredibly, was the young man she sought, walking with a book in his hand, his posture less than erect, his eyes squinting, his straight black hair falling over his ears. Rachel stopped running, and turned to walk toward Leone Ha-Levi, not even looking back to where Mordecai had been. It was enough to know that she had escaped.

"I have to talk to you," she said when she'd come up to him. For all his scholarly eyes, his less than magnificent stature, Leone had a physical charm that never failed to work its power over Rachel. His dark eyes had a way of looking right into her, giving her his full attention; an attention that was not merely intellectual but seemed to search for an emotional framework to give sense to one's words. Like many Portuguese Jews, he shaved his beard, and the bones of his face stood out with the sharp outlines of beauty.

He was a businessman, and successful for his years; but instead of a fat, complacent face, his was agitated, contemplative, ineluctably open to pain. It was the face of a poet, of a lover. Still, he could talk sharply to make a good sale. He knew the way to buy cheap, and sell dear. He knew when he was standing on firm ground, and when he was floating on air. He knew that he had fallen in love with Devorah for her beauty, and for her spirit; a spirit that refused to accept the limitations of her life. He knew that he loved Rachel, but in another way. He loved her for her kind heart, and for the kind of mother she would be to their children. But even he—reader of romances and legal texts, dreamer of future fantasies and crafter of sharp contracts, even he who should have understood at once—did not realize that he loved Rachel simply because she was Devorah's sister.

When Leone saw her coming to him on this quiet street, she was like a desire suddenly materialized out of the air. He went to her, his face alive with gladness. There could be no doubt in his mind that he loved this young woman and wanted to be with her at that moment. His face expressed this so clearly that, for a terrible second, Rachel's decision to refuse him turned to dust. For a terrible second, she believed that her love for him was answered by one as pure and as simple for her. But the second passed. There was Devorah. Rachel allowed a vision of her sister's face to pass between Leone and herself, and there was nothing to believe now, nothing other than the fact that the man she loved, loved her sister best.

"I was looking for you," she said. "I need your help."

She was so agitated that Leone had to put out his hands to keep her from falling. Rather than badger the girl with a hundred questions in the middle of the street, Leone guided her firmly to the street of his parents' house. "It's all right," he said. "We'll talk once we're inside and you've had some hot wine."

Leone's mother served them, chasing the curious servant away; and then Leone had to chase his mother away, who was just as curious. At Rachel's express desire, Leone had mentioned to no one that he had offered his hand in marriage to the Cuheno girl; Rachel didn't want the offer known unless she was going to accept it. Leone watched her drink some wine, and then slowly, looking directly at her with intense kindness, he said, "Don't be afraid, Rachel. You can tell me whatever you like. I'll help you in any way I can. It doesn't matter what you've decided about me. Whether or not you'll marry me, I'm the same Leone."

Rachel couldn't speak. She would not tell him of the indignity that had just occurred with the Portuguese stranger, but the incident still confused her. She would not tell him of the decision she had made, with so little thought, to create a life for herself, on her own terms, with her own money, as an independent person. This was not what he was waiting to hear. She must speak about her answer to his proposal of marriage, but that was not why she had come to him now either. Devorah was what she had come about. Devorah and the emerald.

"Leone," she said. She took the emerald necklace out from under her gown and showed it to him. "I need your help."

"What is this?" he said, looking in wonder at the valuable gem. "How did you get hold of something like this?"

"I can't marry you, Leone," said Rachel, unable to bear the weight of the words unspoken a moment longer.

"You can't or you won't?" said Leone.

"I don't want to," said Rachel. "I don't want to marry you."

"May I know why?"

"I need your help, Leone," said Rachel.

"I love you," he said.

"Please, Leone. Will you help me?"

"I just want you to know that I love you. I thought we could be happy together. There would be no waiting for a dowry. I would insist this time with Yehezkel. I don't want a dowry, and I don't expect one. We could be married almost at once. I want a family. I thought you would have liked that. That's what I imagined. I thought you liked me."

He was so upset by the refusal that his words wandered up and down the musical scale, like a misplaced dirge, a confused lament. The usual clarity of his statements was gone. He looked at the emerald necklace, as if this might be relevant to the issue at hand, and touched its surface with a finger. "Sometimes love is less important than respect in a marriage, but I didn't see our marriage in that way. I wanted to take you from that little shop and make you comfortable, I wanted you to be able to read the books you want, I wanted you to be the woman to teach my children. But not just out of respect. I love you, too. This is what I mean. I'm all right, Rachel. I'm sorry if I'm not making sense. I don't understand why you don't want to marry me, I confess I don't. I don't know why you've brought this here, either. Did you say you need my help with this necklace? Forgive me if I'm not myself."

"It's I who has to be forgiven."

"No."

"I'm lying, you see," said Rachel. "I don't mean it when I say that I don't want to marry you."

"But why . . .?" said Leone, letting his sentence trail, unable to formulate a question when he couldn't understand her words.

"This emerald necklace belongs to Devorah," she said. With all her strength, she kept her eyes on Leone now, and his eyes revealed everything: the shock of memory, the raw power of his loss. In his eyes, Rachel could see that his love for Devorah remained as strong, as obsessive, as ever. Blindly, she went on, her love for him strangling the words in her throat. "I met with Devorah. She is well. She asked for my help, and of course I would do anything for her. Devorah wants to leave Venice, and she asked me if I could sell this necklace for her in the ghetto. She needs money, a great deal of money to suit her plans. I've tried to sell the emerald, but I've so far failed."

Leone picked up the necklace and, without thinking, fondled it, as if it were a living thing. "Devorah," he said. "I'm glad to know that she's well."

"Will you help me?"

"You said that she wants to leave Venice?"

"Yes."

"May I ask you why she wants to leave? With whom she plans to go? I'm sorry if these are difficult questions."

"You may ask nothing about Devorah," said Rachel. "Either you can help me, or not, as you see fit. Helping to sell this necklace will be a service to me, as well as to Devorah. But I do not wish to discuss her life or her plans."

"I'll help you," said Leone.

"Thank you," said Rachel; and quickly, while he watched her with his beautiful, omniscient eyes, she told him about Rabbi Yakov's revelation to her father about her possessing such a stone. Leone dismissed this as a reason to fear. He would say that it was his emerald, and that he had given it to Rachel to sell for him. Rachel saw that his hands could not let go of the necklace, that his fingers continued to stroke the stone, to weave the chain about his knuckles, his wrists.

"Is this why you won't marry me?" said Leone.

Rachel was shocked by the question. That he could include her in his thoughts at all, at a time when Devorah's name and presence was invoked from a two-year silence, was barely to be believed. It was the shock that allowed her to speak with more frankness than she would have otherwise dared.

"I don't want to marry you because you don't love me the way I want you to."

"How do you want me to love you?"

"The way you loved Devorah," said Rachel. "The way you still love her."

Leone understood at once what Rachel was saying, and, in his understanding, he became aware of her pain. The young man knew that she loved him, and that the quality of this love was unmatched by his own, because Rachel loved him with passion, without reason, the way he loved her beautiful sister. There was nothing more he could say. He loved Rachel, and wished she would consent to be his wife. But his passion was for Devorah, the woman who lived in sin, away from her people.

He unwound the necklace from his hands and placed it on the table. Leone Ha-Levi could not yet conceive of a world where a whore could be returned to her family, to her lover, to her religion. Life was not a meaningless set of experiences that were not to be paid for, either in this world or the world-to-come. Living involved choosing, deciding between goodness and evil, accepting commandments or breaking prohibitions, performing good deeds or sinning. Rachel had chosen a good path, Devorah an evil one. Marriage was a commandment, as was the bringing forth of children into the world. Rachel suited this commandment, and he loved her for this. But all his sure knowledge of life and the world seemed to get up and dance in his head now, a macabre dance, a dance of howling phantoms, of crossed chances, twisted meanings, inchoate feelings that transcended any sure knowledge of right action.

Rachel had not only refused him, she had brought to the surface something that had festered in some black corner of his mind. He could not stop loving Devorah, regardless of her freely chosen sinning. Yet he could never forgive her, not within the boundaries of his world. Leone's agony lay in not being able to see a compromise between blind love and perpetual condemnation. And there was no compromise, not in his world, perhaps not in any world, no matter how modern. When he spoke, he knew what he was saying. He wasn't offering forgiveness, he was giving in to passion. He wasn't performing a good deed, he was entering into an evil one. In a moment, he had decided not to change the world but to be cast from its congregation of devout, honest men.

"Yes," he said, "I do love her."

"Then you'll help to sell her necklace?"

"Yes," said Leone. He didn't have to ask what was written in his face.

"You want to see her," said Rachel.

"I want to see her," said Leone.

"I'll arrange it," said Rachel.

CHAPTER TEN

For twenty-four hours after David Ha-Cohen's encounter with
Devorah, he waited. John Clement had asked him how the whore
had been, and Ha-Cohen had said nothing. Pietro Bellini tried to
make conversation with him at the lavish evening meal, but Ha-
Cohen refused to be baited. He ate the unclean food of the
Gentiles, he drank their wine, and waited.

"Will you talk to the doge, or will I?" said John Clement, as
he watched his friend finish dressing the following day.

"I will," said Ha-Cohen.

"You are not angry with me, David?"

"No."

"With whom then? You are angry, aren't you?"

"I will talk to the doge," said Ha-Cohen, and he turned his
back on the conversation. Clement wondered if Ha-Cohen might
have been insulted by the whore the day before, or if he had
suffered from some temporary impotence. If so, Clement knew
that he should speak to him about it, as an older, more experienced
man. But before he could think of words innocuous enough to
broach this delicate subject, a servant arrived to announce the
readiness of the gondola for the trip to the Doge's Palace.

Bellini accompanied them in the gondola, thus making the small quarters cramped. He talked incessantly, pointing out the sights to Clement, as Ha-Cohen had shut his eyes, as if to underline his disinterest.

"You'd better be careful not to get my uncle angry," said Bellini, pointing his words in Ha-Cohen's direction. "It's not just a palace we're going to. We've got courts and council rooms to sentence you, and torture chambers and prison cells to punish you, so do him the honor of letting him speak. He fancies himself a Rabbi Yakov of Modena."

Ha-Cohen suddenly came to life. For a moment, it seemed that his body would bristle forth with enough energy to capsize the little flat-bottomed boat. But all he did was grab Bellini's chin and say, "What is this about a rabbi?"

"I didn't say anything insulting!" said Bellini. "As Jesus is my witness, Rabbi Yakov isn't God that his name can't be mentioned in vain."

"Who is Rabbi Yakov?" said Ha-Cohen. "And why is it that you make use of his name as a figure of speech?"

"Please let go of me," said Bellini. "Clement, surely you've heard of Rabbi Yakov?"

"No," said Clement.

"He is famous," protested Bellini, and then went on to explain that Yakov was the greatest orator alive in Venice, and that he'd meant nothing malicious by using his name. "I didn't even think of him as Jewish when I mentioned the name. I think of him first as an orator, second as a Jew."

Ha-Cohen let go of Bellini's chin and returned to his dull silence. The explanation was satisfactory, but it was not for mention of Rabbi Yakov's name that he waited for a chance to wreak vengeance on Bellini. He had left the whore called Diamante as soon as he had dressed, not looking at her once after hearing her secret. Ha-Cohen didn't know if Bellini was privy to the knowledge of Diamante's Jewishness, or if it was because of the knowledge of her Jewishness that he had taken him to her bed. It was enough to know that a Jewish girl had fallen into the hands of this Venetian pimp. It was enough to know that Bellini had almost brought him into carnal knowledge of a Jewess. Never before had Ha-Cohen felt the coarseness of his flesh, the ugliness of his life, the injustice of the world with such force. Intercourse with the Jewess would have been as sinful as incest.

All the prideful lessons of his father came back to him, not in summary but in a flash of revelation: They were the people of the Book, and were chosen to carry out its commandments. It was unspeakably horrible to imagine a daughter of the chosen people a whore in the palace of this Bellini. Only if she had thrown out all knowledge of her past, all alliance with her people, could she have stooped so low; and this she must have done, for she was indeed a whore, indeed naked at her master's command.

Ha-Cohen felt her perfect humiliation before him, because he himself had lusted after the same things: to be an *Am Ha-Aretz*, an ignoramus of all things Jewish; to be broken apart from his heritage, his race; to be free of all knowledge of commandments and prohibitions, free of the myriad restrictions of the Jews. This is what she had lusted for, and she was a whore. Not only must she be avenged for the humiliation forced upon her, but the world that had brought her to lust for this false freedom—Venice and its ghetto and its restrictive laws against the Jews—must be twisted now to his will. It was for this that Ha-Cohen waited. The doge of Venice would not know that this diamond merchant's demands would be fueled by the plight of a Jewish whore.

Soon, they had alighted from the gondola, and followed the chattering Bellini through the crowded Porta della Carta, into the palace's courtyard. Everywhere, gaily dressed young men, and their more sober fathers, swooped down upon Bellini to greet him. Clement more than once had to insist on hurrying, worried lest Ha-Cohen explode at the needless delays. The three walked quickly up the magnificent staircase leading to the first-floor loggia of the palace, and Ha-Cohen noted with satisfaction that Bellini was out of breath, simply from the climb.

"Before we leave," said Bellini, "I must show you the carvings in the lower arcade. None of this pagan splendor we have here." He was pointing to the massive statues of Mars and Neptune guarding the staircase they had just climbed. "Down there we have Noah, and Adam and Eve, and even Solomon, judging between the mothers."

"Take us to the doge," said Ha-Cohen. "I care nothing for art."

"All right," said Bellini. "But in Venice, like it or not, we are always walking in it, and on it." He exchanged quick greetings with soldiers at the foot of the Scala d'Oro, the great golden staircase, with its gilt stucco reliefs executed by Alessandro Vittoria and its painted panels by Battista Franco, and as the three climbed up to the second floor, Bellini seemed to relish the thought that Ha-Cohen, clod though he was, could not help but be moved by the force of beauty around him.

Bellini took them into a little waiting room, watched over by overweight soldiers, and exchanged a few words with a secretary. Immediately they were all ushered into the adjacent, much larger room, where they were asked to sit by another secretary.

"We will wait five minutes," said Ha-Cohen. "More than that, and we shall return at once to Amsterdam. Tell that to your doge. We have not come to beg favors, but to offer them."

The secretary bowed at this outburst and hurried out of the great room, as oblivious as Ha-Cohen to the magnificent paintings and statuary about him.

"I see why you've been silent," said Clement. "You've been saving up your venom for this moment."

But the secretary returned soon enough, and quickly ushered the three men through a series of magnificent rooms, leading deeper and deeper into the doge's private apartments. The room where they finally found the doge was surprisingly small, but it was suited for conversations of a practical, as opposed to a ceremonial, nature. Bellini rushed to kiss his uncle, who remained sitting in a very democratic sort of chair at a tiny desk whose beauty was obscured by a quantity of papers.

"Good day, gentlemen," said the doge. "I trust your stay in Venice has thus far been pleasant."

"Very pleasant, Your Grace," said Clement, his courtier's manner burning bright.

Ha-Cohen grunted and found himself a chair. No one else had sat down, but he saw no reason to remain standing during a business discussion. Clement handed the doge two elaborately lettered pieces of paper bearing greetings from a Hapsburg prince and an adviser to the sultan of Turkey. "We've come with sincere recommendations, Your Grace," continued Clement. "Both from the North and from the South."

The doge looked up from the papers with a smile. "You Jews trade everywhere. Did you know that the word for Jew was once, long ago, used in place of 'trader' throughout the Italian peninsula?"

"This man is not a Jew, Your Grace," said Bellini.

"Not a Jew?" said the doge, looking in surprise at Bellini.

"I am an Englishman," said Clement. "And I work with the Ha-Cohen family of Amsterdam."

"I thought they were sending one of their own," said the doge.

"Your Grace," said Clement, "allow me to introduce David Ha-Cohen, son of Master Ha-Cohen of Amsterdam."

"Your Grace," said Ha-Cohen, getting out of his chair and approaching the doge, "you will forgive me if I don't stand on ceremony. I am not a courtier, nor am I a counselor to great princes. I am a simple, direct man of business, and my mission here is very easy to understand."

The doge, even from his sitting position, gave the impression of being of short stature. His shoulders were narrow, and his complexion sallow. The face, framed in a severe black skullcap, had once been handsome; but it seemed tired, thin with cares. The doge had a reputation abroad as a scholar, but the face had nothing to suggest great intelligence, or even diligence in the library. The eyes were blue, and clear. The tiredness in the face was not from reading, or reflecting; this duke was weary of rule.

Looking at the heavy fur stole about his neck, the voluminous sleeves of his velvet costume, Ha-Cohen had an impression not of power but of constraint. The man seemed trapped in his ceremonial clothes, his useless paper work, his exalted position that was merely a shadow of what the office of the duke had once been. The Republic of Venice was really ruled by the Great Council, and the doge who presided over this patrician assembly could do little more than sign whatever legislation they had written, either with or without his participation. Still, a powerful doge, one with the right friends, and of good family, could exert a great influence on the decisions of the Great Council. And this doge was more powerful than his predecessors of the last one hundred years.

"I don't admire your attitude, young man," said the doge. "The quality of brazenness is sometimes useful in battle, but never in entering into a commercial arrangement with the oldest government in the world."

"I assure you, Your Grace," said Clement, "young Ha-Cohen means no disrespect."

"Perhaps we should demand an apology," said Bellini, smiling at this latest evidence of Ha-Cohen's boorish nature.

"I don't want you to interfere," said Ha-Cohen, pointing his finger into Bellini's face. "I have no business to conduct with you, but only with the doge, and the Republic of Venice. And I do not apologize for being straightforward in my dealings. If you are ready to hear my proposal, I shall make it. If not, I shall go at once."

"Your Grace," said Bellini, raising his hands as if in an expostulation toward heaven, "I have put up with this Jewish brute long enough. His manner and his insults have nothing new to teach me. He is an envoy who should be sent back to the family who sent him with his arms broken and his tongue cut out. It is absurd that we continue to listen to him for another moment."

"I have something to show you, Your Grace," said Ha-Cohen, and from about his neck he removed a leather cord, to which was attached a leather pouch the size of a fist. John Clement took a step between Ha-Cohen and Bellini. He knew that when Bellini saw what was in the pouch, he would come close to it, without thinking, and the tempestuous Ha-Cohen might be unable to restrain himself from striking the man who had just insulted him.

"This is what we are to talk about," said Ha-Cohen. "This is the sort of beauty and commerce my family represents." And out of the pouch he took an object wrapped in black velvet, and when he had spread out the velvet wrapping on the doge's crowded desk, the object was revealed in all its glory.

It was a diamond, and for a moment it broke apart all thoughts of insults and anger. It was sixty carats, and flawless, a pure white stone, table-cut and polished, and it had nothing in common with any stone the doge had ever seen.

In Ha-Cohen's family, it was known as Rachel's diamond, or the Cuheno diamond, retaining the older family name from the time they had lived in Spain. It had been his father's sister's stone; she had been born Rachel Ha-Cohen, and the stone had remained with her even after her marriage to a doctor from Augsburg. Though she had daughters, none of them carried her name, as Jewish children are never named for the living, and they couldn't have inherited the diamond anyway since the stone was to be passed along the male line of the Cuheno-Ha-Cohen family. In David Ha-Cohen's time, all the children born after his aunt's death were—blessedly—males. The diamond rested with the head of the family, Master Ha-Cohen of Amsterdam, until such time as a Rachel from his line would be born. David often borrowed it, however, believing in its great value as a luck piece, a talisman of strength and fortitude. Master Ha-Cohen was reluctant to allow the immensely valuable stone to leave Amsterdam at all, but took his son's interest in it as one of the few marks of his interest in the family's heritage, if not its religion. Besides, even the cautious, worldly John Clement acknowledged the power of the diamond in negotiations of this sort; it stopped all talk dead, and concentrated attention on absolutes of light, beauty, enduring power.

"I have never seen a diamond shine like that in all my life," said the doge, reaching out his hands to touch the stone. Ha-Cohen let him bring his fingers to the diamond. It would take more than that to scratch its surface.

"This is the diamond of my family," said Ha-Cohen. "It was cut by my ancestor, Judah Cuheno, more than a hundred years ago. It is the way we cut diamonds to this day, and there is no one in the world who cuts them better."

"It's true," said the doge, lost in admiration of the stone. "No one understands the nature of gems better than the Jews. Even under the weight of restrictive legislation, our own lawmakers, of the most noble families, continue to run to the ghetto in search of precious stones, rather than buy jewels from Christians in the city. It is a strange thing that you people, who profess to be the People of the Book, are in fact the People of Precious Stones, Money-lending, and Jewelry."

"It's not strange at all, Your Grace," said Ha-Cohen. "If you exclude Jews from every occupation but moneylending and dealing in secondhand merchandise, do not be surprised that we excel in these things. And from what we in Amsterdam understand of our brethren in Venice, the dealing that Jews here do in gems is strictly legitimate, as the Jews of the ghetto buy and sell only gems that are secondhand." Ha-Cohen carefully began to wrap up the Cuheno diamond in its black velvet, and replaced it in the leather pouch. "Amsterdam is prospering, Your Grace, and our diamond cutting and distribution is one of the reasons for her prosperity. Under the right set of circumstances, we will do the same for you here in Venice."

"*You* will make Venice prosper?" laughed Bellini. "We have need of Jews to make the city rich? That's like telling the ripe, perfect apple that what it needs to be healthy is the caress of a worm."

Clement looked at Ha-Cohen nervously, surprised that he hadn't already struck Pietro Bellini across the face. Clement decided to turn away the brunt of an attack by stealing his friend's own thunder.

"I don't think your nephew is being either wise or friendly, Your Grace," said Clement. "I address these comments solely to you. Venice's glory has been sorely shaken during the past ten years. If you want to look at her history, this is not the best of times for her. Your colonies are in revolt, your trade routes are being usurped, your famous ship arsenal is outdated. The Austrians pay the savage Uskoks to prey on your ships, and your Dalmatian ports are in need of defenses and commerce alike. I don't consider that a healthy apple. Neither do I consider Jews analogous to worms."

"Well spoken, sir," said the doge. "You paint our republic in very gray colors. And you defend the religion of your employer with loyalty. Still, it is quite incorrect to think that Venice is an old lady in dire need of assistance. Our trade routes are strong. We remain the essential link to the East. When a country or a state comes to us with a commercial proposition, we review it from the point of view of a flourishing state, not one ready to collapse. We are not dictated to, we are not advised."

"Perhaps," said Clement, "if you are ready to hear the proposal of the Ha-Cohen family—"

"Wait a minute, John," said Ha-Cohen in English. Then he turned to the doge and spoke in Italian. "Your Grace, there are two things I have to propose: One is of value to the Republic of Venice; one is of value to yourself." Ha-Cohen, who had replaced the leather pouch around his neck, now removed a small diamond ring from his hand. "This is what my father wanted to give you as a present. It is a ten-carat diamond, and of rare quality, mounted in a band of gold. I say that it was my father's wish to give it to you as a gift, but, as I was to be the representative of my father in your city, I insisted that I be allowed to reserve judgment on whether or not you shall get this ring as a gift, or as a bribe. It is a diamond fit for a king, Your Grace, and I am not the sort of man who gives away something for nothing."

"I will not be bribed, sir," said the doge, though his eyes remained on the glittering stone. "And as for a gift, sir, the doges of Venice are not allowed to accept gifts unless they are gifts to the republic."

"Yes," said Ha-Cohen. "And your sons are not allowed to serve in the government, and you yourself cannot engage in trade. It is a difficult business being on the doge's throne. But I shall tell you what my father said. 'Talk too much and you talk about yourself. A donkey has long ears, and a fool has a long tongue.' We're not fools, Your Grace, and we don't tell other people our business. If we did, we could mention the names of princes across the face of Europe who have been gifted by us, and who did no disservice to their people in accepting our offers. I have not even made you our offer, Your Grace. Do not refuse in advance what could benefit Venice, and leave your sons with a large, portable fortune." Ha-Cohen returned the diamond ring to his finger. "But I won't press you. I tell you that I have something to benefit you. Do you want to hear it?"

The doge continued to look at the ring, his eyes following it even as Ha-Cohen moved his hand through the air. "I want to hear anything of potential benefit to the republic I serve."

"All right," said Ha-Cohen. "We both know that Spain and England are more powerful every day. Countries that were once weak have suddenly become strong. Their power lies in being able to sail to the New World and bring back gold. No one needs the galleys of Venice now, the way they did a hundred years ago. Ships needn't hug the coast to sail round the Mediterranean. This is a time of the open sea, and new markets, and new quantities of precious metal. Spain will become so rich with the gold of her conquests that any other nation must be a pauper by comparison. Only England has had sufficient vigor to strike out at Spain, and take for herself what Spain has already conquered. Venice cannot hope to fight these giants, but she can retain her glory, she can retain her riches at a time when gold is flooding the world. She can be a city of diamonds."

"Your Grace," said Clement, "Venice is at the heart of our trade route from India, the only place in the world from which diamonds come. The demand for them grows all the time, and the cutters of Amsterdam could work twice as much and still find a market for all their stones. Amsterdam is called the Venice of the North. You can become the Amsterdam of the South, with your own diamond-cutting industry here, and with your galleys carrying the finished diamonds throughout Italy and Dalmatia and Spain and the south of France. The city's treasury will swell with your share of the profits. Great princes will come to the new source of finished diamonds to be the first to bid for them. As for us, we will be saved the effort of carrying uncut diamonds to Amsterdam, only to be shipped back the same way after they are cut. There will be enough diamonds for both cities, and enough profits for everyone."

"And Jews shall control it all," said Bellini.

"The Ha-Cohen family, and its shareholders, will control the importation of uncut stones, the cutting and polishing of diamonds in the city, and the distribution and sale of the finished diamonds in those parts of the world where Venetian-cut diamonds will go," said Clement. "I might add that not all the shareholders in our Amsterdam company are Jewish."

"Of course we haven't discussed any details," said the doge, "as to the city's participation in profits, and the control we would have to exert on various aspects of the industry. But, in general, I find nothing objectionable in the proposition."

"There is something else," said Clement.

"Yes," said Ha-Cohen. "There is something that might cause a bit of controversy in the Grand Council. It is for this that we rely on your judgment and persuasive powers. And it is for this 'something' that we will thank you with our gift."

"Well?" said the doge.

"It shall be a Jewish industry," said Ha-Cohen.

"What do you mean?" said the doge.

"I mean that the Grand Council will remove all restrictive legislation against Jewish participation in the gem trade. We will not trade only in secondhand jewels. We will set up the diamond-cutting industry in the heart of the ghetto, we will teach Jews to cut the stones, we will allow the poor shut-up Jews in Venice a chance to earn a decent living." Ha-Cohen paused for a moment, an image of the Jewish whore crossing his mind. "It is very simple, Your Grace," he said. "Either diamond cutting in Venice will be a Jewish industry, or we will take our proposal south. There are other cities in Italy, anxious for commerce."

"Listen to me, Ha-Cohen," said the doge, and Ha-Cohen could see that he wanted the diamond on his finger, and he wanted the diamonds of India to be cut in his city, but he wanted to have nothing to do with the Jews. The doge explained that he had no special authority over the Grand Council, and that while he thought he could help effect the Ha-Cohen family's proposal in Venice, even to the extent of allowing new Jewish immigration from Amsterdam to help teach the cutting trade, he would never have any success with creating a new Jewish industry.

"You don't understand, Ha-Cohen," said the doge. "We have nothing against the Jews here in Venice. They enjoy their lives here, and many of them become rich and are invited into the homes of patrician families. As for the ghetto, Jews like to live there. They like to be among their own kind, and it affords them protection. It's true that they're locked up at night, but that's the fate of any foreign population in a great city. We can't have Jews roaming around all night with their endless schemes. There has to be an end to the business day, too.

"Now, I know that you rich Jews in Amsterdam hear some grumbling from Jews here that they don't have enough opportunity, but that's just not true. The secondhand-merchandise market is a great opportunity, otherwise there wouldn't be so many rich Jews in Venice. Any talk of a new industry for Jews would be laughed out of the council. No matter how many restrictions you put them under, they always manage to flourish. There are too many Venetians who owe Jews money, too many priests who want the ghetto closed down and the Jews expelled from the city altogether to even begin to think of a new Jewish occupation.

"Venice is the great artisan capital of the world. You can work with Christians, and we will allow members of your family the right to remain outside the ghetto after the regular curfew, but more than that would be impossible to obtain. You must remember, Ha-Cohen, that this is a city of great churches, and that we Christians remember the great crime of your ancestors. We will tolerate the Jew, and we will allow him to live in the ghetto, but we cannot possibly pass into being a law that would increase his numbers and prosperity within our midst."

"I have only one thing to add to that fine speech, Your Grace, and that is this," said Ha-Cohen. "I am glad that my father allowed me to present this ring as a gift for services rendered. I am glad that I leave no diamond for such a man as you."

David Ha-Cohen turned his back on the still-seated doge, and as Clement turned to join him, Bellini realized that there was no longer to be a deal, that he was no longer under any obligation to cater to these men on behalf of his uncle, the doge.

"You have not yet been dismissed, you swine of a Jew," said Bellini.

Ha-Cohen stopped, and turned slowly about to face Bellini. He was done waiting. "Are you hoping to be slapped?"

"A verbal challenge will do as well, Jew," said Bellini.

"David, don't be ridiculous," said Clement in English. "If you challenge him, he'll choose that light little Italian rapier, and all you know how to do is slash with a German sword."

"Is he telling you to beg my forgiveness?" said Bellini.

"He's telling me," said Ha-Cohen in Italian, moving past his friend and close to Bellini, "that a verbal challenge is perhaps less clear than what we need." And Ha-Cohen slapped Bellini's face with enough force to bloody his nose.

"Where shall I send my second?" said Bellini. "You can no longer stay in my house."

"There is a hospice for Jews," said the doge. "In the ghetto. If you are not to do business with us, you are no longer guests of the republic. See to it that you're inside the ghetto walls before dusk."

"Your Grace," said Clement. "I appeal to you. Young Ha-Cohen has been provoked. He is a hot-blooded young man, that is true, but it is also true that his name and his religion have been maligned by your nephew, and not only during the course of this meeting. If he is wounded, or if he is killed, there will be serious consequences. His family is not without influence, not only in the North, and with the Hapsburgs, but with the Sublime Porte, and also in Italy. Think how it will look if it becomes known that he was sent to the ghetto, given no honors worthy of his station, and then killed in a duel. It will appear that he was deliberately humiliated, deliberately drawn into a combat of which he knows nothing."

"For a Jew," said the doge, "he looks like a healthy enough specimen."

"They're not fighting with fists, Your Grace," said Clement, but now Ha-Cohen urged him to silence.

"In the interest of saving time," said Ha-Cohen, "you needn't send your second to look for me in the ghetto. Clement will arrange details as to time and place and your selection of weapons, and then he can report back to me. I would appreciate it if we could meet tomorrow, because I don't enjoy lingering in this old wet rag of a city."

"Tomorrow will be fine," said Bellini. "As to time and place, I suggest we meet on the Isle of the Dead. It's in the lagoon, near Malamocco. Gentlemen duel at dawn. As the challenged party, I select the Italian rapier. It's been a year since I killed anyone in a duel, but I still manage to practice almost daily with my master." Bellini smiled. "It's true that men will speak disparagingly of me for running through a clumsy brute like you. Some will even think me guilty of a crime for dueling a Jew at all. But I shall not think of this as a contest, simply as an execution. You should know that my fencing master considers me the best in Venice." Bellini turned his once handsome face to Clement. "You may call at my house today, sir." To Ha-Cohen, he said: "Till dawn tomorrow, on the Isle of the Dead."

CHAPTER ELEVEN

David Ha-Cohen walked the Street of the Mercers, extending from the great clock tower in the Piazza di San Marco to the Rialto Bridge, brooding over his fate. John Clement was to meet him on the Rialto Bridge after his meeting with Bellini's second, and then the two of them would have to share the ignominy of a night's sleep in the shut-up ghetto. All about Ha-Cohen were the most beautiful shops of Venice: clockmakers, haberdashers, perfumers, apothecaries, sellers of tapestries, gold cloth, silk, and damask, sellers of nightingales. Merchants had pushed their wares into the streets, vying for space with the numerous painters displaying canvases of their portraits to potential customers. Cages filled with gorgeous-colored birds sang amid the cries of the street hawkers. Even the wind was heady with exotic perfumes.

Ha-Cohen wondered what his father would think after the events of tomorrow's duel were revealed to him. If Bellini killed him, would Master Ha-Cohen assume that the affair was his son's fault? The fact of David Ha-Cohen's temper was not a secret in the city of Amsterdam, and his father had expressly warned him to be careful in his dealings, to try and wrest an advantage for the downtrodden Jews of Venice from the doge—but not to insult, not to challenge a patrician to a duel, using weapons with which he had no skill.

But I won't die tomorrow, thought Ha-Cohen, pushing his way through the crowd. He felt so strong at that moment that he half-fancied a rapier wouldn't be able to break the surface of his skin. It was infuriating to imagine that a fat-faced, thin-limbed weakling like Bellini could dance rings around him with that womanly weapon, with his womanly fencing-master skills. If only *he* had been challenged, thought Ha-Cohen. Then they would be dueling with German swords. He'd like to see Bellini pick one up and try to lift it over his head!

All about the lovely street, he saw, like specks of ill-matched color in an otherwise harmonious painting, the crimson hats of the Jews. Some of them were rather well dressed and except for the crimson that, looked much like their Christian neighbors in dress and manner; they had the haughty attitudes and pretty faces of men like Bellini. But there were other Jews, too, old and be-draggled, their faces red from the sun and the wind, from the constant exposure to the elements as they peddled their used clothes, raising plaintive eyes to passersby as if in expectation of a coin, or a crumb. Occasionally he'd see one of the fabled Jewish beauties of Venice, dark-haired, with light eyes and modest manner. With their eyes on their wares, or looking at the ground, they scurried about at the commands of father or brother as they prepared a bundle of clothing, or tied together some ancient pots and pans.

Ha-Cohen knew that no one took him for a Jew. He wore his blond hair long, and was hatless; this alone, without his foreign clothes and great size, marked him as a stranger from the North, a German or a Swede perhaps, but not a Jew. Jews visiting Venice tended to mix with local Jews. They stayed in the ghetto, and if they ventured into the city, they put on the hats of shame as a mark of community with their fellow Jews. Ha-Cohen didn't understand how they could bear the humiliation. Because he had been born into a house that was both powerful and wealthy, a house visited by men of honor and rank, he could not understand why all Jews didn't feel the way he did. He had no conception of what it was like to have been born in the ghetto, to have grown up accepting your lot, accepting the hat of shame as a mark as per-sonal as the color of one's hair, accepting the restrictive laws against the Jews as one accepts the laws of nature. All he could think of was that these Jews were despised by the Venetians around them, and that they accepted their lot like slaves.

He could not have known about the few Jews who had unlimited entrance to the homes of the Venetian nobility, be it as fellow gamblers, rakes, or businessmen. He could not have conceived of a situation wherein Jews and Venetians, friends for years, didn't think once of their different places of residence, didn't wonder about the ghetto as a restrictive way of life, but saw it only as a fascinating neighborhood where the Jews happened to live together. He could not have imagined that there were Christians as blind to the indignities forced on the Jews as Jews themselves were often blind to their own limitations.

What Ha-Cohen knew was that the doge wouldn't assent to his family's plan to set up a Jewish diamond industry in Venice because he had a repulsion for Jews. What Ha-Cohen knew was that Bellini, the doge's nephew, hated Jews, and would try to kill him on the morrow not only out of personal hatred but as a mark of contempt for any Jew who stepped outside the boundaries of the ghetto.

"Watch where you're going," said Ha-Cohen in his gruff Roman Italian to a young gentleman dressed in a multicolored doublet with red hose, who had stepped into his path.

"In Venice, sir," said the dandy, "we all look where we walk. This is not like the northern wastes where you come from, where an oaf might walk with his eyes closed and never meet another man in his way."

Ha-Cohen didn't know that the young man's hose indicated membership in a particular club, one of the city's Companies of the Hose, and one noted for its expert rapiermen. All he knew was that he had once more been insulted, by another man of Bellini's type, and rather than dignify him with a slap, Ha-Cohen simply struck him a blow to the chest, and then to the side of the neck, that sent the man crashing senseless into a rickety cart laden with old cloaks. In a moment, the young dandy came back to life. Slowly, looking dimly at the crowd around him as if he didn't quite know where he was, he pushed himself away from the cart, and, in so doing, knocked it over, sending its garments crashing to the filthy street.

Immediately a wailing went up from the old Jewish woman whose cart it was, a wailing that struck Ha-Cohen more profoundly than all the shouts and cries of the onlookers around him. Realizing that he must help this woman, and at once, he again struck out at the advancing dandy, as if he were a fly, a minor impediment to the task at hand.

"No," said Ha-Cohen, not letting the man fall toward the cart. "You get on your way, you son of a whore." And he pulled at the man's right hand and wheeled him about, letting him feel the incredible strength of his own grip. "Just go," said Ha-Cohen, and the half-conscious dandy, feeling his hand and his shoulder gripped with an almost inhuman force, forgot about being challenged to a duel, or slapped across the face. He merely wanted to go, and he stumbled on in the direction that Ha-Cohen pushed him, not daring to delay or look back.

When Ha-Cohen turned fiercely about to look at the crowd, men and women alike stood back, out of his reach, as if he were some sort of monster, capable of mindless destruction. Only the old Jewish woman continued to wail as she picked up the old clothes and placed them back in the cart. Ha-Cohen now saw that the dandy, in falling, had dislocated the cart's axle from its wheel, and the old woman was not strong enonugh to right the connection.

"Excuse me," said Ha-Cohen to the old woman, and, bending low, he took hold of the axle and returned it to the wheel.

"Thank you, sir," said the old Jewish woman, just at the moment that Ha-Cohen was rising to his full height. It was at that instant, as the astonished thanks of the woman reached him, as he was almost at his full height and thus towering over the crowd, that he saw, at the edge of the crowd that had gathered about him and was now dispersing, the Jewish whore.

Diamante. Her made-up name rang in his mind with a force that deadened all else. Clumsily, he turned from the old woman, unable to take his eyes off the girl, afraid that she would too soon disappear into the crowded streets. He took a step after her before he realized that he had not done what he wanted to with the old woman; and he stopped in his tracks, and found the leather pouch of ducats beneath his cloak and extracted ten ducats—more money than she had probably made in the last three months.

"I don't understand, sir," said the old woman as he gave it to her. "What do you want to give me so much money for?"

"Take it," he said. And then he added, because she didn't

understand who he was and why he cared for her, "Take it for *mazel.*"

The Hebrew word for luck, mispronounced by the blond giant, struck her like a fist. "*Mazel,*" she repeated, clutching the ducats, watching Ha-Cohen push off through the crowd.

Diamante was dressed in a yellow and blue silk gown, of sufficient distinction and quality to mark her out in the crowd. Of course, she wore no scarlet hat. Ha-Cohen was about to call out to her because she seemed about to turn up an adjacent alleyway where he risked losing her from his sight; but she stopped, ostensibly to examine a painting set up on an easel in the street. As he drew closer, and she had still not seen him, Ha-Cohen slowed down. What would he say to her? Why precisely was he coming up to her in this crowded place?

"Diamante," he said, calling it out without thought so that his voice carried over the two-score people milling about between them. "Diamante," he said again, and there was an absurd softness in his voice, as if he wished to reassure her that his intent to approach was not to harm but to help. Still he had no idea what to say to her; he only knew that he must approach her, must bring his presence close to hers.

The girl turned, her face reddening at the sight of the giant blond man as he came toward her with inexorable speed. Ha-Cohen could understand the blush, but he could make no sense of the fear that flashed across her face, and gave it purpose. Instantly, without pausing to appeal, Diamante turned from the painting and ran.

"Wait!" said Ha-Cohen, and he chased her along the Merceria dell' Orologio, into the Merceria di San Giuliano, his eyes fixed on the shining mass of her dark hair, dressed in a wide, fashionable roll atop her head. High heels had been the fashion in Venice for nearly twenty years, for both men and women, but Ha-Cohen came from less flamboyantly dressed Amsterdam, and anyway had no need of heels to add to his great height. Even with his considerable bulk, he began to gain on the girl, taking enormous strides, landing on his flat, solid heels, and pushing off on his toes.

Diamante ran poorly. She took a flurry of steps, then had to pause, gasping for breath, then rushed on, swirling into people, into stands set up with food and flowers and dry goods. Ha-Cohen saw her take a false step, as if her knee had buckled; then she began to run with a limp, and as he got closer he saw that she had lost the heel of her right shoe.

"Wait!" he called after her again. "Please, wait!" and though it was obvious to a hundred passersby and onlookers, shoppers and strollers and shopkeepers, clergy and laymen, Jews and Gentiles, that this great blond man was chasing a young woman who did not want to be stopped, no one did more than look, and observe to each other that this was a strange sight, even in Venice.

"All right," said Ha-Cohen, slowing his step as he reached out to grab her shoulder, so close was he to his quarry. "All right, now stop," he said. But before his hand could touch the girl's shoulder, a light force struck him from behind, and the big man stumbled forward, almost losing his balance. Ha-Cohen wheeled about to see his attacker.

"Leave her alone," said a young Jewess, her crimson hat awry, her eyes flashing defiance.

Ha-Cohen turned to see Diamante stopping, and coming slowly up to where he and this strange Jewess confronted each other. For some reason, the chase was over, and this girl's appearance was the cause. Ha-Cohen didn't know what a Jewess who wore shabby clothing and the hat of shame could have in common with Diamante, but he did know that this girl was not his enemy. As a crowd from the Merceria di San Giuliano began to gather, Ha-Cohen turned his fury on it. "Get out of here!" he screamed. "Go back to your business!" And he made as if he would knock them all over, send a score of men and women into the waters of the canal.

"What do you want with her?" said the young Jewess to Ha-Cohen as Diamante approached, her breath racing, trying to walk steadily on her broken shoe.

"It's all right," said Devorah.

"I only wanted to talk to you," said Ha-Cohen.

"Yes," said Devorah, weary with running. Ha-Cohen saw her take the young Jewess's hand, openly; and he saw the crowd, still all around them, watching this with intense interest.

"*I said to move*," said Ha-Cohen, and he took hold of a large greengrocer and lifted him into the air as if he were a sack of potatoes, raising him over his head and turning round and round to dizzy the man as the crowd roared. Ha-Cohen dropped the man at the feet of the crowd, and then lashed out with his right leg, kicking at whomever dared linger around the scene.

"Who is this man?" said Rachel Cuheno, who had come to meet her sister along the Street of the Mercers, only to find her being chased by this blond giant.

"It's all right," said Devorah again. She couldn't say anything else at that moment. She didn't know why the enormous Jew wanted to stop her on the street; she couldn't imagine how she could explain to Rachel who he was, and how she had met him. But Ha-Cohen was bearing down on them once again, and he had some definite idea. His whole face glowed with a purpose that ran through her indecision.

"She is your sister?" he said to Devorah, and when she nodded, Ha-Cohen turned to Rachel and said, with obvious admiration, "You are very brave to try and stop me."

"What do you want with me?" said Devorah.

"Come," said Ha-Cohen. "Come where these curious pigs will not disturb us."

Rachel exchanged glances with Devorah. It had been difficult to send a message to the palace of Bellini, difficult to arrange a meeting here with Devorah in plain sight of the world. Rachel needed time with her to plead her cause; she had come to convince her to meet with Leone Ha-Levi, to explain that Leone had need of seeing her only once to agree to throw up his life in Venice and run off with her as his wife to any part of Europe where Jews were allowed to settle. But now this subject could not be broached. This strange man, who had been chasing Devorah through the streets as if she were a wild animal, now looked at her with gentleness, with a kindess that made no sense to her at all.

They wandered up a new little *rio*, an ancient canal that had been filled in to make a street. Ha-Cohen seemed to be steering them in silence to smaller and smaller thoroughfares, until they finally arrived at a tiny alley between two courtyards. They were alone.

"We can talk here," said Ha-Cohen.

Devorah, who had recovered some of her spirit in the course of the walk, now stepped between Ha-Cohen and Rachel. She spoke firmly, so that there would be no mistake about what she meant.

"Listen, sir. If I ran before, it's for a reason you can understand very well. You know that I am a Jewess. When I walk alone in the streets of Venice, no one knows who or what I am. I was afraid to meet with anyone who knows me at all. This is my sister. She, too, knows that I live with Pietro Bellini. When we meet, we meet in secret. You saw me only minutes before she was due to arrive. Naturally, I ran."

"I'm sorry if I frightened you," said Ha-Cohen. It occurred to him that she had been scared that he might say out loud that she was a whore; first to the denizens of Venice, and now, even worse, to her pale little sister. "I mean you no harm."

"How does he know that you're Jewish?" said Rachel, unable to conceal her curiosity.

"Because he is a Jew himself," said Devorah.

Though this was no answer, it satisfied Rachel; or at least it diverted her from thinking about anything other than that incredible statement.

"How can you be a Jew, sir?"

"It is very simple. I was born of a Jewish mother. I was not born with a crimson hat, or a desire to blind my eyes in a house of study. But that makes me no less a Jew. I eat the food of the Gentiles, and I attend the synagogue only once a year, but I am nonetheless a Jew, no matter what anyone else might think."

"I am sorry for striking at you," said Rachel. "I thought you meant my sister harm."

"What is your name?" said Ha-Cohen.

"Rachel," she said, and at once the name conjured up all that was mystical about his family's history, even to the diamond he carried in a pouch close to his heart.

"There have been many women of that name in my family," he said.

"What is your family?" said Devorah. "Where are you from?"

"My name is David Ha-Cohen, and my family is from Amsterdam."

Seeing Rachel's confusion that her sister didn't even know this much about a man who knew that she was Jewish, Devorah said, "The gentleman and I were never introduced. He was a guest at Pietro's table, and Pietro let it be known, to amuse the table, that I was a Jew, along with this great gentleman from the North."

"Pietro amuses himself by talking of your Jewishness?" said Rachel, the revulsion in her voice striking a responsive chord in Ha-Cohen.

"It is about Pietro Bellini that I want to speak," said Ha-Cohen. Ever since he had felt the full force of Diamante's humiliation, he had been drawn back into a great feeling of kinship with Jews, into a heightened awareness of his own family's origins. Although the ancient Jewish prohibition against graven images had allowed for few portraits to have been painted of his ancestors, there was one that hung in his father's study that he remembered now.

It was of his father's older sister, Rachel, whose diamond he carried on his person, whose name had the impact of both history and legacy in his tightly knit family. The portrait wasn't pretty. His aunt Rachel had had a severe face, strung together with creases. She had had black eyes and black hair, showing none of the influence of the Ashkenazi Jews whom the Ha-Cohens had been mixing with their Iberian blood for the last three generations. The Rachel who stood before him now in this quiet Venetian courtyard had no such severe face, no lines of age or sorrow. And though not a beauty like her sister, she had more to recommend her looks than had Ha-Cohen's aunt.

Still, beyond the differences of age and beauty, there was something to the features of both Rachels that Ha-Cohen saw as in common. Something brave, something hard; there was desire in the faces of both Jewish women, a desire that would not be stifled. This desire impaled him. Their dark hair and little noses, the way the bones in their cheeks stood high in their faces—these were characteristic of both Rachels; and their eyes—those of the portrait and those of the young girl of Venice—were of the same limpid depth, the same terrible intensity.

Rachel and her more beautiful sister looked at Ha-Cohen now, but it was to Rachel that he spoke, to Rachel that his eyes were drawn.

"I think you should know about what tomorrow will bring for Pietro Bellini," he said.

"What?" said Devorah.

"You're going to kill him," said Rachel, the words tumbling out of her mouth without conscious effort.

"What are you talking about?" said Devorah.

"Why did you say that?" said Ha-Cohen to Rachel. He was not a superstitious man, but on the eve of dueling to the death, the spontaneous outburst startled him.

"I don't know," said Rachel. "It's just the way you looked. You hate him, and I can see that you have the desire for murder in your heart."

"I don't understand any of this," said Devorah. "What have

you to do with Pietro? I don't understand even that. Why do you hate him? Are you really going to kill him? Are you a Jew or are you a spirit? Who are you that you can make my sister think of murder?"

"I told you who I am," said Ha-Cohen. "As for Bellini, I was a guest in his house, and he insulted me. We are to duel tomorrow. I hate him enough to kill him, and if God guides my hand, I hope to drive my rapier through his heart."

"Don't," said Rachel.

"What?" said Ha-Cohen.

"Don't invoke God's name in the desire for murder."

"Why on earth not?" said Ha-Cohen. "He's my God, too, isn't he? I want to live, and I want to kill Bellini. Don't you want him dead, too?"

He was speaking to Rachel, but Devorah spoke over her sister's silence: "Yes," she said.

"Devorah, please," said Rachel, "it's a sin to wish for another man's death."

"You wish it, too," said Devorah.

"No," said Rachel, but she had shut her eyes, as if to ward off the temptation to wish for evil. "I wish there was another way."

"Do you have parents?" said Ha-Cohen abruptly.

"Yes," said Rachel.

"I need a place to sleep tonight, in the ghetto. For myself and a friend, a Christian friend."

"What will happen if he kills Bellini?" said Rachel suddenly, looking past Ha-Cohen's question to the life of her sister.

"I don't know," said Devorah.

"Leone wants to meet you," said Rachel, almost as if Ha-Cohen had vanished into thin air.

"I said I don't know," said Devorah. "What has Leone to do with it? I must leave Venice sooner or later. If Pietro dies tomorrow, I shall steal whatever is small and easy to carry and flee the city. If he lives, I shall wait a little longer."

"Who is Leone?" said Ha-Cohen.

"He is a young man of the ghetto who wants to marry her," said Rachel.

"I see," said Ha-Cohen.

"You don't see," said Devorah. "Or if you do, you see with blind eyes. No one can marry me. You know that, Rachel. And you know it, you know it better even than she."

"He loves you," said Rachel. "And he wants to meet you. That's why I'm here to see you. It's all because of his love that I came here today. Only because of his love for you, and my love for you."

"I can never marry," said Devorah, the words striking more powerfully for the soft whisper in which they were expressed.

"Let's go now," said Ha-Cohen. "It's time we go to the Rialto."

"I must go back," said Devorah. "I've been gone a long time."

"We haven't spoken yet," said Rachel.

"I won't meet Leone," said Devorah. "That is an end to our talk."

"You're coming with us," said Ha-Cohen.

"What?" said Devorah.

"You're coming with us to the Rialto Bridge," he said, his ideas running together, so fast did they come to him now. It became clear that he would have to kill Bellini, because that was now intrinsic to the needs of other lives, not simply his own. Devorah was a whore who could become a wife; Rachel was a poor girl who could become a rich ward of his family; the young man who loved Devorah could be given the keys to a world of influence and power. Yes, he would kill Bellini and take them all under his wing. "Listen to me," said Ha-Cohen. "You must both do what I say, because I know what is best for you. First, tell me, do your parents have a place for me and my friend to sleep tonight?"

"It would be better if you were received by Leone Ha-Levi," said Rachel. "My father is not a man of hospitality, neither is he one of enlightenment or understanding."

"And is there a place for your sister to sleep this night?" he asked, letting the comment about her parents take hold in his mind.

"Yes," said Rachel, believing more and more in this man of violence and death. Devorah could wear a hood over her pretty face and climb up the narrow steps to her tiny room; their parents never entered the tiny space adjacent to their own. "Yes, of course, for one night it shall be easy."

"You're both mad," said Devorah. "Either mad or stupid. I will never return to the ghetto, not unless I am dead. And then even the Jews are allowed to leave the ghetto, to be buried under some less populated bit of sand."

"If you don't want to go to the ghetto, girl," said Ha-Cohen, "then you won't. Pray do me one favor, though, and accompany us to the Rialto Bridge."

The sudden acquiesence, coupled with the curious favor, made no sense to either sister. The Rialto was the center of the city, in view of a thousand eyes. It was not a place to which either sister would want to go together; Jewish and Gentile eyes both would see them there together, and this fact could get back to their parents, or to Bellini. But Rachel felt as if she were being swept up by some great force outside of any ordinary experience. If this strange Jew from the North wanted them to accompany him there, that must be enough for her; she felt that his way would help them both.

"Why must we go to the Rialto?" said Devorah, but Rachel took her sister's hand and urged her on, to satisfy the gentleman.

"He means to help us, Devorah," she said. "Don't you at least understand that?"

As they walked, they lapsed into silence. Ha-Cohen led the way, the two sisters walking abreast, though not holding hands. They attracted attention nonetheless: the enormous blond man, his belligerent eyes sweeping clear the street before them; the great beauty in fashionable silks, her hair carefully done up, limping along on a heeless shoe; the young Jewess, her eyes burning under the crimson hat.

When they had gotten halfway to the Rialto, near the entrance to the Merceria di San Salvatore, Ha-Cohen heard an English voice: "David, wait a minute! David, over here!" And there, in the water of the little canal that led up past the procession of palaces a little less grand than those on the Canal Grande itself, was John Clement, in an open boat propelled by one swarthy oarsman. All at once, Ha-Cohen knew what to do.

"Who is the man in the boat?" said Rachel, but Ha-Cohen didn't have time to answer her. He had to speak of something else, even in the seconds that it took the boat to approach the quay on which they watched.

"I am very rich, you know," he said, "and I plan to help you both, in every way I can."

"I must go," said Devorah, her spirit rising in some nameless fear.

"Of course," said Ha-Cohen. "Go if you must." And in a single fluid movement he grabbed Devorah's wrist and pulled her hard into his chest, knocking her breath away; in the same instant,

he lifted her off the ground and jumped with her onto the surface of the boat.

"Jesus," said Clement. "What are you up to now?"

"Give me a rag, will you?" said Ha-Cohen, his hand clasped
tight over Devorah's wide-open mouth as she struggled to scream.
Rachel looked down at them from the quay as if she were in the
middle of some mad dream. Only the gondolier remained aloof
and unconcerned; he had seen stranger happenings with members
of the upper class.

"Well, get in," said Ha-Cohen impatiently to Rachel. "Don't
you want to help your sister?"

Slowly, Rachel moved along the quay to where the boat
shifted uneasily in the water. Then, with a sudden clarity of decision, she moved quickly, lithely stepping into space, and landed
flat on her feet on the deck of the boat.

"What the hell are you doing, David?" said Clement.

"What is the purpose of this boat?" said Ha-Cohen with a
smile. "Don't you know that we can walk to the ghetto?"

"I haven't said that you shouldn't duel the man," said Clement.
"But he is an expert, and the duel is going to solve nothing in this
world. It will only kill someone, and create more problems."

"Father won't have your head if I die in Venice."

"It's your decision. I just think you should know that this boat
can easily take us to Mestre on the mainland, and from there we
can be free and clear of Bellini and any and all problems."

"That's good to know," said Ha-Cohen, his hand still pressed
over Devorah's mouth, though she had finally stopped struggling.
"But we're not going to Mestre. We're going first to the ghetto,
where we shall drop off this young woman"—here he indicated
Rachel, looking frankly at him, without fear—"and then you
and I and this other young woman—I believe her Hebrew name
is Devorah—will proceed to our quarters for the rest of the day,
and the evening and the night as well."

"Where?" said Clement.

"Would you please get a gag for this girl's mouth?" said Ha-
Cohen. "She's actually trying to bite me."

"Here," said Clement, ripping off a bit of his own blouse. "But
where? Just tell me what we're doing. Where are we going?"

"Going?" said Ha-Cohen. "I suppose you have a right to know.
I hope you're not as superstitious as I am."

"*Where?*"

Ha-Cohen finished gagging Devorah, and now, her arms gripped behind her back in his left hand, she raised her eyes to his. Rachel and Clement watched him, too, and the great blond man enjoyed the suspense he created. "Oh," he said, "tonight we sleep on the Isle of the Dead."

CHAPTER TWELVE

Rachel's story was barely credible to Leone Ha-Levi, but he was prepared to accept it, in the same spirit in which he had prepared to change the course of his life.

"But what about the gates?" she said. "Will you be able to arrange the opening of the gates?"

"I can do that and more," said Leone. He had expected to hear from Rachel that day about whether or not Devorah would consent to meet with him. Though he was prepared to sin, it was not at all sure that Devorah would be prepared to draw him into a life outside the world he had always known. Waiting for hours near the main gates to the ghetto, hoping to catch sight of Rachel's flushed face, he understood that he was not simply hoping to meet Devorah; he was hoping to go off with her as his wife. But Devorah could be so bad now that the thought of leaving her life of sin made no sense to her; or so good that she could not bear to dirty his life with her own. Leone waited at the gates because he thought that at his first sight of Rachel he would know what Devorah had said, and what he must do.

But Rachel's face, when he saw her coming through the gates, was not like anything he had expected to see. She was excited, yes, and happy, and he supposed that those were very good signs for him, as Rachel was eager to press for his happiness; but there was more to her expression than just this. Her eyes were lost in a sense of inner satisfaction, in a celebration of self. Her joy was contained within her small frame, and blazed out from her eyes. When she saw Leone, she could hardly restrain herself. "We must talk," she said. And when he had walked her quickly into the Portuguese section of the ghetto and into the parlor of his parents' house, she had told him of Ha-Cohen and Devorah and Bellini, all in such a rush that the only thing that was clear was that Rachel was to be free.

"I am to go to Amsterdam," she said. "They are taking me to Amsterdam, where I can study, where I can be free to master my own life."

"What are you talking about?" Leone said, but her talk had gone on in mad circles. There was so much to say, so many incredible things to relate. Could he imagine that there were Jews such as David Ha-Cohen? So rich that they walked with kings? So powerful that they commanded commercial treaties from India to Amsterdam, from Russia to England? So physically strong that they could fight a dozen men all at once, and win?

"We are to go, we are all to go," said Rachel. "Devorah and you and Ha-Cohen and John Clement and myself—we are all to go to the Ha-Cohen family of Amsterdam."

Slowly, Leone had gotten the story. Of course, Devorah had not agreed to marry him; she had not even agreed to meet him. She had been abducted by a Jewish gentleman, of rich family, who was to fight a duel tomorrow with Pietro Bellini. If the duel ended with Ha-Cohen still alive, he had promised to take them all to Amsterdam, to help Devorah begin a new life, to allow Rachel a chance to study and meet Jewish men who could appreciate a woman of scholarship.

"What if he dies?" said Leone.

"*He can't die,*" said Rachel. "You haven't seen him. Such a man can't die."

But Ha-Cohen had spoken of the possibility. In the event of his death, Clement was to escort them, in his stead, to Master Ha-Cohen of Amsterdam. This would be his final request of his father, and certainly the charitable old man would not hesitate to help Jewish refugees under his son's support.

Of all these things Rachel spoke as if they were written down in a contract, as if they were divine writ. Leone knew very well that in a few hours the young woman of twenty had latched on to a dream, and taken hold of it fiercely. And to this sort of blind faith, his pragmatism could yield no compromise, no sense of caution or alternative. Rachel had understood that her life in Venice was bound up in a marriage to someone that her father would choose; to a life of sewing up secondhand mattresses; to respecting her husband, no matter how doltish; to gobbling up bits of knowledge from whatever books might fall her way, like a beggar picking up the courses of his meal from table scraps.

Leone could not help being a practical man; he was experienced in the vagaries of international travel, of broken promises, of persecutions and massacres. He knew that a great many miles separated northern Italy from the city of Amsterdam, and each mile contained a story, a threat, a space of danger and uncertainty. Still, he knew there were powerful Jews in the world, believed that some Jews would do just what this Ha-Cohen had proposed; and if this man of Amsterdam was as little religious as Rachel had indicated, perhaps he would be particularly willing to close his eyes to Devorah's sins and allow for her salvation in this world, without punishment. In any case, he would not go unprepared. Leone had money, and he had gems, and he would take these as his safeguards for the voyage to come.

Rachel had asked him about the gates to the ghetto. He would have to find a way to get the guards to open them early, before dawn. They would have to get to the Isle of the Dead before the city began to stir, and make their escape with Ha-Cohen and Devorah.

"I have often bribed the guards at the gate to let me leave early," said Leone. "But what I shall also be able to do is help all of us out of the republic before the doge sends out his men to avenge Bellini's death. I have a boat at Mestre, ready to travel, with all necessary trading permits. We can be in Trieste before the doge learns the results of the duel, and out of the republic before anyone can trace us across the Gulf of Venice."

But though he could imagine the early-morning walk to the ghetto gates, the swift opening of those gates in exchange for his coin, the prearranged gondolier waiting for them in the dark, the silent trip across the lagoon to the tiny island off Malamocco, the flight in a larger vessel to Mestre on the opposite side of the lagoon, where his boat, and his captain, would serve them in the flight to Trieste—though he could imagine all these things with his poetic fancy and his merchant's exactitude, he had no feeling for what else would transpire, for those things that would make the whole mad adventure worthwhile. Would Devorah smile at seeing him? Would Ha-Cohen live? Would Leone's family ever forgive him for what he was about to do?

"Oh, Leone," said Rachel. "Just think of it. You'll be free to marry Devorah, and I'll be free to live my life, and we'll all be free of the ghetto forever."

And that is just how Leone Ha-Levi now thought of it. He let Rachel's reckless joy sweep him along, prepared for the best, eyes closed to disaster. He did not know that Rachel herself, in the middle of the night, dreamed of a blade piercing her hero's chest, and that she leaped out of bed screaming, her hand over the stabbing pain in her heart.

That night, on the Isle of the Dead, Devorah talked. The little island was a gravesite, reserved for victims of plague more than a hundred years before. Bodies that had been burned and shoved into shallow graves were accorded more respect when the plague hysteria had passed; thus when Ha-Cohen, Devorah, and Clement went ashore, they were greeted with marble memorials to the long-departed: Cherubs and saints, crosses and angels stood guard among the tombs as the dying sunlight played through the cypress trees. Two monks were supposed to live on the island, but they were nowhere in evidence; neither was there any sign of shelter. The only sign of life was a swift-moving black cat, and when Devorah was freed of her gag and sat down calmly with Ha-Cohen and Clement against the tombstones, this was the first thing she spoke of.

"For a Jewess, you have very Christian fears," said Ha-Cohen. "In my family, we've always allowed the Gentiles their own superstitions. And what's a bad omen for a Gentile often turns out to be a good sign for a Jew."

"Then perhaps *I* should worry," said Clement.

"Let Bellini worry about the black cat," said Ha-Cohen. "I take her as my friend."

"It seems you take whatever you want," said Devorah.

"Often," said Clement.

"I didn't take you for myself," said Ha-Cohen. "I took you because you and I are of the same race."

"That's hard to believe. You seem to belong to a race all your own," said Devorah. "For myself, I would never have the courage to take charge of so many people. For myself, I would never fight a useless duel. I am neither so generous nor so foolhardy."

"You're a Jewess nonetheless," said Ha-Cohen. "I'm a Jew. And so, somehow, our families are related, even if it is as far back as Abraham."

"You don't look like a sermonizer."

"You should hear him sometimes," said Clement. "Mostly speeches about the injustice done him by the world."

"You know who always talked about injustice?" said Devorah. "My father. I think it was he more than Pietro, that got me out of the ghetto. I couldn't bear his self-pity, and his talk. He loved to say that he couldn't stand talk about legends, about how rich and powerful the Jews were, so he used to let my mother have the speeches all to herself. She'd talk about his father, and the stories he told her about his ancestors, how rich they were. And then he'd get furious, really angry, as if she'd made the whole thing up to taunt him.

"He was so religious, my father, but that didn't stop him from beating up my mother. He'd beat her up, and then talk about the Gentiles, how they didn't let him get ahead in the world. He was crazy, he was. He never wanted to admit the possibility that we really did come from some great family in the distant past, so he let my mother say it out loud instead. Then he beat her for it. That's one reason I called myself Diamante. To remind myself."

"Remind yourself of what?" said Ha-Cohen.

"About my mother's story about a diamond. More than anything else it drove my father to a frenzy. His father was in Venice himself, as a young man—that's the story my mother used to tell, anyway—and he had a diamond to bring somewhere. It wasn't his—it belonged to the great family we're supposed to come from. Anyway, the Gentiles found him wandering around the city, a foreign Jew—he was German I think, but he was born in Egypt—the story was never told the same way twice."

"Yes?" said Ha-Cohen, with surprising intensity. "What happened in Venice?"

"Oh, he wasn't dressed properly for a Jew," said Devorah.

"No red hat. I think in those days it was supposed to be yellow, but it's the same thing. And my father's father, like my father, was a great big man. Not as big as you, but at least as big as Clement. He was attacked for not wearing his Jewish hat, and he fought back and was beaten. They took his diamond, and according to my mother it's for that reason we're poor today. My grandfather was too embarrassed to have anything to do with the family again—he was afraid they'd think he stole the diamond. Just the word 'diamond' drives my father crazy. Still and all, he always drove my mother to tell these stupid stories. Just to mock her, and abuse her."

Ha-Cohen didn't know what questions to ask. He knew that the questions he needed were safe with his father and brothers in Amsterdam. Their family history was important to them, and well remembered. All Ha-Cohen had was a terrible fear, a terrible wonder that this Jewess might be more to him than just another daughter of Abraham.

"Your father," said Ha-Cohen. "What is his name?"

"Yehezkel," said Devorah, not understanding the intense expression in his face.

"A name is longer than that," said Ha-Cohen.

"Yehezkel of Nürnberg?" said Devorah, wondering what else he'd like to know. "The family name is Cuheno. If you want to know his whole princely name, it is Yehezkel Cuheno of Nürnberg." Devorah laughed. "You see, sir, my father is a Cohen just like you." Both Cuheno and Ha-Cohen were names that indicated a descent from the priestly tribe of the ancient Israelites.

"*That is not to be laughed at,*" said Ha-Cohen, with such sudden force that for a moment the girl remembered the wild look that had been in his eyes when he'd first entered her room in Bellini's palace. But she had no time to look at his eyes now; for the young giant of a man stood up and walked away from Clement and the girl.

"It's all right," said Clement to the pretty Jewess. "When you know him, you'll get used to his moods. He just needs to be alone for a while."

Ha-Cohen was alone till after dark. He walked through the fields of white marble gravestones as the wind picked up and the cold descended on the tiny island. In the distance, a fire blazed— Clement's work, to keep their bones warm till morning. Ha-Cohen found the fire inviting, but more pressing was his need to stand alone, in the wild space, amid the dead, their hearts and bowels and eyes and hair long since gone the way of their memories—only their bones remaining under the uneven ground, under the eyes of sculpted angels. Perhaps his father's long-dead sister was really a relation of the Rachel of Venice; perhaps that was why they shared the same brave look. Perhaps Devorah Cuheno was his kinswoman, and the sin they had almost shared was thus tenfold more powerful. Nor was this the only thing made more awful; Bellini's crime in humiliating a Jewess, turning her into a whore, was now more personally insulting to Ha-Cohen.

His hatred ran through his great frame in waves, like the undulations of a terrible fire. Still, he was cold amid the cold bones. The black cat didn't scare him, and when he heard its cry and caught its bright-eyed look beneath the bust of a cherub, he knew no fear. He was cold with fury, and he had to conquer this fury so that he could wield its force at dawn. No matter what he had told the others, he was sure that, if he lost the duel, Bellini would slaughter his friends.

Ha-Cohen knew few prayers, but he needed a prayer now. His walking about, imagining the joy of his father in discovering a lost family connection, imagining the face of Rachel of Venice when she would be told of the ancestors who shared her name— he had need of all this musing, but it didn't substitute for his need to pray.

Then suddenly, from the depths of memory, the words of a psalm came to him in a rush. It had always been his favorite part of the morning service, coming on a Wednesday, when he would intone, with the rest of the congregation of students at prayer in the Study House at Amsterdam: "Today is the fourth day of the week, counting from sabbath, as the Levites in the temple used to say." He whispered the words now; then, louder, speaking the words in a Hebrew that was mispronounced, but nonetheless understood, David Ha-Cohen prayed, shouting the psalm into the wind.

"O Lord, thou God to whom retribution belongeth, thou God to whom retribution belongeth, shine forth. Lift up thyself, thou Judge of the earth. Render to the proud their desert. Lord, how long shall the wicked, how long shall the wicked triumph? They prate, they speak arrogantly; all the workers of iniquity are boastful. They crush thy people, O Lord, and afflict thine heritage. They slay the widow and the stranger, and murder the fatherless. And they say the Lord will not see, neither will the God of Jacob give heed. But the Lord is become my stronghold; and my God the rock of my refuge. And He bringeth back upon them their own iniquity, and in their own evil shall cut them off; the Lord our God shall cut them off."

Pietro Bellini arrived on the Isle of the Dead at dawn. He wore stockings decorated with clocks, he wore shoes with heels of two and a half inches, he wore a leather jerkin over a white blouse. His face was pale, but he spoke with confidence. When he saw Devorah, he gave no indication of surprise, though he told one of the three men who had accompanied him and his second to return her to the palace at the conclusion of the duel.

Devorah walked away from the group of men and waited for a boat to come from the city; she expected her sister and Leone, and could not bear to watch the duel take place. But her back bristled with a thousand sensations, as if the skin under her silks longed for eyes to see.

Bellini removed his leather jerkin, and Ha-Cohen removed his thick doublet, revealing a much soiled blouse.

"Even the rich Jews are filthy," said Bellini.

It was the only time he spoke to Ha-Cohen that day. Clement and Bellini's second examined the Italian rapiers, and the two adversaries took up their weapons.

Clement said, "The duel will end when one of you draws blood."

"No," said Bellini, looking at Ha-Cohen but talking to Clement. "The duel will end when the Jew is dead." And with that, Bellini struck his on-guard pose, his thin limbs and fat face frighteningly graceful.

He and Ha-Cohen bowed, struck each other's swords, and then jumped back. Ha-Cohen's hatred was so intense that he had to blink his eyes to clear his vision. In the dawn light, he saw Bellini as a true devil, taunting him with a vision of hell, wherein the evil held sway.

Then, in a second, Bellini advanced, his rapier extended by a floating wrist, his legs moving like springs.

All Ha-Cohen saw was the smile on Bellini's face as he advanced, almost to within striking distance; and Ha-Cohen lunged.

Bellini parried the clumsy thrust, and then twisted his own rapier with lightning speed. Ha-Cohen heard the ringing of steel, felt the flash of pain in his powerful fist, but had no sensation of letting go his weapon. Still and all, it was gone.

Bellini, laughing, was advancing now, slashing lightly at Ha-Cohen's belly, at his retreating legs, at his upraised hands—but only to draw a little blood, only to scare. And there was nothing to be done. Ha-Cohen did not have his rapier, and, in his fury at losing it so easily, he could feel no pain, only rage that this man before him was alive, and had no right to live. Bellini continued to flash his rapier in front of Ha-Cohen's face, forcing the giant man back until he was stopped by the trunk of a cypress tree.

"You can't kill him," screamed Clement. "You've drawn blood. The man has no sword. The duel is over."

But Clement was restrained by the other men, and Bellini raised his rapier for the last time, ready to strike. Ha-Cohen, his back to the tree, felt as if this were a dream. He bled, but he was strong. This man was about to drive a blade through his heart, but he could not die. Bellini smiled, arched his back, raised his free hand behind his neck, for balance; then he lunged for David Ha-Cohen's heart.

The steel blade drove through Ha-Cohen's blouse, and met the Cuheno diamond, hanging in its pouch about his neck.

Bellini, expecting the yielding of human flesh, met the perfect resistance of diamond. Ha-Cohen turned his massive body from the glancing blade and struck at Bellini's skull with a bloody right fist. There was shouting now, all about Ha-Cohen, and he could see the other men advancing upon him; but though Bellini had dropped his rapier, Ha-Cohen had to make sure that there was no life left in his body. Swiftly, he grabbed Bellini at the neck and drove his head into the trunk of the cypress. Bellini's skull cracked, and then Ha-Cohen smashed the head into the trunk a second time, and a third time, with such force that only bloody pulp remained about the mutilated scalp.

Clement shouted at him, and Ha-Cohen stepped back from an advancing Venetian, and since his head was now clear, he knew what must be done. He ran from the men with their flashing rapiers and picked up the German sword that Clement held out for him. Together, he and his English friend fought the four Venetians; two German swords against four Italian rapiers—and Ha-Cohen and Clement slaughtered all four.

Minutes later they left the island, and its new dead, and together with the just-arrived Leone and Rachel, and with the calm, deathly pale Devorah, they made their way across the Lagoon of Venice to Mestre, and set out the same day for Trieste in a great vessel.

A month later, after many hardships, they arrived in Amsterdam. Devorah and Leone were married almost at once. Two years later, Rachel Cuheno married a pious German scholar. Her family origin had long since been established by Master Ha-Cohen, and David Ha-Cohen made no complaint when his father desired to give Rachel the stone that was her birthright. On her wedding day, Master Ha-Cohen presented the diamond to Rachel, the only girl of that name among the male-blessed Ha-Cohens and Cuhenos of that time. When Rachel touched the diamond's glittering surface, a wealth of family thrilled her soul.

THE FAMILY OF DAVID HA-COHEN
1615–1772

David Ha-Cohen, the youngest son of Master Ha-Cohen of Amsterdam, was married to Sophie Oppenheimer of Vienna in 1615. They had ten children—six boys and four girls; the lastborn girl, the child of David's old age, was born in 1645, only months after Rachel Cuheno of Venice, and later of Hamburg, died. David's youngest daughter was thus given the name Rachel, and the Cuheno stone became her birthright.

In 1660 the Jews were expelled from Vienna, where David had made his home, and Rachel emigrated to Amsterdam in the company of two brothers. Here she was married to Jakob Levi of Berlin, and returned to that city with her husband, where she died of old age in 1727, the year that George II ascended the English throne.

Rachel's grandnephew, Haim, son of her brother's son, had accepted the invitation of the English Crown to become court jeweler, and his firstborn daughter, born within a week of her great-grandaunt's death, assumed her name, and her birthright. This Rachel, wild and reckless, was poisoned by a rival to the affections of an English baron in 1750, when she was only twenty-three. Though the Ha-Cohen family—now known in various cities as Cohen, Cuheno, and Cohn, with a single family unit known as Cogan in St. Petersburg, jewelers to the Imperial Russian Court—had many young married men among its members, no Rachel was born until 1753.

Rachel Cohen, the second child and first daughter of Samson Cohen of Berlin—who was himself a first cousin of the Rachel of London and a great-great-grandson of David Ha-Cohen of Amsterdam and Vienna—was born on Berlin's Wilhelmstrasse, into a life of luxury. The Seven Years' War, the occupation of Berlin by Russian troops, the horrors of anti-Jewish riots and massacres during her infancy and childhood—none of these catastrophes were allowed to disturb her careful, enlightened upbringing. From an early age, she learned that she was a Jewess, of an old and distinguished family, and that while there were many other Jews in the outside world, few were born with her privileges. She had a string of governesses—Jewesses of Berlin and of Vienna; a young Christian lady from Metz; an old maid, of noble family, from Paris itself. Men, both Jewish and Gentile, tutored her in German, English and French. She studied geometry and philosophy, the history of Greece and the history of Rome. She memorized Voltaire, who lived at the court of Frederick the Great in Berlin during much of her childhood.

But Hebrew had to be forced upon her. First the alphabet, then the grammar, then the words of the Five Books of Moses were thrust upon her at her father's command. Rachel's desire for knowledge encompassed all that was secular, all that was outside the pale of things Jewish. For while her father tried to mitigate the shock of her situation—a singularly emancipated Jewess in an overwhelmingly Gentile world—by calling upon her to thank God for her freedom, her mother taught her to loathe the accident of her Jewish birth.

Frau Cohen's outlook was simple: She came from a family as Jewish and nearly as old as her husband's, and every single one of her five siblings had embraced the Protestant Church. Only she was still cursed with the Jewish mark, and this only because of her husband's obstinacy. They lived in an age of enlightenment, when the shackles of superstition were beginning to fall away; it was time that they embraced the form, if not the substance, of the religion of their equals. And Frau Cohen did not see anyone other than Gentiles of the upper classes as her equals. The Jews who wandered into Berlin for a day's gawking, either from the South or the East, were an embarrassment; she wished she could make them disappear. Their dirty clothes and ragged beards, their terrible Jewish German, their worn-down boots and dusty hats— all these were a personal affront to the dignity of Frau Cohen of Berlin. She wanted her daughter to have the things she had always aspired to: a noble Christian husband, as blond as a yellow brick; a title; and a salon that received not Jewish bankers and Christian poets but one that was open only to the landed aristocrats of ancient family names.

Frau Cohen died in 1770, when Rachel was seventeen and still unmarried. But her work had not been in vain: If Rachel knew Hebrew, she hated the sound of it; if she remembered the legend of her family's descent from the Jews of Spain, she wished she had come from the Hohenzollern instead; if she thought of the restrictions that prevented any more Jews from settling in the city of her birth, or even any but the oldest son of an already settled family from starting his own family in Berlin, she was glad of it. There were two thousand Jews in Berlin, and, as far as Rachel was concerned, they were the only Jews worth knowing in all the world; of the hundreds of thousands in Germany and Poland, she knew all that she cared to, and she hoped that they'd stay where they were put, mumbling their prayers and bowing their necks to their Jewish God and Christian oppressors.

Herr Cohen gave his daughter's hand to Phillip Meier, the son of a banker and jeweler, and when he gave the bride the Cuheno diamond that was hers by right of her birth, he cried.

This was a Rachel who understood nothing of her people, and who had no interest in anything but Christian poets and sensual pleasures. Herr Cohen cried, because he knew his daughter was unworthy of her inheritance, unworthy of her name.

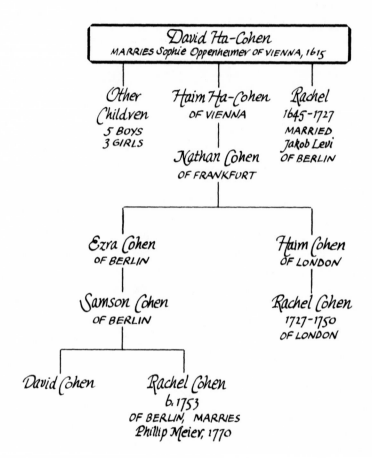

PART THREE

BERLIN, 1772

CHAPTER THIRTEEN

In the home of Phillip and Rachel Meier of Berlin, on the lovely Jagerstrasse, there were two salons—one for men of business, and one for men of the arts. Phillip Meier, banker and diamond merchant, held court in the larger salon, that of business: Here the talk was of the price of gold, the instabilities within the Prussian court, the flooding of the European gem markets with diamonds from the new mines in Brazil.

Rachel Meier, his nineteen-year-old wife, held court in the smaller salon, that of the arts: Here the talk was of Rousseau and Voltaire, English painting and German music, the politics of revolution and the poetry of love.

It was not infrequent for a bearded envoy from the East, dressed in the black gabardine of an Orthodox Jew, to mix freely in the large salon with Protestant landowners, Jewish bankers, Catholic merchants. Here were men of substantial girth, in dark clothing, often wearing long-haired wigs, the long back-hair caught in once-fashionable silk bags. Men smoked cigars, drank whiskey and brandy, often drifted into a quiet corner for a private business negotiation. A physician from Hamburg with a diamond to sell might carry it in his pocket to the Meier home, in hope

of meeting an honest dealer. A Bavarian aristocrat, with an introduction from a mutual friend, might appear with a family heir-
loom clutched in his fist. A Berlin textile manufacturer, rich from
clothing Frederick the Great's regiments, might hope to convert
Prussian currency into a gemstone of lasting value. A Dutch
jeweler, perhaps a distant relation of Meier's wife, would seek a
connection to one of the many German courts to procure a contract to mint coins.

In the smaller salon there were fewer Jews, no bankers, no
merchants. If two men drifted into a corner for a private talk,
it was usually to talk of a mistress, or a play, or an impossible
adventure. One or two women other than their hostess were often
present, and the men didn't smoke. They were poets, writers of
plays and pamphlets, opera singers, painters. The men were young
and slim, and wore leather breeches and even riding boots into
the genteel salon, sharing their hostess's contempt for conven-
tion. Here a penniless poet might read his lines to an atheist, a
collector of Italian paintings, an apostate Jew, a Polish count, an
English actress. A painter might shout out insults to the reigning
masters of his profession, looking among the egalitarian members
of the salon for a rich patron; a hungry musician might demand
a meal; a poet might call for the abolition of marriage and religion, and the institution of free love in their place. The two
salons had as much in common as their respective host and hostess;
there was as much harmony and connection between greater and
lesser salon as between husband and wife.

"Do you know that I've never seen him?" said Count von
Kauthen to Rachel one late winter's afternoon. "I must have
met a hundred Jews since I've come to Berlin, and still I've never
met your husband."

"Please," said Rachel. "In my salon we engage in wit and intelligence, not talk of jewelers and husbands."

"He is not at all a Jewish type," said Andreas Wolff, a young
German poet who wrote all his poetry in French. "He is blond
and straight-backed, and he does business without devious motions." The young poet moved his hands in a description of
curves.

"I don't think that a very proper way to talk about our hostess's
husband," said the count. He had been looking for a chance to
demonstrate his manliness in this clever little assemblage for the
better part of an hour. Every time someone spoke, it was either

to quote a line of Rousseau's or Shakespeare's or Dante's; no one wanted to quote a German, except perhaps to make fun of Frederick the Great's latest pronouncements. Count von Kauthen had spent most of his thirty years on the family estates, and in the army. He could not get used to the Berlin type—the *verwegener Menschenschlag*, the audacious man who spoke without thought of consequences. The count was used to being honored simply because of his name and his rank, and here he was honored for nothing other than his turn of phrase.

"I think that for a man who professes principles of equality," continued the count, "it is a mark of perfect ignorance to refer to devious business practices as Jewish characteristics. I think that you should apologize to our hostess."

"Why is it, Rachel," said Andreas Wolff, "that you insist on inviting aristocrats to your salon? They don't write, they don't paint, they don't compose music. All they do well is ride horses, and anyone can do that."

"I insist that you apologize to our hostess," said the count, rising to his full height. Across the room, a pretty singer turned from contemplating a painting by van de Velde, a theologically suspect pastor looked up from a beautifully leatherbound edition of Plutarch, a painter who had been stirring up the flames in the white marble fireplace turned and stared.

"Sit down, Count," said Rachel. "And don't make yourself ridiculous on my account."

"I think I had better leave," said the count. He had offered protection to this young woman, and she had turned it about and thrown it into his face with this comment.

"Don't leave," said Rachel.

"Only politeness prevents you from asking me to leave," said the count, his face reddening. "It is obvious that I am not wanted here."

"I am not polite," said Rachel. "Sit down, Count von Kauthen."

"Whatever you command, madame," said the count. And he sat down, avoiding the insolent eyes of the Berlin poet.

"I am a Jew," said Rachel. "And I didn't take offense at what Wolff said. In this room, we can say whatever we like. I can tell you that I dislike counts, or that I like the color of your hair. You can tell me that you are an atheist, or plotting the overthrow of the Prussian government, and that shall be all right, too."

"Then I tell you this, madame," said the count. "I dislike the color of Andreas Wolff's hair. I loathe the lines of his face, and I hate his poetry."

"This is serious," said Wolff. "And I didn't even dream you understood French."

"Perhaps," said Rachel, "it would be safer to talk about something else, gentlemen."

"Hyprocrisy," said Andreas Wolff. "We shall talk about hyprocrisy. This is the one place in Berlin where I can go and not worry about being slapped down for dishonest statements, so we shall discuss hypocrisy with the Count von Kauthen. Why are you here, Count?"

"He is here because I invited him to come," said Rachel.

"I am asking the count for a reason, my dear," said Wolff. "I shall tell you why I'm here, Count, and then perhaps you can be honest with me. I am here because I love Frau Rachel Meier. All the black-haired temptresses in my poems, who are they if not Rachel? You shouldn't get angry, Count. Half the poets in Berlin are writing of no other woman. That is why I am here. I am here because she is here. Why are you here?"

"I am interested in philosophy," said the count.

Wolff burst out laughing. "Hypocrisy," he said. "Hypocrisy, my dear Count! You are still new to this sort of thing, new and stiff, and not at all privy to the rules of the game. You are here because you wanted to look at a famous black-haired Jewess. You wanted to see for yourself why she was famous. Count, can't you at least be truthful enough to admit this? Please, Count, you are among friends. Didn't you seek your invitation here to see Rachel Meier, just like everyone else does?"

"I am interested in philosophy," said the count. "A friend of mine, who is in communication with Kant himself, suggested that a visit to Frau Meier's salon would be interesting. I was told that here some of the best minds in Berlin gather."

"Hypocrisy!" screamed the audacious Berliner. "Your friend didn't only say that! He said that Frau Meier was beautiful, did he not?"

"Our hostess *is* beautiful," said the embarrassed count, nodding to Rachel as a mark of obeisance. "My friend did mention that, but that was not the point of my coming here."

"Look here, Count," said Andreas Wolff. "I like you. We're all Prussians under the skin, though some of us act more like Frederick the Great, Old Fritz, than others. I used to be a lot stiffer, too. But I've learned. I came here to read my poetry and hear other poets, and I still come here for that reason. But that's not the main reason I'm here. I love Rachel. Everyone in this room loves Rachel. Not romantically—only some of us love her romantically. But we all love Rachel, and that's why we're here, and that's why you'll be back."

"It shall be an honor for me to be invited again," said the count.

"You don't need an invitation," said Rachel. "Not anymore. Come whenever you like, Count."

"Then I shall be here every day."

"You won't be here every day to discuss philosophy!" said Wolff.

"Perhaps not," said the count. "Perhaps I shall come here to make loud noises as you recite your poems."

"That, too, is allowed here," said Wolff. "Anything is allowed here. Do you know, I was forced to visit Jena two months ago. What a godforsaken place, Count! No Jews! No Jewish salons! Not a single black-haired Jewess for miles around! What a bore! The only salon was so stiff, I bruised myself on the whalebone dresses. Everyone dresses like it was 1750, and the only Jews one ever sees are the peddlers, who'd kill their own mothers for an extra penny."

"I wish you would think of something other than the accident of my birth to discuss, Andreas," said Rachel. "I was born a Jewess, yes, but that is not why I am what I am."

"Ridiculous!" said Wolff. "You don't mean to tell me that I can't discuss the Jews in a Jewish salon?"

"You can discuss what you like, but the subject of Jews bores me," said Rachel. "I am a Berliner. What difference does it make if my ancestors were slaves in Egypt, or ran around slaughtering each other two thousand years ago? What has it to do with me? What have I got to do with peddlers, speaking that atrocious Jewish German? What have I got to do with beggars and superstitious peasants, any more than you or the count?"

"Are you serious?" said Andreas Wolff. "Who else but a Jew could be rich enough to live on the Jagerstrasse, hang Rubens on the wall, walk around with diamond-studded walking sticks, be prouder than a duchess, and still be positively daring, revolutionary, open-minded, egalitarian, and snubbed by all the real aristocrats in the country? Only the Jews have salons like this! Every

Christian with money and a title invites only bores, gentlemen to talk about dogs and horses, ladies to talk about French millinery. They can't invite poets and rakes and actors and scoundrels to their homes. Only the Jews can. I thank God for the Jews! And I thank God for being alive to enjoy them while they're still here —because mark my words, Count, the next generation of our hostess's family will be as Christian and as boring as the rest of us. No more salons where a crazy poet like me can sit with the likes of you. No more superstitious beggars and peddlers. Every-one's going to be emancipated, and no one is going to care about going to church. You can't have a Jewish beggar with a proper mind, any more than you can turn a man with a proper mind into a Jewish beggar! Once the Jewish rabble is emancipated, once we shave off their beards and teach them to speak, we won't have any more Jews left. Everyone will be like everyone else. We won't have any more decent salons, but then we won't have any more penny-stealing Jewish pawnbrokers either!"

"I know a Jew," said the count," who wears a beard, attends the synagogue daily, and is a doctor of medicine, a student of Plato and Aristotle, and a teacher of Hebrew to princes of the Church."

"Such Jews are a dying breed," said Rachel, sitting up straight in her seat. "My father is like that, or thinks he is. My brother doesn't attend the synagogue, but he would never marry a Gen-tile either. My husband also thinks us a separate race. He also thinks it possible for a fanatically superstitious Jew to be learned. Just because he deals with religious old Jews who are also crafty in business, rich from gems and banking, he thinks they're wise.

"Well, you can't be wise and superstitious at once. You can't learn to be anything except a slave and a beggar until you throw off that old religion. The wisest law in Berlin is the one that keeps the Jews out of the city, unless they're specially privileged. I wouldn't want my city filled with little humpbacked peddlers hawking old clothes in Yiddish. If my mother had lived a little longer, I'd probably be baptized today. I'd probably be baptized and the wife of a count."

"The Countess Kauthen," said Wolff. "Yes, that would sound well over your entrance. And I'm sure you'd be a terrible enemy of the Jews."

"I'm not an enemy of the Jews," said Rachel. "I just don't feel like I have to be made to suffer because I was born one."

"You only suffer because you're ridiculous," said Wolff. "If I'd had the misfortune to be born a woman, I'd wish I were a Jewess. They're the only ones who ever run off to Paris with poets! You can't find a Christian girl to do that, at least not an educated one!" Andreas Wolff stood up and bowed. "I shall allow the two of you time alone. In Rachel's salon, the tête à tête is everything! Next time we meet, Count, I hope you shall tell me everything you like, without restraint. When I said that Herr Meier was not a Jewish type, I meant it as a compliment to our unseen host, not as an affront to peasants and peddlers! If you fall in love with Frau Meier, perhaps you and I can write a poem together."

Wolff backed away, and picked up a brandy. There were about a dozen others in the salon at that moment, most of them familiar to the young poet from previous visits. His friend Dieter was there. Dieter, swearing him to secrecy, had told him that he had made love to Rachel in his own home less than a month before. Andreas had kept the confidence, but had also spontaneously slapped his friend across the face at the news. There had been no duel, of course; Dieter and Andreas were both enlightened men, and had no desire to kill over a confession of passion. Besides, surely there were other men with whom Rachel had had affairs. Andreas exchanged greetings with one possible lover, a younger son of the rich house of Nathan, whose recent baptism had led to his loss of a job in his father's bank, and a life of dissolution.

He wondered if Rachel was at that moment conquering the heart of Count von Kauthen. It was maddening to be infatuated with a woman as amoral as he was himself.

Andreas walked over to his favorite painting in the room, a portrait by Jordaens of a young, fair-haired girl. He wondered how much of the trappings of this magnificent home came from the fortune of the Meier family, and how much was the product of the much greater Cohen fortune. The paintings were all Dutch: two by Jordaens, a small Rubens, two by van de Velde, and a brilliant series of landscapes with peasants by the religious painter Teniers. He knew that Rachel's father, Samson Cohen, was of Dutch descent, and that the Cohen house on the Wilhelmstrasse was filled with the works of Dutch masters. Andreas had met Rachel's brother, David, in this very room, and he had been as dour and Dutch as the paintings on the wall. But perhaps it was because David Cohen had disapproved of the company in his sister's salon; perhaps he felt that poets were not as fascinating company as men of business.

Andreas took a large sip of the brandy. Across the room, he saw Rachel's little hand reach across her painted calico dress and touch the Count von Kauthen's arm. The poet felt the blood rise to his face. What could the Jewess see in that aristocratic clod, other than his ridiculous name? He put down his brandy glass with a little bang, and went to talk to the only other woman in the room, an Italian actress with a stupid face. It was just like Rachel to allow women to mix freely with men at her salon, but to introduce only a few at any one time, and always these would be women such as this actress—beautiful, of a dangerous class or calling, and stupid. She liked to have ornaments at her salon, but only those that served to emphasize her own uniqueness.

There were other women in Berlin who were beautiful, who were rich, who were famous, who had had affairs; but only Rachel was as aggressive as a man. Only Rachel had the mind and the spirit of an adventurer. When Andreas had asked her if she would leave her husband and go to Paris with him, she'd laughed in his face. "Do you think I'm the sort of woman who needs to follow *you* to go to Paris?" she'd said.

Rachel would follow no one and nothing except the dictates of her own will, and this was her attraction to the poet, and to a hundred other men. This was a Jewess who was free from the restraints of religion, a wife who overshadowed the strength of her husband, a woman who could not be abandoned or controlled. If she were to have an affair with the Count von Kauthen, it would be the count whose heart would be broken, he whose innocence would be crushed.

Andreas didn't understand where Rachel's spirit came from, but he liked to imagine it was a product of confusion and inner conflict. He liked to believe that he could teach Rachel to strip away the turmoil within her soul. If she could love the way she had never loved, if she could give herself completely to a man worthy of her spirit, she could learn happiness. It seemed to Andreas Wolff that all her talk was bright without brilliance, all her lovemaking was diversion rather than fervor. It was no wonder she hated being a Jew, he thought. Rachel lived so much on the surface of things that the surface branding of her Jewish name was something repugnant to her. Until she learned who she could be, she would be condemned to this obsessive suffering on the surface of things.

"I am a deist," Count von Kauthen was saying, still red in the face from the moment when the Jewess had touched his arm. "I believe that God exists, but I don't think he takes much notice of us. I don't think we're important enough."

"You don't think I'm important enough?" said Rachel. "You think I'm too insignificant a creature to be paid much mind to?" She smiled at the count, to let him understand that this was all to be taken without offense. "Do you read Spinoza?"

"Yes, of course, I think he's fascinating. That's one of the reasons I took such exception to that man Wolff's remarks about Jews. Spinoza was a Jew."

"Spinoza was born a Jew," said Rachel. "But he wasn't a Jew any more than I am a Jewess. He didn't live as a Jew, and he didn't think as a Jew, otherwise he could never have developed into the genius that he was. Have you ever been to Leipzig, Count? Or to Frankfurt?"

"Many times," said the count. "I've been to the fairs."

"If you've been to the fairs, you've seen the Jews there. Can you imagine any of those superstitious, greedy little people to be a Spinoza? There's a difference between being born Jewish and remaining Jewish. I am an enlightened woman, Count von Kauthen. I have the courage to use my reason, and I am therefore an enemy of close-minded men and institutions. I am glad that you read Spinoza."

"I have read Mendelssohn as well," said the count.

"You needn't give me the names of all the Jews you've read."

"I only mention him because he believes that morality is possible without revelation," said the count. "I believe that, too. I believe that there are good men in every religion, and even outside of religion. I am a deist, but I believe I am moral, and I believe it possible for all of us to be moral without subscribing to anything other than a faith in the order of the universe."

"Do you think I'm beautiful?" said Rachel suddenly. She sat back with a languid motion on the stuffed chair.

The count had never seen a rich and beautiful woman in such a rustic dress before; it was part of Rachel's daring to wear clothing only accepted in Paris. Painted calico was still worn in Prussia by servants, but of course Rachel's dress was not the frumpy domestic issue. Its bodice was tightly fitted, revealing the soft curves of her breasts. A simple gold chain hung about her neck, descending into her cleavage. Just above the cleavage, where the line of the dress rose and fell as she talked and gestured, was a small beauty mark. The count wondered what was resting between her breasts, supported by the golden chain; he wondered if any other woman had been blessed by nature with such a beauty mark; he wondered if she could possibly love her husband and sit here and touch another man's arm.

"It is wrong to flatter a woman indisputably beautiful on the fact of her beauty," said the count, aware that he was outdoing his usual eloquence. "I would rather flatter you on your intelligence, madame."

"You have already flattered me on both," said Rachel. "Are you staring at the mark above my breasts, or at the chain round my neck?"

"Forgive me, madame," said the count. "I did not mean to stare."

"Michelangelo thought that any beautiful object raised the desire of man from earth to God," said Rachel. "But you have no devout look about you, sir. Do you like gardening?"

"Gardening? You change topics so swiftly, madame, I hardly know what to say."

"Shrubs, flowers—do you like them?" said Rachel.

"Yes, I like flowers."

"Good, then perhaps you would like to visit the Tiergarten while you're in Berlin. It's being replanted and it's going to be beautiful one day, more beautiful than anything in Paris or Vienna. If you like flowers, you must go and see the flowering shrubs. I have been there a hundred times, and I can never have enough of it."

"You would like to go again?" said the count, hardly believing his daring.

"Yes, certainly," said Rachel. "I plan to go again. I love to ride down Unter den Linden, from the palace to the Tiergarten. I love to walk between the tall trees."

"May I ask you a favor?" said the count, bowing gravely.

"Yes," said Rachel, sitting perfectly still.

"You won't think it amiss, I hope," said the count. "I only ask because you seem interested. In trees and flowers. And I am in Berlin only for a few more weeks, madame. So please forgive me if I seem forward."

"You don't seem forward, Count. You are very old-fashioned, even if you are a deist."

"May I take you out to the Tiergarten in my carriage one day?" said the count.

"Perhaps," said Rachel. "I would enjoy it very much, Count von Kauthen, but until you show me the spirit of your regard for me and my family, I am afraid that I shall have to go to the Tiergarten alone."

"I don't understand, madame," said the count. He had gone so far as to ask a married Jewess to come with him in his carriage; and this much in an age where, in his own principality, Jews were still forbidden to ride in carriages at all. Of course, rich *Jews* were different; and Berliners, Jew and Gentile alike, were different. It was not enough to be of noble descent, and a deist. He knew he was on the verge of being mocked by half the people he met in this fast city of one hundred thousand souls.

"Your uncle is not a deist," said Rachel.

"My uncle?"

"The prince," said Rachel.

"But what have I to do with the prince?" said Count von Kauthen, blushing. He had seen his uncle once whip an old Jew across the face, when the man had not taken his hat off at the prince's approach. In the written laws of the principality was the injunction to all Jews to get out of the path of all Gentiles, to doff their hats at any Christian's intoning the words: "Your manners, Jew!" The count had always been embarrassed by these outrages, and his principality's reputation for backwardness was not based only on its treatment of the Jews.

"The prince is your uncle," said Rachel.

"I don't know how you in Berlin know of the ways of my uncle, but I assure you, madame, that his views on life and religion are totally different from my own."

"The prince is your uncle, and you can therefore approach and speak with him."

"I seldom speak with the prince," said Count von Kauthen. "It's true we hunt together, but that is because it is an activity requiring little communication."

"My husband wants to provide him with jewels," said Rachel.

"Jewels?" said the count, thoroughly confused. "What have you and I to do with jewels?"

"The prince is going to issue his own paper currency. It is to be a currency based on his reserves of gold and jewels. He is turning great quantities of land into cash, and cash into gems for the treasury. I understand that he is making a great many mistakes. My husband can help him, and he can help my husband, but it shall be up to you to effect the introduction. Then I shall be able to go riding with you in the Tiergarten. I find you very intelligent, and I can sense that you are a sensitive man."

"Madame," said the count, "I don't know much about these matters of coinage and currency, but I shall be happy to do anything I can for you and your family. You need not accept my offer to ride with you in any case. You have only to tell me what to do, and I shall do it."

"You are very, very kind, Count von Kauthen," said Rachel. Again, the little hand reached out to touch his wrist, and the contact thrilled him. "And I want you to know that I find you charming, and that I want very much to go riding in the Tiergarten with you."

"Thank you, madame," said the count.

"You seem a bit flushed," said Rachel. "You feel well, I hope?"

"I feel fine."

"You're surprised?"

"No," said the count. "It is natural for a wife to ask a favor for her husband."

"It is a favor for myself as well," said Rachel. "I am a woman, but I still know something of business. And I know quite a lot about jewelry."

"Well," said the count with a smile, "that is the prerogative of all women of means. I can think of more than one of my female cousins who knows quite a lot about jewels. I never thought of that as a business sense, I always thought of it as a way to spend the family's money."

The count couldn't understand why anger suddenly flared across the young woman's face. He had lapsed into a familiarity of tone, and had, without thinking, belittled her claim to a knowledge of business. In the count's world, this could hardly be an insult to a man, much less to a woman, since an aristocrat had nothing to do with business, except when he selected a financial adviser. A woman of the upper class would hardly even know of the existence of the financial adviser. But Rachel had not been brought up as a member of the count's class. Even if her far-flung family had more money than his, it had never lost touch with its sense of self: If they were princes, they were merchant princes; if they were powerful, their power was based on the substance of their diamonds.

"I want to show you something," said Rachel. "I want to show you something I understand." And with a single easy motion, she lifted the gold chain out from under the bodice of her dress, so that he could see the great diamond to which it was attached.

The diamond rested against the bright painted calico of the tight bodice, a shining center of white light against a background of tawdry colors. It was more beautiful than anything the count had ever seen, and, without thinking, his hand went out to touch its surface.

"No!" said Rachel, and she drew back from the count and slapped his hand away from her chest.

Immediately, the count got to his feet and began to apologize. "I'm sorry, madame," he said. "I didn't mean to offend you."

"It is not for you to touch," said Rachel, her heart pounding. Out of the corner of her eye, she saw the rakehell young poet Andreas Wolff, so sharply dressed in his gleaming riding boots, turn from a boring talk with the pretty actress and look up at an apparition behind Rachel's back. Simultaneously, the pleasant buzz of a dozen cultured voices suddenly stopped short, filling the room with an ominous quiet, punctuated by the crackling of the fireplace logs. But the quiet had nothing to do with the showing of the sixty-carat diamond, named for the Spanish family from whom the Cohens of Berlin, Rachel's family, were descended. "I only wanted to show you what I know of gems," she said, and her words ran loud and clear in the hushed salon. Because the count, too, was now staring, Rachel turned about. She saw at once why everyone in her salon, the salon of the arts, had stopped talking.

Herr Phillip Meier, her husband, had entered the salon. With him was a young beggar, dressed in the filthy gabardine of the lowest class of Jew. Never before had her husband, lord of the large salon, dared enter this place of wigless poets. It was scarcely possible that he would do so now, particularly in the company of this lowest species of Jew, unless he had predetermined to humiliate Rachel, to humble her before her witty companions. Herr Meier was smoking a cigar, and when Rachel finally spoke, to welcome him, she said only: "My dear husband, there are women present. We do not allow smoking in here."

Herr Meier removed the cigar from his mouth and looked about the salon, as if in search of a particular man. "I need some-one who understands Latin," he said. "Who can understand it when it's spoken out loud."

"What is the meaning of this, my dear husband?" said Rachel, her eyes blazing. "Who is this man that you bring him into our company, wearing his cap like a Polish peasant? He stinks of the stable, and I want him out of here at once." She checked her anger for a moment and forced a little smile for her husband and their audience, adding, "If you would be so good, my dear Phillip."

Herr Meier, Rachel's husband for one year, a man of forty years with little physical grace but with a stolid, confident bear-ing, slowly turned his eyes from his very young wife to the attentive members of her little salon. "I need someone who under-stands Latin," he said again. "I can read it, but I can't understand it when it's spoken."

"The least you can do is tell the beggar to take off his hat," said Rachel, her harsh words directed at her husband, but spoken within inches of the beggar's face.

The beggar, who had thus far kept in Herr Meier's shadow, his features obscured by his large fur hat, suddenly straightened up and threw off this cover, his face radiant with understanding. "My hat," he said, in terrible German. "My hat—you want I should take off my hat!"

The young Yiddish-speaking beggar was so happy at having understood this request that, for a moment, all the attention in the room was fastened on his joy. But this recognition of joy quickly passed, overwhelmed by the sudden revelation of the young man's beauty. His hair, dirty, matted, and long, lay in thick curls that ran to his shoulders. His face was bearded, and covered with dirt and dust. But his dark green eyes, bright with joy and understanding, fired the features of his face, giving an intensity of presence to what was more pretty than handsome, more fragile beauty than strong good looks.

The young man turned from one to the other of the company, repeating, "My hat, my hat!" as if this would be the key to all future communication with these wondrous creatures, and threw the hat into the burning fire, laughing maniacally. As the mem-bers of the salon turned from looking at this apparition to stare at each other in an acknowledgment of disbelief, the young man ripped off the four fringes of his *talis kattan*, the religious undergarment worn by Orthodox Jews, and threw these, too, into the fire.

"Is he mad? What is he doing?" said Rachel, unable to take her eyes from the young man's beautiful face. "He's crazy!"

"I speak Latin, sir," said the Count von Kauthen, approaching Herr Meier. "I can understand it when it's spoken."

But already the young man was whirling about from the fire, stepping between the count and Herr Meier, his eyes reaching for Rachel's. He pointed a finger at his chest and said, in rapid Yiddish that no one understood, "I am not crazy, beautiful lady. And I will show you that I am more than simply sane." He looked in wonder at her diamond. In Hebrew he said, "The sin of Judah is written with a pen of iron, and with the point of a diamond!" Then, laughing and looking into Rachel's eyes, he said, "*Tantum religio potuit suadere malorum*," quoting Lucretius in Latin.

The Count von Kauthen stared at the young man, astonished that a beggar could speak such clear, excellent, church-accented Latin.

"What did he say? Can you understand him?" said Herr Meier. "Does he know how to speak Latin?"

"He said that religion was strong," said the count, slowly putting the sentence together in his mind. "Religion was strong in persuading us to do evil deeds."

The young man, smelling of gutter and stable, of a hundred nights on the hard frozen ground, knew enough German to see that he was understood, and impulsively threw his arms around the count. Even as he embraced Count von Kauthen, the young man's eyes searched out Rachel. He wanted to see the diamond against her white flesh, he wanted to break out of one world into another, he wanted to talk and to learn and to teach. He wanted so many things at once, so many things that suddenly, for the first time in his life, seemed possible to attain, that he nearly crushed the count's backbone before he was pried away by Herr Meier's strong hands.

Mordecai of Mir had arrived in Berlin, and his lust was as big as the world.

CHAPTER FOURTEEN

Sometimes the son of a wise man is ignorant, and the son of an ignoramus wise. A grandson will often inherit his grandfather's capacity for wisdom, but be thought of as a dullard if he is the son of an ignorant man.

When Mordecai's mother was pregnant with her first child, she used to pronounce his name on sabbath eve; this was to insure the arrival of a boy, rather than a girl, into the world of men. Mordecai's father placed sweetmeats under their bed to appease jealous demons. Father and mother both wrapped a string seven times around the grave of the last Chief Rabbi of Mir, and the mother wore this string next to the skin of her belly, to insure the survival of the unborn child. When she went into labor, all the doors of their tiny house were opened, all the knots and ties in both parents' clothing were undone; still, the delivery was not easy. A boy was born, large and healthy, but the mother died three days later. He was called Mordecai, the son of the butcher, and it was not until he was nearly three years old that his genius became known to the town of Mir.

The butcher's son, raised in a harsh dialect that was a composite of Yiddish, Hebrew, Polish, and Russian, had only to look at a page of the Pentateuch to memorize every word. Without comprehending what he knew by heart, he could sing out every portion of the Torah before he was four. He was raised to the highest seat in the one-room school, higher than the boys of eleven and twelve, who were afraid to bully him, afraid lest he cast a spell upon their souls.

The town of Mir, on the river Niemen in the Lithuanian section of Poland, was too small for a boy of genius. When he was six, he was sent to the Talmud academy at Iwenez, and he learned Aramaic and Hebrew and the Syrian dialect in which the holy book of the Zohar is written. The other boys at the academy used to joke that Mordecai was worth three hundred thalers, because this was the price of the printed Talmud, the forty-volume edition printed in Venice and estimated to contain two and half million words, every one of which the genius was supposed to know by heart.

Mordecai tried to discover why the Aramaic of the Palestinian Talmud was different from the Aramaic of the Babylonian Talmud; why the Babylonian Talmud sometimes had a section in beautiful Hebrew, then digressed into inelegant dialect. But the rabbis at the academy were of no help. They praised him for his powers of total recall, saying that he was one of God's chosen, to have been given this gift. But they weren't interested in the differences between the Aramaic of the Palestinian and the Babylonian Talmud, because he was supposed to study only the Babylonian. He was reminded that language was but an instrument to put him into closer touch with God, and not to be investigated for its own sake. Hebrew was not to be spoken between classmates in a casual manner. It was the holy tongue, and used when reading the Torah, or parts of the Talmud, or in prayer.

When Mordecai was twelve, he was returned to Mir to marry the bride picked out for him by his father, the butcher. Her name was Mirrel, and she was eleven, with dull blue eyes and a woman's body. Her mother, a widow, owned the local inn and had paid Mordecai's father a dowry of one hundred thalers for the right to have a son-in-law of such distinction. The whole town of Mir was at the wedding feast, and while two hundred people ate the food provided by the widow, Mordecai and Mirrel went to the smallest room in the inn and did what their respective parents had told them to do.

Mirrel took off her white wedding clothes and shook loose her

long blond hair. Mordecai undressed slowly, trying to comprehend the changes taking place in his body: His heart pounded, an
enormous pressure built up in his genitals, a promise of ecstasy
outside the sphere of the Holy Law blew up in his chest.

"Here," said Mirrel. "I will show you where you must go."
She was ready for a pain, so frighteningly described by her
mother, and then an explosion. She was strong, and she could
endure what her mother had endured.

Mirrel had been told often enough of the great honor that her
mother had been able to procure for her. Marriage to this young
rabbi, the best pupil at Iwenez, would never have been possible
without her skill in tricking the butcher into a contract. The
young man was worth much more than a hundred thalers; if the
butcher had taken the trouble to inquire at Iwenez, he would have
gotten offers of a thousand thalers for his son's hand. But a contract was a contract. This would be Mirrel's husband. She would
have the honor of supporting him all the days of his life, as he
studied Torah and Talmud for the glory of the Name. Mirrel
would be insured a portion of the world-to-come.

All this would have been enough for Mirrel. She had taken her
mother's words as statements of fact. She had expected to greet
a twelve-year-old boy who knew nothing of play, whose eyes
were hooded with the fatigue of the classroom, whose back was
bent and whose skin was sallow; she had expected to meet a young
boy who was already an old, holy man. Mirrel expected this,
and was prepared to accept Mordecai with all her heart. When she
saw his face for the first time, when they were placed side by
side under the wedding canopy, she turned red. Try as she might,
throughout the long ceremony, she could concentrate on nothing
other than the fact of his beauty. She was led around him seven
times, pledging devotion to her new master, her head in a fever of
disbelief. Next to him, she was thick and coarse. Not simply dull
and uneducated, but plain and ugly. He was the most beautiful
boy she had ever seen, and when she spoke to him in their wedding bed, her eyes brimmed with tears, and her hands were
clumsy.

But Mordecai noticed none of this. He was about to fulfill the
first commandment, to be fruitful and multiply, to bring about
the next generation of children. As the young girl tried to help
him enter her body, he was aware that he was on a plane of
experience far superior to anything he had ever encountered in

the synagogue or the study house. The ecstasy he had achieved when he had fasted for three days and three nights, staying up through the entire ordeal to study the Torah, was now seen as empty and weak. Mirrel's body, perfectly formed, young and white and smooth to the astonished touch of his fingers, was holier to him than a hundred fast days; the ecstasy he was experiencing was more profound than the brightest bit of wisdom he'd ever gleaned from the endless years of his youth of study.

Mordecai entered the young girl with a difficulty that seemed part of nature's design; there was no doubt but that God was all around him, because he remembered nothing of what his father had told him about a woman's body, heard nothing of what his wife said to him, he only felt the desire to enter the holy space that was her body, to spill his seed into the awesome place where man and woman create a new being, according to God's plan.

Mirrel screamed at the pain, and she screamed again when he pulled away from her and she saw the blood that her mother had prepared her for. The widow entered their room and took away the bloody sheet to display to the assembled guests. A half-minute later, as a cheer went up among the crowd at this ceremonial display of the end of virginity and the beginning of woman's role in the world, Mordecai turned to his bride in their little room and kissed her for the first time.

Mirrel's mother had never told her about this. She was astonished at the sensation of his lips on hers. No one had told them about love, and they didn't understand the feeling running through their youthful bodies; they didn't know what part was lust, what part holy, what part a feeling for which there were no words at all.

Mirrel had expected to be slave to a genius, to honor his footsteps, to anticipate and cater to his physical needs so that he could exist in the world of the spirit. Instead, she felt a slave to his physical being. He taught her that she was beautiful, and she taught him that there was a world of endless wonder outside the Talmud. They made love, and they fell in love, and they grew one with love. Mordecai thought nothing of the study house, but only of the pleasures of Mirrel's beauty. Even when she was forced to follow the custom of the Orthodox and shave her head, and wear a wig, so that her beautiful hair would entice no strange man, she still enticed her husband. They lived only for each other. They thought of nothing but their love.

A month after their marriage, though she was not yet twleve years old, Mirrel became pregnant. Because the Talmud states that the fetus lies in the deepest part of the womb during the first three months of pregnancy, making intercourse painful for the mother, Mordecai abstained from lovemaking during this period, regaling his child bride with stories from the Bible: Daniel in the Lions' Den, Joshua and the Battle of Jericho, Joseph and His Coat of Many Colors. From the fourth through the sixth month of pregnancy, the Talmud explains, the fetus moves to the middle part of the womb, and intercourse, though difficult for the mother, is beneficial to the unborn child; and so Mordecai and Mirrel fulfilled their duty as parents, making love constantly, surprised that Mirrel felt no pain. The last three months of pregnancy, when the fetus moves to the top of the womb, was supposed to be an ideal time for intercourse: The Talmud explained that it would be beneficial to both mother and fetus. They made love so frequently that Mordecai's absence from early-morning prayers in the synagogue came to be noted with alarm.

His mother-in-law, who provided their sustenance, and with whom they lived at the little inn, rebuked him. "I thought you were a holy man, Mordecai," she said. "Are you become too holy to go to the *shul* anymore?"

When Mirrel took sick in the eighth month of pregnancy, there was talk in the town of God having punished Mordecai for his lack of religious devotion. Mordecai soon quashed this talk with a zealous appeal to God on Mirrel's behalf: He fasted three days out of every week, ate meat only on the sabbath, stood on his feet from dawn till dusk, rocking in a meditative trance before the Ark of the Law in the synagogue. But every night he returned to his bride to find her worse: pale, breathing with difficulty, with beads of sweat along the bridge of her little nose.

Mirrel delivered a stillborn child at the end of the eighth month of her pregnancy, and died a few hours later. Mordecai sat *shivah*, staying in the home of his mother-in-law for the required seven days of mourning. He spoke to no one, and no one spoke to him; in the house of mourning, it was customary to remain silent until the mourner initiated conversation.

This silence lasted far past the *shivah*—the seven days of initial mourning—through the *shloshim*, the thirty days of mourning, during which one is allowed to sit on an ordinary chair instead of the floor, and may leave the house and return in part to the mainstream of life. Mordecai, though he left the house of his mother-in-law, did not return to his daily routine. He was too young to have a beard, had no profession other than sage, but refused to share his knowledge, even to answer the simplest Talmudic question.

His father, the butcher of Mir, found him another match at once; more than one family had a daughter whom they wished to marry to the genius of Mir. But Mordecai refused to even listen to his father's plea. He was silent not only from grief; he was shaken to the core of his belief in the God of the Torah and the Talmud. He had found a heaven while still in the world, and this heaven had been replaced with torment. It was unspeakably cruel to have learned to love Mirrel, and the pleasures of the flesh, and then to have been thrust back into the world of the study house, intoning the Kaddish, praising God's name.

Mordecai left Mir, and went to the Chief Rabbi of Iwenez. The rabbi told Mordecai that he was too young to understand the ways of the world. He questioned him on difficult points in the Talmud, and was not impressed with Mordecai's answers. "It is not enough to know the words by heart," the rabbi told him. "You are not the first Jew to have that gift. You see the page of Talmud like a picture, and you can bring this picture before your eyes at will. But that does not mean that you understand its deep meaning. If you want to learn solace, you must first learn to be humble before the sages. You must study with an open heart, and an understanding of your own ignorance."

Mordecai remained in Iwenez for four years. When he walked into a room in the Talmud academy, the other students rose, out of respect for his knowledge. Visiting scholars came to Mordecai to ask a question, or pay homage. The Chief Rabbi treated him as if he were his own son. From a total recall of the Talmud, Mordecai progressed to an enormous wealth of understanding. He could cite numerous examples, from various tractates, of decisions about boundaries, moneylending, astrology, the sabbath, marriage. But he came no closer to understanding the reason for his loss of Mirrel, and the inability of knowledge to bring him to the same plane of ecstasy as love.

"There is a love of God," said the Chief Rabbi of Iwenez. "There is a love of God that is stronger than any love of woman. But such a love can't be taught, it can only be experienced. It can't be derived from the pages of the Talmud, it must overtake your spirit. But the *Ruah Ha-Kodesh*, the Holy Spirit, can only enter your soul when you empty your body and mind of the evils of this world. If you want to love God, so that you can experience the ecstasy of his spirit, you must cease looking. You must give up something. You must empty yourself, like a flask filled with impure water. You must empty yourself, and wait for the spirit to fill you with purity and love."

So Mordecai was not to look. He was not to study. He was not to search the endless reaches of his memory, trying to put together a logical commentary to the story of his seventeen years. He was not to try to know God. He was not to think of love.

Following the example of other great men of Iwenez, Mordecai of Mir left the Talmud academy and undertook the penance of Kana, a cabalistic means of self-purification dating from four-teenth-century Spain. Shimon of Iwenez had suffered this pen-ance for five years before joining the Hasidim. Every day Mordecai fasted, drinking no water, eating no food, until the sun had set and he could see the first three stars of the evening. Only then could he eat, and what little food he tasted could not come from a living being: no meat, no milk, no honey. Mordecai ate nuts and berries, and his body grew lean and weak. Yet a strange glow seemed to illuminate his skin, like a power radiating from his heart. Though his experience taught him of the fact of his weakness—the light pack of clothes on his back grew heavier day by day—he felt strong, healthy.

To the penance of Kana he added the penance of Galut, or con-tinuous wandering: Mordecai could stay in no one place longer than two days. The rare Jewish village that learned of his holi-ness—most Jews and Gentiles mistook him for a simple beggar, worthy of contempt—could not honor him for more than forty-eight hours. Even then, it was difficult to honor the penitent. Mordecai slept on the floor of the meanest hovel, or on the bare ground. Only on the sabbath would he break his fast, eating a small portion of carp, to make the sabbath different from the rest of the week.

For six months Mordecai of Mir wandered, fasting every day, ignoring the cold and the damp. It was only the sabbath that pre-vented him from succumbing to illness during that time. Unlike the hordes of beggars drifting from miserable villages to the poorhouses of established towns, Mordecai had the advantage of bathing once a week, in the ritual bath of the Jewish community.

It was ungodly to be filthy at the approach of the sabbath. So while his body grew thinner, and his eyes seemed to be searching a feverish inner tableau instead of the world before his trodding feet, his skin was not covered with sores, festering under layers of dirt.

Still, after all those months, Mordecai came no closer to spiritual ecstasy. He prayed without words, meditating on the beauty of a leaf, the joy of the seasons, the wonder of waking in the morning light. Nonetheless, he could not forget Mirrel's love. Hungry as he was for food, he was far hungrier for his child wife's hands, her little breasts, her belly, her knees, her eyes. Lying under a tree, wrapped in rags against the cold, his lust reached out for her across a hundred nights of dreaming. His clothes, soiled with his sperm, his seed, the stuff of life itself, greeted him in the mornings, reminding him of what he had lost, reminding him of his lack of purity. All that fasting, all that wordless prayer, had not left him an empty vessel, ready to accept God's spirit. All that wandering had not left him too weary to remember his desire for what had been taken, without reason, away from his life.

After six months, the young Mordecai entered the town of Lubtsch, and demanded a meal in the house of the Chief Rabbi. He was questioned on his origins, and then tested on his knowledge of the Talmud. For the first time in half a year, Mordecai ceased dwelling on great abstractions, and called to his mind particular laws from specific pages in various tractates. He had forgotten nothing, and quoted decisions without hesitation from every section of the vast commentaries of the sages.

The Jews of Lubtsch honored him. Mordecai exchanged his rags for a decent rabbi's suit and ate at the Chief Rabbi's table. The richest man in the town prepared a room for him in his house and Mordecai slept on a bed of feathers. Matchmakers approached him from as far away as thirty miles. Letters reached him from the Chief Rabbi of Iwenez, and from his father, the butcher of Mir.

Still, though he ate well, and slept well, and received all manner of honors, Mordecai was depressed. He spoke to no one, unless it was to answer a question. He attended the synagogue and recited the daily prayers, but these words were from memory, and not from his heart. The penance had been difficult, and it had achieved nothing. Mirrel's face, exhausted and beautiful in her last hours on earth, tormented him. He could not go forward with his life until he could understand why she had lost hers.

One day another penitent entered the town of Lubtsch. His name was Elijahu, and he had been found near death by some merchants of the town. Elijahu had fasted daily, had wandered from town to town, and had tormented his body. He had rolled naked in the snow every morning and had plunged himself into a lake covered with a thin sheet of ice. In addition, he tried to stay awake all the time, pinching himself, and propping himself up against tree trunks. The first thing he asked the men around his bed was whether he was dead or alive. When told that he was alive, he burst into tears, ashamed at having slept. Elijahu was brought to Mordecai in a litter, and the genius of Mir wept at the sight of the sick man.

"How long have you been a penitent?" asked Mordecai.

"I only count the days till the sabbath, not the days of the year."

"Don't you observe the holidays of our people?"

"Only the sabbath," said Elijahu. "Sabbath is the only day on which the Lord rested. It is the only day I break my penance. I know nothing else of time—not my age, not the month, not the year."

"And what have you learned?"

"That I am sinful."

"You didn't know that before?"

"I don't know what I knew before. Before I was a penitent, I learned from books."

"And God? What have you learned of God?"

"Nothing, master."

"And desire? What have you learned of desire?"

"Nothing, master," said Elijahu. "All I have ever desired was to know God better, to bring myself closer to him. But I have come no closer, I know God no better, I have failed. I am the same man I always was, only frailer, forced by illness to lie down in the presence of my betters. All I pray for now is to be able to regain my feet, so I can continue wandering, so I can continue my penance until death."

That night, after prayers and the evening meal, Mordecai left the house of his patron and walked out of the town. He felt an enormous hunger, a hunger for knowledge that would appease the pain around him. Elijahu the Penitent was holy, but he was not the sort of man Mordecai wished to be. Mordecai understood that he had come closer to God's heaven in Mirrel's embrace than he could ever hope to by tormenting his body till mindless death. No longer would he grow proud with reciting the memorized knowledge of the Talmud to his fellow Lithuanian Jews; no longer would he grow humble by mortifying his flesh and emptying his mind of thought. Mordecai had resolved to leave penitence to men like Elijahu, and Talmud to men like the Chief Rabbi of Iwenez. He himself would have to take another direction, because all he knew now of the world stifled his soul.

Mordecai became a woodcutter. He traveled from village to village, carrying an ax and offering to cut firewood in exchange for his supper. In this way he traveled through Poland, visiting the Jewish towns for more than two years. He learned many Russian phrases, and purchased an alphabet book where he learned the German, Latin, and Greek letters. Nowhere could he find a Latin grammar, though he had heard that Latin was the language of learned men; the Jews of that part of Europe still thought of Latin as the cursed tongue, the language of the Romans who tore down the Second Temple.

Mordecai was eager to learn, but he allowed the time to pass, because for the first time in his life he had begun to revel in the strength of his body. He swung his ax in the open air, and the local Jews, assuming him to be unlearned, ignored him when he sat in their little synagogues, unobtrusive in the last row from the Ark of the Law.

Traveling through the country of the estates of Prince Radziwill, Mordecai one day fell into the company of a wandering monk. They were each glad of some company and chattered in the way of strangers, trying to pass the time. At nightfall they shared a fire, and Mordecai told the monk of his desire to learn Latin. The monk explained that it was a difficult language to learn; he himself had no knowledge of it, and didn't for the life of him see the necessity of learning it.

The next day they approached the border of a neighboring principality, and Mordecai had to pay the *Leibzoll*, the customs toll required of Jews. Neither the monk nor Mordecai took much notice of this humiliation; there were three hundred borders to cross in the complicated network of territories that made up Poland, Prussia, and the rest of the Germany, and it was common practice at most of them to extract money from each enter-

ing Jew, and for each head of cattle. Still, neither the monk nor
Mordecai had been prepared for the special humiliation of this
principality. After the *Leibzoll* had been paid, the guards at the
customs house demanded a pair of dice from Mordecai.

"I'm not a gambler," said Mordecai.

"But you are a Jew, stupid," said the guard. "Here you pay
with a pair of dice, or with the money to buy them."

"I don't understand," said Mordecai. "What have I got to do
with dice?"

"I think we shall have to teach him," said one guard to the
others. And at once they all fell on Mordecai and began to beat
him.

Mordecai, without thinking of the numbers against him—there
were four guards—began to fight back, using his fists against their
clubs. But though he was far stronger than he had ever been, he
knew nothing about fighting. Almost at once he was knocked to
the ground, and kicked at, and pummeled. Were it not for the
monk with whom he traveled, the genius of Mir might have been
clubbed to death and thrown into a ditch. But the monk ordered
the guards to stop, and they listened to him, preferring to cut
short their fun, rather than risk the wrath of the Church.

"He doesn't know," said the monk, taking Mordecai by the
arm. Later he explained to the young Jewish man that the toll of
a pair of dice was imposed on Jews entering this backward principality, as a symbol of atonement for when the Jews cast lots at
the time of the Passion.

Mordecai didn't know what he was talking about.

"I am talking about Jesus Christ," said the monk, and while
Mordecai knew that this was the name of the Christian god, he
explained that he knew nothing of his story. "Perhaps," said the
monk, half to himself and half to Mordecai, "this is why you
want to learn Latin. Perhaps it is God's will that you come close
to his church."

"I am a Jew," said Mordecai. "I am a Jew who wants to learn
the language of the world's scholars."

But the monk wasn't listening. He knew very well that a Christian who becomes responsible for the conversion of even a single
Jew is granted a place in heaven. "You want to learn Latin?" he
said. "You shall learn Latin, and then you shall be able to learn
of all the works of the fathers of the church."

The monk and Mordecai traveled together for two weeks,

walking all the way to the outskirts of Königsberg, in Prussia, and every day the monk's notion of saving a Jewish soul increased. Not only had he saved Mordecai's life at the border, not only had the Jew approached him to ask about Latin, the language of the Church (even if he, like most Prussian monks, knew none of it), but day by day he began to understand that Mordecai was not a simple Jewish woodcutter. It was obvious that the young man was intelligent, far more intelligent than any Jew he'd ever met. And he was handsome, as handsome as an angel. It wasn't possible that Mordecai and he had met for no reason. It had to have been preordained, a special task prepared for him by God.

The monk took Mordecai to the abbot of the monastery outside Königsberg, and told him of his plan to save Mordecai's soul. Mordecai was given the use of a tiny hut outside the monastery— it was not thought proper for him to use a monk's cell until conversion had been effected—and the abbot assigned a monk to teach Mordecai the rudiments of Latin, as a preparatory inducement to conversion. But within a week, the flabbergasted monk, who could not believe that the Jew was learning the grammar and vocabulary without the help of a demon, went to the abbot for assistance. "He has only to look at a page and he knows it by heart," said the monk, and the abbot soon learned that this was true. Mordecai was brought to the abbot and questioned by him.

"I am a Jew," he told the abbot, "and I have been a teacher of Torah and Talmud. I am not here to be converted, but only to learn what I was never taught. If you can help me, I shall be forever grateful."

Like the monk, the abbot was certain that God had brought Mordecai to him for the purpose of conversion. The Jew had a formidable intelligence; it was clear that Mordecai had only to learn to read Saint Benedict, and Saint Augustine, and Saint Vincent of Lerins, and Saint Thomas Aquinas, and he would be saved. The abbot sat with Mordecai for the next two weeks, reading to him in Latin, teaching him to pronounce the words of the Latin Bible. It was hardly possible, but the abbot was sure that Mordecai carried the spirit of an angel within his breast, speeding him on to great knowledge, whispering the names of words, the meanings of phrases, into his inner ear.

Before the end of a month, the abbot gave Mordecai his copy of Saint Augustine and, quoting him, said: "*Tolle lege, tolle lege!*"

"I shall," said Mordecai, taking the thick volume without

fear. The abbot had simply said, "Take up, read!" and this was not an injunction to convert but simply to absorb what someone else had written, in a language Mordecai had come to understand.

He retreated to his hut with the book, glad of his decision to retain the appearance of a Jew. He had been afraid to shave, and to change his garments, lest the abbot think this a symbol of his desire to convert. Mordecai wanted knowledge at this point; and if this knowledge was at odds with what he had learned in the Talmud academy, he would be prepared to meditate on both sides of the argument. But this was hardly the same thing as wanting to accept the Christian Church.

Mordecai read Saint Augustine through the night. To succor himself against the possibility of being swayed by the writer's brilliance, he recalled the words of Rabbi Meir, who was able to learn much from a heretical teacher. "He found a pomegranate, and he ate the fruit, but cast the rind away." This is what Mordecai would do with Saint Augustine, with the abbot, with the Latin language.

Before dawn, Mordecai woke with a start, the unfinished volume of Saint Augustine open on his lap. There were monks outside his hut, and they were singing. The Latin was strangely familiar, and he realized that he had been hearing the same hymn since his arrival, but now for the first time understood its meaning. "O saving Victim, opening wide/ The gate of Heaven to man below,/ Our foes press on from every side,/ Thine aid supply, Thy strength bestow." Mordecai stood up and grabbed his ax. He had heard about forced baptisms, but didn't think his teacher could be responsible for anything like that.

"Go away!" he screamed at them, as the monks, two dozen of them, grew nearer to the entrance to the doorless hut. "Go away!" he howled, and he leaped out wildly, his ax above his head.

The monks remained where they were, but drew no closer. They continued to intone the hymn, *O Salutaris Hostia*, their faces expressionless, inexorable. All at once, Mordecai realized that he had within himself the possibility of murder. The ax shivered in his hand. He understood that he could crack a man's skull, that he could swing his weapon into the path of anyone who would try to contain his life. Mordecai had learned a little

Latin, but in this moment he learned much more: He might give up the form of Judaism, but never his allegiance to it.

"I am a Jew!" he screamed, and he waved his ax and ran into the monks, who got out of his way. He made good his escape, and killed no one in the process.

Within a day, he sold his ax and bought passage on a ship from Königsberg to Stettin. He worked chopping wood and cleaning stables as he made his way overland from Stettin to Frankfurt. When he found a Jewish village, he made known his rabbinical status and stayed long enough to answer talmudic questions, but only in order to beg for some herring, dry biscuits, perhaps a bit of brandy. Whatever coins he earned, he used to buy books: Lucretius and Virgil and Horace, as well as Latin translations of Aristotle and Plato. He could not speak or understand spoken German well, but his knowledge of Yiddish and his reading of Adelung's *German Grammar* taught him to read the language of the Prussian nation. In Frankfurt—whose five hundred Jewish families were only allowed to marry off five sons a year, to restrict the growth of the Jewish population—Mordecai was able to trade his Latin texts for German books: Sturm's *Physics*, Kulm's *Anatomical Tables*, the German translations of Locke and Bacon, a tattered copy of Leibnitz, a pamphlet about the new work of Kant.

Mordecai became intoxicated with reading. He could not get enough of this new knowledge, for it took his mind to places it had never been, and now it wanted to go everywhere, all at once. He learned geometry and geography, he learned about the politics of Machiavelli, the life of Frederick the Great. The bookdealers of Frankfurt took pity on his worn and hungry appearance and accepted his old books at overvalued prices to make it easy for him to procure new books. One of these bookdealers, a Catholic of Portuguese descent, asked him if he'd ever read Spinoza. The bookdealer lent Mordecai a copy of the *Ethics*, and advised him to go to Berlin. "It is the only place for a young Jew who wants to learn," said the bookdealer.

"I want to learn," said Mordecai, and that night he read in his borrowed Spinoza: "Avarice, ambition, lust, etc., are nothing but species of madness."

Two months later he arrived at the Rosenthaler Gate to Berlin, where the rich Jews of the city had erected a house. Here he was examined by an old religious Jew, who told him that he would have to go on his way, as Jewish paupers were not allowed in the city.

"I am not a pauper," said Mordecai. "I am worth three hundred thalers, because I know the entire Babylonian Talmud by heart."

This extravagant claim proved to be true. Within a day, the rich Jews of Berlin vied for the honor of patronizing the Yiddish-speaking genius of Mir. The honor was won by Phillip Meier, who took Mordecai into his home. He would show his wife that a Jew could be something more than a superstitious peddler, that behind a beard and fur hat could lurk a powerful mind.

CHAPTER FIFTEEN

Mordecai slept for two days and two nights, and woke up with a start. It was dark, and he didn't know whether it was the dark before dawn or the dark just after dusk. He was in a bed, and the room he was in smelled of pine. When he tried to get to his feet, he stumbled, and fell to the floor.

In a moment the room was flooded with light.

"Rabbi, are you all right?" said an old man, running to him from across the great room. The man spoke in Yiddish, with a heavy Prussian accent. He took hold of Mordecai's thin arm and helped him to his feet.

"I am no longer a rabbi," said Mordecai, speaking with a weak voice. As he was helped back into the bed, he remembered that he had collapsed, to his shame, in the presence of Herr Meier and his exalted company.

The old man had pulled back enormous wooden shutters to let in the sunlight. As Mordecai sank back in the bed, he could see the evergreens of a little garden through many panes of sparklingly clear glass.

"Am I still in the home of Herr Meier?" Mordecai said.

"Yes, of course, Rabbi. He was not about to throw you into the street."

"What is this?" said Mordecai, grabbing a bit of the fine fabric of his nightgown. "What is this I am wearing?"

"It is Herr Meier's, Rabbi. It is I who washed you and dressed you. You were in need of cleansing. And as it says in the Talmud, 'Physical cleanliness leads to spiritual purity.'"

"It's true that it says that," said Mordecai, his head clearing after the long rest. "But I prefer the talmudic saying, 'Zeal leads to cleanliness, cleanliness to ritual purity, ritual purity to self-control, self-control to holiness, holiness to humility, humility to fear of sin, fear of sin to saintliness, and saintliness to the Holy Spirit.'"

"Rabbi, my daughter is sick," said the old man, and he got to his knees before the young man on the bed.

"Get up," said Mordecai. "I have already told you, I am not a rabbi."

"Please, Rabbi, don't make fun of an old man. It is well known that you are Rabbi Mordecai of Iwenez. Your fame has spread far. Your ways are strange, but none can deny that you are a holy man. My daughter is sick, and I beg you for your blessing."

"I am not a rabbi, and I am not a holy man," said Mordecai. "And if I am a guest in the house of Herr Meier, I would like to press his hospitality for some food."

The old man tried to kiss Mordecai's hand, but he pulled it away. "Please, Rabbi, if you don't give her your blessing, she will die. She is a mother, with seven children, and she will die without your holy blessing."

"What is going on here?" said a cold, high-pitched voice, speaking in the harsh rhythms of Berlin German. Frau Rachel Meier walked into the room, unescorted, and took hold of the old man's arm. "Get up, you old fool! What do you think you're doing? And how dare you speak Yiddish to this man? He's not here to learn Yiddish, and you're not allowed to speak that filthy language in any case!"

Mordecai didn't understand everything the young woman was saying, but he could see that she was angry, and that the old man was afraid. He started to get out of bed, but then remembered that he was dressed only in a nightgown.

"The old man didn't mean any harm," said Mordecai, as mildly as he could, speaking in his own Lithuanian Yiddish.

"I said don't speak that language!" said Rachel in German, almost as furious with Mordecai as with the old man. Then she remembered that he didn't know German, and she said more slowly: "No Yiddish. You must learn German."

"I learn German," said Mordecai in German, but with so thick a Yiddish accent that the words were indecipherable to Rachel. "Do you know Latin?" he asked, in that language.

"No, I don't understand," said Rachel. Turning to the old man, she said in a tone of command: "Now get out of here at once and bring him something to eat! Hurry!" And she moved him along with a sharp tap on his back.

"Wait," said Mordecai to the old man, and he stopped in his flight from the room and turned to Mordecai.

"I told you to go, you old fool!" said Rachel, but before she could strike at the servant, Mordecai, thin as a spirit, as beautiful as an angel, got out of the bed and stood between her and the old man.

"Please," he said to Rachel in German. And then to the old man he said, in Yiddish, "What is your daughter's name?"

"Deborah," said the old man. "Her name is Deborah, Rabbi Mordecai."

Mordecai put his hands on the old man's head, and the old man lowered his eyes. Mordecai asked for the Lord's blessing on the sick woman Deborah, beloved of a devout father, herself the mother of children in need. The old man raised his head at the conclusion of the blessing, and then knelt before Mordecai, grasping the young man about the knees. Rachel said nothing as the old man finally left the room, his eyes filled with tears of gratitude.

"What was that supposed to be?" said Rachel finally, as Mordecai remained standing, his eyes fixed on a point in space. She took a step closer to the young man and looked unabashedly into his face. He had been bathed and his hair had been washed before the servants had put him to rest in bed; his eyes, whose irises were a lighter shade of green at the bottom than at the top, shone from a frame of lustrous beard, a clean head of wavy hair. "What was that supposed to be?" she repeated. "Are you trying to bring superstition into an enlightened home?"

Mordecai snapped out of his reverie. He had been reproaching himself for pronouncing a blessing when he could feel no communion with God. But even in the heart of the reproach, he could feel the old man's joy. Surely, if God cared not at all what man did on earth, what harm could there be in Mordecai's insincerely offered blessing? Perhaps the greatest rabbis knew this, he thought with a start. Perhaps they all knew that their congregations were praying to an empty sky, filled only with their hopes and dreams. Perhaps the rabbis knew this, and encouraged a deception that could lead to bliss. For a man of great devotion was a happy man. A man who believed in the coming of the Messiah, in God's goodness, in justice for all in the afterlife—this man was happy.

"Why are you looking at me?" said Mordecai in Yiddish. He looked the young woman in the eyes, suddenly reacting to their concern with his own.

"You don't understand me at all, do you?" she said in German.

"I understand," he said, remembering to speak in German, trying to pronounce the terribly accented words as slowly as possible. "I understand, but I can't speak."

"I asked you what you were doing with the old servant."

"I blessed his daughter," said Mordecai in German, but she didn't seem to understand. "His daughter is sick," he said. "And he wanted me to bless her."

"You sound like an old Jew," she said. "I hate the sound of your accent. I shall get you a teacher—you understand what I'm saying? You don't speak French, do you?"

"No, but I shall learn it," he said. "Wait. Do you know Hebrew?"

Rachel blushed. She had been forced to learn Hebrew at an early age—as all the Cohen family always had—and even without use, the early teaching had stayed with her. She could read the Bible in Hebrew, and she could speak, in a stilted, biblical fashion.

"We can't speak the language of the Bible," said Rachel in German. "The religious Jews will have us excommunicated. It is a language for prayer, not talk."

"We can speak it to each other, if it is the only language we share," said Mordecai in Hebrew.

She understood every word. In that language, his accent, broad and Germanic, was identical to hers.

"Welcome to my house," she said, after a lengthy hesitation, the Hebrew words strangely comfortable on her tongue.

"You are the wife of Herr Meier then?" he said in Hebrew.

"Yes."

"I thank you for your hospitality. I am Mordecai of Mir."

"Mir? What is Mir?"

"Mir is the town in which I was born."

"Yes. I didn't understand. I was born here. In Berlin."

"What am I to call you?"

"Frau Meier."

"I want to stay in Berlin. To learn."

"Yes."

"Why do you look at me like that?"

"I don't look at you," said Rachel.

"Yes, you do, Frau Meier."

"It's what you have on your face," she said. She had forgotten the word for beard, and now she made motions as if to shave one off. "Your beard," she said in German.

"My beard," he said, repeating her German. Then, in Hebrew, "I shall shave it, if you want."

"Yes."

"You are young, Frau Meier. Do you have babies?"

"No."

"Who will teach me German?" he said. "Will it be you? I have read a German grammar, and I understand the grammar perfectly, but do not know how it should sound."

"Did you have a wife in Mir?"

"Yes," said Mordecai.

"She did not come to Berlin?"

"She is dead," said Mordecai.

"I'm sorry."

"I don't believe that God cares about us," said Mordecai, in the language of the Bible. He felt his heart race, and a lust for this young woman, alone with him in the great room, thrilled him.

"I will teach you German, if you will be a good pupil."

"There are forty-eight attributes demanded of the good pupil of the Torah."

"So many? What are they?"

"Understanding and discernment of the heart; awe; reverence; meekness; cheerfulness; sedateness; laughter; perseverance, a good heart; faith in the wise; recognizing one's place; rejoicing in one's portion—"

"Stop," she said. "Please. I don't understand all that."

"It's from the Talmud."

"It's not Hebrew?"

"No, it's different."

"You will be a good pupil," she said, and she stepped closer to him, and his heart beat faster, and a flush crept across his beautiful face.

"Yes."

"I am sorry that your wife died. Was she young?"

"She was very young."

"My husband is old."

"He is my savior," said Mordecai. "It is Herr Meier who lets me stay in Berlin."

"It is Frau Meier," said Rachel, "who wants you to stay."

"Thank you," said Mordecai, and then he remembered that lust was a form of madness, and that he was mad.

"You're shaking," said Rachel, speaking in German.

"What?"

"Shaking," she repeated, and Mordecai turned his back to her and walked across the room to a desk under the windows. His heart was beating so hard, it seemed about to leap into his mouth. He grabbed a pen on the desk and dipped it into the inkwell.

"Please," he said in Hebrew. "Can you write the word?"

"Yes," said Rachel, and as she came up to him at the desk, he kept his back to her. His penis was erect, and surely visible through the flimsy nightgown; it seemed to Mordecai that he was about to take hold of the young woman and do with her what he had done with Mirrel. She took the pen from his hand and said in German, "Your hand is shaking, too." Rachel bent low over the desk, and wrote in German: "Why are you shaking?"

"Please," he said, in German, and took the pen from her hand. As he began to write in German, she stood very close to him at the desk, and the smell of her perfume was stronger than incense; the warmth of her body seemed to pass through her clothes directly into his skin. He wrote: "I was shaking because I am mad."

"Yes," she said, almost in a whisper. Her fingers brushed his as she took the pen from his hand. She wrote: "But how can a good Jewish rabbi be mad?"

Mordecai took the pen out of her hand and dropped it on the desk. He looked at her. Her full lips were parted, and it seemed as if they were open to devour him He remembered Mirrel's lips: thin and blue with cold. If beauty was something physical, something that could be decided upon with a glance, this young woman was beautiful, far more beautiful than Mirrel had been. But Mirrel had been a child. Perhaps she would have grown into something as soft, and as wicked, and as wise as this young woman. Mirrel had never expressed anything to Mordecai but her perfect love, her complete devotion. Whatever lust she had felt had been overwhelmed by this love. Mirrel had not wanted to sleep with him to fulfill a carnal desire; her desire was religious, fanatically devout—and Mordecai had been her god.

If Mordecai didn't rush to kiss Rachel in that moment, to crush his lips to hers, it was because he didn't quite understand what was being offered him in those parted lips. It was not love, not as he had thus far experienced it. It was not devotion. But he would have yielded to his own desire, even in that confused moment, had not the old servant returned with his breakfast, and Rachel's husband.

"Good morning, Rabbi Mordecai," said Herr Meier. "We didn't know if you would want to attend to your prayers before eating. We didn't know when you'd want to leave your bed." He motioned to the servant to put down the tray of hot food.

"Tell him what I said, Joseph," said Herr Meier. But as the old man nodded and began to speak, Rachel cut him off.

"No!" she said. "I don't want Yiddish spoken in this house!"

"This is my house, woman," said Herr Meier.

"If it's your house, it's because you have the help of *my* money."

"Your money is my money," said Herr Meier. "You're my wife, and your possessions are mine."

"There is no reason to speak that gutter language in this house," said Rachel, with icy calm. "You don't speak it, your father didn't speak it, and I don't want to live in a house where it's spoken."

"Your father speaks it," said Herr Meier maliciously.

"My father also speaks Latin and Greek."

"Your father speaks Yiddish, and is proud of it," said Herr Meier. "And since neither you nor I speak Latin, we must allow Joseph to ask our guest if he'd like to eat now, in the language of the Jews."

"My husband would like to know," said Rachel in Hebrew, "whether you would like to pray to your God or eat your breakfast."

"Hebrew!" said Herr Meier with amazement. "That's Hebrew you're speaking!"

"It's better to speak the language of the Old Testament, written by poets and scholars, than the language of beggars and peddlers, spoken in ignorance," said Rachel.

"Please tell your husband," said Mordecai, "that I will eat now."

"Your rabbi will eat now," said Rachel.

"I am not a rabbi," said Mordecai. "Your husband doesn't speak Hebrew at all?"

"Not a word," said Rachel.

"Serve Rabbi Mordecai," said Herr Meier to the old man, Joseph.

Before he began to eat, Mordecai said to Rachel in Hebrew: "If you are my teacher, I shall learn very fast."

And Frau Meier did become his teacher.

She had never read Adelung's *German Grammar*, as he had, but reading it through with her, he learned to pronounce the words of her language. He learned to shave, and to sit still while a servant shaved him. She took him in her carriage, pulled by six horses, with two liveried servants riding in front and one behind. Rachel told him about Frederick the Great, about the new fashions from Paris, about the plays of William Shakespeare, about the European colonies in America and Africa, and the savages who lived there. She taught him about silks and satins and velvets, about white marble and polished mahogany and rubies and emeralds and diamonds. Rachel showed him a map of the world that was a hundred years old and full of mistakes; and then she showed him the true world of 1772, with its distant horizons, its unconquered lands.

Mordecai pressed her for information about her family, and she told him how they lived, as *Schutzjuden*, privileged Jews who were allowed to remain with their families in the cities of Frankfurt, Leipzig, Breslau, Dresden, Brunswick, Hanover, Dessau. There was a branch of the family in Vienna, and in several smaller cities in southern Germany. She showed him where Brazil was on the map of the world, where a distant cousin had gone to buy diamonds.

He wanted to know what her father was like, and she told him that he was very wise, but old-fashioned, and believed that the Jews must keep apart from the rest of society or risk assimilation into the Christian world. It was her father who had arranged the marriage between herself and Phillip Meier, a year ago, and she tried to explain the complicated commercial negotiations between the rich Meier family and the richer Cohen family in effecting this union of houses.

Rachel spoke about the poets she knew, about the artists and musicians and aristocrats and theologians; she spoke about opera and theater and architecture; she spoke about the Count von Kauthen and Andreas Wolff, and why the count was shy and the poet forward; she spoke about the life of Voltaire, and the need for enlightenment of the backward world; she spoke about love.

Everything she said he remembered. They spoke only in German after the second day of lessons, and by the second week of lessons his German was as fluent as his Hebrew, his Latin, his Polish, his Yiddish. He read a dozen volumes a week—books of philosophy, mathematics, politics, history. Rachel had started up a thousand curiosities that could not be stifled. He was not thinking of surprising or pleasing his teacher, but only of satisfying his own endless appetite for knowledge. From the moment before her husband had interrupted their first meeting—when Rachel had been sure that the beautiful young man was about to take her into his arms—there had been no hint of passion on his part in anything other than a desire to learn.

After four weeks of lessons, he was exhibited to the world. "He learns everything," she told the Count von Kauthen. "He remembered that I had promised to ride with you this week, and that I had told him you were blond and shy. Anything I tell him he remembers. If he says something incorrectly in German, it is because he remembers an error that I taught him as fact."

"I scarcely recognize him," said the count. "He could pass for a gentleman of old family."

"I *am* of old family," said Mordecai of Mir.

Phillip Meier had invited the Chief Rabbi of Berlin, and he looked suspiciously about the others at table, as if they might be unclean. Besides the count and Rachel, Phillip and Mordecai, there were several decorative cousins, male and female, children of Rachel's converted aunts and uncles; their second generation of Christianity was almost as listless as Rachel's Judaism. In addition, David Cohen, Rachel's older brother, was there, strictly to discuss business. But all heads turned to the handsome young man, who had miraculously taken on the trappings of civilization in the space of a month.

"I *am* of old family," he repeated. "We are all of us from old families. How can a family be anything but old? Don't we all have mothers and fathers? Even a bastard is of old family, even if he doesn't know his name."

"I beg your pardon, sir," said the count. "I was attempting a compliment in my own clumsy way. What I was trying to do was compare your appearance the last time we met to what it is now. *Poetarum licentiae liberiora*—the 'freedom of poetic license,' as Virgil put it."

"Cicero," said Mordecai. "Marcus Tullius Cicero, in his *De Oratore*, part three."

"I'm sure you're right, sir," said Count von Kauthen. "But I really must insist that there is a difference between a family whose history is known and a family whose history is not."

"Your family, for example?" said Mordecai smiling. His voice wasn't angry, and his smile seemed to suggest a friendly feeling for the count, indeed for everyone at the table. But he was angry. And he had little friendliness for those around him, save Rachel, his teacher.

"My family is old, yes," said the count.

"Its history is known?"

"Yes. For four hundred years."

"When did it become old?"

"Excuse me?"

"When did it become old?" said Mordecai. "Four hundred years ago it wasn't an old family, not by your definition. Did it become old three hundred years ago? Or two hundred years ago? How many years does it take for it to be considered old?"

"This conversation is unpleasant," said Rachel. "I think we should discuss something else."

"I think all families are old," said Mordecai. "I am the son of the butcher of Mir, of very old family. We've been Jews for three thousand years. And before that, we were a family, too. Maybe we were kings, maybe we were beggars, but we were a family, and we're related to you. You're my cousin, Count von Kauthen."

"Mordecai," said Herr Meier. "The count's family is of the purest blood."

"There is no such thing as pure blood," said Mordecai. "There is only false pride, and blindness, and vanity. Either all men are brothers, or all men are not created by the same God."

"This must be your work," said Herr Meier, pointing to his wife. "It seems like our genius has been left too long in your salon."

"Your wife has been kept too long in her salon," said Mordecai; and with that strange statement, he got out of his chair at the table before a servant could rush to assist him.

"What on earth is that supposed to mean?" said Frau Meier, but Mordecai wouldn't deign to reply, or even to look at her. His long hair had been brushed back from his forehead, and the ascetic lines of his beautiful face seemed fit for an angry Old Testament prophet. He stomped out of the vast dining room without another word.

"Please forgive me if I am the cause of any of that," said the Count von Kauthen.

"It is we who must beg your pardon, Count," said Herr Meier, "myself and my wife. Mordecai is our guest, and we should have realized he was not ready for company yet."

"Perhaps," said the Chief Rabbi, "he is possessed by a spirit."

Rachel laughed out loud. "Dear Rabbi," she said, "I think it's enough that we've humiliated the Jews by Mordecai's actions in front of our Christian guests, without you adding to their ideas about our manners and superstitions."

"Spirits aren't things of fancy," said the Chief Rabbi. "They are real, and they can destroy a man or woman as easily as you can crush a fly."

"Nonsense," said Rachel.

"Rachel, you're not to speak like that to the Chief Rabbi," said Herr Meier, but Rachel shook her head defiantly.

"I won't listen to superstitious nonsense, no matter from what source. There are no spirits floating around here; there's only a lot of ignorance, and bad manners."

"It's all right, Herr Meier," said the Chief Rabbi. "I'm not offended. Enlightened people don't believe in spirits. I understand their feelings. But they're wrong. Did you see how Mordecai stood up? Like he was pulled from behind. Like he had no control over his body. Did you hear the things he said? The lack of respect? The lack of reason? A spirit has taken control of him. I'm sure of it. Men of genius are always the most prone to attack by evil."

"What evil? What has he said or done that's evil?" said Rachel in a high-pitched voice. It seemed for a moment that everyone at the table, in particular her brother David, was looking at her in a different way.

"I don't think we should criticize him so much," said David Cohen. "The man is obviously under a great strain. From what my sister tells me, he's absorbed a year's study in four weeks, and he never sleeps. Even if he's been a scholar all his life, nothing could have prepared him for Berlin. I think our hosts have done a work of mercy in bringing such a brilliant man into such a comfortable home."

"And I think," said Count von Kauthen, "that our hostess should be especially commended for what she's done in instructing the man. I have never seen anything like it in all my life. Even the most brilliant man in the world couldn't have learned to speak German so well without such a brilliant teacher."

"Aren't you gentlemen here to discuss diamonds?" said Rachel. Suddenly, she caught a hint of what had brought on Mordecai's anger: Everyone about her was slow, and obtuse, and given to formal speeches rather than impulsive thought. Mordecai had left because he was a man of passion, and all about him were men and women of cold, plodding spirit. All these weeks he had been devouring volume after volume, thought after thought, sensation after sensation; his world was changing before his eyes, in his heart. He must have felt like an animal trained for a circus and put on display before creatures worthy only of scorn. And so scorn was what Mordecai had given them all. Rachel wanted to get out of her seat and tell him that she was not part of the company at table; that she was not like them, she was not cold, she was as full of passion as her pupil.

"This is not a business meeting, my dear," said Herr Meier. "I am grateful to the Count von Kauthen for his help with Prince Alexander."

"Please, please, Herr Meier," said the count, "I have done nothing."

"The only reason the count is here with us is to let us have the pleasure of his company."

"The Count von Kauthen is my friend," said Rachel. "He's

at our table tonight because he's getting you a contract with his uncle, the prince. My brother is here because he knows more about diamonds than all of us, and that's what your contract with Prince Alexander is all about."

"Rachel, please," said Herr Meier with a pleasant voice, and a face that seemed to be twisting itself into a fist.

"That is why I'm here," said David Cohen. "The count understands that, I'm sure. This is not my sister's salon."

"There are women present," said the count. "Perhaps we should wait until the brandy."

"There are sometimes women present who have things to say worth listening to," said Rachel, touching the Cuheno diamond hanging from a chain about her neck.

"Of course," said the count. "I was simply trying to spare you and your cousins the boredom of a discussion about the price of gems."

"I want to discuss the price of gems," said Rachel. "My family's fortune is in gems, particularly in diamonds, and if no one listens to me, we all stand to lose a great deal of money."

"We're listening," said David Cohen.

"The Brazilian diamonds are destroying the price of diamonds," said Rachel. "A diamond is only as valuable as it is rare." She touched the Cuheno diamond. "This is beautiful and strong, and if there were a million like this, they would all be beautiful and strong, too—but they would no longer be valuable."

"There is only one diamond like that in all the world," said her brother.

"True," said Rachel. "But diamonds are coming into Europe in too great a supply. People are buying them too cheaply. Every diamond that we sell today for a thousand guldens we could sell for ten thousand, too. It's all a question of how we control the market. As long as people think there's a limitless supply of diamonds pouring into Europe, the price is going to be low. As long as every jeweler in Germany is selling diamond rings to little shopkeepers, we're losing money. The count's uncle wants to use diamonds to protect his currency. We can't do that for him until we protect our diamonds ourselves."

"How are we supposed to do that?" said Phillip Meier, looking at her with exasperation. "Lock them up in a secret safe? How can you protect something's price when everyone else in the business is selling them cheap?"

Rachel looked at her husband as if he were a fool. It was not enough that he was thick and methodical, stolid and dispassionate; with all these businesslike qualities, he was not even a good businessman. "You have to see to it," she said, looking from her husband to her brother, "that no one else sells diamonds at a cheaper price than you do."

Herr Meier laughed at this, as if his wife were saying something outside the realm of possibility. But he realized that David Cohen was listening to Rachel with more than brotherly interest.

Rachel went on. "The Cohen family brings in diamonds from India and Brazil. We've been cutting stones in Amsterdam for three hundred years. We've controlled the diamond trade routes for longer than that. Almost every other family in Europe with an interest in diamonds is related to us by marriage. Even some of the Christians who deal in gems are related to us. But most of the men who buy and finish and sell diamonds are Jews. The most powerful among them can organize them. We are the most powerful among them."

"There are more powerful families than ours," said Phillip Meier. But David Cohen cut him short.

"Rachel is talking about the family of her birth. Our father's family. There is no family more powerful than the Cohens in diamonds—not in Prussia, nor among the Dutch or English. Perhaps Rachel is right."

"I *am* right," said Rachel. "If we fix a price for a diamond of a certain weight, anyone who sells the stones will benefit. If we all compete, we all lose."

"What of the political implications?" said Count von Kauthen. It was the first question he'd raised since Rachel had initiated the discussion. "Won't there be powerful men, kings and princes, who will resent the increase in price of what they buy for their queens and their treasuries?"

"They shall have to understand, Count," said David Cohen, "that it is better for them to buy a stone that will retain its value, no matter how many new mines are discovered in Brazil."

"Of course," said Rachel. "No one ever thought that diamonds would be found anywhere outside of India. Even when the boats came back from Brazil with the first New World diamonds, fifty years ago, there were diamond dealers who wouldn't buy them— they were certain that if they weren't Indian, they couldn't be true diamonds. My father tells a story of a cousin from Amsterdam who traveled three months to Brazil, spent half the year there buying diamonds, and sailed back to Portugal, and from there to India itself, all the while keeping his Brazilian diamonds. When he returned from India, he sold the Brazilian stones at an enormous profit, passing them off as diamonds from the Indian mines.

"But those days are over. People can't see the difference between Brazilian and Indian diamonds. And everyone knows that diamonds are flooding in from the New World. You can't sell diamonds embedded in the lid of a snuffbox and hope to sell the same stones as the rarest and most valuable gems in the world. We will have to buy up the diamonds now on the market and sell them only to kings and princes. We have to hoard diamonds till the demand for them blows up their price. And if we have political problems, as the count wonders about, then we shall have to look to good and powerful friends, like the count, and Frederick the Great, and the French and English kings, to understand and protect our prices, so that we may all benefit."

"Where are you going?" said Herr Meier, for Rachel had suddenly gotten to her feet, and now all the men at the table had to get to theirs.

"I am going to leave you to discuss your business," said Rachel.

"But is that all?" said Herr Meier. "Have you nothing else you wish to tell us? Surely what you've begun so well you must want to continue."

"No," said Rachel. "I have already told you what I think. I shall leave you, who have the power to act, to decide what to do with my ideas. The count is right. There are some things that should wait for the men to be alone with their brandy. Excuse me."

Rachel walked quickly away from the table, leaving a husband more alive with the possibilities of what she had said than with the humiliation of having been lectured by his wife. She ran down the wide steps from the first to the main floor of the great house, not consciously following in Mordecai's steps but aware that her sharp suggestions to her husband and brother were a reaction to the way in which Mordecai had taken leave of them. If she had browbeaten them, she had done so in a language they could understand: the language of business. If she had wanted to express dissatisfaction, she had done so by taking them to task on matters for which they were responsible. If they could not be poets, like Andreas Wolff, or men of genius, like Mordecai, they could at least be swift and sure in the area where her family had always been preeminent, otherwise they were assimilating in the worst way—into mediocrity.

It was particularly repulsive, she thought, that her Jewish husband remained stubborn and strong in his resistance to conversion although he had nothing Jewish about him, no reason for his faith. He was not only assimilated in his dress, his speech, his culture; he was assimilated into the safe, boring confines of a family of inherited wealth.

Rachel's family had always made their fortune by virtue of their position on the edge of society, not safe within it; each generation was like a rebirth, as the forces of history had moved them from land to land. She not only loathed the Jews of Eastern Europe, embarrassingly backward in custom and dress, she loathed the Jews of Berlin who refused to accept the modern world, who fancied themselves different when they were just as boring and dull as everyone else. Had Rachel's father been younger, he would have seen, in a moment's reflection, what her brother had not; all this clever talk of controlling the diamond trade would be obvious to anyone with a true stake in the world. But Samson Cohen, Rachel's father, now was more concerned with the world-to-come, and thought only of his daughter's heretical pronouncements and hatred of Jewish superstition. And David Cohen had not been brought up to be fast on his feet; he had been brought up to be a rich man's son, heir to a great fortune of a great family. He was not worried enough to have a mind like a razor's edge.

Rachel wondered why she was different. She was a rich man's daughter, a rich man's wife; but she was fast, and she was not satisfied with what she had. Perhaps it was because she was a woman, she thought. Perhaps that was the source of her strength. Her womanhood kept her at the fringe of society still. She was not safe; she was still the property of her husband, traded to him by her last owner, her father. Her opinions were offered at her hazard; she might either be scolded for being out of order, or laughed at for being frivolous. Perhaps that's why she had to have an edge! It let her have a chance at being heard, it gave her an outlet to express her dissatisfaction with the world. If she was not sharp when she finally was heard, she would be just another silly woman offering foolish complaints from a bed of roses. Still, if this explained her sharpness, it did not explain her passion; and it did not explain the fury she'd felt when Mordecai had left the dining room—the fury and the shame.

Suddenly, as she entered the library, she heard someone call out her name: Not "Frau Meier," and not the harsh German-accented variation of her first name; someone called out, "Rachel," in Hebrew, the way her father had always pronounced it, and the sound was urgent, a cry. She turned to see Mordecai staring at her with his beautiful, intelligent eyes, staring at her with pity and hate, jealousy and love, staring at her with passion.

"Rachel," he said. "You love the Count von Kauthen. Why didn't you tell me that you love the Count von Kauthen?"

She didn't understand why he used her Hebrew name, but everything else was perfectly clear to her. Everything flashed through her, and it was as if she could suddenly see through a night that had been black and heavy with fog.

"Mordecai," she said. "I don't love the count."

He reached out and touched her hand, his fingers deathly cold, his eyes burning into her as if he hoped to find some eternal secret locked in her soul. "Rachel," he said, and he dropped her hand, and was no longer gentle. His body, almost as thin as when he had finished his six months of daily fasting, was surprisingly strong; he took hold of her hips and pulled her lower torso to his, like a demon, a ravaging incubus.

She kissed him, not to slow down his lovemaking but to express an urgent need of her own: She had to kiss that beautiful face; she had to pull at the thick hair that fell over his forehead; she had to press her breasts against his hard, flat chest; she had to force her tongue between his clenched teeth. Her eyes open, she watched his open and close in a mad, involuntary rhythm as his penis swelled and rubbed against her groin. She wanted to ask him if he was mad, if he loved her; if this was an expression of contempt, or desire. His hand grabbed at the tight bodice of her French-made dress, grabbed at her breasts and pulled at the silk fabric. She wanted to tell him that it was madness, what they were doing—dangerous, stupid. But the madness and the danger made her stupid with passion, and all she'd ever wanted was to be passionate, without a thought running in her head; to be instead a wild, driving force.

They fell onto the carpeted floor of the library, beneath a wealth of leather-bound volumes, summaries of all that men have thought and aspired to in five languages, over three thousand years. Mordecai held her, caressed her, and Rachel kissed his eyes.

Upstairs the men talked about diamonds, and Rachel's female cousins retired to the salon, talking of the perfect beauty of the young man from Lithuanian Poland. Rachel was nineteen, and Mordecai of Mir a little older; they made love clumsily, like the children they were. In their youth, and in their passion, there was no way for them to see the danger that was forming, dark and mysterious, and of their own creation.

CHAPTER SIXTEEN

Later that night, Phillip Meier got drunk. It was one of the many qualities that Rachel's father thought of as Gentile in his daughter's husband. To Samson Cohen, to assimilate into Christian society meant accepting moral sickness, drunken and riotous behavior, a disregard for scholarship, and a love of war. "There must be rabbis who drink," Rachel used to tell her father, only half believing it. But Samson Cohen thought of the Jewish law as a preventative of disease, physical and spiritual; eating pig was as bad for the body as lighting a fire on the sabbath was bad for the soul.

Rachel lay in her bed in her large, overheated room, wondering what her father would think of Mordecai. Here was a young man so learned in Jewish tradition that he had been accepted as a rabbi, a teacher, among the most Orthodox, from the age of twelve. And yet he was a deist, as much as she was; he believed with Spinoza that the Five Books of Moses were written by many men, and not by Moses, as dictated to him by God. But in conflict with his deism, he called her by her Hebrew name, took pride in his Jewish birth. He would not pray if he could no longer feel that a god listened to his words, but he would not reject the fact of his birth, and believed that the Jewish people were something worth saving. Anyone who converted to Christianity for the sake of social acceptance was a hypocrite and a coward, according to Mordecai. It was one thing to exclaim that your religion was outmoded and your people degraded by the weight of oppression; it was something else to be humiliated by their presence, and long for a life apart from them.

And now she had made love with him.

All their talk, the questions and answers, the love song of student and teacher, had been a prelude to their lovemaking in the library. She had taught him to pronounce German words. He had taught her to believe that Jews could be brilliant, that Jews could be proud. He had wanted to learn, to fill the empty part of his soul. But only lovemaking could fill that emptiness, and when they had come together, they were no longer teaching and learning, no longer representatives of different camps of the Jewish world; they were a couple, united on the wings of an identical impulse. Passion was what they had together, what they longed to live with, what even at that moment was making Rachel twist and turn in her bed; reason was what kept her there, for a moment longer, enumerating the dangers of going to Mordecai in the middle of the night.

But passion won.

As she got out of bed, she reminded herself that Phillip was drunk and impossible to wake, and the servants would say nothing to their master; in the Meier home, they had far more to fear from Frau Meier. She washed her face with cool water, dabbed her neck with perfume. What difference did it make if Phillip did know? she thought. This was not to be the last time with Mordecai. She had to see him constantly, to feel his heart beating against hers. He was beautiful, he was wise, he was brave; he was a man who had suffered, and had been reborn, and she had been a part of that rebirth. This love she felt was greater than poetry, greater than lust.

Yes, she wanted to feel him inside her again, she wanted to feel the waves of passion rise up to the point of breaking, and stay there, lost between heaven and earth, stay there in an unbearable expectation, stay there while she felt his eyes hot on her body, reading through her mind and soul, stay there till his own desire broke into a thousand movements, a thousand bits of pain and bliss, stay there and break; all at once, she'd come to life, her brain bending back to infinity, feeling older and younger than ever she'd felt before. What difference did it make if Phillip found out? He'd have to know. Rachel wanted Mordecai for her own, and she knew that she would have to leave her husband, no matter what the consequences.

Mordecai slept on the ground floor, in a room next to the housekeeper's. Rachel walked through the dark in a fog of expectation, her bare feet warm on the carpeted floor of the hallways between three drawing rooms and her shut-up little salon, and then cold on the stone floor of the conservatory. Out of breath, she opened Mordecai's door and found him hunched over a book, a candle burning, sitting cross-legged on the bed. But he was not reading. She could see at once that his eyes were somewhere else, not on the text before him, and his back swayed back and forth, as if acceding to some interior rhythm, perhaps the rhythm of an ancient Hebrew prayer.

Rachel took the book from him, and he looked up at her, not in surprise but in calm, measured understanding. "I wanted you to come," he said.

Rachel blew out the candle, and they made love. It was late, and their first exhaustion had long since passed. Their bodies were in a state of excitement that was dreamlike. They shut their eyes against the dark, and where before their lovemaking had been urgent, it was now gentle, hovering between bright sensations and dark spaces of quiet, like an interlude between images, stepping through a dream. They made love, and she fell asleep in his arms, but only for a minute. Mordecai watched her, watched her face grow childlike as it sank into sleep; even in the nearly total dark, he could see the lines of her face soften, relax, return to a moment of perfect peace. He lit the candle, and she woke.

"Will you leave your husband?" he said.

"Yes," she said.

"I have been thinking where we can go."

"Paris," said Rachel, and at once he could see the lines forming, the childishness vanish. In the sounding of the name of that sophisticated city, she was at once the young woman of the world, of the salon.

"Not Paris," he said. "We don't want a place filled with dandies. We're not running off to go to balls, Rachel. If we run, we run to be free."

"We can be free in Paris," she said. "You don't know what it's like there. It's the most enlightened court in Europe."

"You don't understand," he said. "You don't understand what it means to leave your husband and to come away with me. You don't know what you'll have to leave behind."

They didn't talk more that night. And in the morning, when she woke up past noon in her own bed, it seemed scarcely possible that she had told the young man from Lithuanian Poland that she would leave her husband, her riches, her name, and run off with him. It seemed even more absurd that she had proposed running off to Paris. If she left her husband, she would leave her place in society; and only under the protection of a rich nobleman could she hope to enter into any aspect of life in Paris. As Mordecai's mistress, she would be relegated to a life she could scarcely imagine. She wondered if she could bear living with him in a wretched hovel while he earned their bread by teaching, or even by the labor of his hands.

Later that day, while sitting alone in her room, her husband entered, with a curious expression on his face. "I'm sorry if I was drunk last night. I didn't do or say anything wrong to you, did I?"

"No, Phillip," she said, realizing that he must have confused the previous evening with another in his memory, when, drunk and slobbering, he had come into her room and tried to rape her. "You let me sleep in peace."

"I wondered why you didn't come down for breakfast."

"I was tired. I was up reading late."

"Like your pupil," he said. But there was no sarcasm in his voice. "Do you know he came to see me an hour ago?"

"To see you?" she said, trying to keep her voice level.

"Yes. It seems he's getting tired of scholarship. From rabbi to deist to businessman."

"Businessman? What on earth are you talking about?"

"He wanted to know about diamonds."

"He might have asked me," said Rachel.

"You flatter yourself too much, my dear," said Phillip. "Rabbi Mordecai was my discovery. If it had been you who examined him at the Rosenthaler Gate, you'd have thrown him back onto the road from the city. It just goes to prove my point to you! There's plenty of Yiddish being spoken by wise men."

"What did he want to see you for? Precisely, I mean."

"Brazil."

"What?"

"He's curious about the diamond mines in Brazil. He wanted to know if he could work at all on the accounts coming in from the mines. His mathematics is excellent. I'm going to use him as a bookkeeper."

"No, you're not!" she said, her voice breaking. "How dare you even say such a thing? You're supposed to be his patron! He's a scholar, not a servant! He's only begun to learn the great plays! The great poems!"

"Rachel," said Herr Meier, "he wants to work as a bookkeeper. I told him he could. That's all there is to it. I thought you'd like to know, but the matter is not open to discussion. Oh—thank you again for your performance yesterday. You said some interesting things."

"Excuse me," she said. "I must talk to Mordecai."

"Mordecai is working," said Herr Meier with a laugh. "He's studying our accounts already. I don't think he wants to be disturbed."

When Rachel stood up, her husband blocked her way. "But I'm not working," he said.

"Will you let me pass?"

"I want you," he said. "Right now."

"No," said Rachel.

"What?" he said. "What do think you're saying to me?"

"I don't want to, Phillip."

"You can't refuse me."

"Please let me pass," she said again, and tried to move past him.

He grabbed her wrist and twisted her arm. "No," he said. "You're my wife. No matter how rich or how beautiful or how young, you're still my wife."

Phillip took her to her bed, and she was forced to submit, lying flat on her back, her eyes on her future. He made love to her quickly, without any other thought but his own need to master her.

That night he got drunk again, but it was two days more before Rachel could gather the courage to go to Mordecai's room.

"If we don't go to Paris, where do we go?" she said to him a week later, when they were alone in her salon, reading Lessing.

"I'm not sure," he said.

"Brazil?"

"Your husband told you?"

"He told me that you're more interested in Brazil than any other part of the business."

"Brazil is wild," he said. "It's jungle, Rachel."

"I can't stay here like this."

"I can only go to a place where I can be accepted for what I am. That is why I am thinking of the New World. I think of it for us, but I don't know. I don't know if you could stand it."

"I could stand anything better than this."

"Rachel," he said. "You must understand. I want to go somewhere where Jews are accepted."

"You don't look Jewish—any more than I do. I don't see how someone who doesn't pray, who doesn't wear a skullcap, who doesn't care about God, can take so much concern over being born Jewish. We can go anywhere if we have a little money. No one will have to know who we are."

"I don't want to hide what I am."

"You're a scholar. You're the handsomest man in the world. You're gentle. You're brave. I'll call you something other than Mordecai. Perhaps Frederick. You look like a Frederick. I can be Dorothea or Marie. I like Marie."

"I am a Jew, Rachel," he said. "A Jew should be able to be anything. And if I can't be what I want in Europe, then we shall have to think about the New World."

"But what do you want to be?" she said. She could not know how all his life had been a search for passion, filled with little moments of spiritual clarity: when he had learned the Torah, and understood that, if all men were good, the kingdom of heaven would be one with the earth; when he had made love with Mirrel, becoming a man in the same breath, understanding passion to be superior to reason; when he had given up his penitence, understanding that one couldn't hope to appeal to God on a human level; when he had learned to read in new areas, when Spinoza had taught him that God existed but did not concern himself with humanity; when he had learned that all religions were invented by men.

"I want to be free," he said.

"Free?" she said with exasperation. "But what does being

Jewish have to do with being free? It's not as if you want to observe the Jewish law. You're free right now in Berlin."

"No," said Mordecai. "I am not a protected Jew. I am not allowed to settle here. I could not legally marry here. I could not buy a house. I could not enter a university. I could not make love to a Christian woman. That is not free."

"But then do not announce your Judaism. I'm not even asking you to hide it. Just do not announce it."

"My name is Mordecai of Mir."

"You can be Frederick. We can get your papers, birth certificates—even a certificate of baptism. With money, you can do anything."

"Are you listening, Rachel?" said Mordecai. "Do you know who you're talking to? Don't you understand that I've rejected living like an Orthodox Jew but I haven't rejected my whole life? I am the son of a Jew and the grandson of a Jew, and I am proud of the Torah and I am proud of the Talmud. Our books are holy, not because they were inspired by God but because they were inspired by men. Our men. Jews. I am a man who has the Talmud and the Torah by heart, in my mind, in my soul. I don't believe in the world-to-come, and I don't believe in devils and demons, but I do believe in the brilliance that is there. My mind is sharp, and it was made sharp by who I am, where I come from. I am not an accident, not a man without roots, who came out of the air.

"And you, Rachel, you with all your fine German and black hair, who do you think you are? We are a people, Rachel, and if you want to run away with me, you must know that you are to run closer to Judaism. Wherever I go, I will not disguise—to myself or to others—who I am. The Count von Kauthen is my cousin, because we are all men, no matter when his tribe came down from the North and embraced a new god, but if he is proud of his four hundred years, I am equally proud of my three thousand. I am Mordecai of Mir, Rachel, and my father is a ritual butcher, and my first wife shaved her head when we were married—married as children. And if I reject eating ritual meat, and I reject the customs of a wife shaving her head or covering her hair, it doesn't mean I reject my origins."

Mordecai had come closer to her now, and held her hands, and fixed her with his eyes. "I want to be free," he said. "Free to read and understand something of why I am here on this earth. Free to make love to you, though you are another man's wife. Free to ignore old customs and create new forms, new fashions, in which to honor our past. I want to be free, and I can't be free by lying about who I am and how I came to be."

He had finished his speech with such force that Rachel felt she must answer him, even if it was only to acknowledge his words.

"I love you," she said. "But I am not what I am because I'm a Jew. I am what I am in spite of being Jewish. I am a prisoner in a Jewish frame, and I wish you could see that you are, too. I wish you could know what I know. I wish you could see that we are exceptions, you and I, people who were born without connections to their past, people who were born only for the future."

"Rachel," he said, saying her name in Hebrew, "I am much wiser than you. No Jew can ever forget where he comes from, no matter what he says. Neither you nor the world will ever fully let you alone with your lie."

Rachel didn't answer him at once. She was too confused to make a statement, and too afraid. She was not afraid because she believed him; she was afraid because she knew him to be firm in his useless convictions.

"I don't believe you," she said finally. "But I will follow you." It was at once the weakest and the strongest thing she'd ever said.

"If you follow me, you'll learn to believe me," he said.

A week later, it was Mordecai's idea to seek out the assistance of Rachel's father. Rachel did not think it wise, but both knew that the situation in the Meier home could not continue without some explosion: Mordecai, working in Phillip's office, growing more insolent to Phillip as he saw his clumsy treatment of Rachel; Rachel unable to conceal her distaste for her husband; the affair no longer a secret to any of the great house's servants.

"But what on earth do you expect my father to do?" she said.

"He is a religious man, a man who knows some Talmud," said Mordecai. "I can talk to him in his language."

"Talk to him of what?"

"Talk to him of what we want to do in terms of Jewish Law," he said.

But what this was, Rachel couldn't imagine. Certainly no Talmudic law could sanction their affair, allow for a love between a man and another man's wife; or allow for a divorce simply because a wife no longer could bear life with her husband. She envisioned her father, whom she hadn't seen in months: Samson Cohen wore a black silk skullcap while in his own home on the Wilhelmstrasse, and the black stood out sharply on his white hair. He had been in his late forties when Rachel was born, and she had always thought of him as old; it had been an irony that his much younger wife died before he.

In the end, Rachel agreed, and she and Mordecai set out in her carriage for the Cohen house. On the way Rachel asked if they could change direction; she needed time to prepare for the visit.

"Listen," said Mordecai. "There is nothing to fear. Either he will help us with the Chief Rabbi, and with money, and with a passage to some safe place, or he won't. In either case we shall be better off than we are now. In either case we shall be together, and we're not together now."

As forcefully as he expressed himself at that moment, Mordecai still allowed Rachel time to calm herself. They drove to the Forum Fredericianum, with its opera house and palaces, and Rachel chattered about the low cupola of the Hedwigskirche, as if a description of its stately beauty would chase away her fears. Of the residences connecting the great forum to the Royal Castle, she liked Prince Henry's the best. Only last month, Count von Kauthen had promised to escort her to Henry's palace and introduce her to the prince. Rachel remembered the flush of satisfaction she'd felt when hearing the invitation. It seemed incredible to her now that she could have cared so much about something so shallow.

They drove about the Zeughaus, the famous arsenal of Berlin designed by Andreas Schulter, himself a distant relative of her friend Andreas Wolff. Andreas had interested her once, too, she remembered, looking at the statues of dying warriors, valiant in their last breaths, all about the Zeughaus. He had seemed to her to have been capable of anything from war to poetry, from patriotic sacrifice to amoral dissolution. She had thought him romantic, and free of any resemblance to Jewishness. She had thought of Jewishness then as something closed-in, unintelligent, unattractive. But when she looked at Mordecai, next to her in the carriage, she saw a Jew who was none of these things, and who clung to the fact of his Jewishness with all his strength.

When they were admitted into her father's presence, she started at the sight of him. His skullcap had always seemed to push him down, hunch his back, make him a slave compared to the more fortunate, bareheaded Gentiles of the world. Now his old, sharp-eyed face, looking coldly past her to Mordecai, reminded her of how much she had hated him, and for how long. Samson Cohen opened his arms for her, remaining in his chair. She walked quickly into his embrace and kissed the white-bearded cheek. Then she stepped back from him, returning to Mordecai's side.

"Father, may I present Mordecai of Mir," said Rachel, and before Mordecai could execute a little bow, the old man had shot out of his chair.

"Rabbi Mordecai?" he said. "You're not Rabbi Mordecai of Mir and Iwenez?"

"Yes," said Mordecai. "But I do not call myself a rabbi, sir."

"But Mordecai!" said Samson Cohen with a note of wonder. "The genius of Mir who lives in your house!"

"Yes, Father," said Rachel. "This is he."

"It is an honor to have you in my house, Rabbi Mordecai," said Samson Cohen, but he was looking askance at the young man: This was a rabbi dressed like a German dandy, without a wig, or a covering for his head, without any look of piety at all. How could the legends of this rabbi's genius be true? He looked too thin for struggle, too pretty for scholarship.

"Sir," said Mordecai, "so that there shall be no misunderstanding, I want to say once again, once and for all, I do not consider myself a rabbi. In Poland, most of the young men in towns such as I come from are rabbis. It is a term that refers to a certain standing in the community, based on spiritual zeal and the accumulation of knowledge. I retain my knowledge of Torah and Talmud, but I have no spiritual zeal. I do not pray in the synagogue. If you were to offer me the honor of reciting the blessing over a glass of wine in your house, I would refuse to accept the honor. I am not a rabbi, sir."

Samson sat down in his chair, his eyes turning from the intense young man to Rachel. "Are you well, child?" he asked, retreating to a question with no meaning. He could not imagine why his daughter was here, and why she had come with this man. "I am well, so you needn't ask. It is a shame that you come here so seldom. Here, too, we serve the fancy food of the French, my dear. White bread and asparagus, cauliflower and artichokes. Mordecai speaks excellent German. Perhaps you would like to explain why it is that you've come?"

"I want to divorce my husband," said Rachel.

Samson picked up his skullcap, as if some interior force had necessitated its being driven into the air. Then he replaced it on his head and stared at his daughter. "Is it because you are childless?" he said.

"No."

"Because that is not sufficient reason. Not after only one year of marriage. You're just nineteen, though you pretend to act the great lady of forty-five. This is a great marriage you're talking about, Rachel. There are few Jewish families greater than the Meiers. How can you think about divorce when you've hardly been together long enough to know the man? Children will come, mark my words."

"This has nothing to do with children, Father."

"You're sure?"

"Yes."

"Why does he want to divorce you then?" he said.

"I don't know if Phillip wants to divorce me, Father. I haven't asked him. I'm telling you that *I* want to divorce *him*."

"You?" said Samson Cohen, perplexed for a moment, then beginning to understand and growing angry. "You want to divorce your husband? Just like that?"

"I want to divorce him—yes."

"A woman can't divorce her husband, you know that."

"No, I don't," said Rachel. "I think she can."

"Still the same!" said her father. "Still telling me what you can and cannot do! I can see where that's all gotten you! I bring you the twenty most promising Jewish bachelors in the city, and you choose Phillip Meier."

"I made a mistake, Father."

"A mistake! You think you can say that it's a mistake and that'll be the end of it? I should have selected your husband for you and not given you a choice. You would have been happy with Nathan Raphael."

"He was a typical backward fanatic!" she screamed, forgetting that Mordecai was standing next to her.

Her father got out of his chair and towered over her. "And

Phillip Meier wears his hair like a Prussian and eats pig in the morning, and now you want to divorce him! Why? Isn't he Gentile enough for you? What do you want now? To marry a bishop?"

"She wants to marry me," said Mordecai of Mir.

"You," said Samson, turning from Rachel, and looking at the intense young man with an expression of wonder. "My daughter wants to marry you?"

"Yes, sir."

"That is why you are here."

"Yes."

"Who are you?" said Samson Cohen, looking at him as if he might be a friend.

"What?"

"Who are you if not a rabbi? Who are you if not Rabbi Mordecai of Mir? What is your family? What is your name? What is your position? If you are no longer a rabbi, are you still a Jew?"

"He is a Jew, Father," said Rachel with surprising force, but Samson Cohen turned on her with violence.

"Quiet, girl! You've given me enough misery! Now that I know why you're here, I shall be the one to speak, the one to ask questions!"

"No," said Mordecai. "I am afraid I cannot allow that, sir."

"You?" said Samson Cohen. "Who are you to tell me what to do in my own house?"

"I am a man who knows Torah and Talmud. And I know that we have a right, both of us, to be treated with respect."

"Respect? You had better treat me with silence. As it says in the Talmud, 'Silence is good for the wise, how much better for the foolish.' You had best be quiet and never breathe a word of this nonsense to another soul. Phillip Meier is my daughter's husband. He would never want to divorce her, not when he profits so much from my house. And the Talmud says, 'A woman may be divorced with or without her consent, but a man can only be divorced with his consent.' "

"That is a stupid law," said Rachel.

"Don't you dare call the Talmud stupid!" said her father. "You won't stay another minute under my roof if you call the Talmud stupid!" His eyes condemned them both as evil.

"Herr Cohen," said Mordecai, "you've quoted the Talmud,

and so shall I. 'If one has a bad wife, it is a religious duty to divorce her.'"

"Herr Meier will never divorce my daughter," said Samson Cohen. "And I shall see to it that you don't last the day in Berlin."

"Are you a God-fearing man, Herr Cohen?"

"Of course I am," he said. "No man or spirit can change that in me."

"Then you shall have to listen to what I say," said Mordecai. "It is not a question of desire only, it is a question of right."

"If you are no longer a rabbi, you had better not lecture me on the talmudic law."

"I am not a rabbi, but I have the authority of a sage. And the Talmud tells you that the curse of a sage, even if not deserved, will come to pass."

"I am not afraid of your curses, or of your wisdom."

"Do you know the penalty for immorality in the daughter of a priest?"

"Stoning," said Samson. "Death by stoning."

"You're wrong, sir. Death by burning. It's in the Sanhedrin tractate, section seven. Do you know how that death by burning was carried out?"

"Yes, of course," said Samson. "I am a learned man."

"Tell me, as you are a learned man."

"Molten lead was poured down the throat."

"No," said Mordecai. "That is the remark of one who studies only on the sabbath. That is the common misconception. The Talmud tells us quite clearly how the death by burning was carried out. Shall I tell you, sir, since you doubt my knowledge?"

"I'm not interested."

"A religious man must always be interested in the study of our holy books."

"Not when the devil is speaking," said Samson, his eyes blazing.

"Death by burning!" said Mordecai in a powerful voice. "You should well know how it is done, for you are a Cohen, are you not, Herr Cohen? A Cohen is a descendant of the ancient priests of the Israelites, and even to our own day has the rights and liabilities of the priestly class. Death by burning, sir! Listen: The immoral daughter of a priest is to be sunk up to her knees in manure. The immoral daughter is then subjected to a partial strangulation. A cloth is wrapped about her neck, and two men pull at it from either side. When she is forced to open her mouth, the executioner steps forward and throws a lighted wick into her mouth. The *Gemara* mistakenly refers to this wick as molten lead, but it is clearly a wick, only a wick. The wick burns up the interior organs of the immoral daughter. That is the way burning was carried out, according to our laws."

"You defame our laws, simply by voicing them," said Samson Cohen. "I can see the spirit of evil all about you. Leave my daughter alone. Bad as she is, she's not as bad as you!" His voice trembled.

"Some of our sages think that an evil spirit can change his appearance, that he can be invisible. Yet I stand clearly here before you!"

"Get away!" screamed Samson, waving his arms at the young man.

"What are you afraid of? Do I have wings? It says quite clearly in the Talmud that 'like the ministering angels they have wings, they fly from one end of the world to the other, and they know the future.' I've never even been to France, much less the other side of the world! And the only future I know about is that I shall remain with your daughter!"

"Shofar!" screamed Samson Cohen. "Shofar!"

"Father, have you gone crazy?" said Rachel. For Samson had gotten out of his seat and now stood waving his arms, his eyes shut, screaming this single word "Shofar!" again and again.

Mordecai laughed out loud, laughed like a true demon. "He says 'Shofar,' dear Rachel, because he thinks I'm a devil!" laughed Mordecai. "The sound of the shofar is supposed to scare away any spirit, any demon, no matter how evil, no matter how strong!"

"Shofar!" screamed Samson Cohen, and his daughter turned her face from him in shame.

"Now you see how degraded are the Jews," said Rachel. "Even the rich and powerful Samson Cohen is a superstitious old fool."

"Shofar!"

"Don't talk like that of your father," said Mordecai. "He is your father, no matter how foolish."

"Shofar, shofar, shofar!" screamed Samson Cohen, shutting his eyes with all his strength, conjuring the picture of the shofar, the ram's horn blown on the High Holidays of the Jews, hearing its sound blow through his terrified body. Never before had he been so stricken with a sense of evil. Never before had he been so conscious of a presence from the world of spirits.

"Look up Kethubot, Herr Cohen," said Mordecai. "Look up what it says in that tractate about when a woman must be divorced."

"Shofar!" screamed Cohen, so he would not have to hear his daughter accused of adultery by this demon.

"In section three," said Mordecai, bringing the words from out of his perfect memory. "Section three has it: 'A woman who has committed adultery must be divorced.'"

"No, Mordecai," said Rachel gently.

"No!" screamed her father, and he opened his eyes, eyes that were dark and full of madness, and turned round and round in a frenzy till he found Rachel, and then he lunged at her, as if he would strike at her neck. Rachel jumped back. "Shofar!" screamed her father, and he lunged again and tore at the necklace she always wore, the gold chain that supported the Cuheno diamond, the diamond which Herr Cohen had never thought her fit to wear.

Rachel pushed him back and away from her. "We're going, Father," she said.

But her father was yet enraged, and came at her again, screaming, "It's not yours! Give it back! Shofar, shofar, shofar!"

Rachel pushed him so hard that the old man fell back against the arm of his chair and cried out in pain. Still he was not through; he rang for the servants, and one of them came running and threw himself at Mordecai. Rachel moved away from her father, but he backed her into a corner of the room. As he came at her, she could see that the servant had wrestled her lover to the floor.

"No, Father," she said, "the diamond is mine." And she pushed him away, thrusting a palm into his chest, and the old man tripped over a footstool and fell, his head striking the wood floor. Rachel didn't pause to help him. She grabbed at the servant who was continuing to struggle with Mordecai, and pulled him away with force. "Look after your master," she said, in a voice he had long been used to obey. As the servant rushed to the fallen Herr Cohen, Rachel helped Mordecai to his feet, and together they fled the house.

Two days later, at a post stop on the way to Königsberg, they learned that Herr Samson Cohen of Berlin had been murdered. The two who had been fleeing for their love were now fleeing for their lives.

CHAPTER SEVENTEEN

They had little money, no provisions, and a diamond worth more than a kingdom. Rachel's family in Berlin was but one branch of the great Cohen/Ha-Cohen/Cuheno clan, spread all over Europe and other parts of the world, who would spend their fortunes to ransom the diamond first cut by Judah Cuheno of Zaragoza, but the lovers had no intention of ransoming the diamond. Their plan had been to run to Königsberg, to the east, rather than the more expected flight to Hamburg, where Phillip's agents might be waiting, either with a force of law or a force of arms, to take Mordecai from her. From Königsberg they had hoped to sail to Copenhagen, where distant relations of Rachel's lived. Perhaps they would help a kinswoman get passage to England, before the entire family knew the story of her abandonment of Phillip. From England to Lisbon, from Lisbon to Brazil—such had been their dream. But when news of the murder reached the post stop on the way to Königsberg, their plans suddenly had no shape, no sense, no hope.

"Come," said Mordecai, and he took Rachel with him away from the coach, away from their fellow passengers, away from the post road. They went into the woods, somewhere between Stettin and Königsberg, and they walked for hours without speaking.

"I can't," said Rachel, exhausted, stopping to rest.

"You can't?" said Mordecai. "With a full belly and in good health you're going to give up now? Come on." He took her hand and dragged her forward.

They went on along a footpath that Mordecai was sure pointed north, until darkness descended, and with it, the cold of a late March night. He made a great fire, being as wasteful as he liked with the enormous quantities of deadwood all about them.

Rachel warmed herself, and he spoke. "This is the situation. We have to hide. They will be looking for us, for two well-dressed Berliners of our description. No one could know that your father's death was an accident. And we ran on the same day. We can't go anywhere now, not as Mordecai of Mir, and Rachel, the daughter of Samson Cohen."

Walking through the woods by day, sleeping in filthy, inhospitable inns by night, letting a layer of dust and a hundred little rents in the fabric of their clothes disguise their station, was no hardship to Mordecai. He who had slept on wet ground for six months, who had eaten only after dusk, and then only berries and carrots and beans, had no trouble eating the local cheese and eggs and bread of the villages, or sleeping in a bed that was not made up for a king.

For Rachel, it was another matter. She could not bear to be treated rudely, by an innkeeper whose German was so poor it might as well have been the grunts of an animal, by a farmer's wife who fingered the clothing on Rachel's back as if it might be for sale. She could not stand the smell of the inns: manure, urine, sweat, beer. She couldn't swallow the thick crusts of black bread, the terrible sausages, the sour wine. She seemed always weak, always hungry, always tired. Mordecai grew back his beard, and it looked well on him now that he walked tall, spoke excellent German; if his clothes were becoming threadbare, at least they were the clothes of a Berlin gentleman, and not those of a Polish Jew. But Rachel felt ugly, wasted. In a week of wandering, she felt she had aged ten years; in a month of hiding, she felt ugly and old.

"Brazil!" she said one day. "It was a stupid dream to think we could ever get to Brazil! Why don't you just kill me right here and let me die in peace!"

"I won't kill you," he said.

"Why not?"

"I love you," he said, and when she looked at him, he was as beautiful as he had ever been, and she couldn't understand how he could still love her, with her beauty gone, her fortune unattainable, her temper wild with self-pity.

Mordecai held her in his arms as they rested near a stream, somewhere near the Lithuanian border, on that sunny day at the end of April. He told her what he had learned of Brazil: how besides the European Jews who had penetrated its territory for the sake of diamonds, there was a *Marrano* community, strong in secret Jewish faith, and powerful in that remote country; how the king of Portugal had renamed the town of Tejeco in Brazil, near where Brazilian diamonds had first been found, Diamantina; how powerful slaves of mixed black and Indian blood mined the diamond beds; how any slave who discovered a diamond of more than eighteen carats would win his freedom.

"Eighteen is the numerological value of the Hebrew word for 'life,' " he said. "I'm sure that it was a Jew who made up that law about eighteen carats. We shall get there, Rachel, and we shall live as Jews. But we must not be too hasty to get to a great port here. Perhaps by the beginning of summer we will have been forgotten enough to take the chance of sailing from Königsberg."

"By the beginning of summer, I shall be dead," said Rachel.

As if in corroboration of her words, a storm suddenly broke and the sky turned black. They ran to take shelter under a cluster of trees set back fifty yards from the stream.

"What a storm," she said. "It's like a punishment."

"A punishment from whom?"

"You know what I mean," she laughed.

"If God made this storm, it had nothing to do with you and me," said Mordecai, embracing her under the thicket.

"Maybe we will get to Brazil," said Rachel.

"Of course."

"I would love a hot bath."

"All we have to do is find diamonds."

"That should be no problem for a Cohen."

"I want to marry you."

"We're getting wet, Mordecai," she said, looking nervously up at the wet branches that showered them with water with each gust of wind.

"A man not married is not a man in the full sense," said Mordecai. "That is what the Talmud teaches us."

"I'm still married," she said. "You know that."

"No, I think not," said Mordecai. "You have no bill of divorcement, but I'm sure that Phillip has arranged for a divorce in your absence."

"I'm sure he hasn't," said Rachel. "As long as he's my husband, he is connected to the Cohen name. That is something he will never willingly give up."

"But you have committed adultery. He must divorce you, according to Rabbinic law."

"There is no proof, and we're not about to submit it to him," she said. "Besides, it makes no difference. We are married already in everything but name."

"Then we shall have the name, too," he said, his eyes burning. "By the authority of Mordecai of Mir and Iwenez." Mordecai rummaged in his wallet for some token, and finally found an odd Russian coin that he had found as a boy, and now he gave it to her.

"Thank you," she said, and the rain crashed down through the trees.

"Do you take me to be your husband?"

"Yes."

"I take you to be my wife," he said, and he clasped his hand over hers, and they kissed, and Rachel felt how cold his lips were, and shuddered involuntarily; as if this, too, like the sudden storm, was a premonition of bad luck.

That evening, they could find no inn. Just before the dark set in, they came across a very mean shack, a hovel really, with black smoke coming out of its ramshackle chimney. "We can't go in there," said Rachel, but just then the rain picked up again, and a cold wind howled at them from the North.

"I know the man who lives there," said Mordecai, surprised at recognizing the place. He hadn't realized that they had gone so far into the principality of Prince Alexander. "I've been here before. He's a trapper."

"I won't go into that place," said Rachel, as the rain poured down.

"Don't be ridiculous, the man is a Jew," he said, and he took her by the arm and ran to the hovel and punched at the little door. "Hello!" said Mordecai in Yiddish. "It's a friend!"

The trapper's dog was barking now, but the man's voice, harsh and unfriendly, was at least speaking Yiddish, too. "What do you want? You can't come in!"

"It's Mordecai. Mordecai of Mir," he said, and at once the door was flung open from the inside and Mordecai and Rachel were pulled inside by a little man, covered with fur and soot and a long beard.

"Mordecai," he said in Yiddish. "Mordecai, my teacher."

Rachel was struck with the warmth of the tiny space. It smelled of smoldering fur, and she couldn't tell if it was hunger or heat that made her stagger at once for the only chair in the hovel.

"No, no," said the trapper to Rachel. "You'll get too filthy up there. Don't you know that it's best to stay low? It's smoky, and smoke rises." And he dragged her off the chair and onto the hard floor.

Rachel looked up at him from the ground in a daze. In the tiny hut, every surface—wall and floor and ceiling—was black from the soot of the fire. There were no windows, only the little chimney hole. The trapper had blue eyes as small as pinheads. They seemed to glitter at her through the smoke.

"Who is this girl?" he said to Mordecai, his eyes never leaving Rachel's.

Mordecai had sat down next to Rachel on the floor, and now he placed his arm about her. "My wife," he said. "Hazka, this is my wife."

"I am honored, madame," the trapper said, speaking Russian.

"She is from Berlin. In Prussia," said Mordecai.

"I am honored, madame," he repeated, this time in Yiddish.

Rachel looked about her once more at all the black, at the walls that seemed to be moving closer together, at the smoky fire in the tiny fireplace, at the cracks in the black ceiling where water dripped through into the hot air. Even the man's dog, some kind of fearful animal, was black with soot. This dog watched her every motion, and Rachel knew that it could throw itself across the tiny room, leap at her neck, and tear out her throat in less than a second.

"Have you any food here, Hazka?" said Mordecai. "We've got money and can pay you for your hospitality."

"Don't insult me with such an offer," said Hazka with a laugh. "If you go to bed without supper, you'll rise without having slept.

God has given me bread. Let me share it with my betters."

Mordecai had met Hazka and his hospitality during his six months of penitence. The unlettered trapper had been impressed with the holy young man, and Mordecai had spent much of his forty-eight hours with the man in teaching him the basic prayers of his fathers. "This time I am not a penitent, Hazka," said Mordecai. "I can eat everything. As for my wife, she is not used to very rude food."

"I will give you the best, only the best, my dear teacher," said Hazka. "I have today slain a duck."

"A duck? What was a duck doing wandering through the woods?"

"There are farms nearby. West of here. Sometimes the ducks get away from the farmers and come to the trappers. You know the saying—'Ducks for a penny? And if you haven't a penny?' I don't have a penny, but I've got us a duck."

"I won't ask how."

"But why are you here? How did you manage to stumble across this miserable little hut of mine again? Surely not just for a visit?"

"It was raining. Fate brought us here, fortunate fate. You give us shelter and food."

"Shelter now," said Hazka. "We must wait for the duck. Even in this miserable weather, I am expecting a friend."

"Perhaps some wine, or some water?" said Mordecai, motioning to where Rachel sat in an exhausted stupor.

"Of course," said Hazka. "Forgive me for not offering it. I am thinking too much about my visitor. He is not really a friend, he is a colleague." This last word was said with a cynical little smile; and then the short, dirty man moved with a fascinating speed and grace to where a great goat wineskin hung from a peg in the wall. The wineskin was as black as everything else in the room. "Is she a Jew, your wife?" said Hazka.

"Yes," said Mordecai.

"I thought she must be," said Hazka. "Seeing as you're her husband." He took a great squirt of the wine. "It's good," he said, and he passed it to Mordecai.

"Rachel," said Mordecai, and he squeezed her chin so that she would smile. "Come on, it's good for you."

"What is it?"

"Wine," said Mordecai, and she opened her mouth, and he squirted it into the back of the throat, and Rachel never tasted it. She swallowed and swallowed, looking at the black room, wondering when this nightmare would end. "Wine for our wedding day," he said, glad that she was drinking.

"Since when do you give your wife to drink before you?" said Hazka.

"It is a custom of the Berliners," he said, and then took a squirt of wine for himself.

"It is strange that she wears no covering for her head," said Hazka. "And you no longer have a hat. If I didn't know you're Yiddish, I could mistake you for Polish gentry."

"I could mistake *you* for a Polish trapper," said Mordecai.

"That's you," said Hazka. "Everyone around here knows who and what I am, even if I eat unclean food. But you should be different. I mean, everyone should be able to see at a glance that you're not an ordinary man. Why do you dress that way, my teacher?"

"I am a Jew, Hazka, but I no longer cover my head," said Mordecai.

"But if you don't cover your head, who will?" said Hazka. "You're a holy man. You have to cover your head."

"I am not a holy man."

"Mordecai of Mir not a holy man? Don't be ridiculous. I met a trapper who had fled into these woods—he'd been poaching beaver—and he was from two hundred miles away. When I told him who had taught me the *Shema Yisroel*, he nearly went crazy. He told me you were the greatest Jew who ever came out of Poland. He told me you could heal the sick, delay the setting of the sun—all kinds of crazy things. Mordecai of Mir! Everyone knows you're a holy man, even an ignorant trapper like me!"

"Do you still remember the *Shema Yisroel*?" said Mordecai, hoping to divert the conversation from an examination of his change in belief. He wouldn't want the trapper to eject them into the cold and rainy night.

"Of course," said Hazka. He took the wineskin from Mordecai and squirted a great quantity of wine into the back of his throat. Rachel stirred from her stupor. The wine had brought her back to awareness. It was her wedding day, even if the wedding had been without proper ceremony, without witnesses, without the sanction of law. Hazka cleared his throat, and sang out in a surprisingly beautiful voice: "*Shema Yisroel, Adonai Elohenu, Adonai Ehad!*" The trapper turned to Mordecai eagerly. "It's right, isn't it? I say it every morning to greet the sun, but I was afraid that perhaps I was missing a word. In Yiddish, it seems longer: 'Hear this, O Israel, the Lord our God, the Lord is one.' Am I missing anything?"

"No, it's right," said Mordecai.

"It's not my fault, madame," said Hazka to Rachel. "My father was a woodcutter and he never taught me a thing. Maybe he didn't know much. He knew that he was a Jew, all right. My mother died when I was a baby. Maybe she knew more. All my papa used to know was to hit anyone in the eye who said anything he didn't like about the Jews. Most of the Jews I met before Mordecai wouldn't even talk to me. They thought I was scum because I didn't know any prayers.

"This past year was the first time I ever had the nerve to go to a synagogue. I got all cleaned up, and I even went and bought a shirt in town—a white shirt. They let me into the *shul*, and I had to stand in the back row. No one talked to me. Then I heard the *Shema*, and I joined in. '*Shema Yisroel, Adonai Elohenu, Adonai Ehad!*' I sang louder than any of them, and even those who before had shunned me now smiled at me.

"When they asked me who I was, I told them that I was a Jew who lived in the woods, and knew almost nothing, but that I was still a Jew and wanted to be a good one, in my own way. The Chief Rabbi of the town took me to his own home for dinner and sat me at his right hand. *Shema Yisroel, Adonai Elohenu, Adonai Ehad!*"

Almost against her will, Rachel was smiling. Even with the heat, and the wine, and her hunger, she understood enough of the simple trapper's Yiddish to know that he was telling her much the same thing that Mordecai had been saying for weeks: that there was pride in acknowledging one's origins. Still, her smiling lips did not open to echo the trapper's words. And hardly had the trapper finished singing out the short prayer than her reverie was broken by a sudden violent knocking at the door.

"That's my friend," said the trapper softly, raising a finger to his lips. "Be quiet or you'll scare him away." The trapper moved silently to the door and opened it halfway. He spoke Polish to whomever was at the door, and only Mordecai could understand what was being said: Hazka's "friend" had brought the "pelts" he'd promised, but did not want to stay to discuss prices. Hazka explained that there were friends inside and that he had nothing to fear from them. At this, the man outside the door became fearful. He told Hazka that this was a dangerous business they were in, and that they could trust each other to discuss prices the next day. He only wanted to leave the pelts and run off.

"Don't you trust me?" said Hazka in Polish.

Mordecai heard the man answer: "Of course I trust you. I wouldn't leave you valuable pelts if I didn't trust you, would I? There's enough in there to send us both to the gallows. I go now, my friend."

And then he was gone, and Hazka was left at the half-open door, holding onto a coarse trapper's bag, soaked through with blood. The rain seemed to be coming down in torrents, and Hazka hesitated, wondering if he dared bring the bag inside. His dog, who had heeded its master's sharp order to remain in the corner when the knocking had begun, now began a low, dangerous growling. No matter how stern its training, the dog scented something remarkable and wanted to investigate. Hazka turned from where he stood in the half-open doorway and hissed at the dog: "Stay!" The dog slowly relaxed its legs and sank to its belly, but continued growling, its eyes on the bloody bag. Hazka said, "I'm afraid to leave this outside. My friend just might come back for it."

"All right," said Mordecai, "then you must bring it in."

"They're only pelts, they won't smell so bad, even if she's not used to it," said Hazka, embarrassed in front of Rachel. "And the rain is really fierce just now."

"Please," said Mordecai. "She won't mind, Hazka."

The trapper nodded gratefully and turned from the doorway, dragging the big bag inside. The dog began to rise again, and Hazka shouted at it again: "Stay!" For a moment, it seemed as if the dog would obey, but then it stood up, and seemed to quiver in expectation. "Sit!" screamed Hazka, but the dog growled and advanced toward its master, and the bloody bag. "I said sit!" yelled Hazka, and he let go the bag and turned to shut the door.

In that instant, the dog sprang for the bag.

"Down!" screamed Hazka, and he kicked at the dog and

grabbed at its neck so that it would let go its hold on the bag. Hazka seized the bag and pulled it away from the dog. The dog glowered at him and continued to growl. "Get away from here!" screamed Hazka. "Get into that corner! Go!"

"What's in the bag anyway?" said Mordecai.

"I told you—pelts," said Hazka. Slowly, the dog backed away from its master. "I've never seen the dog like that."

"I know they're pelts. But of what animal?"

"Oh, that's what you want to know," said Hazka with a smile. "If you can keep a secret, I'll tell you."

"I can keep a secret."

"Beaver."

Beaver was royal game, and poaching it on the prince's land could be punished by death. The dog was growling again, its eyes on the bloody bag. "So that's what beaver smells like," said Mordecai.

"Is that going to be here all night?" said Rachel.

"What did madame say?" asked Hazka.

"Yes," said Mordecai to Rachel. "They're animal pelts." In Yiddish, he said: "She wanted to know if it's to be here all night, but she doesn't mind." In German, he said: "He's got to keep them inside. They're valuable, and he's afraid of being robbed. Besides, it's a real storm out there."

Rachel hid her face in her sleeve. One more awful smell wouldn't kill her. She was more likely, she thought, to die here from suffocation than from the awful odor.

"Actually, it shouldn't smell like this at all," said Hazka.

"Maybe he didn't skin them."

"He always does. That's our deal. He kills and skins them, and leaves them with me. I know how to sell them safely."

"Why do you think the dog is acting like that?" said Mordecai. "You must have brought pelts in here before."

"Old age," said Hazka. "Sit!" he screamed again, for the dog had gotten back up, and was beginning to advance. "Sit!"

"You want me to hold the bag?" said Mordecai.

"It's old age, it's a crazy old dog," said Hazka, and in that moment the dog lunged at the bag with enough force to knock Hazka down. The trapper howled with rage, but before he could rise, the dog had torn into the bag, and Mordecai could see a hand.

The hand of a human child, small and perfectly shaped, free of its wrist, its stump caked with black blood.

"Oh, my God," said Rachel.

Hazka, back on his feet, grabbed his dog and pulled him across the hut, where he tied its neck with a thick rope to a pole that supported the cracked ceiling. Mordecai backed away from the bag and sat with Rachel, trying to comfort her. Hazka returned to the bag and opened it from the top, so that only he could see what was inside.

His eyes registered no shock, not now, for in the instant of seeing the hand, he knew what would be in the bag, and why it must be there. "I am sorry, my friend," he said to Mordecai. "Fate did not bring you to a good place. I am sorry for all of us. We are all of us in the trap."

"It's a boy in there?" said Mordecai in Yiddish.

"Yes, no more than five or six. Mutilated. They paid him. They must have paid my friend to do this. He would cheat me with his pelts, but he would never want me dead without reason. They must have paid him well." Hazka closed up the bloody bag and stared sadly at Mordecai. "You and madame could try and run away on your own. They are not after you. But they will be if they see you here, and know that you're my witnesses. And worse, that you're Jews."

"What is he saying, Mordecai?" said Rachel. The wine had made her sleepy, then very clearheaded; now, all at once, it made her feverish. "I saw the hand! You can tell me what he said! Where are we, Mordecai? How did we get to such a place? I can hardly breathe, and I saw the hand!" Then Rachel got sick, throwing up a thin gruel from her nearly empty belly. Mordecai tried to help her, but he could do nothing about the way her frame shook as her body tried to vomit out what was not there. It seemed to Rachel as if the whole room's contents—the two men, the dog, the blackened chair, the bloody bag—all had gotten up and begun to dance around her head. It was smoky, and black, and hot, and the blue pinhead eyes of the trapper and the green eyes of her lover seemed to shine through the turgid air, as if they were demons and she had died and gone to hell.

"Listen, try to listen," said Mordecai, but all she could hear was the low growling of the beaten dog, the wretched crackling of the burning logs, the shaking of roof and walls as gusts of wind and rain battered the hovel in the middle of nowhere. As Mordecai talked, she tried to imagine Unter den Linden in Berlin, she tried to imagine her bathroom—her pretty little French maid helping her from the hot, perfumed water of the enormous tub and wrapping her in towels for a late-afternoon nap. "I think we should try and run," Mordecai was saying. "I don't know if you're strong enough, but I think we should try. You might feel stronger once we're outside, in the cold and the rain."

"I'm sorry," said Hazka. "I can see she is not strong."

"Please, Rachel," said Mordecai. "They don't know we're here. We can live."

But she had begun once again to throw up a tiny stream of spittle and air, to clutch at her belly and cry against the pain. Unlike Mordecai, she had no conception of what was about to take place. She could see no significance except perfect horror in finding a boy child in a bloody bag in the hovel of this Jewish-Polish trapper in the middle of the woods. Horror such as this was as foreign to her as Turkish or Sanskrit. All she knew was that she could not get to her feet, she could not throw up the awful remnants of a long-since-digested meal, she could not listen to Mordecai's words as he tried to help her to leave this hellish place. "You're beautiful," she told him in German. "I love you, my beautiful Mordecai, I love you."

A moment later, there was a knocking at the door, and both Hazka and Mordecai stood up in the smoky room, on either side of Rachel. "Say you are not Jewish," said Hazka in Yiddish. "And speak only in German or Polish. I will say nothing."

The door was thrown open, and three soldiers, soaking wet with rain, entered the tiny hut. They seemed shocked to see anyone other than Hazka inside, especially this couple in the dress of gentlefolk. But their leader didn't hesitate. "Don't move," he said. "I don't want anyone to move." Ignoring Hazka's tied-up, pathetically howling dog, the soldiers opened the bag, looked inside, and blanched with a horror that was not feigned.

"It's true," said one of them.

"I am the one you want," said Hazka. "The bag was given to me."

"Quiet, Jew," said the leader, and he slapped the trapper across the face.

"It was an accident that they came by," said Hazka. "They're travelers from Germany, and they got lost in the storm."

The leader punched Hazka with all his might, hitting him in the belly, then in the neck. As the trapper fell over, near the open door, another soldier kicked him with a muddy boot. Mordecai couldn't restrain himself from speaking. "Wait," he said, speaking in Polish. "You don't know what happened. Let me explain."

The rain was pouring down Hazka's face, mingling with the blood that drooled from his mouth. Rachel said in German, "Who are these men, Mordecai? What are they doing in this place with us?"

"There is nothing to explain," said the leader of the soldiers. "You will all come with us, and you can explain to the magistrate. You can tell him how it is that the Jews continue to kill Christian boys for their blood."

"That is a lie," said Mordecai. "Even the pope has condemned the blood libel against the Jews."

Hazka was stirring, and tried to raise his head from where it caught the rain. He opened his eyes and began to speak, to tell Mordecai not to say anything to these men. But before he could utter a word, one of the soldiers kicked into his jaw, silencing him.

"All that happened here is a man came to sell animal pelts," said Mordecai.

"What man?"

"I didn't see him, he was outside. They spoke Polish."

"Jews know Polish. Hazka is a Jew, and he knows Polish. What about you? Are you a Jew, too?"

"I am from Berlin," said Mordecai. "And this is my wife, also of Berlin. We were lost in the woods."

"Are you a Jew?" said the soldier.

"What difference does it make?" said Mordecai, and all at once the soldier lashed out at him, slapping his face three times in quick succession.

Rachel didn't understand what was happening; all she knew was that her lover was being attacked. She cried out to them to stop, and she tried to get to her feet, but the soldiers had no sympathy for her, for they saw only the horror of the martyred child.

"He's a Jew," said one of the soldiers. "Only a Jew would be here with this Jewish murderer."

Rachel was knocked to the ground, and one of the soldiers stepped on her chest to keep her there. She screamed at them in

German, demanding to be released, playing the patrician lady that only her delirium was able to preserve. "You're a Jew, aren't you?" said the leader of the soldiers to Mordecai. "You're a Jew, and you came here to buy the boy's body!"

"The man brought the bag—he said it was pelts, animal pelts," said Mordecai, and then he went to help Rachel, pushing at the soldier who rested his foot on her chest. "Leave her alone," said Mordecai, and he was struck on the head with a stick, and collapsed into a moment of red pain, then a longer space of white, dreamless sleep.

Rachel saw him fall, saw the tied-up dog flash his teeth, saw a soldier's fist grab for her neck, and then softly raise her head and dash it back against the floor. She didn't feel the soldiers lift her body and throw it into the open wagon; she wasn't aware of the ride through the howling storm, the blood from the murdered boy's body washing away next to where she and Hazka and Mordecai lay. Rachel sensed nothing at all until there was sun and light.

She woke up with chattering teeth in a sunlit stone cell, her ankles manacled together, her eyes focusing in horror on two male bodies in a heap against the far wall. It was cold, she thought, but she didn't know if it was the cold of the air or the cold of fear.

She got to her feet awkwardly, struggling against her chains, but before she could take a step, she fell to the hard stone floor. "Mordecai!" she cried, but there was no answer from the bodies across the room. Rachel crawled, dragging her manacled ankles, to where Hazka and Mordecai lay. "Mordecai," she whispered when she was close enough to see what they had done to his beautiful face. Rachel kissed his green eyes and stroked his bloodied hair.

There was a wind through the barred window, and it carried more than cold; she could hear the voices of a mob, but could not understand what they were saying. In a gesture of despair, she raised her hand to her heart, and realized that her diamond was gone from about her neck. She always wore it; its loss made her feel more naked than if she had been stripped of every last stitch of her clothing. In the heart of her sorrow, she suddenly let out a laugh. What difference did it make that the Cuheno diamond was gone? She had no purpose, no life. Mordecai's lips didn't move, his heart didn't beat, the corners of his eyes were caked with blood.

Rachel shut his eyes with the tips of her fingers and kissed his dead lips. For him, she sang in her heart: *Shema Yisroel, Adonai Elohenu, Adonai Ehad.* It was not an affirmation of faith. It was a eulogy, a tribute to her lover. If they were to ask her who and what she was, she'd tell them, whoever they were: She was Rachel Cohen of Berlin, and she was a Jew.

CHAPTER EIGHTEEN

The Count von Kauthen came across the Cuheno diamond five days later. It had gotten speedily from the backward little Polish town in the prince's mostly German-speaking territories to the royal palace in the usual fashion: The jailer who tore it off her neck sold it for a pittance to the magistrate of the town; the magistrate showed it to a baron, who confiscated it as property of the Crown; the baron tried to sell it to a Jew from Stettin, who recognized at once that it was a magnificent—and hence easily identifiable—stone, and certainly stolen; he refused to buy it, and instead sold the information of its existence to a certain count, who took a force of soldiers to the baron's residence and took it away from him; the count presented the diamond the next day to Prince Alexander, and he in turn showed it to his wordly nephew, recently of Berlin.

Count von Kauthen recognized the diamond that Rachel Meier wore around her neck—he recognized it with terror. The prince, his uncle, explained what he knew about where the diamond came from.

"You don't understand these things," he told his nephew. "It's Easter time. The peasants are hungry. I'm not about to send my troops in to prevent them from killing some Jews. This is the season when they remember who killed Jesus Christ. Your problem is that you understand nothing about politics."

"What are you going to do with the diamond?" said Count von Kauthen. He was certain that the lone survivor of the blood-libel outrage was Rachel. But the diamond did not belong to her, not by the laws of Prince Alexander. The count would have to wrest it from his hands to give it back to its owner.

"The diamond?" said Prince Alexander. "I'll sell it to a Jew."

The count took two dozen seasoned troopers with him to the little town where Rachel was being held. The magistrate came out to greet him before he had dismounted.

"Is she alive?" said the count, and when told that she was, he rode past the magistrate and jumped off his horse at the entrance to the Town Hall. A guard escorted him to the cell, and the count urged him to walk faster with a crack of his riding crop. These men were no better than animals, he thought, and when he got to the cell and saw Rachel sitting there in her chains, he nearly went mad with rage.

"You," said the count to the guard, "unchain the woman, bring her decent clothes, and bring her food. Do this with speed, or I will have you flogged." The guard, terrified, began to run off, but the count stopped him. "First the manacles, you fool," he said, and the guard opened the door to the cell, got to his knees before the Jewess, and began to unlock her irons.

Rachel stared directly into space, taking no notice of the man at her feet, or of the Count von Kauthen, standing before her in tears. "It'll be all right, madame," he said. "Madame, I swear to you, I will take care of everything, and you shall be well, and this nightmare will have passed forever."

He had come into her line of vision, but she took no more notice of him than if he had been invisible. In a week, her thin frame had become emaciated; her terrorized eyes stared out from a face of tightly drawn skin, harshly defined bones. Her clothes were in tatters, and her breasts showed through a bodice that was merely shreds. She had mourned Mordecai, she had been raped, she had been interrogated for hours in a language she didn't comprehend, she had been beaten, she had been starved, she had been left alone.

"This man Hazka," the count was saying, "was apparently hated by the local trappers. That's what the magistrate thinks. He thinks he was framed by another trapper, a foreigner, who poaches on the prince's land. No one believes the blood libel anymore, only the most ignorant. This is an enlightened time. Even the prince was appalled to learn of what happened. The trapper either killed the child and brought him to Hazka, or found a dead child, sick from some disease, and mutilated him. All he had to do was leave the child in a bag and report Hazka to the authorities. Imagine how they must have felt—it was Easter time, and it seemed as if a Jew had murdered a Christian child. Rachel, please try to listen to me, you'll be all right."

The guard was sent for the food and the clothing, and the count turned again to Rachel. He had seen men come out of a battle this way, in shock that seemed as profound as death; but most of them came around to life and laughter once again.

"It's the peasants here, not the soldiers—that's what the magistrate says, and I believe him. They're not even proper Christians here, the peasants. They go to Mass, but they still pray to the gods inside trees and rocks. They pray to the sun god and the moon god. No wonder they believe that nonsense—that Jews need the blood of Christian boys to mix into their Passover food. They think that it is at Easter time that they must be most careful, for that is the time of the Jewish Passover and they believe that the Jews are abroad, looking for Christian boys, to take their blood and bake it into their matzoh bread. The peasants believe this, Rachel, and it is they who killed Mordecai and Hazka, not the soldiers. Peasants, Rachel, not Christians. Please believe me. You'll be all right. I'm taking you with me to Berlin, and you'll be all right once again."

But Rachel Cohen Meier was never all right again.

She continued to look into space, seeking some reason for her pain, and some reason for her life. If God was there, all around them, but didn't care, why didn't the continents sink into the ocean? Why didn't fire and plague and wars finish off the suffering population of the earth? Why did everyone want to live if life had no meaning, if death was simply sleep?

Samson Cohen had never died.

The irony of this would have been unbearable for Rachel, had she enough reason to comprehend it. But she had lost her reason—at least the reason with which one can communicate with other men. Samson Cohen had struck his head on the floor, but had not died; his murder had been a rumor, based on reports of the scuffle between daughter and lover and father in the richest Jewish house in Germany. But he had not died. And when Rachel was brought back to Berlin, it was Samson Cohen, and not Phillip Meier, who took her to live in his house. It was Samson Cohen, and not Phillip Meier, who paid the ransom for the "lost" Cuheno diamond to Prince Alexander.

Count von Kauthen continued to visit her for the next year, feeling intensely responsible for the outrages committed on her in his uncle's principality. But she never got better. Rachel never spoke, and she ate only enough to keep her alive. Her maid dressed her in the finest silks, and she wore the Cuheno diamond about her neck, but all these worldly things could not disguise that she was of another world, another life.

She died when she was twenty-one. Her father was amazed to hear her utter the Jewish affirmation of faith, in the soft, sepulchral tones of a spirit, only minutes before she died. "*Shema Yisroel, Adonai Elohenu, Adonai Ehad,*" she whispered, and Samson Cohen was sure that in her last moments she'd discovered her God, she'd repented for her bad life, she'd become one with the Rachels before her.

THE FAMILY OF DAVID COHEN
OF BERLIN
1774–1850

The untimely death of Rachel Cohen Meier of Berlin was not reported to all branches of the Cohen family. David Cohen, her brother, wanted the Cuheno diamond to stay within the Berlin family. It was inevitable that the Cohens of Germany and Austria, even of Amsterdam, hear something of the death of young Rachel, but no sad dispatches were sent to Cairo or Baghdad, where descendants of Abraham Cuheno of Zaragoza lived. David Cohen had a vision of his Levantine cousins: They must be swarthy and squat, with red turbans and black, pointy beards.

It would be unfortunate if the diamond passed from Berlin to London or Paris; it would be intolerable if it passed to distant relations living in the East.

David Cohen didn't realize that his Levantine relations had forgotten that the Cuheno diamond was their legacy as well. Ha-Cohens from Constantinople or Alexandria weren't sure if they were related at all to these Western Cohens and Cohns and Kanes; they were sure only that they were all Jews. Most had never heard of their common ancestor, dead for nearly three hundred years. The family who lived in England and Germany and France had intermarried with Ashkenazi Jews, Jews whose origin had nothing to do with Spain; while the family in the Ottoman Empire, and in India, had married their children into other Sephardic—that is, Spanish Jewish—families, and thought themselves purer, more aristocratic, than these Western Cohens.

But the Ha-Cohen bankers of Baghdad, the Cohens of Antwerp and Amsterdam, the Cohns in Strasbourg and Paris, the Kanes in London, all kept the story of a relationship alive: It was good business. The Jewish diamond brokers of the world took their contract-sealing words from the precedent set by the Cohens: *"Mazel un bracha!"* "Good luck and blessing" was all that the young Kane from England needed in the way of a contract from his Ha-Cohen banker in Baghdad to buy a diamond from an Indian mine—that and a handshake; and whether or not each believed that the other was a cousin mattered less than the fact that the world did.

David Cohen's wife gave birth to a girl in 1780 in Berlin, and she was named Rachel. News of the death of Rachel Cohen Meier went out simultaneously with the news of this latest Rachel's birth. Presents and congratulations flooded into Berlin from a dozen countries, from three dozen cities and states, in honor of the birth. Condolences, tersely expressed, were dispatched separately. Those Cohens from Amsterdam or Vienna who might have known how David Cohen had insured that the Cuheno diamond remain with him did not scruple to protest. The Berlin family had grown very important of late, and, besides, no one from the Dutch or Viennese branches of the family had given birth to a girl in the last few years.

David Cohen had ten children, all of whom survived infancy. Within the larger framework of the diamond world, his seven boys established their own small network of gem trading. The boys went to Naples and Vienna and Paris and London and Copenhagen and even as far as New York. One of the girls married a Rothschild; another a Warburg; and Rachel, the next to youngest, married a scholar from the Annenbergs of Frankfurt.

Both Rachel and her husband were liberal, enlightened people, with a desire to reform the backward Jews of Eastern Europe. As representatives of Prussian Jewry, they accepted the invitation of the czarist government to participate in a meeting on the Jewish problem in Russia. Both husband and wife were believers in the cultural assimilation of the Jewish people into the greater culture of Europe. They were Germans of the Mosaic faith, not Jewish people living in the land of Germany.

Rachel and her husband visited Russia in the spring of 1830 and spoke to the backward communities in the Jewish pale of settlement. They urged the Jews to shave their beards, to send their children to the schools set up for them by the state, to put aside the Talmud and study mathematics, philosophy, geography, medicine.

Only the imperial troops that traveled with them prevented the fierce, sandy-bearded Jews they lectured from rioting. These Jews of the pale did not want enlightenment, not if it meant abandoning their identity as Jews; they looked at Rachel and her husband as agents of the Czar, agents of treachery and oppression.

Broken with disappointment, the enlightened Prussian Jewish couple went to St. Petersburg, where a distant relation of Rachel's —a Cogan—was a jeweler to the court. Before they had been in the half-savage, half-fairytale city a week, Rachel contracted pneumonia. She died in the winter of 1831, and her husband arranged for her burial in a Jewish cemetery in Vitebsk, hundreds of miles away. When he returned to Berlin late in the spring, he brought the Cuheno diamond with him; that and the story of the death of Rachel at the age of fifty-one.

A grandson of David Cohen, Daniel Cohn of Paris, was in Berlin at the time, concluding a purchase of diamonds. The late Rachel had been his aunt, but he had never met her, and whatever sorrow he felt was mitigated by the knowledge of his wife's advanced state of pregnancy. Daniel Cohn had already been blessed with four sons. Surely, he thought, this time he would be blessed with a girl.

He decided to wait in Berlin, with his cousins, until he had news of the child's sex. He didn't want to return to Paris and receive a message about some new female cousin having just been born in Rhodes or Bombay or Philadelphia. Two months later he got the news from Paris: He was the father of a baby girl.

"Rachel," he said. "Her name is Rachel Cohn," and he returned to Paris with the Cuheno diamond in his fist, anxious to see his youngest child.

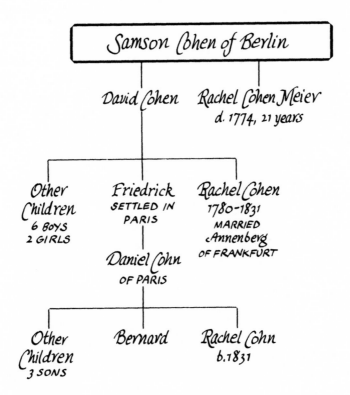

PART FOUR

JERUSALEM, 1852

CHAPTER NINETEEN

Rachel Cohn had traveled so quickly that she had not yet had time to be afraid.

She had been in trains before, both in ordinary first-class cars and in the private cars of her family. She had sailed before, both on steamers between Calais and Dover and on sailing yachts off the Côte d'Azur. But she had never traveled, in one direction, without lingering to see the sights, or take the baths, or visit the gambling houses. She had never traveled without her parents, or one of her daring brothers. She had never crossed the borders of France without being met by some member of her great family from Germany, or Holland, or Italy, or England. She had never before run away.

Run away, she thought, and the words chilled her, even as the sun reflected white light off the clear blue waters of the sea. I *didn't* run away, she thought to herself, twisting her mind out of a guilty shadow, rearranging two heavy blankets about her on the deck chair. Rachel resolved to clear her mind of any thoughts of guilt. She knew that what she was doing had a purpose, a value greater than fulfilling a dull obligation. It was not as if her father had arranged a marriage for her from which she was fleeing. It was not as if the task she had set for herself was selfish, or ignoble, or even something that her parents would condemn as wrong or foolish. It was simply something that her father had forbidden her, because he was afraid it might prove too difficult for a young, unmarried woman. She wasn't so much running away as she was defying her father.

After all, she had left both her parents a carefully written letter—though it would be only her father who would read it with reason—and she had taken a sufficient sum of money, and two servants: Marie, her personal maid for the last dozen years, and Marie's husband, Henri. Both servants understood that she was ignoring the commands of her parents and taking advantage of their trip to Deauville to go off on her own. But Marie and Henri had been made to understand that she would go with or without them, and they had decided to risk the wrath of her parents by accompanying her, and protecting her, rather than leave her to her own devices. Besides, Marie was forty-two, and her husband older; they would never get another chance to visit the Holy Land.

Rachel shut her eyes and breathed in the sharp sea air. In less than a day they'd dock at Beirut, the threshold to Jerusalem by land or by sea. As long as her destination was just a name, or an ideal—Jerusalem was both—it hadn't enough reality to threaten or to frighten her. No matter what her father had said about Turks or poverty or danger, all melted away under the power of that ancient name. She had money, she had intelligence, she had will, and she had a purpose: to help the poor Jews in their once-glorious capital. No matter how angry her father would be with her when he read her letter, he would forgive her, and he would learn to respect her.

These thoughts were consoling, and they were easy to keep alive during the incredibly swift train ride from Paris through France, Belgium, and Prussia, stopping in Berlin not to rest but to make a connection. After a day in the Prussian capital, Rachel and her servants had continued their rail journey through Bohemia and Austria, arriving finally in the port city of Trieste only six days after leaving her home in Paris. Racing from the train to the port, they were able to catch the Austrian Lloyd steamer leaving for Syria, Athens, and Constantinople.

Even these fabled cities could not divert her from her dream of Jerusalem, or bring her down to a sense of the realities of the East. Rachel saw nothing of these places as she rushed from train to steamer, and she had no intention of leaving ship until she reached Beirut. So there was no taste of the Orient to prepare her for what she would see in Syria or Palestine. She didn't join the rush of passengers who braved customs at Constantinople for a glimpse of ladies behind veils, of human beings for sale in the famous slave markets of this capital of the Ottoman Empire, of endless beggars and cripples and thugs swarming through the twisting, fetid streets. Rachel remained aboard, her eyes on the sea, served by her maid, protected by her manservant, thinking only of her dream.

After Constantinople, the steamer stopped at Smyrna, Rhodes, and Larnaca. These were short stops, and for the first time Rachel felt a tremor of uncertainty: There was only a short space of calm sea between herself and the Promised Land, the land of Israel, the land of her fathers. What would she see there, she wondered, and how strong would she be?

No, there had not yet been time to be afraid, for all her energies had been directed to the next city, the next port, preparing the proper papers, the proper moneys. The terrible noise of the train had kept her awake for most of two days out of Paris; the rest of the train trip had been taken up by fitful naps, and a poor digestion. Their steamer had experienced a mild storm in the first hours of leaving Rhodes; regaining her appetite and her sea legs had occupied her for two days after that. But her appetite was fine once again, and the Mediterranean was perfectly calm. If she shivered now under her blankets, it was not from the weather, but from the lack of turbulence, from the presence of peace, and light; she shivered because she was able to think of the end of her journey, and she was becoming afraid.

"Beirut in twelve hours, miss!" said a large man in an old white explorer's suit hovering over her with a smile. He took off his hat and bowed his head in a way that suggested that this custom was absurd. "My name is Rex Mitchell. Do you speak English, or am I barking in the wrong language?"

"I speak English," said Rachel Cohn, blushing. A strange man had never before spoken to her without introduction. She was sure the man was an American. He had long blond hair and big white teeth; a scar ran faintly from under his left eye to his chin. He was not very handsome, but he was a little handsome; and he had the frame, and the spirit, of a man who would be charming to women. Such men had no interest in a girl like her, Rachel knew, unless they were after her family's fortune.

"English?" said Rex Mitchell. "Is that a British accent? You've got to talk more if you want me to guess."

"I am French."

"French? I never would have guessed that. *La mer est tranquille*. I could've said that. If I had guessed you were a French mademoiselle, I would have said that to let you know I was educated. But if you speak English, that would be a lot better, I think. I've been practicing Italian. Do you know that Italian is the most widely spoken European language in the Holy Land?"

"No," said Rachel.

"Then this must be your first trip. Am I speaking too fast for you? I can probably slow down. It's just that I'm an American, and we're fast. I know you're probably thinking I'm not much of a gentleman coming up to you like this without an introduction, but that's how I was brought up. If it'll make you feel any better, I studied theology at Harvard for two years. I almost became a minister. I won't pretend this is exactly a *religious* pilgrimage, but then again, I'm not a Turk. Are you from Paris?"

"Yes," said Rachel, looking around at the few first-class passengers who walked their deck. They were exclusively Oriental, and whether Turk or Arab or Jew, she had no way of knowing.

"I loved Paris!" said Rex Mitchell. "Didn't know anybody, and the hotels sure were expensive, but it was pretty! That's a pretty city! I loved the orchestras they've got playing all night off the big avenue—you know, the Champs-Elysées, with all those palaces. That's where I'd like to have a little place. Stay up all night drinking wine, dancing, listening to the music, talking to friends. Listen, I hope I'm not disturbing you. You look like someone who's got something to say. Do you read a lot?"

"Yes."

"Have you read Lamartine?" he said, mispronouncing the great romantic's name.

"Yes."

"He came here, you know. To the Holy Land. Crazy man, like all romantics. Should have spent ten years in Texas, get it out of his system. I've been to Texas, I've been to California, I wanted to go to India, but here I am, on my way back to the Holy Land. This is my second time. First time I went through Egypt. Saw

the pyramids and the sphinx, and then I took the steamer from
Alexandria to Jaffa. I'm a writer. Not too famous, not too rich,
but I sure travel a lot. That's what I like best, traveling. Don't
exactly know why. The Council of Protestant Churches sent me
here—they paid. I'm writing a guidebook for pilgrims. In ten
years, you're going to see more Americans on the road from Jaffa
to Jerusalem than you see sitting in the cafés in Paris. You don't
talk much. Are you married?"

"No."

"I didn't think you were. This is a religious pilgrimage, right?
Listen, don't mind me if I say something stupid about the Romans
—I mean the Catholics. I have nothing against them. It's just that
I tend to speak my mind, that's how I am. I think it's crazy that
you get these girls who want to renounce the world before
they've even seen it. I know nuns do lots of good in the world,
but it's crazy. You see these pretty young things and they get a
crazy idea in their head that the world's not pure enough for
them, or the only way to Jesus is to stay locked up in a cell the
rest of your life, and, hey, I feel sorry for them. That's all I've
got to say on that subject, and I hope you're not offended. You're
here with your parents?"

"No."

"Not your parents? Who then? You don't mean that you've
come here all on your own?"

"Yes," said Rachel. "On my own." She had not forgotten the
existence of Marie and Henri; it was just that the way she was
brought up had led her to discount the existence of servants in
any list of traveling companions.

"A young girl like you?"

"I'm twenty-one," said Rachel Cohn, as if to correct a wrong
impression.

The American stared at her, shaking his head. "You probably
don't know the first thing about it," he said. "What's a young
girl like you going to do when she gets to Beirut? You don't
know what they're going to do to you at customs. They can
take your baggage apart and leave you with nothing. You can
end up in a miserable *khan* tonight, if you even know what that
means."

"I know what a *khan* is," said Rachel, who had read numerous
travelers' accounts of the filthy Arab hotels, housing men and
animals together with their fleas. Something about the American's

attitude released her rising resentment: He was talking to her not as a young man flirting with a girl, but the way her father lectured her, from a pedestal of manly experience. "But I don't know why you're so angry."

"Angry? Of course I'm angry. It's because of this infernal religion. It makes people do crazy things. You've got no business going by yourself to the Holy Land."

"Why does that concern you, sir?"

"Oh, Jesus," said Rex Mitchell. "I may not sound like a gentleman, but now that I've found you, I sure as heck can't just pretend I never met you. Here you are, a white woman all on her own, and ready to land in the middle of a city run by Turks. What am I supposed to do, close my eyes and pretend you're not here? I wish I could. I wish your daddy was here, but he's not, and so naturally I've got to be the one to worry about you."

"Mr. Mitchell," said Rachel, "we have not been introduced. I do not really exist for you except as a nameless person on the same ship on which you found yourself for a few days. It's absurd to think that you have any responsibility toward me."

"That's just what I mean about Catholic education!" said the American. "Pardon me, miss, but this is just exactly what I mean! I hate to offend another person's religious beliefs, but the way I was brought up was to think sensibly about religion, not to be fanatical to the point of putting my life in danger. Only a school run by zealous nuns could make you crazy enough to want to come all by yourself to the Holy Land. And now it's a crazy Protestant like me who's got to make up for that crazy Catholic mistake!"

"I don't want any of your help, thank you," said Rachel.

"I have no choice, damn it. I'm a gentleman. I'll have to help you through that customs-house madness, and I'll have to help you find a convent, and a group of pilgrims who'll take another woman with them, and that's not going to be easy. Even among Catholics, what you're doing is a little unusual. But I've got no choice. I've got to help you get yourself out of this predicament before I can get myself a good night's rest. That's my way. I'm just going to have to keep my eyes peeled for some kindhearted nuns on the way to Jerusalem."

"I am not a Catholic," said Rachel.

"Not a Catholic?" said the American, momentarily at a loss for words.

"I'm going to the Holy Land to see about the condition of the Jews."

"Oh, no!" said the American. "Don't tell me you're a missionary! Don't tell me you're going to try and convert the Jews!"

"I am a Jew," said Rachel.

"What?"

"I am a Jew," she said again, looking at him squarely. "I am going to the Holy Land, and I need no one's help."

"What do you mean you're a Jew?" said Rex Mitchell. "Do you mean a born Jew?"

"Of course."

"I met a Jew in Jerusalem," said the American, covering up his surprise at her words by speaking rapidly, as rapidly as he could. "An American. From good family, too—he was born a Quaker, in Boston, I think. Very religious. He went on a pilgrimage to the Holy Land, and he went crazy. These religious people are always a little crazy. I don't care what they are—Christian, Jew, Muslim—if you carry it too far, it's crazy. He married a Jewess in Jerusalem. He divorced his wife, an American, and he converted—became a Jew—and married this Jewess. It was sad, because it didn't make any sense. I don't have anything against the Jews. I just can't stand when you carry these things too far. Like when I was studying theology, I woke up one day and realized that everyone around me was *crazy*. I mean, I was studying *stories*, and everyone else was *believing everything*. You still haven't told me your name, miss. Or should I say 'mademoiselle'?"

"My name is Rachel Cohn."

"Cohn? I knew a Cohan—he was an Irishman, an Irish Catholic. Born in Ireland, but he lived in New York. But you said Cohn. That's different. My family's from England, but that's a hundred years back. I know some Jews. You don't look very Jewish. I mean, most of the Jews I know are pretty dark in the hair. There's a man I met out West once, his name was Kauffman, from Germany originally. The talk was that he was Jewish, but he was blond, blonder than you. The Jews in Jerusalem are pretty dark, except for the ones from Poland and Russia. The ones from there are pretty pale, with yellow beards. I wouldn't know they were Jewish if they were dressed differently. Usually I'm a pretty good judge of nationalities, because I travel so much. This is a religious pilgrimage then, what you're doing? You must be pretty religious if you'd go to all this trouble."

"I'm not religious at all," said Rachel.

"Not religious?"

"No," said Rachel. "I'm not going to Palestine to look at tombs. I understand that the condition of the Jews there is terrible, especially in Jerusalem, and I plan to see what I can do to help them."

"You?"

"Yes."

"You plan to go by yourself from Beirut to Jerusalem to help the Jews?"

"Yes."

Rex Mitchell was about to say something, but his laugh overpowered him. He had been standing with a bent back, looking down to where Rachel sat wrapped in a blanket in her deck chair, but now he stood up straight and raised his eyes to the sky and howled. His large frame shook with uncontrollable gusts of laughter; and with each new series of laughs, Rachel felt herself growing angrier and angrier.

"There is nothing amusing about what I propose to do," she said. "But since you find the idea of helping Jews so laughable, I'd appreciate it if you would leave me alone. I don't like to be laughed at."

"I'm not laughing at you," said Rex Mitchell, trying to contain his laughter.

"Please leave me alone," said Rachel again, as the big American started to bend low over her again with an ingratiating smile.

"Monsieur," said a low, growling voice behind Rex Mitchell; and as the American turned, he was astonished to see a short, squat man, dressed in black, pointing a knife at his chest.

"Henri," said Rachel in French, "that's not necessary."

"You asked monsieur to leave," said Henri, also in French. "He has not yet left."

"Who is this man?" said the American, looking from the point of the knife to the young woman he'd thought was traveling on her own.

"Henri," said Rachel, speaking sharply now. "Put away the knife. This man means no harm. I said *put it away*."

Henri returned the knife to the sheath on his belt and closed his black jacket over it. "Oui, mademoiselle," he said, bowing his head. "Would mademoiselle like her tea now? It's half-past four, and it would be good to settle your stomach. One never knows when the sea will rise up in anger."

"Would you like some tea, Mr. Mitchell?" said Rachel.

"Tea? Is that what you were talking about? When I learned my French, no one ever told me how *fast* you people speak. Who is this character?"

"Please, Henri," said Rachel in French. "I would like some tea. And bring a cup for Monsieur Mitchell as well."

Henri, with severe disapproval in his eyes, walked off. An old Turk, dressed in bright silks and green-glass spectacles, sauntered past them, his hand clutching the arm of a beautiful young girl of thirteen or fourteen. Rex Mitchell pulled over a straight-backed chair and sat facing Rachel, his blue eyes squinting into the sun.

"You asked him to bring me some tea, didn't you?" said the American.

"Yes."

"He's a servant?"

"Yes."

"I thought you said you were traveling alone."

"Well, yes," said Rachel. "Alone except for Henri and Marie."

"*Two* servants?"

"Yes."

"That's quite a lot of servants for just one person," said Rex Mitchell. "Especially in America. Am I to take it that I'm forgiven?"

"Forgiven for what?"

"You were angry with me for laughing. Now you've invited me to tea. I'm really very flattered, Mademoiselle Cohn."

"I thought it better to ask you to tea than to let Henri think I needed his help to get rid of you."

"Then I am not to think myself flattered?"

"Think yourself whatever you want," said Rachel. "Only please don't laugh at me, or think me incapable of doing anything. I am not an idiot. If you would like to help me by giving me some advice as to how to get to Jerusalem from Beirut, I'd be very appreciative. But don't talk to me as if I didn't know the first thing about it. I've studied Arabic, and I know the geography of the region, and I'm very hardy."

"Are you rich, too?" said the American.

Rachel started at the words. Was it her imagination, or was the American now being openly flirtatious? At twenty-one, Rachel had never been in love, except with idealized characters out of Lord Byron's poetry. Her older brothers, all four of them, were handsome, adventurous, rich young men who had insisted on traveling to America, and Australia, and Mexico without benefit of great sums of money and without carrying the name that opened doors without effort. They had long since impressed upon her the fact that she would be seen first as a Cohn, as an heiress, before anyone could see through to her own character. She was warned of fortune hunters, favor hunters, men with slick hair and toothy grins who would try to make her love them so that her fortune could be theirs. Even more than her father, her brothers had been able to convince her of her essential plainness: little, undistinguished features; dark blond hair without a bit of curl; too thin; too quiet; too ordinary in every way. What man would want this woman, she was made to believe, unless they knew her to be the daughter of Daniel Cohn of Paris?

"Why do you ask me if I'm rich?" said Rachel, her voice more than harsh—it was as if she were complaining of an injury, or an insult. "What does money have to do with it?"

"When I was so worried about your welfare, mademoiselle," said Rex Mitchell, "that was before I learned of your servants. If you have enough money, you can travel quite well in the Holy Land. But the amount of money I'm talking about is not small."

"I am not carrying a fortune, Mr. Mitchell," said Rachel.

"I was afraid of that," said the American. "But perhaps your idea of a fortune and mine are not precisely the same."

"What if I am not rich? What shall I do then? You said something about my joining a group of pilgrims?"

"Such pilgrims that I was thinking of are not usually Jewish, and traveling with servants."

"Perhaps a caravan?"

"What?"

"A caravan, a trading caravan," said Rachel. "I have heard that there are still trading caravans going across the Judean deserts. Perhaps there is a trading caravan going along the shore from Beirut to Jaffa."

"Do you mean that you would like to travel with a pack of Arabs?"

"Perhaps. I am asking you for advice."

"You are asking me for advice," said the American, screwing up his eyes to heaven. "When I hear a question like that, I begin to hope your manservant is very handy with his knife."

"You think it unsafe to go with a caravan. Very well."

"Very well!" said Rex Mitchell, turning his eyes from heaven to earth and twisting them in comic anguish about the sunny deck. At that moment he saw the old Turk draw the young girl with whom he traveled close to him, clutching at her little breasts. "Look!" said the American in a whisper. "Do you see the Turk and his girl?"

"What?" said Rachel; but when she turned to look, the Turk was once again standing upright, his arm loosely about the young girl's shoulders. "Over there, you mean?"

"Yes." Rex Mitchell lowered his head so that his eyes were level with Rachel's. "Do you know that she is his slave?"

"What do you mean?" Rachel was horrified.

"You didn't know?" said the American. "You see why it is that I'm afraid for you, Mademoiselle Cohn? Anyone else on board this ship would know at a glance that the old lecher had bought her."

"Why did he buy her?"

"Why?" said Rex Mitchell with exasperation. "I thought it was just the Catholics who brought up their daughters in the dark."

"You don't mean that she's his *mistress*?" said Rachel.

"That's not quite her status. She's a slave. He bought her at the market in Constantinople. An Arab told me about him. Every year he goes to Constantinople to buy a new slave girl for his harem. Every year they get younger."

"But we've got to do something," said Rachel.

"Do something? That's not why I'm telling you this. I'm just trying to show you that the East is different from what you're used to. Insidious, evil, corrupt. You don't know the first thing about it. What if I weren't here and you wanted to join a caravan? You and your servants could end up with your throats slit. I don't understand how your parents could have ever let you go alone, especially since your family is a little well-off."

"We've got to do something," said Rachel again, and she got out of her deck chair and started to walk toward the Turk and his slave girl.

"What are you doing?" said Rex, going after her.

"In France we don't have slaves, monsieur," she said, and she would have gone over to the old Turk had not Rex barred her way.

"No," he said. "You don't bother the Turk."

She was looking at the slave girl's little form, her bare feet on the rough deck, her childish profile set against the Turk's old, massive shape.

"Even if you were to kill him," said Rex, "that girl would remain a slave. Even if you could buy her yourself, there'd still be a thousand slaves just like her."

He had taken hold of her arm, and guided her back to the deck chair, and for the moment Rachel steeled herself. Henri was coming up from the galley where he had brewed good China tea, brought from Paris, and he quickly set out the tea service for the silent Rachel and Rex. "Shall I pour, Mademoiselle Rachel?" said Henri, and Rachel shook her head, saying that she would do it, and as soon as the manservant left, she lifted up the teapot and began to cry so much, with such sudden force, that the American had to grab the pot from her little hand to prevent serious scalding.

When she had finally stopped up her tears, Rex felt her eyes on him, as if they were taking the measure of his worth. There was something in the way this almost-handsome big American looked at her that made Rachel stop worrying about fortune hunters. He had a kind face, an open face, and she had a need to explain herself, here on this quiet, almost deserted first-class deck in the sunshine.

She poured out the tea, and she spoke in English, all in a rush, telling him too many things: that she was rich, and that others were poor; that she came from a people despised by the world; that her life could be as easily led by a tailor's dummy as by a living person—dressed up, paraded about, sat at table, presented at palaces.

Did he know, she asked, that the Papal States refused to allow Jews to practice medicine and law, that the Jews there still had to wear the Jew badge, that in the year 1852 the pope still kept her people locked up in ghettos? Did he know of the ravages of the cossacks in Russia and Poland? Did he know that the czar was drafting Jewish children into pre-army camps for brutal indoctrination from the age of twelve to eighteen? That the Jews were kept in the czar's army by law for twenty-five years after their eighteenth birthday? Did he know of the mass murders in Damascus? Did he know that every time the Jews tried to start a farming community in the Holy Land, the Arabs or the Bedouins massacred the farmers and burned their crops? Did he know how ashamed she felt to live without fear, or want, or even desire?

Rex Mitchell knew enough about young women to know when not to interrupt. It was not so much what she was saying now that was important, but that the fire within her had to be let out. So while he was confused by much of what she said—he couldn't keep straight her brothers' names, or who and what her family was, or whether or not her father had given her his blessing to take this pilgrimage—he was resolved to let her talk herself to exhaustion.

What remained in his memory that night, when he had gone below to the cabin he shared with an old Armenian Christian, was the sound of her voice cracking from too much use. He was struck with an idea of her as a recluse, a pretty girl made plain by staying always in the library, afraid to retreat from the stacks of books. She was young, she was a dreamer, she felt the pain of the world, and of her own people in particular; but most of all she was herself in pain, herself infinitely vulnerable.

Rachel had spoken of the old Jews in steerage who had saved their pennies to be able to touch their lips to the Holy Land's soil. She had spoken of the Jews who lived without chance of work, living on charity and under the yoke of the Turks, and how she wanted to help them. She had spoken of the Jews who for nearly two thousand years had never forgotten *Eretz Yisroel*, the land of Israel, and its capital, Jerusalem, who remembered the Holy Land every day in their prayers. But Rex Mitchell felt that her intense desire to help her people was also a means to helping herself; she was looking for something to do that would lift her into some new realm of satisfaction, of happiness. She was stifled, unformed, and her soul longed to be shaped into something noble, strong. Her soul was looking for struggle, so that it would be able to live.

This is what Rex drew from her rambling confession; this is what attracted him to her with such force as he conjured her face in the middle of the night.

The American woke with a start at five o'clock in the morning. His Armenian cabinmate had already packed up his few possessions and left, and Rex was suddenly terrified that he had slept too long. The horrible landing in Beirut would be more than Rachel could bear alone, he thought. As he ran out and up to the first-class deck, he felt the madness all around him: The anchored steamer was besieged by a score of little boats, and the beautiful view of the Lebanon Range was obscured by the shrill shouting of a dozen languages as merchants, boatmen, hotel runners, local officials all tried to sell something to the latest arrivals.

A tall Syrian grabbed his arm and showed him a scimitar. "Good dragoman," he said. "Speak five languages. I've killed many men, many men, and I'm not afraid." Behind him, a short Turk in a red fez chattered at him in Italian, extolling the virtues of a pest-free hotel. An Arab boy held up a watermelon and begged him to buy it. Other children were pulling at his legs, urging him to take their fathers' boats to get to the shore. Rex could see that other passengers, most of whom had already brought their bags on deck, were similarly besieged. Every moment it seemed that more raggedy children were clambering from their little boats onto the ship, their hands out, begging for *"Baksheesh!"*

But Rachel Cohn was nowhere to be found. Rex wondered if she could still be asleep, or if, by some unfortunate chance, she had already fallen victim to one of the boatmen and was even now wandering through the customs-house madness on shore. What could she do without him? She would not know anything about giving *baksheesh* to the half-arrogant, half-obsequious customs officials, who would take apart her possessions, demand to see her money, confiscate and steal whatever they could, all the while bullying, begging, demanding, recommending.

"Baksheesh!" said a one-armed beggar, his toothless mouth grinning at him with what was supposed to be friendship. The old Turk and his slave girl were surrounded by porters, picking up their bags as the old man howled indecipherable abuse at them. A group of old Jewish men and women, dressed in black, squinting in fear at the rising sun, stood huddled together, looking fearfully across the narrow band of water separating them from the port. Three Russians of the Orthodox Church stood

silently, with infinite patience, ignoring the cries about them as so much dross from the material world.

Rex moved through the crowded deck, pushing aside beggars and hawkers and pilgrims, searching for Rachel. Finally, when he was just about sure he had missed her, and that she had managed to fall into evil hands, he caught sight of her, amid the bright flashing of a dozen brilliant uniforms. The girl was being escorted off the ship, onto an official-looking tender of the local authorities.

"Mademoiselle Cohn!" he called out, but she was too far from him to hear. She was on the opposite end of the ship, and as he made his way through the crowd, she was already going down to the tender, followed by her servants and the dozen armed men of her escort. "Mademoiselle Cohn!" he called out, and he called it out again and again, and finally, as the tender pulled away toward shore, she turned and saw him.

"Mr. Mitchell!" she cried, looking very pleased to see him. But then her face screwed up, as if afraid to disclose something. She waved, and he waved back at her, and then she turned to talk to an old Turkish official standing next to her on the tender.

Rex stood at the rail, watching the tender dwindle into the rising sun. Suddenly, he grabbed one of the boys hawking for boat passengers. "You!" he said. "Let's go!"

"Yes, sir," said the boy in Italian. "Right away, sir! Right away in five minutes."

"Now!" said Rex Mitchell. "Let's go now!"

"Five minutes!" said the boy, as the tender dwindled in the blaze of light.

The captain of the steamer was standing next to them, and he turned to the American and said, "No one can leave the ship until the inspectors come. You know that."

"But that girl just left," said Rex.

"The French lady, you mean?" said the captain.

"Mademoiselle Cohn, on the tender!"

"But, Mr. Mitchell," said the captain smiling, "that's different. Only she is allowed."

"Why? Why can she leave and no one else?"

"Because the Turks want it that way. They were here to greet us. Orders from the governor. Orders from Constantinople. Very important. I don't know who the French lady is, Mr. Mitchell, but I'll tell you something—she is a special case."

CHAPTER TWENTY

Rachel was taken at once to a villa outside the walls of the city of Beirut, and given a suite of rooms. Marie used sign language to indicate to the villa's servants that a hot bath was required for mademoiselle. After the bath, Mademoiselle Cohn was put to bed by Marie, in a ventilated room with great wooden slats beating back the force of the sun. At midday, fruit was brought her by Marie, then Rachel ate and dressed and brushed her hair.

"You are expected to join the governor's party, Mademoiselle Rachel," said Marie. In the years that she had been Rachel's maid, she had never learned to hide anything from her: curiosity, fear, disapproval. They were in the villa of one of the richest men in Syria, with the governor of this provincial backwater of the Ottoman Empire waiting for her below; but through all this excitement, Rachel could sense that her maid had something else on her mind.

"What is it, Marie?"

"Nothing, mademoiselle. You needn't hurry yourself for these Turks. They will wait for you as long as they must. I only wanted you to know that they expected you."

"That's not what I mean."

"May I, mademoiselle?" said the maid, taking the hairbrush from Rachel's hand. Marie began to brush Rachel's long, straight hair, sighing in disapproval.

"What are you mad about, Marie? Please don't torture me. I haven't the time or the patience. If you're angry with me, just tell me the reason why."

"Why would I be angry with mademoiselle? What has mademoiselle done?"

"Marie, *please.*"

"It's not for me to say, perhaps. I am not your mother. But then again, she is not here. She is in France, where you should be, where I should be with Henri, and it is only because I love you that I'm here at all. You know that, don't you?"

"Of course I do."

"Well, your mother is not here."

"I asked you to just tell me what it is. Pretend you're my mother. Why would my mother be angry with me?"

"That species of gentleman . . ." she said, her French sinking into the *midi* accent she reserved only for contemptuous expressions.

"I am listening, Marie," said Rachel.

"An *American*," she said.

"I was simply talking to the gentleman."

"That's not what Henri told me."

"Just talking to pass the time."

"He said you were crying. I myself saw what you looked like last night. It was hard to get you up this morning, and no wonder. I can imagine what you must have been dreaming all night. What do you think you are, a lowborn girl, just off the farm?"

"I'm glad you've told me what was on your mind, but I think I'd better join the governor's party."

"Wait!" said Marie. "I am to act like your mother, so let me finish! You were not brought up to speak to strangers! The man could be a thief, a murderer!"

"He's a nice man, that's all."

"A nice man! Oo-la-la! You are talking trouble now, my Mademoiselle Rachel! You are talking dangerously, and I do not like it. You do not know the world, not the way I do. You are too good, too openhearted, and you don't pause to look at the finer things that give one away! The man you call a gentleman had frayed cuffs on his trousers, his hair hasn't been washed in two weeks, and his eyes are hard—he would kill you for your money."

"He doesn't know my family."

"How do you know? Because he said so?"

"A man can talk to me without knowing me to be rich, can't he?"

"Perhaps. But who hasn't heard of your family, who in the world of men?"

"I mentioned my name, and it meant nothing to him. He is an American. Americans don't know very much about these things. All we did was talk, that's all."

"What is he?"

"What do you mean?"

"His profession, his family, his religion?"

"He's not Jewish, of course, but neither are you."

"He's not Catholic, either, is he?" said Marie.

"He's an American Protestant."

"They're the worst. They're worse than nonbelievers."

"He's a writer, a travel writer, I think. And he can't be a non-believer, because he's writing a guidebook for pilgrims to the Holy Land."

"A Protestant guide, no doubt. Making fun of all the Catholic shrines. I know that type. He doesn't have a sou to his name. All he can do is smile, and hope you don't notice his frayed cuffs. Did he ask you how you're going to Jerusalem?"

"Yes. He wanted to help me."

"I'm sure. And did he ask you if you had enough money to make the trip? Did he happen to ask you if you had a good deal of money with you?"

"He pointed out that the trip can be expensive."

"I hope he doesn't try to ambush us, kill us en route for your money. Maybe he doesn't know your family, and he only thinks it worthwhile to kill you right now for what you've brought from France. Mademoiselle Rachel, you are never to see this man, you are never to talk to him again!"

"Marie, please! I'm not a little girl."

"You are. You are a little girl, and foolish besides—I don't care how old you are! You are a foolish little girl, and you are not to talk with that man ever again!"

The maid's tirade was interrupted by a knock on the door, and in a moment Marie opened the door to Henri.

"Are you perhaps ready yet, mademoiselle?"

"I am very ready, Henri. Please calm your wife. She thinks I've become infatuated with an American."

"Of course, mademoiselle," said Henri. "But if mademoiselle would allow me, I have something to say on that subject as well."

"Not now, Henri," said Rachel, and she left her two servants alone in the room and went down the stone stairs to the five men who awaited her.

She had been first shocked, then dismayed, when she realized that her family's influence had beaten her across the Mediterranean to provide this reception in Beirut. Shocked because she had been sure that the family would have no way to trace her until she had written them from Jerusalem; dismayed because she had hoped to accomplish something on her own before being given the aegis of the family's influence.

But the shock and dismay had yielded at once. The officials who greeted her had seemed merely to know that she was a Cohn, and should be greeted with the hospitality due her position. After all the warnings of the American, Rex Mitchell, it was comforting to know that at least for one night she'd sleep in a feather bed, eat decent food, be protected from desert marauders by armed men. It was not as if she'd been greeted at the border by distant relatives bearing angry messages from her parents, demanding that she return home at once. She'd simply been helped through customs, and welcomed to the city of Beirut.

Rachel entered the room where the men waited. The governor, a very fat man with oily skin, remained sitting on his bank of pillows; the other four men got to their feet. It seemed as if they were practicing an unfamiliar custom, a custom that had something amusing in it—getting to one's feet to greet a woman. One of the men seemed not Turkish but Arab. He was tall, bearded, wore embroidered trousers and a rich vest, decorated with silver buttons. Two of the others were of medium height, dressed in Turkish robes, and seemed to look at her as if she might be a piece of meat in a butcher's shop; they didn't know how to show respect for a European woman.

The last of the four had been the first to get to his feet, and now was the first to speak. He was short, bareheaded, and wore an outlandish costume: an Arab skirt over English boots; an Indian belt with a great silver scimitar thrust into it; an embroidered shirt; a thick embroidered vest shot through with silver designs and delicate braiding; a great multicolored cape, with which she imagined him to cover his head when on horseback. Crisscrossing his chest were other belts, attached to cartridge pouches, a leather water cup, a wineskin, a sheathed knife. He wore a great moustache, turned up at the ends, and his black hair was very long and glossy. His facial features were a mix of European and Asian. He couldn't be an Arab or an Indian; he was probably not a Turk; he was certainly not a Frenchman.

"I am Avi," he said in English. "I am the famous Avi the dragoman, I am here to translate for everyone. I am sorry I do not speak French, but you speak English, yes? I also speak Italian, Arabic, Turkish, and Greek. I do not speak ancient Greek, but I read it very well. I also can read Latin tablets, if you go to the ruins. I know the ruins. You have never heard of Avi? I also know Hebrew, the language of the Jews, but I know no Ladino, or the language of the Jews of Germany and Poland. I know all the languages of the Holy Land. I was born in Russia, but I came here to Syria when I was a baby. I am a Jew, like you."

"A Jew?" said Rachel. The mention of Russia had explained the face: He could be a mixture of Mongolian and Muscovite, of a Tartar on horseback and a European man of books.

"There is more than one Jewish dragoman, but not many. I am the best, and the most famous. I translate for all honored guests. That is what 'dragoman' means, you know this? From the Arabic 'targuman,' a translator. But I am not just a translator. There are dragomen who speak only one language, too." Avi patted the hilt of his scimitar to explain what he meant. "But these gentlemen don't understand a word. The governor is fat, no? Much too fat," said Avi, and he laughed out loud, as if sharing some wonderful secret with the young woman.

"I thought the dragomen were the ones who arranged trips," said Rachel. "Organizers. The men who got the tents and the horses and the servants."

"I get you the best," said Avi. "I organize everything. I translate. I fight. I organize. I set up the tents. I take down the tents. I can cook, too, but if you're rich, we'll get a cook."

One of the Turks suddenly turned from contemplating Rachel's face to Avi, and spoke to him sharply in Turkish. Rachel couldn't follow the words, though she'd studied the language for months in Paris.

"He says I should stop talking about myself," said Avi. "He wants me to tell you why you're here."

"I'm here to go to Jerusalem."

"We talk about that later. I mean here, in this house. He's the owner of this house, and he wants a favor from you."

The Turk turned to Rachel and spoke rapidly to her, shaking his hands and bowing his head for emphasis.

"He says that you do him honor by staying here in his house, because you are the daughter of a great man and a great family. But he begs to know if you have the knowledge of that great family. If you possess the knowledge, you can honor his house with a great favor."

"What knowledge?"

"The knowledge of diamonds," said Avi, and he turned to the governor and made a little bow. The governor reached into his loose blouse and took out a silken bag, jabbering in Turkish at Rachel.

"I know something of diamonds," said Rachel. "If I can be of help, I should be glad to." She smiled at the governor.

Avi started to take the bag from the governor, but the fat, unattractive man pulled away from the dragoman and got to his feet, clutching it in his hands. Avi said something in Turkish, smiling from Rachel to the governor. Before the governor could open the bag and exhibit the gems inside, the richly dressed Arab laughed out loud, looking at Rachel with contempt. The governor said something to him in a high, clear voice, still speaking Turkish; the Arab responded in the same language, stroking his beard and shaking his head.

"The governor has bought these diamonds," said Avi, "and he wants to know if he's paid a proper price for them."

"Why is that man laughing?" said Rachel, going up to the governor and taking the first gem from his hand.

"He doesn't think a woman can know diamonds," said Avi.

Rachel nodded, and glanced at the diamond the governor had given her: It was fairly large, perhaps ten carats, and mounted in a heavy gold setting on an ugly gold ring. The governor was explaining something to her in Turkish, and Avi was quick to translate.

"He wants you to look at it in the sunlight. It's very nice, he says. It's pure white. He wants to give it to the sultan."

Rachel thought it odd for such a large stone to be so clumsily mounted; the setting hid too much of the diamond—unless there was something that the stone's seller wanted to hide. She took the ring to the open French doors, and the two Turks—looking at her hair, her hips, her ankles—and the tall, bearded Arab followed Avi and the governor and Rachel as she stepped through the doors onto a patio in the full light of the sun.

"Ask the governor if I may take the stone out of its setting," said Rachel to Avi.

Avi spoke to the governor, and at once the Arab interjected violently, pointing to Rachel with contempt, demanding something of the governor. The governor said one word to the Arab, and the Arab quieted. Then the governor took the ring from Rachel's hand and gave it to Avi, who at once began to pry loose the diamond, using the point of his knife with speed.

"Here," he said to Rachel when he had freed the diamond. "Please be very careful about what you decide, mademoiselle."

Rachel had no need to think twice. She held the diamond before her eyes, turning it to catch the sunlight. It was a diamond, table-cut, and cut very well at that; but it was not pure white. The diamond's girdle, which had been hidden by the heavy mount, had been painted with a light shade of violet.

"It is not pure white," said Rachel.

The governor said something to Avi in Turkish, and the drago-man answered him at once. The Arab turned pale.

"Look," she said, and she turned the stone round in her fingers as the governor and Avi watched. "You couldn't see the painted girdle when it was mounted," she said, showing with her hands how it had been concealed by the setting, so that Avi didn't even translate. "People put some violet on a small part of a stone that's not pure white; if it's got yellow in it, the violet makes it disappear."

"Yellow and violet together make white," said Rachel, and as Avi translated this incomprehensible statement to the governor, the two other Turks took hold of the tall, bearded Arab, making sure that he was not about to flee. "The colors blend together. An expert knows just how much violet he must use to erase the amount of yellow showing in the stone. Look." Holding up the diamond before the governor's eyes, she was able to show him the hint of yellow seen through its sides, and the way the yellow disappeared as she turned the stone upright and he looked through the table into pure white.

The governor understood, and he turned from the stone to the Arab. Without a word he slapped the Arab across the face. Then he turned to Avi and barked out a series of high-pitched questions. Avi translated: "The governor thanks you, and wants to know if this filthy, lowly, yellow stone has any value at all, or is worth its weight in the camel dung that these dirty Arabs used to adorn their huts?"

"It is a valuable diamond," said Rachel. "But it is not pure white. If it were pure white, it would be immensely more valuable."

Avi translated, and the governor interrupted him and shouted out a question. "He wants to know if the diamond would be an insulting gift to present to the sultan," said Avi.

"I don't know," said Rachel; but before Avi could translate this, the governor had reached into the silken bag and taken out another diamond, this time a loose stone of between six and ten carats.

"What about this?" said Avi. "He wants to know if this is a proper gift for the sultan."

Rachel took the stone in her hands, turned it about in the sun, touched it to her lips. "This is not a diamond," she said.

Avi hesitated before translating, but when he did, the governor went mad with fury. He slapped the tall Arab again and again. Avi said, "That is the man who sold the diamonds to the governor."

The Arab was protesting now, screaming back at the governor as he was slapped. Avi never left off translating: "He says you are a whore and a slave, mademoiselle. He says you are blind and you are stupid. He says that your eyes see only what they want to see, like all Jews. He says that you only say all these things so that your family can sell diamonds of inferior quality to the governor. He says that he will kill you, mademoiselle." Here Avi paused, held up his hands: "No need to worry, mademoiselle. You make me your dragoman, no one gets close to you. Everything clean and safe and fast—ask anyone. I'm famous."

There were more fake diamonds in the silken bag: whether of glass or of paste, Rachel was not sure; they were fine copies. But as her eyes and fingers had been privy to the best diamonds in the world ever since childhood, she never hesitated. She knew a diamond in a moment, and these were not diamonds.

"I must reward you," the governor said through Avi. "I must make clear to you that you have done me a great service."

But the Arab—though held securely by the two Turks, though

he had been told that he would not be killed, but only whipped, and deprived of his license to traffic in gems, and that he must repay the governor twice the amount he had paid for the jewels —was not through. He insisted on his innocence, demanded that Rachel prove her statements, repeated that any jeweler in Beirut would confirm the authenticity of his merchandise; even the violet hue painted on the diamond's girdle, he swore, was put there not by him but by nature.

"I believe you, mademoiselle," said Avi. "The fat, stupid governor who understands not a word of what you and I say—he believes you. But how much better for you if you can prove to him that this Arab is crazy! He wants to reward you. Let's make sure you get the proper reward."

"I don't want a reward."

"I'll tell you what you want," said Avi. "You are too young and too rich to know what you want here in the Holy Land. You want an Arabian steed—something powerful, yet gentle; something that never tires, yet doesn't need to eat every half-mile. You should see the horses the pilgrims get out here. Only the governor can get you what we need for our trip. Even to fancy English lords, he sells only half-dead horses who only know that there are stones in the road and that they are broken from fatigue. Make a miracle with the diamonds, and the fat governor will be very impressed. Avi, the famous dragoman, will do the rest."

"Can you get me some water?" she said.

When it was brought, she placed the yellow diamond with its violet-painted girdle and the two fake ones on a flat surface. "If you put a drop of water on the table of a diamond, it will stay there in the shape of a drop far longer than when placed on any other gem."

As Avi translated, Rachel dipped her finger in the cup of water brought her and placed a drop on the table of the true diamond; quickly, she did the same with the two fake diamonds. In a moment, the drops collapsed on the fake diamonds; but the globule of water remained on the table of the real diamond for half a minute more.

"Also," said Rachel, "a diamond can scratch glass, but glass can never scratch diamond." Swiftly, she drove the real diamond against the fake ones, scratching them deeply, while the Arab cursed her. Just as swiftly, she drove the bigger of the fakes against the real diamond, producing no blemish.

"I have still more proof," said Rachel. "A true diamond is colder when exposed to the air than a fake placed next to it."

The governor touched his fingers to the stones, and exclaimed in wonder at the girl's knowledge.

"And if you hold a diamond close to your heart, or to some warm part of your body, it grows warmer much more quickly than any fake," she said, and she gave the governor one of the fakes and the real diamond, and he held them close to his heart, and in seconds the diamond was warmer than the fake.

The Arab stopped shouting. Avi made a low bow to Rachel and said in English: "Now we shall be able to take what we want from this big ugly Turk of a governor. An Arabian steed for you, and one for your faithful dragoman, guide, and defender."

Avi quickly made the request, speaking in Turkish and continually pointing to Rachel and the real and false diamonds. The governor made a great show of reluctance, pressing his hands to his forehead, bowing, and clucking his tongue, but after a while he clapped his hands and turned to Rachel and said to her in Turkish: "I am glad to reward you in the way you wish."

Avi translated, and Rachel thanked the governor, and then Avi said, "The governor congratulates you on making a wise choice of a dragoman for your trip to Jerusalem. It is all settled. You stay here, and I arrange for everything. We can leave in two days. I know that you are rich, but do you have money with you?"

"Not so very much," said Rachel. "Perhaps your fee might be too much for me."

"Then your father will send it. He would want the best for you, and I am the best dragoman in the Holy Land—everyone knows Avi. If you are very, very rich and you have no money with you, I still trust you. I will get paid. But you must be careful. Dragomen always love very rich lady travelers, and if you are staying here, and know so much about diamonds, then I will love you very much."

Rachel wasn't sure if he was joking, but, whether or not the speech was meant in fun, it was not to her liking. "I do not want talk like that, not if you work for me."

"I work for you, mademoiselle, it is all settled," and the short, very attractive Jewish dragoman, born in Russia and raised in the land of his forefathers, twisted his brows into a gesture of mock-compliance. "I do what you like, and I work very hard. You will be very happy."

"And I have not yet said that I'm going to hire you. That remains to be seen," she said.

Avi looked at her as if her words were to be taken as a mere formality of reluctance, and that the two of them knew perfectly well that they were joined together for the pilgrimage up to Jerusalem. But there was no time to dwell on the expression on the dragoman's face. At that moment, the furious Arab, who had been placid in the grip of the two Turks for the last minutes, suddenly broke out of their hold; he tripped one to the ground and took the other's knife out of his belt. Howling in Arabic, he grabbed at Rachel's wrist and pulled her to his chest, raising the knife to her throat.

"Do not be frightened," said Avi, his face abashed.

The Arab held her so tightly that she thought more about the pressure on her belly from his encircling arm than the threat of his knife at her throat. He shouted at the men in Turkish, and all of them removed their scimitars and let them fall to the floor.

"Dear lady," said Avi in a steady, cheerful voice, "when he turns you about, if you hear me shout out suddenly, do what you can to protect your throat."

The Arab shouted at Avi threateningly, screaming in Turkish and cursing in Arabic. Avi nodded his head and moved further away from the captive Rachel, as did the Turks. "He wants you to pick up the diamonds," said Avi in English. "I will shout soon thereafter, dear lady. Do not be afraid."

Rachel picked up the gems, the knife at her throat. When they were in her hand, the Arab tightened his hold about her waist and turned her about, away from the others. He uttered a threat in Turkish, and then capped the phrase with something in Arabic. Avi spoke: "He says to tell you that you will not be hurt if you don't fight. I am going to kill him, don't worry."

One more threat from the Arab, and he began to walk Rachel off the patio. Suddenly, the knife moved away from her throat, and Rachel could see that the Arab wanted her to place the gems in the hand holding the knife; but in that second in which the knife left her throat, she heard a shout that was in no language, a cry that was nothing other than a call for death. Without thinking, she ducked her chin, but the knife that had been gripped so well in the Arab's hand had not even come up to the level of her chest. It fell to the ground, and a great weight fell on her, and in a split second the weight was gone, and she could see that Avi had turned the Arab about and was slitting the man's throat.

"Just to make certain," he said, smiling.

Avi rolled the Arab over, and she saw that there was a knife in his back. Somehow, the dragoman had thrown the knife into the Arab's back from twenty feet and killed him instantly. Somehow, he had done this without fear or indecision. Somehow, he saw nothing strange in the sight of a dead man's body, a knife sticking out of his back, blood pouring out of his slit throat.

"Please, mademoiselle," said Avi. "You see, there is nothing to worry about. I am the famous dragoman, and nothing can harm you." He helped her to her feet, he urged her to be brave, he took the wineskin off one of the belts crisscrossing his chest and filled her mouth with wine. "I am Avi, the famous dragoman, and we go together to Jerusalem, and nothing will ever harm you."

The body was taken away, the Turks prepared a table of fruits and cheese and bread, and her own maid was asked to join her at the table; but Rachel was still not recovered when two hours later a servant entered the room where they dined with their host and the governor and spoke to him in frightened, servile tones.

Avi translated the governor's words to Rachel. "Do you know an American, mademoiselle?"

"What do you mean?" said Rachel, looking from the wild Turkish faces, to Avi, to Marie.

"There is an American gentleman outside who wants to see you," said Avi. "He says you are an old friend."

A moment later Rex Mitchell walked into the room, big and friendly, and eager to be of service.

Nothing that Marie or Henri said could change Rachel's mind. She was frightened, in a strange country, and she hired Avi as her dragoman and eagerly accepted the offer of Rex Mitchell to join their company on the way to Jaffa and Jerusalem.

CHAPTER TWENTY-ONE

Rachel Cohn was naïve in anything having to do with money. Avi the dragoman could have asked for almost anything for his services and he would have been paid without complaint. Rex Mitchell had once traveled the long way to Jerusalem from Beirut: over the mountainous terrain to Damascus on a miserable nag, accompanied by a not-famous dragoman, four fellow travelers, and a string of half-dead mules. From Damascus, the exhausted, dyspeptic, flea-bitten party had trudged on past Mount Hermon, the Sea of Galilee, Nazareth, and along the ancient highway—little more than a rocky path—to Jerusalem. Rex and each of the other travelers had paid the dragoman three dollars a day for providing all services—food and shelter and protection.

But the letter of credit that Rachel's father had made available to her through the Rothschild agent in Beirut was virtually unlimited. Even before Rachel had left Paris, Marie had sent word to Rachel's parents in Deauville about their daughter's headstrong plans. Both parents could not decide on any plan of action other than short-term help; their daughter would need the cushion of wealth in the strange places she was visiting. And so couriers had set out from Deauville, messages were telegraphed, family members visited Turkish ambassadors, and a letter of credit went out from Constantinople fully four days before Rachel had even arrived in that city. This she entrusted to Avi the dragoman, who had probably saved her life.

"I will take care of everything, mademoiselle. I am very happy that you are so rich," said Avi. The next day he hired an assistant dragoman, five Arab servants, and two heavily armed Arab guards.

"Now look here," said Rex Mitchell. "I'm carrying two good guns, and I've ridden back and forth through this country without a guard."

"I am the dragoman, I know what is best," said Avi, smiling. He procured four sleeping tents, one kitchen tent, one dining tent, thirty horses and mules. All the tents were of the finest quality and were very large. Avi ordered good beds, with excellent linen; camp chairs and tables; a great quantity of barley for the horses; tobacco for himself and the Arab guards. The cooking utensils, the cutlery, the plates and cups and serving dishes were all of European origin and absurdly expensive in Beirut. The blankets were of the finest wool, the lanterns had silver bases. The expedition, whose primary purpose was to transport one person—Rachel Cohn of Paris—from Beirut to Jerusalem, was taking on the proportions of a small army. "I know best," said Avi the dragoman. "Mademoiselle is not used to hardship. She is very rich, and she must be made very comfortable."

Marie found herself agreeing with all of Avi's arrangements, even though they had no language in common. Part of Avi's charm was to be always smiling, always complaisant with those who might turn out to be useful; he wanted Marie to tell her mistress that Avi was gentle, good, wise, and charming, and he made himself useful whenever he was around her. The dragoman bowed to the maid, told Rachel how lucky she was to have such a servant, made it a point to apologize for not speaking French; Marie responded by telling Rachel how lucky they were to have found such a good man, in such a pesthole. Rex Mitchell had a different opinion, of course; but then, Marie's opinion of the American was already well known to Rachel.

When they left Beirut—Avi and Rachel splendidly mounted on extravagantly expensive, and surprisingly rare, Arabian horses, galloping to the head of their train of animals and men—Rex's chagrin at being left with a plodding steed, more like a mule than a horse, was not severe. After all, he was paying but three dollars a day—and even that at his own insistence—for a magnificent tour; and on this expedition, only he and the Jewish heiress were not servants, only Rachel and Rex used each other's first name.

They were to take the coast road to Jaffa, and then go inland to Jerusalem. Though the Austrians ran a steamer line between Beirut and Jaffa, the Jaffa port was in bad repair and the service infrequent; moreover, Rachel had had her fill of steamship travel, and had heard quite a bit about the terrible squalls off the coast. The first day of the journey made her very glad of her decision.

Keeping as close to the seashore as possible, Avi led them south toward the ruins of Sidon and Tyre, following a narrow, sandy trail that soon became rocky and hard. Still, the air was fresh and held no hint of rain, though this was the rainy season. Rachel, who had always loved riding, was mightily impressed with her Arabian. She let her gallop, at Avi's insistence, to test the horse's mettle; even where the narrow path was covered with great chunks of stone, or was broken with unexpected cracks, the horse didn't falter.

Rachel could hardly look at the path as the horse ate up the distance, stepping over rocks and cracks and the roots of trees, ignoring a false step into marshy ground, jumping over any obstacle without hesitation. Even after a run that would have exhausted any horse she'd ever ridden before, the Arabian didn't show a speck of foam at her mouth, her chest contained a heart that was hardly racing; only a dark thread of sweat along the dark, silky coat showed Rachel that her horse had strained at all.

But the glories of the day were shaded by the ride past a tiny Arab village. Even before the village was visible past a short rise in the roadway, a crowd of Arab children, many of them naked, descended on the party. Avi slowed the company to a walk. "They are begging," he said, "and it is better to be a little generous with such a large, prosperous party." Rachel noticed that the coins the dragoman threw all landed well off the road, so that the path was soon clear of children.

"Here you see a typical village in the land of Syria," said Avi, and as they came up over the rise, Rachel saw a tiny cluster of square huts, most of them no taller than six feet.

"*Baksheesh!*" came the cry from the beggars who had not

deigned to leave the town and now sat crosslegged by the side of the dusty street. *"Baksheesh!"*

Already, some of the faster children who had met them outside the town were racing after the slower horses and mules and screaming for more. Marie and Henri dropped a few French sous, and the beggars spit at these useless coins, and some of them threw rocks, yelling, *"Frangi!"* the familiar contemptuous name for all Europeans in the Holy Land. When the rock throwing threatened to become more serious, the Arab guards at the rear of the party raised their pistols and fired into the air. At this, the rock throwing stopped, but not the begging, or the importunate cries in Arabic.

A common roof shielded most of the huts, and covered half the town as well. As they progressed through the single street, it became darker in the shadow of this roof, and the smell of dung was overpowering. The most unfortunate beggars seemed to be concentrated here: men and women and children with twised limbs, faces covered with sores; blind children with flies covering their eye sockets.

It seemed to Rachel that the begging was in a different key now: Outstretched hands quivered without expectation, children moaned and whined rather than demanded. It seemed as if the cripples were raising their broken bodies in tribute, or blessing.

"What are they saying?" said Rachel.

"They're praying for our eyes," said Avi.

"Give them money," said Rachel.

"Mademoiselle," said Avi with a smile, "these are not the dangerous ones.

"It's my money. Give it to them!"

The sounds and sights and smells of the village lingered with her for only a while, though they would come back later that evening when they were dining. Avi wisely picked up the pace, so that she and the others had to think about the path and the rush of bleak, yet strangely evocative, scenery. No one had to mention that Abraham had walked this way.

The dragoman set up camp well before dusk. It was incredible to Rachel and her French servants to see the speed with which the Arabs constructed the tents and laid out the camp furniture. Where there had been sand and rock, there was now a comfortable tent village, far more comfortable than the miserable village through which they had passed that day. Marie and Henri shared the pleasures of the dining table in the very large dining tent with Rachel, Avi, and Rex; the dragoman thought it best that the Arab servants serve all the Europeans together. For this unexpected shift in status from servant to fellow pilgrim, Marie and Henri continued to shower the handsome dragoman with praise.

But after a dinner of roast lamb and wine, after Avi had offered both Rex and Henri fresh cigars and old port, Rachel had a sudden vision of the toothless old men and the naked children sitting in the dust, their eyes lost to disease.

"That village we saw today," said Rachel. "Are they all that bad?"

"That was a pretty good one," said Rex, trying to remind Rachel that, if he was not a dragoman, he still knew his way around this part of the world.

"They are bad, all of them, filled with misery," said Avi. "But that is Syria, that is Palestine. And it looks better on the outside than on the inside.'

"It's true, Rachel," said Rex, exhibiting his ability to use her first name. "They're just whitewashed mudplaster, and all they've got inside is disease and vermin."

"I am not talking about the inside of huts, Mr. Mitchell," said Avi. "I am talking about inside here." The dragoman tapped his own broad chest. "They are all sad, all full of despair. No matter what they do, they lose. This is a poor land, and the people have poor spirits."

"I've seen Indians who have much less, and they don't despair," said Rex.

"You've been to India, Mr. Mitchell?" said Avi.

"I'm talking about American Indians. The ones we've got out West," said Rex. "They're proud people. They don't beg like we saw today." Remembering that his audience, except for the hostile French-speaking Marie and Henri, was Jewish, Rex added: "I don't know if you've ever heard this, but there's a theory that our American Indians are the Ten Lost Tribes of the Jews. Do you know, Avi here, with his long hair, could almost pass for an Indian. I never really thought much of that theory, but someone did find stone tablets in Ohio with Hebrew writing on them. I think it was from the Bible, from the Old Testament. Wouldn't that be amazing if it were true? That all our Indians were from the Jewish race?"

"Yes," said Rachel, who had never heard the theory before, though she'd heard others equally preposterous: Pseudoscholarship had placed the Ten Lost Tribes everywhere from China to Timbuktu. "But I'm really less interested in theories like that than I am in what we can know from the evidence before us. I'm not one of those people who've come to the Holy Land to think about the past. I want to see what I can do here in the present."

This would have been an ideal time for Avi to explain that the position of the Jews in the Holy Land was at least as bad, in many cases, as that of the spiritless Arabs in the village they'd passed through that day. But the dragoman didn't want to ruin the evening. The wine was excellent, because the rich girl's money had been enough to supply luxury where often there was only enough to purchase drab necessity. He smoked a cigar, he watched the way the big American tried to talk love to the heiress with his booming voice and friendly eyes, he drank a half-bottle of very good port. Rachel would learn bit by bit about the Holy Land. If she kept her eyes open, no amount of luxury in their own tents could keep out the misery of Arabs and Jews and Bedouins and Druzes; if only her eyes were open, she would know what to expect days before she would see the towers and domes of Jerusalem.

Before dawn the camp was stirring. Swift servants cooked an ample breakfast, and while the pilgrims ate, the tents were taken down and packed up on the mules with lightning speed. The excellent weather of the first day continued without change as they began the routine of travel: up before dawn, traveling at first light; pushing on south past ancient, decrepit cities, little more than rubble, a source of rocks and fragments for the terrible roads.

Sidon and Tyre were disappointing, and the journey had so fatigued Rachel that her only thought was to press on to Jaffa, where they might rest at a real hotel, and then on to Jerusalem itself. Past Mount Carmel, the rains, long delayed, began to fall with a vengeance. The rocky roads were now slippery, and the sandy roads dangerous pools of mud. Setting up camp was now an adventure, and an unpleasant one. The excellent tents beat back the rain for three nights of heavy downpour; but the dampness slowly penetrated, until they all felt it in their bones, and by the fourth night of rain, the tents were all leaking.

When the rain let up, they traveled as swiftly as possible, but now the streams that had been dry were running with furious, overflowing currents. The terrified animals had to be whipped across the raging waters. Rex carried Rachel across one stream on his back; Avi did the same for the half-frightened, half-pleased Marie. When after six days of nearly continuous rain the soggy party reached a small *khan*, there was no discussion about whether they would chance the filth and the vermin inside or remain in their wet tents; the entire company of mules and men and horses took refuge inside. Rex and Avi slept outside the door of the cell-like room where Marie and Rachel slept, and both men kept their hands on their guns through the night. Though the *khan* was small, it was crowded with traveling Arab merchants who had been eating and drinking for days, waiting out the rain; so insolently had they ogled the women when they entered the common courtyard of the place that Avi had had to restrain Rex from drawing his gun right then.

As it was, they didn't remain there all night. Rachel and Marie couldn't bear the fleas and mosquitoes and bedbugs, even sleeping in all their clothes, and hammered on their door before three in the morning to wake up Avi and Rex and urge them to leave. Avi managed to wake the servants and the guards, and by the time they got the animals loaded with their wet baggage, it was almost dawn. In the courtyard of the *khan*, a group of drunken Arabs sat mesmerized before a tall, gaunt figure, who was reciting something by heart to the men before him.

"He's a storyteller," explained Avi as they left the *khan* and pushed on toward Jaffa. "Men pay him to hear his stories. There's always one or two of them traveling about the *khans*."

That day the sun broke through the clouds, and at noon Avi ordered a rest while all their wet possessions were taken out to dry in the suddenly bright, hot air.

"Will the hotel in Jaffa be a decent one?" asked Rachel.

"Very decent, dear lady," said Avi. "It is run by a Jew from Germany, and he keeps it very clean."

"A Jew from Germany," said Rachel. "I'd like to see a Jew at last. I thought there'd be many between here and Beirut."

"Jews stay in the cities, mostly Jerusalem, Tiberias, Safed, Hebron. And they have reason to. There was once a Jewish settlement not far from where we passed near Acre. The Bedouins didn't want the Jews to try and farm, even in that miserable place where the Turks sold them land."

"What have the Bedouins got against the Jews?"

"It's not so much against Jews as it's against anyone who wants to farm the countryside," said Avi. "As long as the land can't be farmed, it's good for their goats. They want to keep everything wild so their goats can roam where they want. Farms mean people, people mean fences.

"I had a brother who was born here, in Palestine, outside of Jaffa. My younger brother. He worked on a farm run by American missionaries. He didn't want to become Christian, he just wanted to farm. The Bedouins burned all their crops, killed three priests, and cut off my brother's left hand. But the Americans sent more priests, and my brother kept farming. The next harvest, the farmers stayed up all night with their guns, and the crop was saved. But during the winter the Bedouins came and massacred everyone—the Americans, the Jews—and burned the farm settlement to the ground."

"Your brother?" said Rachel. "Was he there when it happened?"

"He's dead, yes," said Avi. "And now Bedouins' goats can run wild through the empty fields."

"I'm sorry, Avi," she said, but the dragoman's face was not sad, not even stoic; he was smiling, utterly at peace with the past. She had wanted to ask him about his family, for perhaps it might prove typical of the Jews she had come to Palestine to help. She felt so far removed from his experience that she was afraid anything she might ask would carry the shadow of a spoiled child's curiosity, a dilettante's wonder; and she wanted to impress upon him—upon all the Jews she would meet in this land—her worthiness, her seriousness.

But Rachel felt her credentials were inadequate, especially in their eyes. Avi's family had probably undergone unspeakable hardship in Russia. The proud dragoman might have been born in a wooden hut with a mud floor, with barn animals looking on as he took his first breath in the close air. His parents must have been strong, in body and soul, to have chanced a trek overland from Russia, through the Ukraine, into the territory of the

Ottoman Empire, pushing on with a baby, without proper food or enough money, into Syria and Palestine, into this desolate land filled with crumbling rocks and ancient memories of glory. She refrained from asking the dragoman what she would have liked to: How many children did his parents have? Was he himself married? Was his brother tall or short, handsome or plain? Did he have sisters? Did he feel close to Rachel, feel her to be part of his people? Instead, she shuddered in the delicious sun, and Avi volunteered to explain his smile.

"My brother was the happiest man in Palestine," he said. "He believed in impossible things. When they cut off his hand, he was glad they left him with his stronger hand, glad that he was alive to farm the land. My parents are alive now, alive in Jerusalem, and my brother honored them in their old age. He thought of them as the last generation of Jews who would be without rights in their own land.

"My brother wasn't religious, he was a dreamer. Because the Bible says the land was flowing with milk and honey, he believed that it could happen again. Because the Bible says we were farmers and warriors, he thought the Jews of today could live the same way they did two thousand years ago. He was as crazy as the Christian missionaries. You can find a Jew who'll take up farming, you can find a Jew who can use a gun. But you're never going to make the Jews of the world come back to Palestine. You're never going to make this land green and full of Jewish farmers who can shoot a gun."

"*You* can shoot a gun," said Rachel.

"I am a dragoman, that's different," said Avi. "I am a famous dragoman, the best in the Holy Land. My brother died happy, because he was sure that this land would belong to the Jews, and that it would be beautiful. If he had lived to be an old man, he would never have been able to stay happy. Just look at this land."

"This land can be reclaimed," said Rachel.

"Reclaimed by whom? For what?" said Avi. "It belongs to the Turks, and if the Jews buy any of it, the Bedouins or the Arabs drive them off it."

"Everyone else in the world has a homeland," said Rachel. "Why can't the Jews?"

"Your homeland is France," said Avi. "My homeland is the Holy Land. Your homeland is where your home is. I would like to be rich and live in Europe, with servants and coachmen and fine clothes. My brother was different. He died very happy, he died very young. He didn't know what I know. He never lived the way you do in France, mademoiselle."

Rachel took this as a rebuke. She wanted to claim this land on which they now rested as hers, too—hers by birthright; but she could not, of course. How could she be anything in his eyes but a pampered child, until she had achieved something on her own, with courage, with strength? He had saved her life as casually as she might have drunk a cup of tea; and while her brothers had proved their mettle by traveling in steerage to far ports in the world, his brother had been maimed and murdered for defending his right to live on the land.

For most of the rest of the way to Jaffa, Rachel rode toward the back of the party, slowing her Arabian to the wretched pace of Rex's tired trail horse.

"Are you all right?" Rex asked her as soon as she had pulled alongside. "You're not looking too cheerful."

"I heard a sad story."

"From our dragoman, no doubt."

"Yes."

"I wouldn't pay too much attention to his stories. They might be about as truthful as the ones the Arab storytellers cry over in the *khans*."

"This was a true story, Rex," she said angrily.

"All right, have it your way," he said, riding on in silence. He was convinced she was falling under the influence of the handsome Jew who had saved her life.

Much later that day, he saw the dragoman riding back along the train of horses, his flamboyant silk headdress flying back in the wind. Avi slowed his horse and turned it about, to ride along Rachel's flank. When the dragoman spoke to her, it seemed to Rex that neither Rachel nor Avi was aware of his existence.

"Listen, mademoiselle," said the dragoman. "What I said before. About France. I don't mean it. I don't mean it that I would want to live in France and be rich and all that. I am Avi, the famous dragoman, and my home is here, where we ride."

And then, not waiting for a reply, Avi galloped off to the head of the line. Rex could see Rachel looking after him with what could have been pride, or longing.

They reached Jaffa just before dark, and took over most of the best hotel in town. Rachel was given a spacious room at the top of the house, with windows on three sides. Best of all, she was to be by herself, as Marie and Henri were given a room of their own on the ground floor. It was a luxury to be alone with her thoughts, her feet up on a wooden chair, looking out to the sun setting over the sea. Of course, Marie did not neglect to come up to Rachel's room—to shake out her clothes, to see to her bath, to brush her hair, to question her about Rex, to praise Avi for finding this decent hotel and giving them all some privacy. But Marie had no great wish to linger, as Rachel was so thoughtful as to be almost no company at all. Maid left mistress with a cup of tea and her solitude, and was satisfied with having done her job.

Rachel was pleased to discover a Hebrew Bible in the room, printed in Safed, as well as two devotional works from one of the Hasidic sects who lived near the Sea of Galilee, waiting for the Messiah. It reminded her that the hotel's owner was a Jew; it was an indication of the Jews' presence in their ancient land. Though she had not been very impressed with Herr Goldstein's manners—the hotel keeper was a Jew of German origin—she had been touched by the way he had spoken to Avi in swift, ungrammatical Hebrew, the common language of Palestinian Jews of different origins. Somehow, through nearly two thousand years of wandering, Jews could still on this common ground, in this common language. Avi had not been born in the Holy Land, but perhaps he had children, or someday would have, who would be native to the land of their forefathers.

All her dreams of fulfillment, of dedicating herself to a great, but possible, task, of using her power, her money, her life for something other than pleasure, came back to her with force. She had been fatigued by the trek to Jaffa, worn out by the endless rain, exhausted by the bleakness all about her. But suddenly she found herself exhilarated. They were to turn inland now, to Jerusalem, a journey of less than two days. There she would meet the Jewish community she had come to aid. There she would meet her life's work.

"Mademoiselle?" The voice was Avi's, and it was outside her

door. "Mademoiselle Rachel," he said, and then he knocked softly.

"What is it?" said Rachel, not realizing that she had run over to the cracked mirror over the bureau and was even then trying to fluff out her straight hair.

"May I come in to see you?" he said, and then the doorknob turned and the dragoman entered, shutting the door behind him. "It's all right," he said. "I'm in."

"What do you want?" said Rachel, staring at him from across the room.

"I will light a lamp," said Avi. It was nearly dark now, and she watched in fascination as he lit two old lamps, bathing the room in muted pools of light. "I was worried about you."

"Why did you come in?" she said. His long hair, free of the silk headdress, glistened in the lights of the lamps. He was taking a step closer to her, his eyes wide, as she said again: "I was about to open the door, after all. But it's not right, you really shouldn't have come in until I asked you to do so."

"What?" said Avi, his voice soft, nearly inaudible. She noticed that his scimitar was not attached to the belt that he wore about his waist. "You don't want me?"

"That's not what I said. It's just that you should wait before walking into a lady's room."

"You are a dear lady," said Avi.

"What are you here for, Avi?"

"You were angry before, dear lady. Because I said your home was in France. I do not want you angry at me. That is why I rode back and told you that this was my land, and that I would always want to stay here."

"I want to stay here too," said Rachel.

"You must be very brave then," said Avi, and he took a final step, so that he was standing before her, with his right hand outstretched. "Please take my hand."

"Why?"

"Go on," said Avi. "To be friends."

"We are friends already," said Rachel. "And I'm not angry at you. I'm very happy to be here, and I'm very thankful for everything you've done for me." Still, she didn't reach out her hand.

"I am no longer married," said Avi.

"Yes?" said Rachel, not knowing what to say to this. "You were married once? Is that what you mean?"

"Yes."

She felt impaled to the spot, her eyes forced to look now at his outstretched, indefatigable hand, now at the way the light behind him lit up his handsome face.

"What happened to your wife?"

"She's dead," he said. "A long time ago."

Suddenly, he took hold of her hand. Rachel could not resist his pressure, not as he told of his pain. "She wasn't even twenty. It was in Jerusalem. She was bringing water to the home of my parents. She was attacked by Turks and she resisted what they wanted to do to her, and so they killed her. No one was even punished for her death. I wanted to live outside Jerusalem once. I wanted to be a farmer, like my brother wanted. But I couldn't do it after she died. I couldn't live in Jerusalem, or near Jerusalem. And I couldn't live without it either."

Avi smiled again, the smile she had first seen earlier that day when he had told her of his brother's death. "In two days, we'll see Jerusalem. I'm your dragoman; I wanted you to understand. Sometimes I'm not so happy when I'm seeing Jerusalem again. You will see."

He let go of her hand and backed away from her, not turning his back, retreating as if she were a queen. When he was near the door, he spoke again. "I was going to kiss you," he said. "You are very rich, and I was going to see if you would love me. We are the only ones on this level, up high, alone in this place. I was going to kiss you, but it is better this way. You are a dear lady."

He left her room before she could answer him. She was left with the lamps, the black night, and the image of his sadness.

Rachel could not sleep. She wondered again whether her life could ever be lived with the intensity of heroic fire. She was certain that Avi's wife had been beautiful, with black wavy hair, and that she had been afraid of nothing, even at the point of death. Even when the bearded Arab in the home outside the walls of Beirut had grabbed Rachel, holding a knife to her throat, it hadn't seemed to affect her life; it was like a bad dream, outside her control, and gone in a moment. She had never lived like other people had lived: not like Avi, not like Rex, not like the legends of the Rachels for whom she had been named. He was going to kiss her, he'd said. But he hadn't. It would be better not to kiss her; she was too soft, too ladylike, too delicate—she might break. And there was no reason to kiss her. She was not beautiful, she was not intelligent, she was not strong. She was simply rich, and the dragoman had taken pity on her. But she was too pitiable even for a romance that might bring riches home to her lover. "You are a dear lady," he'd said, meaning that she was too dear to exploit. Only in exploiting her could he find a reason to drive his lips to hers, to tell her that she was a woman worthy of loving.

They left very early the next morning, Avi and the servants having arranged everything in the hours before dawn. She rode with Rex, at the back of the line, over the Plain of Sharon. He could see that she hadn't slept, and his eyes held sadness in them for her. Rachel thought that he, too, was looking at her with pity. When he spoke to her of the flowers he'd seen when riding over this plain once before in the early spring, she thought him kind. Such was her mood that she was incapable of judging the love in his eyes. In the distance they could see the mountains of Ephraim, and Rex tried to cheer her with a story of the night he had spent in a cave full of ghosts not far from Ramla, near where they set up camp for the night.

The next day they rode through desert, up and down little hills strewn with rocks. Rachel remembered the words to a psalm: "If I forget you, O Jerusalem, let my right hand wither! Let my tongue cleave to the roof of my mouth if I do not remember you, if I do not set Jerusalem above my highest joy!" She recited it to Rex first in Hebrew, then in French, and he recited it to her from memory, in English.

The desert glare was frightful, and Rex helped arrange the long white cloth she'd wrapped about her hat to beat back the rays of the sun. Avi rode back to her at one point with one of the white umbrellas that tourists used, but Rachel refused it, afraid of making herself look ridiculous. She wanted to look as natural as Rex in his American cowboy hat, as Avi in his silk headdress, as the Arab guards in their great turbans.

By the middle of the second day out of Jaffa, the party began to ride through a greater concentration of stones and fragments; in the terrific glare the sudden bits of ancient wall and broken-up arches seemed like mirages, like a dream of a ravaged history.

"We're close," said Rex. "We're going up, and it will soon be there."

"Going up," said Rachel, and she remembered with a certain awe how her mother had aways referred to a trip to Jerusalem as an *aliyah*, a going-up, and how all the references to the ancient capital of her people were enshrined in the Bible in that usage. And here were the hills, and the deserted land, and the fragments of the past all about her.

Suddenly, she saw Avi galloping back toward her from the head of the line, the flaming colors of his headdress flying back in the wind, catching the sun, his face radiating intense joy. "Come on," he said. "Come on, mademoiselle, the last hills, we go up! We go up together!"

For the first time, he'd spoken to her in Hebrew. Without thinking, she responded in that language: "We'll go up," she said. "We'll go up, together!"

The two of them, galloping on their powerful Arabians, left the line of hacks and mules, jumping over cracks and bumps and stones, climbing and climbing into the glaring sun, beating back the heat and the light and the dust with an anticipation as old as their people's history.

Then they climbed the last hill.

In the distance, white and radiant, ancient and eloquent, high and austere on its famous hills, was the eternal city of Jerusalem. Slowly Rachel got off her horse and dropped the reins. The beauty of the white domes, massed together under the clear sky, ringed by the ancient city wall, was like a congregation of hopes and dreams, a mass of huddling buildings, each with its history, each standing on a millenium of glory and pain. It was a beauty her soul was striving to see, and so she created it out of the materials before her. Even in ruins, from this distance, she could not be disappointed. The vision within her, compounded from a hundred generations of longing, longed for an object to love, to affirm her past, to direct her present. She sank to her knees, the domes and the towers clouded by tears, as the other members of the party joined her and the dragoman.

There was no talk now; not by the Arab servants and guards, who had conducted pilgrims before and understood their mood; not by Marie and Henri, kneeling before the holiest city in

Christendom; not by Rex, who had no desire to break Rachel's reverie. The American and Avi were the only ones who had remained on horseback; but realizing that these particular pilgrims would not want to proceed for at least an hour, they dismounted at the same time, and their hard eyes met.

As always, Avi had been moved by the sight of the capital of the Jews, but his knowledge of the contemporary city, and his memory of his wife's death, did not let him remain long in a mood of contemplative adulation. As much as Rex, he could see the city in another way: as a small, filthy Turkish city, ringed by dull gray walls that only managed to keep out the sun and keep in the fetid air. Where Rachel saw ancient glory, Avi could see present misery; where Rachel felt the city a link to her biblical past, Avi felt the city a link to his wife's murder, in a city that had not been ruled by Jews for nearly two thousand years.

Still and all, even for Avi, the city was Jerusalem.

No matter how jaded with experience, how privy to the knowledge of the city's miseries, the city still floated its message of hope through the heated air. The dragoman was a Jew, and this was the one place in the world that never failed to release a flood of ineffable sensations. It was as if his ancestors were trying to talk to him through the black corridors in his brain; their muffled voices rose higher and higher as his eyes followed the rising road to the city's heights. Even though he knew that the voices would still as soon as he entered the city, he believed that their spirits remained always about the city, always shouting for a return to Jerusalem's ancient happiness.

"Come," said Avi finally to Rachel. "It's time. Let's go up."

And the pilgrims mounted their horses, and the storybook visions of the Mount of Olives, the Mosque of Omar, the Tower of David, all began to melt together as the perspective changed and they neared the Jaffa Gate. Rex wanted to ride up to her and prepare her for what she would see, but he felt himself excluded from her experience, separated from her by the history of her own people.

Then they entered the city of David, the city of Solomon, the city where Jesus walked to his death and the Jews sacrificed to their One God. Even before they were through the Jaffa Gate, the fetid odors assailed them; even before they could be shocked by the incredibly narrow streets, crowded with beggars and running with filth, they were met by lepers, exposing their sores in hopes of earning a few coins for the sake of pity.

"Jerusalem," said Rachel, her vision assaulted on every side. "Jerusalem." And in that moment she dedicated her life to the spires and domes and shimmering glory she had seen from the other side of the walls. In that moment, she dedicated herself to the dreams of her people.

CHAPTER TWENTY-TWO

At that time, the city walls contained less than fourteen thousand people—perhaps five thousand of them Jews, living in the most squalid part of Jerusalem, the slope of Mount Zion. The rest of the population was divided between Turks and Christians. There were few Arabs within the city, the *fellahin*—peasants—preferring their desolate life outside the walls to the wretched existence offered within them.

The Turks were the masters of the city, and they were contemptuous of the multitude of fanatic sects who suffered so much to get there; they were yet more contemptuous of those who chose to remain as residents. The Christians were Armenian, Latin, or Greek, though there were reputed to be as many as one hundred distinct sects besides, all of whom visited the Church of the Holy Sepulchre and believed it to belong to them alone. The Turks assigned policemen to prevent the Christians from killing each other in the courtyard of the famous ramshackle church, where pilgrims from all over the world went to see Calvary, to see the very hole where the cross had been fixed in the earth. Only the day before Rachel's party arrived in the city, a Coptic Christian had been murdered by two Italian priests, both of whom were hauled off by the Turks to face an impersonally fierce justice.

The Jews had fewer sects, fewer wars, and fewer chances for justice. While the Christians supported themselves with charity from abroad and industry at home—mostly the production of religious articles—the Jews existed almost completely on charity. They were mostly old, having come there to die; mostly tired, having traveled on faith for too many miles in order to get to this stopping place before death. Some of the younger ones, particularly those of the Sephardic community, did engage in selling vegetables and other necessities in the narrow streets; but these merchants were subject to heavy taxation, sudden attacks by Turkish urchins, and the violence of vagabonds. Their quarter was filled with disease brought by a complete lack of sanitary conditions. The narrow alleys of the Zion quarter ran with a wet slime that was never drained, and buzzed with every species of flea and mosquito. About the only good thing that had happened to the Jewish residents of the city of late was the decree by the British government placing all Jews, of any national origin, under the protection of the British consul in Jerusalem.

It was the consul's assistant, a young scholar, who had arrived at Rachel's hotel early the next morning and begun to brief her on this information. Though she was staying at the Mediterranean Hotel, run by a German Jew and reputedly the cleanest hotel in town, she couldn't bear the mosquitoes that seemed to swarm over whatever parts of her body she was not slapping.

"There's a saying in Palestine," said the young scholar, "both among the Jews and the Arabs, that the King of the Fleas lives in Tiberias, but has followers in every village in the country." He went on to explain, in the same maddeningly droning voice, that the open cisterns in the city were what bred the fleas and mosquitoes. "There's not a single sewer in all of Syria," he said with a smile. The mosquitoes didn't seem interested in biting him at all.

He would have gone on to name the various types of insects most prevalent in the city had not Rex knocked on the door. After introductions and excuses, Rachel explained that she had been promised a tour of the city by Rex Mitchell, the famous American tour-book writer. The Englishman extended the consul's invitation to dinner that evening, and left them.

"Now let's get out of here, you poor thing," said Rex.

The city was small, and the entire circumference of the walls could be walked around in an hour. Rex hustled her past the beggars at the gates and joined a small procession of residents, who had the habit of walking around the city every morning. "It's the only way to get any air," said Rex. And Rachel admitted to feeling better at once; outside the walls, there was light, and freely moving air. Most of the horde of mosquitoes had chosen to remain behind, and she could stop slapping at her sorry flesh.

"This is a relief," she said.

"When I was here last, I did it every morning," said Rex. "Otherwise I'd go mad. If the Church was smart, it would hire some brigands to burn the whole city down, and start all over."

"It's not just the Church who has an interest in Jerusalem."

"Of course not," said Rex. "I wasn't speaking seriously anyway. I know how much Jerusalem means to many people. If you like, we can go up on the walls and I can show you some of the sights. I'm writing that guidebook—let me show you what I'm going to include."

"Why don't people live here?" said Rachel suddenly, as they walked about the walls.

"Where? Do you mean outside the walls?"

"Yes. There's so much land outside, so little inside."

"It's safer inside. They close the gates at night."

"Why wouldn't it be safe out here? People could breathe here," said Rachel. "Why couldn't there be a little settlement? A tiny village?" She was pointing to possible places on the landscape, barren save for a tiny cluster of ancient olive trees. "Hasn't anyone ever tried to buy some land out here?"

"Yes," said Rex. "The last time I was here, a rich Jew did. Got a deed from the sultan of Turkey. He wanted to start a settlement here. He got some Jews to move here, ones who were fresh from Poland and didn't know any better. They were all killed the second night they slept in their tents outside the city."

Rachel said nothing to this. If she was horrified, she was used to being horrified. They walked on in silence for a long while, exchanging greetings with several tourists, walking around the walls from the other direction.

"They should have guns," she said finally.

"What? Who should have guns?"

"The Jews."

"What Jews? What're you talking about, Rachel?"

"I am going to buy some land for the Jews, outside the walls."

"But I just told you what happened when I was here last."

"Did they have guns then?"

"I don't know. Probably not. What difference does it make? Americans carry guns when they ride from city to city here, and they still have to hire an Arab guard."

"I'll hire an Arab guard too."

"Hire an Arab guard to protect the Jews?"

"Yes. Why not? The world is becoming more civilized, even if it is taking forever. Did you see those beggars yesterday?"

"Of course I did.

"What am I supposed to do?" said Rachel. "Give them each a few coins and go back to Paris?"

"I am not going to tell you what to do. Not anymore."

"Good."

"Unless, of course, you were to ask me."

"I am not going back. I haven't even seen anything yet."

"You've seen enough. You've seen beggars and filth and crowded streets. You've seen that you could hardly breathe from your high room in the best hotel in the city. What more do you want to see? Do you want to go visit inside the homes of the lepers?"

Rachel refused to answer this question, and then tried to explain. "Do you know that the British consul here knows one of my brothers?"

"No."

"Yes. And several of my English cousins. He's already heard from the family—a letter by way of Alexandria. They're so much faster than I, my family. It would be very easy for me to get home. I could probably arrange something with the British Navy, or one of the French yachtsmen might pick me up in Greece. It would be very easy to go home. That's what my family wants." Rachel looked from Rex to the overshadowing wall. "Look where we are. Jerusalem. I'm not going anywhere. Can you understand that? Can you understand what I want to do?"

"No," said Rex. "I'm sorry, but I can't."

They finished their tour of the walls, and then Rex took her up the stone steps to the top of a wall. He showed her the dome of the Church of the Holy Sepulchre, and the Pool of Hezekiah, adjacent to their hotel. "That's where they grow the mosquitoes," said Rex.

"Where's the Jewish quarter?"

Rex pointed to it, and she looked to another region of twisting streets, so narrow that one could practically jump across the street, from one rickety building to the next. "It looks so poor," said Rachel.

It was the worst time in the world he could have chosen for romance, but Rex was so enamored of what he thought of as her misguided idealism, her heart full of love, that he could contain his own no longer. There, on the top of the wall overlooking the city, he saw her as a noble spirit, full of an urgency to help, to heal, to love, and he wanted to direct this impulse his way. Hardly letting her last words die on her lips, he bent low and grabbed her pale cheeks and kissed her, driving his love through the hands on her face, the force of his mouth on hers. Rex held her so tight that it was impossible to tell if she was yielding or resisting; all he knew was that he was kissing her, that the event was taking place. When he pulled back, he could see that she was in tears.

"I love you," he said.

Rachel looked at him through her tears, looked at him in wonder to see if such a statement could possibly be true.

"Why did you do that?" she said.

"I told you. I love you."

"Why?" she said. She was not angry that she had been kissed, she was incredulous that the kiss could have been motivated by love. "Why do you love me?"

"Rachel," said Rex, "I don't know what to say to that. I do, I just do. It's you, that's all. I love you because you want to cry every time you see a beggar. That's not a reason. I don't know why. I just know I had to kiss you."

"You really love me?" said Rachel.

"Yes."

"Thank you," she said, without thinking.

"What is that supposed to mean?" he said, his voice rising suddenly high in exasperation. He turned about, his back to her, looking down at the city. For the first time, Rachel realized that this big handsome American could actually be hurt by her not loving him.

"Rex," she said, "I didn't think it possible that someone like you would be interested in someone like me."

"Someone like me?" said Rex, turning on her. "Do you mean someone without a penny to his name? Is that what you're talking about? I didn't know your family knew every consul in the East and had a bank in every port in Christendom when I first started talking to you. I'm sorry if I wasn't raised in the same way you were. But I'm a human being, free and alive, and in America we don't care so much who your parents are, so it's not so crazy that I could fall in love with someone as rich and powerful as Mademoiselle Cohn."

"Rex, I didn't mean that," said Rachel. She was smiling, and she knew that it was awful to be smiling in the midst of his pain, but she was twenty-one, and that was very old to have realized for the first time that a man could love her for no other reason than her face, her hair, the words she spoke and how she spoke them. "I meant that you're handsome, and I'm so plain."

"What?" said Rex, looking at her as if she were crazy. He had never seen the beautiful young women of Paris, dancing in the home of her parents, their eyes eager for a glance from one of Rachel's handsome brothers. "Plain? I'm handsome and you're plain? Are you crazy? You're beautiful."

"I am not beautiful," she said, but her lips were still smiling, even against her will. Of course the handsome American was exaggerating, or else he did not know many beauties; but still, there was his statement, his agitation, his profession of love. "Really, Rex," she said. "I'm not beautiful at all."

But then he had bent low over her once again, and this time she understood precisely what was happening, as if it were all slow, laborious action: He shut his eyes, he pressed her face to his, he let out a silly moan from his big, sturdy frame. There were his lips, opening with infinite patience and true devotion; he was telling her again, in his fashion, what he had said before, and what she was now beginning to believe.

She let him kiss her. It was a compliment, not a desecration. No one had ever kissed her before who was not in her family, except for Marie. She loved his kiss, for all its awkwardness. It was a wonderful kiss, and she felt herself swaying through space, floating through a new world that held the possibility of being beautiful. But she was not thinking of loving Rex. Even in the moment of his embrace, her mind swept back to Avi, taking her hand with force, in the hotel room in Jaffa. If Rex could think her beautiful, so could Avi. If there was something about her that a man could love, the dragoman could discover it. Perhaps she'd been wrong to think Avi had pitied her. Perhaps he had pulled away from her in the dark of that room out of respect, or even love.

"What is it?" said Rex.

"I'm sorry," she said.

He had pulled away from her and was looking at her with displeasure, as if he had only just discovered something base, something ignoble about her character. "You don't love me," he said. "You don't care for me at all, do you?"

"I care for you," said Rachel, "but I don't love you."

"Then why did you—" he began, but he never finished his sentence. There were a hundred reasons why she could have allowed him to kiss her. It was not her fault if he had thought of only one. Even as he had kissed her, even when he had felt the beginning of a joyous response quivering through her body, he had feared that the joy was not for him. He was about to turn from her, leave her alone on the wall over the city, but he steeled himself: She could not know his resentment, his anger. "I just thought," he said, "that you were glad when I kissed you."

"I was," said Rachel.

"I don't understand."

"I never thought you'd want to kiss me," she said. "I was very surprised. I was very flattered. All my life, I never thought anyone would want to kiss me like that, especially not someone like you. But if you did, maybe I was wrong. I'm sorry if I said or did anything to hurt you."

"No," said Rex, but there was a pain running through him, a sudden illumination of all that she was saying.

"Because I like you very much. You've been like a brother to me, but even better. My brothers never showed me all that much interest after all. Any interest they did show was because I was their sister. No other reason than that."

"Avi," said Rex, so suddenly that the name was like an execration.

"What about Avi?"

"You're in love with the dragoman."

"I don't want to discuss that."

"You kissed me, and you're in love with Avi," said Rex with disgust. "Come on, I'll take you back to the hotel."

"I don't have to be taken."

"I can't just leave you here by yourself."

"I'm not going back to the hotel."

"All that son of a bitch cares about is how much money you've got," said Rex. "Don't you understand that?"

"Leave me alone. Please. Please just leave me alone."

But Rex would not leave her there. Angry as she was with him for what he had said about Avi, she could see that he was far angrier with her for not having denied that she was in love with the dragoman. They went down the stone steps into the dark, bad air of the city. Instead of turning toward the hotel, Rex led her in the opposite direction, pausing to grab her elbow when they were crowded by Turks in the narrow alleys.

"Where are we going?" she demanded.

"You wanted to see the Jewish quarter," he said.

The alleys they walked on their way to the Jewish quarter were filled with piles of human excrement. Men relieved themselves in the streets without shame or thought of adding to the sanitary crisis of the city. Even the Via Dolorosa, all the way to the Church of the Holy Sepulchre, was crowded with the filth. Only the alleys near the Mosque of Omar, which neither Christian nor Jew could enter—the penalty for violating this injunction was death—were kept at all clean.

"Signora, signora!" screamed a little Jewish boy with a skullcap and long sidelocks, reaching for her hand, trying to pull her to a bazaar. Rachel gave the boy a coin, and he ran with it, running to show his mother. Nearby, Turks were selling Christian religious objects, everything from fake relics of the cross to shells carved with the image of the madonna and child. One of them refused to let them pass, insisting that they look at his beautiful carved bowls made of bituminous stones from the Dead Sea, until Rex pushed him aside with force. Half-starved dogs sniffed at their heels, begging for scraps of food in competition with the swarms of human beggars. Every few hundred feet they'd pass another evil-smelling pile of burning garbage, its smoke unable to pass over the walls of the city.

Wretched as these streets were, however, they were still less bad than the Jewish quarter itself. "If you want to turn back, just say so," said Rex, but Rachel had no intention of retreating.

They entered an alley near the foot of Mount Zion, where the poorest of the Jews lived in crumbling huts, only to be close to the Wailing Wall, the last remnant of the Second Temple. A tall Jew with a yellow beard offered his services as a guide to help them find their way out of the quarter, but Rachel explained to the startled man that she was a Jew and wanted to see the Jewish quarter.

"There is only misery to see here, signora," said the man. "Old people waiting to be buried in the Valley of Jehosophat." But he directed her to the home of Beenyamin Ben-Solomon, high up Mount Zion in one of the few decent parts of the quarter. "He is rich, signora," said the man. "He can offer you the hospitality that you require."

Rex and Rachel continued to walk up the slope of Mount Zion, and Rex observed how easy it would be to drain the filthy streets, due to the steepness of the ground. More than any physical decrepitude, the attitude of the people they passed was depressing to witness. The Jews of Jerusalem seemed positively broken in spirit, as if they'd spent their lives running in a race to reach heaven and, winning the race, had found the promise of heaven to be a sham. Almost without exception, the men and women in the streets seemed to be of the most orthodox, even fanatic, persuasion. Finding Jerusalem to be a hell on earth was not something most of them were prepared to change. They subsisted on charity, and waited either for the Messiah or the redemption of death in the Holy City.

"Signora, signora!" came a voice behind them, and as they turned they saw the same tall Jew with whom they'd spoken before, out of breath from running. "I've spoken to Mar Beenyamin," he said. "Follow me, and he shall greet you with honor."

They were all three out of breath by the time they reached the home of Beenyamin Ben-Solomon, overlooking the famous Tower of Hippicus. A dark-skinned servant stood at the outer door of a modest but well-built home, and opened it at their approach, ushering them inside after they had thanked the tall Jew for his help. Rex and Rachel crossed through a surprisingly large, airy courtyard and were greeted by the master of the house. Beenyamin Ben-Solomon was a man of sixty, but vibrant and clear-headed, with hands that seemed to be always in the act of describing some great feat. He took them into the main sitting room and they all sat on low divans, while Rex tried to find a language in common with the man.

"Do you speak Hebrew?" said Rachel in that language, and Beenyamin smiled.

"Wonderful," he said in Hebrew. "Besides, now we can speak openly in front of this Gentile." He was referring to poor Rex, who was forced to drink strong, overly sweetened coffee and listen to the flow of the language without understanding a word. "I know who you are, of course," said Beenyamin.

"What do you mean?"

"I knew of your arrival almost at once. The consul—the British consul—is a dear friend. He would almost have invited me to the dinner tonight, but, alas, there is still a distinction between a visiting member of the Cohn dynasty and an old Jew made comfortable from selling tenting equipment to tourists on their way to Jaffa or Damascus."

"I shall invite you as my guest," said Rachel.

"No, no, that wouldn't be wise. The British must observe the proper look of things. It's quite enough that they're granting the Jews protection, of a sort. That's really encouraging. The Turks at the consul's table would think he was trying to insult them and their government if he invited a Jew from the Zion quarter to dine with them." Beenyamin Ben-Solomon smiled at this, as if it were to be taken as a harmless joke.

"But that is not what you're here to talk about. You see, I'm at an advantage. When my friend told me you were in the quarter, I knew who and what you were at once. I know you've come to Jerusalem to help the poor Jews. I even know that you want to live in the Holy Land. These are impressive things for me to know, but you know so little about me." Beenyamin clapped his hands together and the dark-skinned servant appeared. He spoke to her in Arabic.

"Where are you from, sir, if I may ask?" said Rachel.

"Russia," said Beenyamin.

"Russia," repeated Rachel in wonderment. She didn't think there were many Russian Jews in the Holy Land, and already she'd met two. "I know someone else from Russia who lives here."

"Yes, your dragoman."

"How did you know that? How do you know so much about me?"

An older Jewish woman entered the room, and with her was a

girl of Rachel's age. Both women wore long veils of embroidered muslin and had thick, lustrous black hair. Around their necks were long strands of gold coins. The younger woman was dressed in black silk and had no jewelry or ornamentation other than the gold coins. But the older woman had a vermilion-colored pomegranate bloom hanging from a chain about her neck, as if it were a jewel. She also wore large earrings, and many rings. Her robe was not black but striped green and gold silk; over this she wore a short-sleeved green jacket. The younger woman was very pale, and very beautiful. She had the look of a tragic heroine, and even as Rex got to his feet to greet the women, Rachel could feel the shock of his desire.

"This is my wife, Naomi, and my daughter, Sarah," said Beenyamin. "Sarah speaks French. Does the gentleman from America know the French language? In Russia, where we come from, only the richest people liked to learn French, but here in Jerusalem she wanted to learn only French. Just two weeks ago we had a French writer, a Gentile, in our house, and she was the only one of us who could translate."

"Why is she wearing black?" said Rex in English.

"She speaks French, Rex," said Rachel. "But I don't think it would be proper to ask."

Rex approached the girl and spoke to her in French, his accent so bad that even the tragic-heroine face had to smile. Unlike the women of the Christian and Muslim community in Jerusalem, the women of the Jewish community were forthright, outspoken. It was Sarah who offered to show the American tour-book writer about their rear garden; Rex stumbled after her, his brow knotted up in concentration, trying to understand every word of her excellent French.

Naomi, Beenyamin's wife, joined her husband on the divan and spoke in Hebrew to Rachel. "You cannot find Jews to farm this land," she said. "It matters nothing how rich you are. That is not the way to help the Jews of this city."

"My wife speaks her mind without ceremony," said Beenyamin. "But she, too, knows why you're here, and has had bitter experience with farm projects."

"Jews are people of the cities," said Naomi.

"Not always," said Rachel. "There was a time when they farmed."

"Only dead Jews farm here. Only dead Jews leave the cities."

"Naomi," said Beenyamin, "this young woman is a guest in our home. She has come to help the poor Jews."

"Let her give money then, like all the others who come."

"I will give money, but I must do more than that."

"That's all the Jews want here in the way of help. With all those missionaries and their farm projects, the most converts they ever made was when they paid the Jews in gold," said Naomi. "That's one of the best ways for a Jew to make a living here in the Holy Land. Convert. Become a Christian ten different times, and you can live well for years."

The woman was touching at her flower with the tips of her fingers, caressing it. Rachel began to wonder if she was a little mad.

"You seemed to have made a comfortable living here, sir," said Rachel. "How long ago did you come from Russia?"

"Twenty-four years ago," said Beenyamin. "I came just in time for the first wave of crazy Europeans, running through the Holy Land for the good of their souls. I was a tailor, a tailor for the Jews, and I knew all there was to know about patching up secondhand material. I worked for an old Turk, who taught me about tents. He died, and the tourists came, and I made a great deal of money for a Jew in Jerusalem. But that's not very much. My wife's jewelry was all bought by my son—he knows it makes her a little bit happy.

"But that's not what you want to know. You want to know how to help the poor Jews. They can't all become tentmakers. And the Turks and the Christians are already making all the trinkets and souvenirs for the pilgrims. If you want to know what Jerusalem needs for its Jews, it needs a business that can employ five hundred men, and give them enough dignity and sustenance to look after their lives on this earth. The only other business this city has for the Jews is the Torah. And unfortunately that's not feeding anyone, and it's not keeping the streets clean."

"Do you think that if the Jews here in Jerusalem had that—a business—do you think they'd change?" said Rachel, speaking so suddenly, her voice so full of excitement, that Beenyamin couldn't fathom her meaning. "What I mean is, everyone has been telling me that it doesn't pay to buy land here for the Jews, because there are so few who can farm. But maybe that's the point. For people who've only lived in cities, it's too fast to start them right off working on farms, trying to defend themselves. I've seen the Jews here today, and they're not the sort of Jews that are going to leave this place. They're too religious, and they've come here to study the Torah and die. But if they had a job here, if they could have a real community that was clean and strong and self-sufficient, then their *children* would be able to farm."

"What is she talking about?" said Naomi. "Why does she want more Jewish boys to die?"

"You understand what I'm saying, don't you, sir?" said Rachel. "My dragoman told me what to expect here, but I didn't really believe it all. I thought everyone would be like you, only a little poorer, a little more crowded. But no one's like you, because they're all on charity and without a trade, and mostly old. There has to be a generation in Jerusalem that can grow up strong before there can be strong young men, and farmers."

"I understand everything you're saying, my dear," said Beenyamin Ben-Solomon. "But even with a huge donation of money to the Jewish charities here, what kind of business can you possibly start in a city of fourteen thousand people with no resources, no real trade except in the junk sold to tourists?"

"There is a business," said Rachel. "Not a little business either. An entire industry."

"What do you mean? What business?" said Beenyamin.

"Diamonds," said Rachel Cohn. "The diamond business."

"What?" said Beenyamin, laughing. "Diamonds for the poorest Jews in the world? Jews who cannot sell old clothes are to buy and sell the world's most precious substance?"

"They won't have to buy and sell," said Rachel. "You don't need five hundred people to buy and five hundred people to sell. You need five hundred people to cut and polish the rough diamonds that my family buys and mines in India and Brazil. We're even hoping to find diamonds in Africa now. Palestine was once the crossroads of the world. It hasn't moved. It's still in an ideal spot for trade. All we have to do is train the people who are here. All we need is time and money and patience."

"All anyone needs is time and money and patience, my dear," said Beenyamin. "But no one has ever seemed to have enough where the city of Jerusalem is concerned. I understand what you're saying. And I believe you to be sincere. But even you would have to admit the possibility of your losing interest in this city, in this little community of poor Jews, even after a few more days or weeks."

"No," said Rachel. "There is no possibility of that."

"They killed my son," said Naomi, speaking softly in Hebrew.

"Not now, Naomi," said Beenyamin. "We have a guest."

"They killed my son," she said again, still more softly than before. She touched the vermilion blossom on its chain. "It is two years ago that he died. This is the week, two years ago, two short years." Naomi leaned forward and touched Rachel's fingertips. "My daughter wears black this week, in his memory, but I do not. He was a dreamer, and he wanted to grow pomegranates in the desert, he wanted to drain the swamps and bring back the ancient terraces. My son was a dreamer and he would have wanted me to dress the way I am."

"I'm very sorry that you lost your son," said Rachel, though she was aware that the woman was no longer listening to anything but her own words, her own thoughts.

"First they cut off his hand," she said, looking at the fingers of her right hand, covered with rings. "He had beautiful hands."

"Naomi, I want you to stop it!" said her husband, speaking to her in Russian Yiddish, his voice wild with emotion. But Rachel understood at once why her son had lost his hand, why her husband knew so much about the rich girl from Paris. She even knew why Beenyamin doubted her willingness to stay on and create the industry she had envisioned in this room.

"Avi," she said. "You're Avi's parents."

Before Beenyamin Ben-Solomon could answer, their son did, entering the room, his eyes alive with purpose.

"Well, my father," he said. "Do you approve? Do you approve of my choice of wife?"

Rachel heard the words, and looked at Avi with wonder.

"Yes, my son," said Beenyamin Ben-Solomon. "She is a brave girl, and she has a warm heart."

Marriage had just been proposed to her, over her head, beyond any wild expectation. The dragoman turned from his father to Rachel now, and there was neither arrogance nor hesitation in his glance. "If I marry you, I will be rich," he said, speaking in Hebrew. "But that is not why I wish to marry you. Do you believe what I say, Mademoiselle Rachel?"

"Yes," she said.

"We will stay here, in Palestine, and we will be man and wife," said Avi.

"Yes," she said again, though there had been no question, only a statement of how things would be.

"I love you," he said, and he got down on his knees beside where she sat on the low divan and took her hand and put it to his lips.

Like a dream made imperfect by a single detail, the figure of Naomi, lost in her mourning, hovered over Rachel's happiness. "I love you," Rachel answered him, and she knew that her love would only strengthen her will, focus the resolve to help her people in their ancient capital.

CHAPTER TWENTY-THREE

One week after Rachel and Avi had agreed to get married, Rachel
fell sick.

Rain had been falling for a few hours every day of the past
week; and as cold, wet air settled in the bones of the city's in-
habitants, the fearful talk was of smallpox, typhoid, and cholera,
all of which had taken their toll of lives in past rainy seasons.
Rachel and Avi had been walking through the Jewish quarter,
their boots splashing through filthy puddles and pools of water.
Under an overhanging ledge of wood, an old man burned garbage, watching to see that the flames didn't consume his own
dwelling. The black smoke bit at their squinting eyes as they
hurried past, trying not to breathe, and at that same moment a
butcher opened the top half of his back door and threw out a
great mass of bloody offal into the middle of the wet alley. It was
not the first time that Rachel had seen animal parts in the streets
of Jerusalem, but still she was shocked at having it practically
thrown into her face. Her reaction was immediate. She let out a
little cry, and fell back against the wall of an old shed, and began
to vomit. Avi held her shoulders in his steady hands as she
shivered and shook uncontrollably, her knees threatening to col-

lapse as she continued to vomit up half-digested food and, when this was finished, air.

"Come on," said Avi. "I want to get you inside."

But she was rooted to the spot for minutes longer, sweating and shaking, and continued to try and vomit what was no longer in her belly.

Because she had wanted to live among the people she would help, Rachel had moved from her hotel to the home of Avi's parents a few days past. Avi took her there quickly now, supporting her with his strong arms as they climbed the wet, steep streets. He was surprised at her reaction to the offal, and worried that she continued to shudder and shake.

When they were finally inside, Avi's mother took one look at Rachel and said, "It's the cholera."

"Don't be ridiculous," said Avi, but Naomi took charge of the weak girl and brought her to the quiet of the small bedroom.

"Get Dr. Kalman," said Naomi; and Avi, who wanted to explain what had happened, how Rachel had simply overreacted to the sight and smell of a butcher shop's refuse, caught the sense of urgency in his mother's voice and left in search of the doctor. It would not be the first time that his mother's common sense had superseded her madness.

He had been gone less than a minute when Rachel weakly lifted her head from the pillow and asked Naomi for help. Sarah, Avi's sister, helped her mother with Rachel's body, alternately heavy with inertia and violently awake with shakes.

"It can't be cholera," said Sarah. "There's been no cholera in Jerusalem for two years."

"God is testing her," said Naomi. "He can bring murderers out of the desert to kill the innocent. He can bring cholera out of the gutters to kill the weak."

"She is not weak," said Sarah, who had come to know and admire the girl whom Avi wished to marry.

"*We* must not be weak," said her mother.

The pain starting up so suddenly in Rachel's abdomen almost drove her to her knees, and Naomi and Sarah had to hold her still as she retched up hot air. Her bowels were on fire, and yet there seemed to be nothing in them. They put her to sleep, a damp cloth on her forehead, the windows shut against the wet, pestilent air.

In the week that had passed since Rachel had discovered Avi's love for her to be true, and not an idealized dream, the insulated world that she had carried with her from Paris had suddenly collapsed.

"Your parents will disown you," Marie had said, forgetting all her previous kind words about the dragoman. "You are under a spell, the spell of a fortune hunter. And when your parents disown you, you will have no money, and then he will leave you, he will wash his hands of you as if you had never existed. He will leave you alone to die in this terrible place."

Their argument had been terrible, and as Rachel lay in the bed in the home of Avi's parents, the angry words that had been uttered by mistress and maid came back to her now, racing through her fever. Rachel had accused Marie of being selfish, unloving, interested in Rachel's welfare only as long as her parents supported her with their vast sums of cash. Marie had accused Rachel of being spoiled, headstrong, ungrateful, unable to take criticism and advice from those older and wiser.

Marie and Henri both wanted to leave Jerusalem at once; they had no interest in looking at any more tombs or relics, not in this atmosphere of beggary and filth. Rachel had urged them to leave. "If you're so afraid I won't be able to pay your wages, go back to Paris," she'd said. "My parents will pay you well for any information you can give them about their runaway daughter.

Rachel had been so angry, so full of resentment at their rejection of Avi, that the French couple had given her notice that they were to leave, within ten days, for Jaffa.

Though Rex Mitchell had been surprisingly pleasant about Rachel and Avi's decision to marry, she knew that the American was due to leave Jerusalem for a tour of Bethlehem and Mar Saba, as part of his travel-book work. Now, in her rising delirium, she felt that she was already abandoned; that Marie and Henri had left for France; that Rex loathed her for having rejected his advances; that Avi had abandoned her to her poverty and disease.

"What is she saying?" said the doctor when he had come and begun to examine the girl, wet and pale and mumbling words and names in swift French to the indistinct faces about her.

"She is calling for her maid," said Avi. "Marie is her maid. The rest I don't understand."

"Send for the maid," said the doctor. "Whatever will make her more comfortable."

Avi tried to speak to her, but Rachel's eyes were shut tight, and no English words, no Hebrew words, penetrated her consciousness. She had written her parents about Avi, of course—a long and loving letter, both about him and to them, loving them for having created in her a love for their people. But her imagination was wild now. The butcher's offal had not created a disease, it had simply been the trigger to release symptoms of an intestinal infection already picked up and waiting to explode. Only enthusiasm, only love, had kept it in check. She would complain of nothing while under the spell of this city, while in the presence of her lover. But her insides were roiling now, and she was sick, very sick, in a foreign place, and her mind ran on with dire possibilities.

"It's the cholera," said Naomi.

"I don't think so," said the doctor, but he was not very forceful in the delivery of his lines.

Rachel's stool had been bloody and filled with mucus. The doctor had seen symptoms like these in cases of dysentery and ordinary diarrhea; but in Jerusalem, in this season, severe diarrhetic symptoms might indeed prove to be cholera.

"What do you think it is?" said Avi. "What can you give her to ease her pain?"

"Nothing," said Dr. Kalman. "Nothing except hot water and hot tea. We've got to starve her for the next forty-eight hours."

"She should have soup," said Naomi.

"No," said the doctor. "We have to starve out her system, and soup will only feed what ails her."

"It's the cholera," said Naomi. "And she should have soup, for strength." As she leaned over the bed, the gold coins about her neck clinked together, and Rachel's eyes opened to a vision of her own mother, blue-eyed and light-haired, with a great deal of powder and perfume: A vision of luxury, of cleanliness, of comfort.

"*Maman*," she tried to say, but the French word never left her lips. As Naomi rubbed the damp cloth along the girl's forehead and temples and dabbed about her tearing eyes, Rachel started in pain. Her mother was shaking her head, castigating her for abandoning her parents in their old age. "How could you do this?" said the mother in Rachel's raging mind. "How could you leave us to die alone? Who is this man, that you love him more than your father, more than your own *maman*? No, we will not celebrate your wedding, we will never celebrate it, and we will never help you with your ridiculous plans!" And at once, her mother's sweet, powdered face, her mother's delicious perfumed aura twisted into something bloody and rank. At once, the pain in her abdomen became so suddenly severe that her eyes opened in shock, and her lips, but there was no sound, there was no strength for sight.

"Bring water," said Naomi to Sarah.

"Hot water," said the doctor. "Only hot water or tea."

Tea was brought, and by that time Marie had come. She entered the little sickroom out of breath, and with fear in her eyes. "What is it?" she said in French. "What is wrong with mademoiselle?"

Sarah calmed her down, speaking in her language, and told her that the doctor was here and that there was no need to be fearful. "It is just that she is asking for you," said Sarah.

"Who else should she be asking for?" said the maid in French, looking daggers at Avi, at the doctor, at the crazily dressed older Jewish woman holding Rachel's hand.

"She was afraid you might have left," said Sarah. "Returned home."

"Was she?" said Marie. "I'm glad she had sense enough to fear that. I'm glad she had sense enough to appreciate those few who really care about her." The maid got to her knees at Rachel's side, taking her hand, feeling her brow, taking the teacup from Naomi and gently bringing it to the girl's lips.

"It's the cholera," said Naomi, but Marie couldn't understand; all she could see was that her poor girl was sick, terribly sick in this miserable quarter of this miserable city. She stopped thinking about running back to the Cohn family in Paris, about begging their forgiveness for having gone off with Rachel, explaining that she had accompanied their daughter only to save her, she stopped thinking about anything other than helping Rachel to feel well.

"Rachel," she said, her accent soft and babyish. Marie stroked the sick girl's face the way she had when Rachel had been sick as a little girl, propped up in her beautiful bed with a dozen pillows, and flowers blazing bright all about the room. "Rachel," she said, more afraid than her mistress of this austere little room, so full of foreign sicknesses, foreign speech, foreign smells. Marie stayed with Rachel into the night, never once letting up her soft, purring words and gentle stroking of the girl's skin, so that Rachel would know that she was safe, in a warm, comfortable place, surrounded by friends. When finally Marie herself fell asleep, Avi gently picked up the maid and helped her onto a couch.

She woke with a start in the early morning to see the dragoman holding a cup of hot tea to Rachel's lips.

"She is not better?" said Marie in French, and Avi, understanding the drift of her words, shook his head. There was so much feeling in his eyes—feeling that had less than nothing to do with hunting a fortune—that Marie all at once forgave him for wanting to marry her mistress. He was kind, he was handsome, and it was obvious that he was in love. Together they watched over the sleeping girl until Naomi came, and Sarah, and the doctor.

The doctor's orders were followed. Dysentery had dehydrated her, so she had to be given tea, as much as she could drink while awake. Gradually, the diarrhea let up, until it ceased altogether. Rachel's eyes were wide with delirium and exhaustion; but after two nights and two days, this, too, passed. She was aware of being awake, not in a dream but awake and lying in a bed in the home of Avi's parents in Jerusalem.

"What happened?" she said in French on the morning of the third day.

Avi rushed to her side, shouting to Marie to join him.

"Avi," said Rachel. As a mark of her sudden clarity she spoke to him in Hebrew. "What happened? I dreamed you had left me."

"I would never leave you," he said.

Marie had come up to her, and watched in wonder as the girl came back to awareness. "Mademoiselle," she said, "you are better! You are getting well!"

"Marie," said Rachel. "I thought you, too, would leave me!"

Marie didn't answer that. It was enough to see Rachel talking to the man she loved in their common language. The maid held her hand and cried.

"I dreamed terrible things," said Rachel, but Avi put his hand to her lips. He asked her not to talk, begged her to rest, but she had to continue, she had to voice her fears so that he could tell her they were without basis. "My parents hated me," she said. "They said I was deserting them, leaving them alone to die. And then I realized that only one thing would let them forgive me. Their faces were so angry, so full of hate and fury, and there was only one thing I could do to please them. I died. I died here and

I never married you. I died alone, without even Marie. I was found dead in an alley, like the animal insides thrown out by that butcher, and when they found me, my parents knew, and they were so sad for me that they forgave me at once. They told their friends that I died all alone in the Holy Land, and they built me a tomb as big as David's, right in the middle of Jerusalem. Do you still want to marry me?"

"Of course I do," said Avi. "But now you must rest. I insist that you rest."

"I am going to die, Avi," said Rachel.

"Don't be ridiculous," he said, but her words had a chilling effect against the pale, exhausted background of her face.

"I am going to die, and I want you to marry me first," she said. "Could you marry me before I die?"

"We will marry, and you won't die," said Avi. "But as I am about to become your husband, I order you to rest. Not another word about marriage until you obey."

Rachel smiled at him, shut her eyes, and slept.

"Oh, my God," said Marie, softly, so as not to wake her. She had not understood a word of what Rachel had said, but the girl's features had spoken out the same message.

"She is very weak," the doctor said after examining her later in the day. "She can have soup now, but in small quantity."

The prescription of soup satisfied Naomi, but it did little for Rachel. Every day she took a step further from delirium, remaining lucid and awake for longer and longer periods, but her strength didn't increase, and she could keep down little food. What seemed to satisfy her most was her time alone with Avi, the man she had hoped to marry. There in the sickroom, from her sickbed, she learned the story of his life, she learned the names of the foods he liked, she learned the Russian-Jewish stories he'd heard as a child, she learned to understand why she had loved him almost at once. Rachel told him stories, too. She spoke about brothers and house pets, about the charities and pretensions of her parents, about Paris, about Deauville, about paintings and parks and horses.

He didn't want her to talk too much. It seemed to him that if only he could overwhelm her with his own strength—talk for her, breathe for her, eat for her—she would get better. "Don't talk, darling," he would say. "Let me tell you a story. I have lots of stories. I am the famous dragoman, and I have the best stories all at my fingertips."

But she did not get better. She tried to eat the soup she was offered. Five different types of apples were made into five different types of applesauce—every apple a delicacy in Jerusalem in that season—but none of these agreed with her. Whatever she ate that could give her strength she promptly threw up; and when she ate nothing at all, she slipped into a serene, dreamy state that terrified everyone who saw her.

"Is there a message from my parents?" she'd ask every day. That and one other question were always on her lips: "When are you going to marry me? Don't you know that I'm dying?"

"You're not dying," said Avi, and Naomi clapped her hands in fury every time the words flew into the air.

Still, there was more than one visitor to the sickroom who began to believe in what Rachel said. Rex Mitchell had come back from Bethlehem, and after visiting with Rachel, went off at once to Alexandria to see if there was mail from the Cohn family that he could bring to cheer up the sick girl. When the American returned, Rachel was no better, and he had come back without mail.

"Take a walk with me," he told Avi, a few hours after coming back to Jerusalem.

"She is no better, my friend," said Avi, and his face was perfectly calm, his eyes shining.

"Why don't you marry her?" said Rex.

"She is dying," said Avi. "I'm afraid what she says is absolutely true. She is another Jew come here to die."

"If she is to die anyway, why do you hesitate to make her happy?"

"I don't understand you, my friend," said Avi. "You don't want me to marry her on her deathbed, do you? I am a famous dragoman, she is a famous heiress. Even on her deathbed, the world will mock her for her mistake. It would be different if she were to live. Our lives could prove that we married for love. But now, it would be terrible. People would think her foolish, and think me bad. I love her too much to let her die like that."

"You love *yourself* too much," said Rex.

"What do you mean?" said the dragoman.

Rex drew his revolver from its holster and pointed the gun at Avi's chest. "Swear that you'll marry her," he said.

"Are you crazy?"

"Swear it," said Rex. "Swear that you'll marry her, or I'll pull this trigger."

Avi looked into Rex's face, trying to understand what was taking place. The American was serious. Not serious enough to shoot him, of course, but it was clear that he thought it right for the dragoman to marry Rachel. Avi looked from Rex's face to the revolver, and then, as he looked back to Rex, catching his eyes, the dragoman's hand reached swiftly through space and took hold of the gun-wielding hand. For a moment, there was a struggle. But Rex had no real desire to put a bullet through the man's chest, and Avi had no fear of any such thing taking place. Each seemed to give up at once. Hardly had the gun been twisted away from Avi's chest than Avi let go Rex's hand. By that time Rex was laughing.

"It's not even loaded," said Rex.

"You would not have shot anyway," said Avi. "I know you are my friend." And the dragoman pulled the American into his arms for a great hug of friendship.

"Yes," said Rex, his face reddening, extricating himself from what he considered an Oriental display of emotion. "And if you are my friend, you shall listen to what I say."

Avi listened. That night he spoke to his father and mother and told them of his decision to marry Rachel, even if she would have to be carried to the wedding canopy. Beenyamin thought the idea unseemly, an affront to decency. But Naomi thought otherwise. "I will make her a wedding dress," she said. "And Sarah will find the women and girls for the procession. Everything will be beautiful. Everything will be beautiful, and she will get well."

The next day the rain let up, and sun filled Rachel's room for a few hours. She sat up in bed and tried to eat some soup. "Why is everyone watching me?" she said in a little voice, for she was surrounded by well-wishers: Avi, Rex, Sarah, Marie, Naomi.

"We are looking at the bride," said Naomi.

"I am not yet a bride," said Rachel. "I am not yet well enough to be a bride."

Before she could begin to cry, Avi was at her side, taking her hand, looking into her eyes. "In two days," he said. "We marry in two days, Rachel. In two days you shall be a bride."

"Good," said Rachel. "Two days is possible. I can live two

days more." She took a last sip of her soup, then sank back into her pillows and slept away the afternoon.

When she woke up, she asked Marie, who was at the bedside, whether it was really true that she was to be married in two days.

"Yes, darling," said Marie. "That is why you must try and eat."

"I shall, Marie," said Rachel, with so much force that for a moment Marie believed that there was still a possibility that the girl could live. "Marie, is there any news of my family?"

"No, darling. But you know how long it can take, you know how far we are from home."

"You don't really think they'll disown me, do you? You said they would, but you don't really think so, do you?"

"Of course not, darling," said Marie. "They would never disown you. They love you. They love you, and they'll love your husband."

"After I'm dead, they must love him."

"Don't say that," said Marie.

"I must say it," said Rachel. "You must remember what I tell you, if you love me. Do you hear me, Marie?"

"Yes, darling."

"After I'm dead, Avi must be helped by my parents," said Rachel.

"He won't want anything from your parents, not unless you're here with him."

"Not for himself," said Rachel. "For the Jews of this city. If you love me, if he loves me, if my parents love me, you must all do what I wanted to do here."

"No more talk now," said Marie. "It's making you tired."

"Listen," said Rachel, sitting up in bed, her eyes blazing with a feverish clarity. "When I die, that is how I want you to show you loved me. I cannot think you love me if you don't honor my very last request."

"Don't talk of dying," said Marie, breaking into tears. "You're not to talk of it. If you don't talk of it, I shall do anything you ask."

"All right," said Rachel. "I won't talk of it, Marie. Just remember what I want. Remember."

"I will," said Marie. "Now, let me see you eat."

Rachel accepted the applesauce that her maid was trying to

give her, and surprised her by finishing most of the bowl. She sat up a little straighter in bed and drank some weak tea with obvious enjoyment. "I feel better," she said. "I feel better because I know that I have not come here for nothing."

She looked still better the next morning. She had a boiled egg and some tea, and she walked around her bedroom with her arm about Avi's waist. "I shall stand under the wedding canopy," she said. "By tomorrow, I shall be able to dance and sing."

Dr. Kalman visited her later that morning. He watched her eat a light lunch with obvious relish, he observed her much improved color, and he patted her on the cheek with a smile of encouragement. But outside her room, he told Avi, "It is not good, my son. She is not at all improved. This is only her soul you see now. It's not her body, it's her soul making a last leap before you on earth. She is putting all her strength into this wedding. After tomorrow, it won't be long. I don't think your bride will last the week."

But Avi was resolved to think about nothing save the present. Rachel, who had been unconscious, wasting away without food, was now standing in her room, trying to eat everything on her plate, making a hundred demands, so that everyone feared for her strength.

"The British consul must be there," she said. "I insist that you invite him. He will be very helpful later, and it will be well for all the Jews if he attends a Jewish wedding. Rex, you see to the Americans. I want every American in Jerusalem to be at my wedding. The American missionaries are the ones with money to bring the Jews to the Holy Land. See that they know what we're doing.

"Beenyamin, you must ask the governor to come. The Turks know of my family in the East. Do not hesitate to hint about future rewards. And the French—the French must all come, all the Frenchmen in Jerusalem must rejoice at my wedding. And Sarah. I know Sarah will gather all the friends of the family, all the Jews of the quarter who will want to share our happiness. This must be a wedding that everyone will remember."

Later that day, she ventured out of the bedroom to take tea in the back garden, wrapped up in blankets under the late afternoon sunshine. "Even the rain has stopped on your account," Avi was saying, watching her clear-eyed face with attention. He almost feared to shut his eyes for a moment, as if he would discover her recovery to be a dream, and find himself talking to a phantom in the garden. "Tonight the women will come and dance for you, round and round the house and the garden. You'll be able to hear everything from your bed. And in the morning, we shall be married. Everything will be done as you wanted. Tomorrow you shall be my wife, and have to obey my wishes. My first wish will be for you to get well."

Suddenly, Rachel felt herself floating. Avi's face seemed to retreat from hers, as if he were being rushed back through space by some divine force. Then he was gone, and there was a murmuring about her, soft and indistinct, and she wondered if perhaps she had already died. She strained against the blackness, trying to move through the soft layers about her eyes, trying to see where she was. But instead of light, she encountered song: A soft, rhythmic chanting grew steadily in force, louder and louder, until it reached understanding.

"*Callah, callah, callah!*" was the chant, and there was much handclapping, and joyous shouting in a score of languages, but always the chant was the same: "*Callah, callah, callah!*"

Somehow she knew that if this chant would make sense to her, she would be awake enough to know that she was alive. It was a familiar word, as familiar as the sabbath eve in Paris; as familiar as Naomi's hands, rushing to drape the soft white fabric of her bridal dress about her; as familiar as Avi's glossy hair. "*Callah,*" she heard, and then she remembered, opening her eyes to a hundred torches and lanterns, and women dressed in white against the black of the night. They were calling her. "*Callah,*" Hebrew for "bride," the word used to describe the sabbath in the Friday-night prayers. She had slept again, she had missed hours of afternoon and evening, and now it was night, very late night, and this was her wedding procession, and these women were singing for her.

She was no longer afraid. She knew that she was alive, and that her strength was flowing back to her, and that she would soon be married. This had all been explained to her, and so she knew that the women around her, dancing and singing around her chair in the large room, its floor-to-ceiling windows open to let in the night, were singing out her name, celebrating her status. Rachel opened her eyes fully, and caught sight of Naomi, dancing with Sarah at the center of the women, all tightly packed into the room, running with the heat of the torches and the bodies and the fever in Rachel's mind. Marie stood next to where Rachel sat, in the seat of honor; Rachel squeezed her maid's hand, so that she would know all was well.

"How much time?" said Rachel.

"Soon, darling," said Marie, her voice breaking. Rachel was dressed in her bridal gown, labored over by Naomi for thirty hours. But there was no bloom on the bride's cheeks, and the white of her gown only accentuated the pallor of her face. The bizarre ceremony had little meaning for Marie, except as a backdrop to their pathetic setting: Rachel about to be married, Rachel about to die.

"Is everyone here?"

"Everyone you asked for, dear girl," said Marie. "Only the Jewish women are here for this special ritual. But in the other rooms, all the guests you wanted are here, waiting for the ceremony at dawn."

"How long have I been sleeping?"

"Not so long. The dancing has only just started. The men of government and business—every important man in Jerusalem, Jew and Gentile—are all here, though it is the middle of the night."

"Thank God," said Rachel, and she shut her eyes again, getting a moment's rest against the crash of sound and light. "*Callah, callah,*" she heard through her shut eyes, and she imagined herself under the *chupah*, the wedding canopy, turning to Avi as he took her hand in marriage. A tear dropped out from under her eye, and then another, and she heard Marie clucking over her, wiping at her tears, urging her not to cry, saying that this was the happiest moment of her life, and that she would be well, very well, and live a long and happy life.

"I would have liked to have heard from my family," she said finally, looking up at Marie, stopping up her tears. "I would have liked to have gotten their good wishes, too."

But she looked from Marie now to Avi's sister and mother, as they danced around and around, wild-eyed with passion, their arms locked together, their voices raised in abandoned song. This, too, was her family, these Jews of Russia, whose history twisted back two thousand years to the same little bit of land where her father's family lived before the Second Temple was destroyed.

Rachel shook off any residue of sorrow and tried to pick up the beat of the singers and dancers, clapping her hands and joining the chanting with her high little voice. Nothing that Marie could say would stop her now from singing; she was not a frail little vessel, she was a woman about to be married, and she wanted to shout in song. Rachel was out of her chair, and she felt her fever rising, but shook off any fear of its force. She clapped till her hands were sore; she sang until her voice was hoarse; she gave herself up to the frenzy of the women in the room, of the torches and lanterns that lit up the sweating faces, of the gold necklaces that whirled about writhing necks.

But, suddenly, she felt as if the room were stilling, as if everyone, from the women at the windows to the dancers at the center of the crowd, were hushing; as if some demon had stoppered everyone's capacity to sing. She was not faint, she was not imagining; everyone had truly quieted; and all at once, like a vision from another world, she saw the reason.

The crowd had parted, so that a corridor existed between the bodies of the women, from the door to where Rachel stood before her chair. And there, walking toward her between the hot, hushed women, was Bernard Cohn.

Her brother, her youngest brother.

In an absurdly foppish suit, with a waistcoat and a gold chain.

Bernard, her brother, was coming toward her in the middle of the night, in the city of Jerusalem, hours before her wedding.

"Bernard," she said in a half-whisper; and then, because she understood that she was not dreaming, she repeated it, shouting, "Bernard, Bernard, *c'est toi*, Bernard!"

"Rachel," he said, and he folded her into his arms. He had traveled fast, returning to Paris from London after getting their father's cable. From Paris to Trieste, and from there, on the family's yacht, direct to Jaffa. He was tanned, he was exhausted, he had a ten-day beard—but he had come in time. "I am in time for the wedding?" he asked.

"Yes."

"Thank God," he said.

For one terrible moment Rachel thought that he had raced there simply to stop the wedding from taking place. But, no, that was impossible, not with that dazzling smile, that little-boy look of surprise and delight about what was to take place. He took out a black leather case from inside his waistcoat. "This is yours," he said. "It would have been a shame to get married without it."

So great was his joy at giving her this gift that he did not notice at first how ill she really was. It seemed natural to him that she was pale and nervous just before her wedding. He opened the box, and brother and sister looked at the necklace inside: On the simple gold chain was attached her legacy, the great Cuheno diamond; the diamond she had always loved, ever since she had first seen it as a little girl and known it to be her birthright. No other message could have so assured her of her parents' approval and love.

"Yes," said Rachel. "Thank you so much for bringing it to me."

Her brother placed the chain about her neck. The diamond beat back the light in the room as she turned it in her hand, feeling the facets, and the centuries.

"Rachel, are you all right?" said her brother, suddenly seeing how very thin and weak she looked—almost as if she were about to fall down.

"Of course," said Rachel. "I am all right. Now I am all right and everything is all right."

She turned to where Naomi and Sarah were watching her in amazement. In Hebrew, Rachel said, "Don't stop! We're celebrating my wedding! Don't stop!" And in a moment there was chanting again, and wild singing and dancing, and the frenzy of abandoned passion in the middle of the night.

Rachel held her hands firmly over the diamond resting against her chest, and through the mad cacophony about her she felt her fever break; she felt her head free, she felt as if the bonds round her body were broken all at once. "I'm all right," she said again.

And two hours later she was married to Avi the dragoman, and within a week she was fully recovered from her illness.

The diamond had not been a false message from her parents: the family's resources and power were put to the help of the city's Jews. Because it was delivered to her just before her wedding, it became a tradition in the Cohn family to give the Cuheno diamond to the family's Rachel at that same time from then on.

Within a year, diamonds were being cut and polished in the city of Jerusalem. As Rachel had envisioned, the children of these diamond cutters were stronger than their parents, and she lived to see some of them, and more of their grandchildren, leave the city to found new communities outside the walls. Marie and Henri eventually returned to France, and were rewarded by Rachel's parents with a pension and a house in the south. Rex Mitchell married Avi's sister, Sarah, and helped found the agricultural community of Kiryat Beenyamin.

The first settlement in the Holy Land financed by the fledgling diamond industry in Jerusalem was built outside the walls of the city, and when the land had been reclaimed and a red windmill had been built to grind the corn they grew, the settlers named their community Matanat Rachel—the Gift of Rachel.

Avi and Rachel had seven children, and these children had forty-six children of their own, and they spread out to every corner of the Holy Land. Avi died a very old man, with more great-grandchildren than he could remember; but his wife lived even longer. Rachel died in Jerusalem in 1920, at ninety years of age, certain that only struggle and faith remained before the time the Jewish flag would fly over the ancient capital of her people.

THE KANE FAMILY
1875–1920

The discovery of diamonds in South Africa in 1866 brought together members of the Cuheno clan from every part of the world. By 1869, when the 83.5-carat Star of South Africa was bought by Hope Town's Lilienfeld Brothers for eleven thousand pounds sterling, and sold in London to the earl of Dudley for twenty-five thousand pounds sterling, more than fifty members of the family had converged upon Cape Town and New Rush (later called Kimberley). These Cohens and Cahanes and Cohns came from Brazil and France and England and Germany and the United States, and they were mostly male, and mostly young, the children of rich men, who wanted to create empires beyond the shadows of those of their parents.

In 1875, Jules Cohn, the twenty-year-old son of Bernard Cohn of Paris, himself the youngest brother of Rachel Cohn of Paris and Jerusalem, arrived in Cape Town. Jules at once began using the surname Kane to differentiate himself from his French cousins, some of whom had already been wildly successful in the diamond rush of 1869. Within ten years, Jules had made the Kane name so distinct that many newcomers to the diamond industry didn't realize the connection between the Kane diamond-buying organization and the famous Cohen family.

A millionaire before he was twenty-nine, Jules Kane had ample time in his thirties to marry and raise a family, and create a philosophy that would accommodate his lavish, self-made manner of living. Unlike his cousins, who took what he considered to be an inordinate amount of pride in the Jewish contributions to South Africa (everything—from the diamond mines to the mohair industry; from the gold mines of the Rand to the Cape's whaling industry; from breweries to factories making steel, glass, brick, and tile—had been originated with Jewish participation), Jules Kane liked to be quiet about his national origin, his religious persuasion.

Born in Paris, he had become in Africa a lover of England, and wanted nothing more than a great English home, a respected English name. While his cousins' children were swept up by the great causes of the time—socialism, Zionism, nationalism, internationalism—his two boys were sent, thanks to the influence of Jules's second cousin, Lord Michael Cohen, to Eton and Harrow. (Lord Cohen's title was hereditary; he was the grandson of a Cohen who floated a very large loan for a philandering prince, and managed to forget to collect it. When the prince's brother became the king of England, Cohen became a baron, and one of the first Jewish peers. The first Lord Cohen, James, was the son of a Cuheno diamond merchant from Amsterdam who had settled in London in the first decade of the eighteenth century. Jules Kane, incidentally, was related to Lord Michael Cohen on both the lord's father's and mother's side; the father's side being the more distant relationship.)

Jules's oldest boy, the Harrow and Christ Church graduate, died for England in the Boer War. His second son, Herbert, had a terrible time at Eton. Though his father had already begun the renovation of the eighteenth-century mansion in the Kent countryside that was to be the family's English home, Herbert's classmates found him neither English nor quite of their class. No matter what his tutors had taught him of the Angles and the Saxons, of the besting of Napoleon, of Shakespeare and Shelley, Tennyson and Byron, these were not his people. He was a Jew, his classmates taught him; and when he wasn't shunned, he was beaten out of his shallow sleep by a half-dozen smirking boys.

So hateful was the Eton experience that Herbert Kane almost

became a Zionist. Shocking his father, the young, very British scholar visited Palestine in 1913, meeting his aged great-aunt Rachel and a score of Hebrew-speaking relations. He was very moved by witnessing Jews tilling their own soil, speaking their own tongue, seeking to create a state in the region which the Bible claimed was theirs. Herbert spent four months touring the country, learning Hebrew, reading the Bible. He returned to England to obtain the blessing of his family—and their financial and moral support—for an extended move to Palestine.

Before his parents had time to give in to his requests, however —his father wanted him to go to Oxford—Herbert fell in love. Love gave him a new lookout on life. His prospective bride, daughter of mildly prosperous Eastern European immigrants, was not at all in love with the idea of a life in Palestine; she greatly preferred the promise of the mansion in Kent. Herbert went up to Oxford, to read history. At Oxford, he experienced nothing of the anti-Semitism that had made life at Eton a hell; he found friends, and he became quickly convinced that England was, after all, the noblest and most civilized place on earth. He took a first-class degree in 1916, and then a commission in His Majesty's Army. Herbert Kane emerged from the First World War a major, and a staunch imperialist. He had not forgotten that he was a Jew. But he had become convinced that his own conduct at Eton, his not having been sufficiently "manly," had been the primary reason for his having been ostracized as a Jew.

He married in 1917. His first son, Robert Kane, was born in 1918. When a daughter was born in 1920, Herbert was astonished to discover his father at the nursery door, wild with glee.

Jules Kane was already a man of sixty-five, and not given to fits of enthusiasm. Herbert had not even known that he was in England, as his father usually spent the first half of the year in Cape Town or Johannesburg. "It's a girl!" Jules was shouting. "It's a girl, and it's just when we needed her! The first girl we've needed in ninety years!"

It was then that Herbert learned that his great-aunt Rachel had died in Jerusalem, and that his own daughter was to take her name, and the legacy of her diamond.

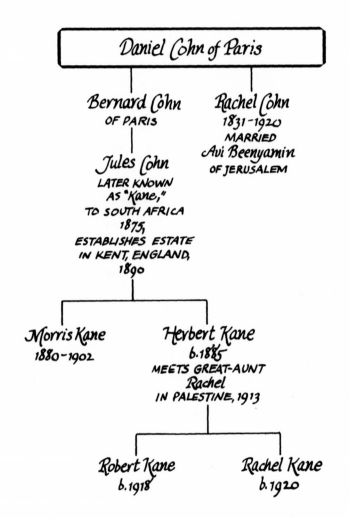

Daniel Cohn of Paris

Bernard Cohn
OF PARIS

Rachel Cohn
1831-1920
MARRIED
Avi Beenyamin
OF JERUSALEM

Jules Cohn
LATER KNOWN
AS "Kane,"
TO SOUTH AFRICA
1875,
ESTABLISHES ESTATE
IN KENT, ENGLAND,
1890

Morris Kane
1880-1902

Herbert Kane
b.1885
MEETS GREAT-AUNT
Rachel
IN PALESTINE, 1913

Robert Kane
b.1918

Rachel Kane
b.1920

PART FIVE

KENT, ENGLAND, 1937

CHAPTER TWENTY-FOUR

Robert had brought a friend down from Cambridge with him late the night before, and Rachel woke early to have a look at the friend over breakfast. Rachel wore pants, Marlene Dietrich–style, and a white shirt flecked with paint. Her mother looked up at her from the breakfast table. "Change your clothes," she said, her beautiful tones determined to be bored. Mrs. Kane returned her eyes to the morning's mail, her thin fingers flattening out a long, thin piece of blue stationery with precision.

"I'm going to be painting," said Rachel, her voice impatient, demanding. She hesitated before a chair, wondering whether or not to join her mother. A servant poured tea into her mother's cup at the head of the long, otherwise deserted table, which glistened in the east light from the great windows overlooking the formal gardens.

"I don't doubt your intention to paint, dear," said Mrs. Kane. "But at my breakfast table, my daughter is dressed properly, or she is not seated."

"I wish to God that you wouldn't place importance on such inconsequential things," said Rachel.

Still, she didn't defy her mother, though she would have liked to do so. A butler stood quietly behind her; it would have been interesting, she thought, to see what he would have done had she inclined slightly forward, indicating a desire to have the chair before her pulled out. It was hardly likely that the butler would have physically prevented her from sitting down.

Suddenly, the girl felt a revulsion at wasting even a moment more on thinking of these things—butlers, mothers, clothing, manners. The entire world was on the verge of collapsing, and she was to be taken to task for wearing pants, or a man's shirt marked with paint. It was too absurd. "I am a painter after all," said Rachel, trying to imitate her mother's regal tones. "It's not too much to ask to be allowed to be seen in my working clothes in my own home."

"You are not a painter," said Mrs. Kane, looking up from her mail with an expression only slightly less mild than before. "You are a seventeen-year-old girl, living in Sanders House, in Kent, in one of the last civilized enclaves in the world. If you want to paint, you may paint. If you want to compose or play music, you may do so at your leisure. If you want to read, there is an enormous library at your pleasure. You are a fortunate girl, you are not a waif, living in an attic in Paris. I will not have you pretending to be something other than what you are. You are Rachel Kane, and your only obligation is not to be an embarrassment to your family. You will please change your clothes and cease aggravating me at once."

"Has Robert come down yet?" said Rachel. It was a question that allowed her to put off for one moment more acquiescing to her mother's demands.

"He is playing tennis with his friend," said Mrs. Kane. She was no longer looking up at her daughter.

Rachel turned and started to run off. "Okay," she said, like an American, and then she added: "I guess I'll change into my tennis clothes." Then she hurried out of the room.

Sanders House had been built in 1702, and renovated eighty years later by its second owner, a vice-chamberlain to the king, with a fortune inherited from his less-than-noble father, an English trader in Indian tea. Jules Kane first saw a painting of the house in Cape Town in 1880, years before he was in a position to buy it. The owner of the painting, an expatriate Englishman, had told the expatriate French Jew with Anglophile tendencies that Sanders House was a perfect example of an English country house, both lavish and simple, rich and understated.

The house had a great Georgian facade with formal gardens at the rear, a kitchen garden with red walls, endless avenues of yew trees, and statues of cupids and cherubs and lovebirds in every nook and cranny. When Jules Kane bought the house, he had thirty new fountains installed about the gardens. One tennis court was built in 1905, and another, a clay court, was built by his son Herbert the year after Jules died, in 1924. When Rachel was ten, a shell grotto was installed at the northern end of the gardens, the work given to a Gentile artisan who had married a daughter of the present Lord Cohen.

What Rachel liked best about the house was what had endeared it to her grandfather—its serene location. The surrounding countryside was so rich with fruit trees, and land under cultivation, that one came upon the house only if one possessed an accurate map and exceptional navigational ability. They were eight miles from the nearest village, where the train station was, but the eight miles between village and house were convoluted tunnels between awesome, endless rows of ancient trees.

The roads were well paved—thanks to the largesse of her father and the neighboring estate owner, Sir Andrew Aubrey—but they were narrow, twisting, precipitously climbing, unexpectedly falling; there were endless S-curves, hairpin turns, and the few intersections were marked with faded signs, impossible to read even in the shady daylight. Because so many friends of the Kanes, and the Aubreys, had been hurt driving those roads, no guests were given driving instructions past the neighboring village. Either one of the family would drive out to the landmark pub and allow their guests to follow them back at a stately pace, or a chauffeur would be sent to pick up those arriving on the train from Dover or London.

Last night, the Kanes' chauffeur had been sent to meet the last train in the family's eight-year-old Rolls-Royce Phantom II saloon. John, the thirty-year-old chauffeur, must have enjoyed the ride back, thrilling the twenty-year-old Cambridge man behind him as he tore about the blind curves he knew so well, anticipating each curve a heartbeat before the headlamps illuminated a rock or a tree on the side of the twisting road. And finally, after the last S-curve, the gentle hill, the space between two oak trees that was the beginning of their unmarked private road, the sudden turn to the left, the first fountain, the sound of its water falling quite audibly over the slowly turning Rolls engine as the chauffeur turned in first gear up to the wrought-iron gate and waited for Malachy, the ancient gatekeeper, to let them in.

Rachel knew there were grander homes, though not within twenty miles of theirs; but even the monumental "Hall" of Lord Cohen's, in Derbyshire, had nothing of this sense of seren- ity. No matter that she was a painter, who reveled in stories of Dionysian abandon in Paris and Berlin; no matter that she longed to model for Picasso, to nurse the wounded in Spain; no matter that her mother was an impossible, unflappable snob, her father aloof with problems and plans—Sanders House was the most wonderful place in the world. If her mother loved to enter- tain a Sassoon or a Montefiore in the Red Drawing Room with its Spitalfields silk–hung walls; if her father could entice a Cab- inet minister into the North Library, which ran almost the entire length of the north wing of the house and was heavy with leather- bound sets with uncut pages, imposing with gilt stucco panels and a Jacobean fireplace removed from a decaying mansion in Middlesex, there was still a tiny reading room on the second floor, with a view of the pond, with a plain little fireplace, with a dear little lamp no older than Rachel. There were the gardens, the benches set out under the spreading trees. There was her own painting studio, with north light. There was a music room, with a wonderful German phonograph. There were the tennis courts, the archery range, the endless trails through manicured grounds, and the wilder walk to the little lake at the border of their prop- erty. Rachel could row a boat, pick herbs in the kitchen garden, find a hundred-year-old hand-painted children's book inherited from a Dutch ancestor and read it under a vine-colored trellis, resting her eyes with a glance to the rose garden, or a flock of birds flying toward Dover.

She knew it was wrong in some way to be so fond of such comfort, but she couldn't help it. She had been to school near London, and had hated it; she preferred her own room at Sanders House and the tuition of her governess. Rachel had hated London, too. She had no use for the theater, opera bored her, museums were crowded with noisy people. Of course she felt guilty when she read about the Civil War in Spain, about the suffering of the

German Jews; she felt guilty about every form of deprivation and misfortune in the world about her. But what was the use? She woke up in the morning and she was in Sanders House. Her mother wanted her to dress decently, her father wanted her to speak with decorum and not intrude her opinions upon those of her elders; but it was still Sanders House, it was still paradise, in the midst of an unholy world.

She couldn't help it, she thought, running without decorum up the wide white marble stairs. Perhaps she was bad, unfeeling. Maybe she was not a painter, but simply another heiress, destined to be as bad a mother as her own. She went into her room and threw off her clothes, letting them fall to the floor. It didn't even enter her mind that this was something else to feel guilty about; servants were not there for decoration, after all. Changing into her tennis clothes, she remembered another reason to feel awful about herself: her father's talk about the Jewish refugees flooding into London from Germany. Major Kane had been eloquent, excessive in his zeal to explain the Nazi menace. As usual, Rachel's comments were not appreciated. She had wanted to include the general sufferings of mankind—particularly those of the Republicans in Spain—in her father's area of concern, but the major had silenced her with an upraised hand.

"What do you propose to do, Herbert," her mother had said, her tones as round and perfect as always, "line up cots in the library? Shall we send the Rolls to London and stuff it with nervous Jews?"

"You will not speak about what you don't understand," said the major. Rachel had wanted to interrupt then, to ask a question, but her father had grown suddenly furious. "And you don't understand a thing! A hundred thousand Jews don't flood into a country without a penny to their names unless they've no alternative."

"There are still Jews in Germany, Herbert," said Mrs. Kane. "Those who are not hysterical. I will not have you standing on that soapbox again. It's talk like that that gives Sir Andrew his ammunition."

"What ammunition?" Rachel had wanted to know, but her parents were ignoring her now, busy with their separate monologues.

"Sir Andrew is an ass," said Major Kane. "He is an ass who should be shot, along with Mosley."

"I will not listen to such language," said Mrs. Kane.

"Sit down," said Major Kane.

But Mrs. Kane remained standing, imperious in her beauty. "It's people like you, Herbert, who don't realize how very precarious our situation is. We're rich, and we're comfortable, and we've got fine friends. But once we start screaming about the poor Jews, there are going to be plenty of people besides Sir Andrew calling us names. If you want your daughter to have to flee this country and grow up in a shack, like my mother had to, keep on in this vein. It's just what the Nazis want, you know. They want to make us all start shouting at the same time, so even the English will think we're foreigners." And then she walked out of the room.

Rachel had looked across at her father, handsome in his white linen suit, his shoulders square, his jaw firm. His blue eyes seemed to be looking right through her, as if she were a window to some vast, contemplative region.

Suddenly, Rachel stood up and said, "I just think we should all be united, Father."

"What?" he'd said.

"United," said Rachel. "I mean that we should look at nazism in the context of all the problems in the world, not just the Jewish ones. It's not as if the Jews have the only problems in the world, is it, then?"

"Rachel," said her father suddenly. "Rachel—don't you know whose name you have?"

"I know those stories," said Rachel impatiently. "But we're talking about *reality*."

Her father stood up, and his suntanned face went white with irritation. She could see that he was sorry he'd even entered into conversation with her; that it was obviously futile to discuss matters that were beyond her ken. "You and your mother both," he said.

"Father," said Rachel, who was sorry the conversation was about to end, "I was only saying what I believe."

"You have cousins in Germany," said the major. He had walked several paces from her now, and Rachel was surprised that he was still talking to her at all. "In Berlin. And in Frankfurt. I am better acquainted with the Cohen family in Berlin. Sigmund Cohen is my second cousin. He was a major, too—on the other side, of course, in the Great War. His family has been in Berlin since the late sixteen hundreds. He knew the kaiser. His wife's father is a baron, a Gentile, from a family that's six hundred years old in Germany. She converted to Judaism, but it wouldn't have mattered to the Nazis anyway; she was born a half-Jew, and compounded her sin by marrying a full Jew. Even the quarter-Jews are persecuted—you have to be *less* than a quarter Jewish to play Bach on your record player. This is what your mother thinks is none of our business. She thinks only the hysterical, the lowborn, the idiotic Jews are leaving Berlin, to plague our position in London."

"I don't understand," said Rachel, interrupting with yet another, to her father, unimportant question. "Why is it that they're not to play Bach on the record player?"

"My God," said her father. "Why am I talking to you about this?"

Major Kane had left her at that moment, and it was only late in the day, when husband and wife and daughter met for high tea, that her father told them both that Sigmund Cohen's wife had committed suicide, and that their son, Wilfred, was coming to Sanders House for a short visit.

As Rachel finished dressing in her tennis clothes, she felt the full weight of her father's disdain, as if it were falling upon herself and her mother for the first time. Hitler was threatening to devour the world, and her mother insisted that one mustn't make a fuss over it. Jews worried about the lives of their children, and Rachel worried about learning to be a better painter. As the world collapsed, her mother never raised her voice, and her distant cousin's wife had just committed suicide, and here she was, all in white, ready to play tennis and see if her brother's friend was handsome.

Rachel looked at herself in a mirror, swept her fingers through her black hair. Even in the moment of being satisfied with how she looked—oh, it was nice to be beautiful, and brunette (which was much more artistic than pallid blond!)—she felt guilty again. What if her father caught her glancing in the mirror, or trying to be charming on the tennis court with her brother's friend? Wouldn't he think it perfectly obscene in the light of nazism? How could she smile when the wife of Sigmund Cohen was dead, a suicide? How could she think about serving tennis balls under the summer sun when other Jews were despairing of life?

Still, Rachel turned from the mirror, picked up her special lightweight racket, and bolted down the great stairs. It was terrible, but she knew in her heart she was selfish and vain. She wanted to play tennis, and be told she was pretty, and paint pictures so strikingly modern that all the world would know her name. What she didn't want was to get on a soapbox for the Jews of Germany. And if she was really true to herself, she would have to admit that this upcoming visit by a cousin of hers from Berlin was dreadful to contemplate. She had never even heard about any Berlin cousins, or, if she had, she had entirely forgotten. Cousins were important to her father, it seemed, only in terms of the diamond business. And no matter how she tried, she couldn't be eternally grateful to some mythical ancestor for having cut the famous diamond she was to inherit on the day of her wedding. The last thing she wanted was some German-speaking bespectacled Jew spoiling the summer at Sanders House. She'd much prefer to have the American cousin her father had mentioned, who was reportedly wounded in Spain. Or better yet —Ernest Hemingway.

Oh, it was terribly selfish to think that way, she told herself, but she smiled brightly as she ran out of the house and took off toward the tennis courts.

"Rachel!" she heard. It was her father's voice, harsh and urgent, and she stopped and turned to face him. "Come here, I want you to do a favor for me, if you please." He stood at a back door, waiting.

"Of course, Father." There were not many favors he had ever asked of her.

"I'm afraid there's been a bit of a foul-up with Wilfred," he said. "He's already arrived. I was expecting him tomorrow at the earliest."

"Wilfred?" said Rachel. She always felt as if she were two or three thoughts behind her father.

"Our cousin," said Major Kane with irritation.

"Oh," said Rachel stupidly. "You mean the cousins from Berlin. They're in England?"

"Look here," said Major Kane. "Listen carefully, please, so I won't have to repeat myself a hundred times. Your cousin Wilfred—*our* cousin Wilfred—is here. Not in England, not in London—he's in town. He just called. He's alone. His father is in Berlin, and his mother, as I told you, is dead. I have a meeting in ten minutes with Lord Clayton. John is just bringing him in from town. Your cousin was apparently on the same train, but no one knew. When John gets back, I want you to go with him to the station and pick up Wilfred. Have you got all that?"

"I don't have to wait for John," said Rachel. "I can take the Bentley."

"Wilfred must have luggage," said the major.

"There's room in the boot," said Rachel. The idea of racing the two-seater home from the station seemed perfectly glorious, better even than playing tennis and flirting with the Cambridge man. "It's not right to keep him waiting."

"You just want to drive," said the major. But he was hesitating. There was an oppressive air about him, as if a hundred problems were clamoring for his special attention. Lord Clayton was an important man; whether he was here to discuss the plight of Jewish refugees or the price of diamonds, her father's attention could not be spared on trivial matters.

"Oh, all right—take the Bentley," he said finally. "If there's too much luggage, leave it with the porters and we can send John for it." He looked at her intently, and then added: "Don't you dare say anything absurd about the Jews in Germany. Don't talk about Mussolini, don't talk about Franco, don't discuss anything that's going to upset him. I don't know anything about the boy except that he's your age and his mother killed herself not two months ago. So please think about that when you drive over. Leave me the racket." The major took her tennis racket and watched as Rachel turned about and ran toward the garage.

The 4½-liter Bentley was a supercharged two-seater with a Gurney Nutting body. It was green, always gleaming: The chauffeur almost never drove it, but he tuned it, he washed it, he sat at the controls and pretended he was in Nurburgring at the German Grand Prix, or at Le Mans, unable to hear the roar of the crowd over the wild engine noise.

For a family that was otherwise conservative, cautious in action and reserved in manner, the Kanes drove at surprisingly fast speeds, though none of them had ever experienced an automobile accident. The major had once nearly driven into a tree when a rear tire burst on his old eight-cylinder Stutz, but he had not considered this worth troubling over. Robert had taught

Rachel to drive when she was fifteen. Mrs. Kane didn't drive, and objected to Rachel's learning to drive; she thought it was undignified. But she didn't give a thought to the speed with which her daughter drove, perhaps because she was used to the sight of the neighboring Aubreys driving at insane speeds along the same roads.

Rachel opened the garage door by herself and quickly started up the Bentley. She drove slowly, in first gear, waiting for the engine to be fully awake. Malachy, the gatekeeper, had plenty of time to open the gates, so slow was her approach. The windscreen was down, and she reached automatically for the goggles on the adjacent seat and put them on as she drove past the wrought-iron gates and entered the narrow private road. Then she stomped on the clutch pedal, shot the engine up to three thousand revolutions per minute, threw it in second gear, and brought up the clutch pedal, gassing mightily.

The Bentley jerked forward, and Rachel held the wheel with all her strength, waiting for the turn. In a moment the twin oaks appeared, and she jammed her left heel on the brake pedal, turning to the right as the tires screamed and the sun caught her full in the face. She kept it in second for the little hill—she didn't want to be too fast coming down it, as the depression at the end of the hill produced a chassis-rattling thud—and with this past, she gassed, threw it in third gear, bringing it up as fast as she could before she would have to slow down for the S-curve.

Smiling without thought, she glanced at the speedometer—she was up to sixty miles an hour in third gear, already faster than most cars could go in top gear—and threw it in fourth, flooring the accelerator. When the clutch engaged, the sudden speed drove her shoulders to the seat back, and she gulped a breath of fright; immediately, she took her foot off the gas pedal, and stepped on the brake. She couldn't see the coming S-curve, but she knew it was almost there, and as she braked, bringing the car back to sixty-five miles an hour, then fifty-five, she tried to clutch and brake at the same time, downshifting to third, wishing she could do it more smoothly, like her brother, knowing she had to get down to second gear before the curve.

Suddenly, Rachel felt as if a great force were bearing down upon her from behind, a wall of strength that would send the little Bentley flying off into space. There was nothing in her rearview mirror, and the car was still firmly in line approaching the curve she could not yet see; but for some reason, she had taken a fright. Clumsily, she threw the car into second gear, and braked, holding on to the wheel as the car twisted left and right and the dreadful sound of grinding gears assaulted her. The curve finally blew up in front of her, but she was now going only thirty miles an hour; it was easy to slip into the curve, her brakes dragging on the slowing wheels. At that moment, she saw a hurtling blue shape loom up in her rearview mirror in a terrible, very long second; with it, the sound of a horn, a familiar sound, as familiar as the shout of the two-seater Mercedes and the man with the shock of red hair, driving her off the road.

Rachel twisted the wheel to the right, braking powerfully. There was no way for the speeding Mercedes to pass her without her driving partially onto the grass, yet there was no thought of not getting out of his way. Sir Andrew Aubrey had already bumped the rear of the Bentley once with his sports car, and Rachel was going too slowly to hope to accelerate out of his way into the S-curve. As she braked the car to a stop, skidding on the grass, the Mercedes roared by, and she saw the baronet laugh. She turned off the engine, and caught her breath. A knot of trees was five yards in front of the car. Had Sir Andrew forced her off the road at a much faster speed, she might have been killed.

"You crazy bastard!" she said finally. "Why the hell did you have to do that?"

Before she could throw off her fear and start up the engine, she saw her family's Rolls come hurtling about the bend, with John at the wheel. The Rolls, coming from the direction of town, slammed to a halt, and John came running out to her. It was only then that she realized how frightened she was, and how the fear was only now building, instead of receding.

"Miss Rachel!" said the chauffeur. "What happened? Are you all right?"

"Yes, of course," she said.

"Did the baronet do this?"

"What?"

"Sir Andrew!" said John. "He almost drove us off the road. Crazy son-of-a—excuse me, Miss Rachel. Are you sure you're all right?"

"Of course I am."

"He's an anti-Semite, that's what I think," said John. "I'd like to see him try to run me off the road in the Bentley! I'd show him, sure I would!"

Lord Clayton, a distinguished man of almost seventy, was laboriously opening the passenger compartment of the Rolls Phantom II by himself when Rachel suddenly started up the Bentley's engine. "He didn't run me off the road, John," said Rachel. "Please don't tell my father that!"

"Sure, miss."

"I was only stopping for a moment, and I saw him come tearing by. That's all."

"I'd like to meet him on the road, Miss Rachel, that's all I'm saying. He's got a lot of nerve, trying to be against the Jews like that. Thinks he's so grand in his Mercedes. I'd run him off the road!"

"You'd better help Lord Clayton, John," said Rachel.

"What?" said John, and he turned to see the old man nearly falling out of the Rolls.

Rachel drove the Bentley off the grass and onto the road toward town. To show them she was unafraid, she threw it in second gear and gassed mightily, whipping out of sight with a roar.

But even in the heart of the curve, she was slowing down, holding the wheel as tightly as she could, her heart thumping. In the seven miles left to town, she stayed in second and third, the engine speed dipping below a thousand revolutions per minute at every curve. Only when she saw the entrance to the town—the red roof of the station house, the cracked sign swinging over the door to the inn—did she relax. As her fear finally subsided, she realized that she had no idea how to recognize her cousin. Was he blond or dark, fat or tall? How would she ever find him?

"Miss Kane?" said a voice behind her.

Because she was sitting in the stopped car in front of the station, she looked first in the rearview mirror, without turning her head. There, greatly reduced in size, but certainly adequately reproduced, was the image of her cousin from Berlin. Even in the mirror she could see that he was tall, that he was very thin, and that he was standing straighter than anyone she'd ever seen, except for the guards in front of Buckingham Palace.

Rachel whirled around in the top-down two-seater.

"I am Wilfred Cohen," he said, nodding curtly. "I am your cousin, your third cousin. Thank you for coming to the station."

"Hello," said Rachel. She tried not to gulp for air, but she did; first almost being killed, now coming face to face with *this*. "Oh," she added stupidly. "I'm wearing my goggles." And she ripped these off, so that he could see her face.

If he found her attractive there was no mark of this in his eyes. Wilfred had a scar that ran from the bridge of his nose to the cleft in his chin. One noticed this at once, though the scar was white and thin on skin that was white and drawn. His hair was cut short, like a soldier's, and it was blond and tightly curled. His eyes were green. His suit was a lightweight flannel, and loose everywhere about him, save at the shoulders. His shirt was white, and immaculate, even after the long trip by rail on this hot summer's day. His tie was carefully knotted, his shoes were shined, he carried one small suitcase of old, beautiful leather.

"That scar . . . " said Rachel, still unable to think out her words.

"It is not from Heidelberg," said Wilfred.

Rachel did not know this was a joke. Wilfred didn't laugh, nor even smile. She couldn't stop staring at him. He was beautiful—he was the most beautiful boy she had ever seen.

"I'm a painter," she said. "I like Matisse."

"I am sorry," said Wilfred Cohen, smiling faintly. "I cannot appreciate modern art."

"Oh," said Rachel. "That's all right. You have more important things to think about." She blushed as soon as she said it; there seemed to be no end to her capacity for making inappropriate remarks. Quickly, she opened her car door—so quickly that she nearly knocked it into Wilfred's legs. Rachel got out, and when she stood up next to him she could see how really tall he was: taller than her brother, taller than the chauffeur. "How did you know it was me?"

"Your father said you'd come. There aren't many cars. There've been none with young women till you."

"I'll open the boot," she said.

"Please, Miss Kane," he said, and he went to open the trunk of the Bentley, the little suitcase in his hand.

Suddenly, Rachel felt as if eyes were boring into the back of her head, and at that same moment she heard the roar of a motorcar. She turned to see Sir Andrew Aubrey roaring up to them from the other end of the village in the fast Mercedes. The baronet braked so swiftly that the rear wheels skidded and the side of his car almost swept into where Rachel stood.

"Listen to me, girl," said Sir Andrew. "If you want to drive my roads, you'd better learn not to dawdle."

"How dare you!" said Rachel, aware as she said the words that they were inadequate to her purpose.

"Don't answer back, Jew-girl," said Sir Andrew. "It's not for Jews to answer back." And the baronet released the clutch of his car and tore off with a screaming of tires.

Rachel stood stock-still. She had never been called a Jew-girl, never been insulted by anyone in her life. Though everyone knew that Sir Andrew was a rabid anti-Semite, a friend of the German ambassador, a leading light in the British Fascist party, a writer of anti-Jewish pamphlets, he had never dared address his own neighbors with anything other than a distant courtesy. She was so shocked that she didn't even realize that her cousin had slammed down the trunk lid and was standing before her.

"He can't do that," he said. "In England, one cannot say that within the law."

"No," said Rachel.

"Get in the car, please, Miss Kane," said Wilfred. "No, here. I will drive, if you please."

Rachel did as she was told. She was about to say more stupid things: that he spoke wonderful English, for example; or perhaps that the scar was really very dashing. But instead she sat down in the passenger seat and watched him as he started up the car, smoothly, effortlessly.

"This is not Germany," said Wilfred, and as he drove off after the Mercedes, his hate was so pure and powerful a force that Rachel was not afraid.

CHAPTER TWENTY-FIVE

Rachel made no protest for the first minute of driving. She was aware of having the wind knocked out of her, either by the shock of speed or the physical action of having been thrown back against the passenger seat of the Bentley. Instead of looking over the lowered windscreen, where the narrow road seemed to be rushing at them in a wild display of power, she looked at Wilfred: His left arm muscled the stickshift, moving it swiftly, but with no sense of jerking or clumsiness. The hairs on his wrist were blond, blonder than the hair on his head, and his fingers were long and elegant. There was a great deal of movement. She was aware of numerous gear changes, almost as if he were taking the measure of the gearbox; she was aware of a rush of power to the rear wheels as he gassed into a turn, steadying the slip of the tires on the twisting pavement. Everything was precise, determined, sure. There was one road to follow out of the village, and Wilfred was taking it, flying after the Mercedes they could not see.

Rachel snapped out of her reverie when they hit the first unmarked hairpin curve. She looked up over the windscreen, and the long hood of the Bentley was rushing at incredible speed—

first toward an ancient stone fence, then toward a great tree. Rachel clutched the passenger grip as her cousin braked with his toe, depressed the clutch pedal with his heel, and ran the car up two thousand revolutions per minute for a double downshift to second gear. Incredibly, the car righted its path, coming out of the curve at seventy miles an hour, back in third gear with no loss of power. But now Rachel was screaming.

"Slow down!" she said, and she said it again, and again, and she shut her eyes against the onrushing road. "There's another curve, you've got to slow down, it's coming, right now, please stop, Wilfred, please stop!"

He was not listening to her. The engine was very loud, straining in the low gears he used to whip out of the curves, the tachometer needle staying steadily on the periphery of the red—danger—zone. She screamed louder as her fear swept away any pretense of decorum. "You don't know this road! Please, you've got to slow down! Please!"

Rachel could not imagine how anyone could drive this road for the first time at such a speed. Her fear built up in the pit of her stomach like a wild, pounding second heart. She was sick with fear, and the fear was growing. "Here, it's coming, slow down, it's coming!" she screamed, but Wilfred didn't slow down until he saw the blind curve: He was listening only to the engine, and the screaming of the tires, and suddenly he could see that the road seemed to end in a thicket of trees. He double-downshifted, pumping the brake, gripping the wheel with only his right hand; even as his left shifted the car into second gear, he picked up the clutch and accelerated slightly, so that the wheels would be spinning as he found the curve—for he knew there must be a curve, a turn, something other than the end of the road—and he found it, to his left, the space between two rows of piled-up stones. Wilfred's left hand joined his right on the little wheel and he turned the car left, directly, at fifty-five miles an hour, hoping that the Bentley's transmission would not rebel at the work he was putting on second gear.

Rachel's eyes were shut tight and her hands were numb from squeezing the passenger grip. But even without sight, she could sense where they were at that moment; the left-hand turn out of nowhere—and the little two-seater twisting wildly in space. She was sure they were about to flip over and die—that only seconds separated her from death. She knew that she was supposed to be able to review the entire space of her life in this expanded moment before death, but all she could think of was that this beautiful cousin knew nothing of her; that she and he would die without his knowing her true worth.

But even these lengthy reflections couldn't fill the second. Time seemed to be reverberating about the moment, waiting for an event. They were not yet dead. There was not yet a crash. She opened her eyes, and the second was over.

The sports car was screaming all over the narrow road. It was as if the wheels couldn't coordinate their actions. They locked back and front, and the Bentley's momentum carried them sideways, leaving rubber over the road's surface. Rachel didn't know when her voice cracked and the crying began. But in the middle of her sobs, the car stopped swerving. It had been flying left and right across the little space of road, but the curve had not defeated them. They had not flipped over. The Bentley was righted again, and the engine had not been allowed to slow down. Like a nightmare that refused to stop, the car grabbed hold of the straightaway, and Wilfred floored the accelerator in third gear. Then they were in fourth, and Rachel looked once at the speedometer, as if to realize her worst fears; just as in a dream she was always forced to open her eyes, and see the monster that was confronting her.

One hundred miles an hour.

It was the fastest she'd ever gone in her life. She'd no idea the Bentley could even hit that high a speed, even on a main highway, working up to it with full acceleration. It was then that she forced herself to look once more at Wilfred, as if it were he, and not the speedometer, that was the monster in this nightmare. And in a moment his eyes, wild with hate, turned from the road to her, and he was shouting at her. She couldn't understand a word of it. Whether due to the engine noise, or perhaps that he spoke in German, she had no idea what he was saying. She continued to sob, and wait for the crash.

"I'm sorry, Miss Kane," he shouted over the engine noise.

Rachel looked up at him. All the hate was gone from his face; it was replaced by a dull fury, a terrible resignation. They had slowed down, slowed down a great deal. She could feel the fear subside in her belly. She looked at the speedometer. Seventy miles an hour.

"Please slow down," she said.

"Yes, of course, I'm stopping," he shouted. Rachel could see that they were no longer on the road to her house. They had passed the crossroads just two miles out of town, and Wilfred had taken the straightaway to the east, instead of the turnoff to the south.

"Please, please, please slow down," said Rachel, aware that she was making a fool of herself with her crying, that it was ridiculous to keep asking him to slow down when she could see that the car was finally in third gear again. She watched him push in second, heard the roar of the downshift, felt the car's acceleration rein in, as if a great hand were holding back the Bentley's snout.

"It's all right, Miss Kane," said her cousin.

"Sure, I know it is," said Rachel. "You don't have to call me that, either."

"What?" said Wilfred, and he finally brought the car to a halt at the side of the road.

"Look—wildflowers," said Rachel. But she couldn't move from her seat.

"I'm sorry," said Wilfred. "It was very wrong of me to do that, with you in the car."

They had stopped, they had really stopped. Rachel felt as if her entire body were heading for sleep; only her mind was functioning. Her limbs, her torso, all seemed to sag with a simultaneous urge.

"Put your head down, Miss Kane," said Wilfred.

"What?" she said.

The beautiful young man placed his hands on her head and gently urged it down, so that Rachel was bent at the waist, her head lowered to her knees in the little open-topped car. "Breathe," he said. "Concentrate on breathing."

"Don't call me Miss Kane," said Rachel. "My name is Rachel."

"Of course your name is Rachel," said Wilfred. "Who in our family would not know that your name is Rachel? You are our royalty, our heroine."

"Can I sit up?"

"No, not yet. You were a little faint."

"I thought we were going to die."

"Oh, no," said Wilfred. "I am sorry you felt like that, but I am very experienced."

"How old are you?"

"Nineteen."

"Seventeen."

"What?"

"I'm seventeen," said Rachel. "It went up to a hundred miles an hour. I'm all right, let me sit up."

"Please, not yet," said Wilfred. "Just one more minute. You were very white. I don't know the way to your house—you have to stay conscious, if only to guide me home."

"Why did you do it?"

"You know."

"No."

"The man in the Mercedes," said Wilfred. "I wanted to kill him."

Rachel said nothing for a moment. It was incredible, but she realized that she had even forgotten the reason for the ride. She had forgotten that Wilfred was chasing Sir Andrew.

"Not only for you," he said. "I wanted to kill him for all the times I couldn't do anything in Berlin. For all the insults."

"What would you have done?" said Rachel, raising her head. "If you had caught him, would you have demanded an apology?"

"I don't want his apology," said Wilfred with sudden force. "What good are apologies?"

"I feel better," said Rachel.

"That's good."

"How many revs was it?"

"How many what?"

"Revs. Revolutions per minute. On the tachometer."

"Do you mean at one hundred miles an hour?"

"Yes."

"I wasn't looking. There was a little power left. I would guess about thirty-five hundred. It must be supercharged. The standard Bentleys only do about ninety miles an hour at thirty-five hundred RPMs."

"You know a lot about Bentleys."

"I drove a Bentley when I was fourteen. And a Mercedes. You forget that I've had a privileged childhood too." Wilfred's face went suddenly hard. "Are you sure you're all right?"

"Yes."

"I lost the Mercedes at the crossroads, I suppose?"

"Yes, he goes the same way we're supposed to."

"Shall I turn around?"

"Can we stop for a moment longer? I could get some flowers." Without waiting for an answer, Rachel opened the car door and got out. Almost immediately she staggered, and had to hold on to a tree for support.

Wilfred vaulted over the side of the car from his seat, and took hold of her elbow. "You see?" he said, his German accent penetrating his English for the first time. "You were not ready to sit up."

"I need to walk," said Rachel. She was afraid he'd want to drive all the way to Sir Andrew's estate. "Please, just a little."

He took her arm and supported her as she walked across a green field to a patch of summer flowers. "Is this mezereon?" she said, stooping down before some purple flowers. "Smell," she said. "I love mezereon."

"I don't think it's mezereon," she said. "Mezereon's usually in the early spring. And it's got more pink to it."

"What is it then?"

"I don't know."

"It doesn't matter, they smell beautiful," said Rachel. "I'll put one in your buttonhole."

"No, please," said Wilfred. "I don't wear flowers."

"It suits you," she said.

"Thank you, Rachel, but I don't want to wear flowers."

There was enough of an edge in his voice to alarm her. Apparently she was making another bad mistake, a blunder such as her father and mother never made, an error peculiar to her impetuousness. "I only wanted to please you," she said. She dropped the flowers, and seemed on the verge of tears.

Wilfred did not pick up the bait. His edge was still there. "Let's go back to the car, shall we?" he said.

"All right."

She walked without his assistance, though he automatically held open her door and waited for her to be seated before closing it with gentle authority. He walked round the back of the car, jumped over the side into his seat, and started up the engine. "You'll direct me?"

"Of course," she said.

"I only went fast because of that man," he said. "I will drive very carefully now." She watched his beautiful hand as he put the car in reverse and turned the Bentley about in a little arc. "It was nice of you to offer me flowers," he said. "I don't want to make a big thing about this, because we are not religious in any way in my family. But there is still a feeling, that is like mourning." He hesitated, as if searching for the right words to make his point. But before he could speak again, Rachel knew why he hadn't accepted the flowers; she knew why she had once again been a fool, and she blushed.

"I'm sorry," she said. "I know that your mother passed away. It was stupid of me to offer you flowers like that."

"She didn't 'pass away.' She killed herself," said Wilfred. " 'Pass away' makes it seem natural. It was anything but natural. My mother was intelligent, charming, loving. Not just a society lady. She kept no silly salon. If she worked for charities, it wasn't to get her name in the paper. She loved history, especially Greek history. There is a lot of opportunity—excuse me, there *was* a lot of opportunity to be a good scholar in Berlin. I would be in university now. She killed herself, so we musn't say things like 'pass away.' Suicide. More than four hundred thousand Jews are still in Germany. One hundred of them commit suicide every month.

"I don't want you to think that my mother was weak. She was not. She was reasonable, and she led her life accordingly. She was only half Jewish, you know. By birth, I mean. Even when she converted—this is what she told me—even when she converted to Judaism, to please my father, her own father was not angry."

He started to drive the car forward. There was not another car in sight, nor a rider on horseback, nor a pack of children running through the fields. Rachel felt her heart beating; it seemed louder to her than the low-revving engine as Wilfred tooled along in second gear, looking from the road to his cousin.

"My mother's father, you see, he is Christian, a Christian baron. Very tall, very straight, very strict, very conservative. But he married a Jewess, my grandmother Carla, and this was a shock to his whole family. Grandmother Carla converted to Christianity, and was always very meek, always allowing all her poor Christian relations to feel that they were her betters. She died before Hitler came to power.

"My mother was nothing like her. She was a Christian, raised as a Christian, though Jewish religion claims her for a Jewess: The child's religion goes according to the mother, and Carla was a Jewess by blood. When she fell in love with my father, my conservative, strict grandfather presented no obstacles. He cared nothing for religion. Besides, his father had known Cohens in Berlin. If the Cohens were not an ancient German family, they were still rich, and powerful. The important thing was that my mother and father were in love. The important thing was that my father was a capitalist, and an enemy of communism. My Christian grandfather never used to equate communism with Judaism. Even when my mother wanted to convert to Judaism, he is said to have created no great fuss: It was important to him that the woman follow the example of her husband."

"You turn here," said Rachel, and she pointed with her finger. Wilfred turned, and his mind drifted a bit, and he smiled at Rachel as if he had been talking to a little child. "I want to hear everything," said Rachel. "We must be very close, and help each other, and you must start by telling me everything."

"Perhaps it would have been simpler if I'd just taken the flowers," said Wilfred.

"I should have thought before I offered them. I never think."

"It is a luxury to be impulsive in Berlin," said Wilfred. "My mother was impulsive, too. She could not get used to thinking out everything she must say and do beforehand. Once, before the Nürnberg Laws, she attacked a Nazi in the street. Not physically. She called him an idiot. She took his pamphlets out of his hands and threw them all over the street."

"What happened to her?"

"Nothing. The Nazi simply picked everything up. He was very meek about the whole thing. He was all by himself."

"Were you there?"

"Yes."

"What did you do?"

"I watched. I did nothing. I just stood there and watched my mother have a bit of a fit. It was incredible for me. I was about fifteen. I would have killed the Nazi if he'd lifted a finger to harm my mother. And yet there were lots of other times when I did nothing.

"I knew a girl, a very nice girl, strictly Aryan, Catholic on both sides, very pretty, very smart, and she fell in love with a Jewish boy from Munich. People knew about it, that she wanted to marry him. This must have been in thirty-four. The girl's name was Lilli. She was very sweet. A pack of Nazis got to her one day. In broad daylight. In Berlin, my enlightened city. They grabbed her. They put her against a wall as if they were arresting her for some terrible crime. They put a sign round her neck. A filthy sign. She had to wear it for eight hours. They forced her to stand against the wall for eight hours, wearing this sign, so that everyone could see."

"What sign? What did it say?"

Wilfred slowed the car even more. "This is a beautiful road," he said. "I can't remember the last time I was on such a road. I haven't even driven a car in almost a year."

"I'm sorry," said Rachel. "I suppose I shouldn't be asking you any questions at all. My father specifically forbade me to ask you questions."

"You can ask me anything," said Wilfred. "I am just a little disorganized. Up here," he added, pointing to his forehead.

"Why do you speak English so well?"

"Miss Woods."

"Who?"

"My governess was English. Miss Woods of London, England. I grew up on the same fairy tales you did, no doubt. We've always had one foot in England. My father never stops berating himself for not going there in nineteen thirty-three. Or thirty-four, or thirty-five. We just didn't know what was happening—and when we did, we didn't quite believe it. More than two-thirds of us are still there. Maybe four hundred thousand, maybe more. A lot of Jews have Gentile blood in them, and a lot of Jews have false papers. But there are at least four hundred thousand Jews left. Full Jews. German Jews.

"You know what's strange? We were all so nonreligious, so assimilated. Now every Jew in Germany is learning Hebrew. Every Jew in Germany goes to synagogue, even when it means walking through a line of Nazis. You know, it's crazy. Every Jew you speak to says that we have to get all the children out. The children must be put in schools abroad. The children must leave, they must be saved. We all agree on that. But as for the adults . . .

"Everyone, no matter what they say, everyone is waiting. No one believes it is all over. No matter what has happened so far, everyone remembers friends at school, favorite singers, favorite foods, books, plays, poems, parks—everything. Don't you feel English? I've an uncle who lost his right leg fighting for Germany in the Great War. A Jewish uncle, but he has always been fiercely German. A patriot. Did I tell you that one hundred Jews a month are committing suicide now? Not only women, of course. Men and women and children."

"What did the sign say?"

"The sign?"

"I'm sorry," said Rachel. "You said I could ask. About the pretty girl, the Catholic girl, the one who was to marry a Jew."

"Yes, they hung that sign about her neck," said Wilfred. "I was not the only Jew who saw it, of course. Or Gentile. Perhaps a thousand people walked by her that day. Even today the streets of Berlin are crowded with pedestrians. Maybe ten thousand saw it."

"What did it say?"

" 'I am a slut, I am a whore, I am a filthy half-breed who lusts after pigs and Jews. Spit on me.' " Wilfred paused, let out a little laugh. "That's what it said. You must think me a coward. I know the English are very brave."

"I'm sure you're brave," said Rachel.

"Oh, no. Not at all. I did nothing. I walked past her a hundred times. Always at the edge of the crowd. I was afraid to look her in the eyes. Perhaps if I had seen someone spit at her, I would have done something. But no one did, not while I was looking. Most everyone looked as embarrassed about it as I did, Jew and Gentile alike. But you see, no one did anything.

"That's how it goes. Bit by bit. First a street fight, where the police look the other way. Then synagogues desecrated. A rabbi stripped naked in the street. In thirty-five, all Jews lost their citizenship, but they remained 'subjects,' a nice distinction. Everyone just said that the Nazis were crazy, making a lot of noise so they could stay in power. No one could believe that they would stay. No one could imagine how far they'd go.

"After the citizenship, we lost other things, one after the other. They called Albert Einstein a cultural Bolshevik. Einstein. Even Einstein is considered impure, inferior! One after the other we lost our rights: to work, to eat, to live. Always, there were exceptions. Always, there were people who felt they would be exempt. And still! Even with my mother dead, there are friends of hers who still won't leave Germany, because the rest of the world seems uncivilized, because German culture is all they know.

"I'll tell you something, it won't be such a problem. Hitler is not about to allow them the luxury to decide for themselves whether or not they want to go. They will have to pay if they want to leave, and they will have to pay more if they want to stay. I have not come here to escape, and leave my father and friends. I am here for a purpose. Perhaps I was not brave before, but now I want you to know that I am not here as a deserter."

"I'm glad you're here," said Rachel. "I'm sure you've come for a good reason, even if it's only a vacation."

"A vacation!" said Wilfred, with real anger. But the anger faded in an instant as Rachel blushed again.

"I know you're not here for a vacation," she said hastily. "You make me nervous. You make me nervous and I keep saying the wrong things."

"It's all right."

"I've never heard so many things—I mean—I haven't been exposed to such stories. I don't really know what to say. I'm very sorry about your mother, but you don't want to hear that. I'm sorry for everything that's happening in Berlin, but I don't understand it. It's so far away from everything I've ever known. What we read and what we see are so different. When Sir Andrew called me that—he called me a Jew-girl—it was the first time in my life I've felt so threatened.

"But being called a name is nothing. Your mother is dead. I'm sorry I keep saying such stupid things. I want to help you in any way I can. I'm sure you're here for a very good reason, something brave and with a purpose."

"I am," said Wilfred. There was no ironic British twist to his line either. If his English was perfect, his delivery was as serious as any German's. He followed her directions about the curves, driving slowly, going up and down the gentle hill on the approach to the Kane estate in second gear, and swinging slowly through the space between the oak trees to enter the private road.

"There's the fountain," said Rachel, indicating it as they approached the wrought-iron gate.

"Very pretty," said Wilfred as Rachel acknowledged the gate-keeper's wave and he drove through onto the estate grounds. But he was not looking about at the fountains and statues and flowers; nor was he looking up to catch the facade of the great house. "May I stop here for a moment?" said Wilfred, turning the car off the path to the house, leaving the Bentley's snout turned into the secondary path to the servants' quarters.

"Of course," said Rachel. She watched as he turned off the

engine, and the car shivered before settling with a slight thump.

"I can tune it, if you like," said Wilfred.

"We have a man who does it."

"It needs tuning. I'd be happy to do it. For the enjoyment of it. Though this is not a vacation."

"I know."

"Look," said Wilfred. "I don't like to leave things unfinished. I was beginning to tell you something, and then I stopped. About my grandfather. I only have my mother's father—he's my only grandparent at all. He taught me to drive when I was twelve. On his estate. It was my favorite place in the world. We hunted together. We rode. We took apart his Mercedes. He taught me how to shift with my heel and brake with my toe. He taught me a lot, and, you see, he truly loved me. He loved me more than he loved my mother, who was his only daughter.

"Anyway, it was his fault. I have to say it. It's complicated, of course—it wasn't *just* him. It was the parades and the pamphlets and the violence in the streets. She couldn't shop in her favorite stores, she couldn't go to the bookshops. And she agreed with my father, as I did, that because it was so easy for us to go—because we have money in other countries, and friends and relations, it would be so very easy—we had to be the ones to remain. To show them. The Jews and the Gentiles. We are German, afer all. We all wanted to show that our presence in the country was sacred, was just. If the Cohens left, it would set a terrible precedent. More than two-thirds are still there. We didn't want to give in. I myself kept believing: Hitler is insane, it's so obvious. Someone is sure to assassinate him.

"But you see, it's not happened. Hitler is alive, he's in power, and every day there are more Jews beaten in the streets, kicked out of jobs, their stores confiscated, their bank accounts taken over by the reich. But it was only after what happened with my grandfather that my mother killed herself. I know it's part of a process, but there it was."

"What did he do?" said Rachel. She wanted to ask him so many things. How did his mother kill herself? When did he find out? Did he cry? How did his father react? Was his father dark or fair? Did Wilfred think her pretty? And she wanted to tell him things, too. To convey to him, in a coherent, intelligent manner, that she was well read, a good painter, enjoyed Mozart. Yes, she wanted to ask him that strange thing mentioned by her own

father: Were Jews not allowed to play Bach on their phono-
graphs?

"He cut us off, all of us," said Wilfred. The handsome young
man took a breath and looked about at the manicured lawns, the
quiet expanse of territory. "Not that his money meant anything.
What he did was he legally disowned my mother. The papers
had to be drawn up by a lawyer. Everything very official, in
typical Germanic fashion. The document had to be presented
to my mother by an official of the court. He was so insulting
that one of our servants—I was not home at the time—a young
man, a Christian, devoted to my family, threw him out into the
street. I mean bodily. He gave the court official a nasty bruise on
the head. All this gave us more trouble than we needed. The
servant was promptly jailed, sent to a detention camp for political renegades, and it cost my father ten thousand reichsmarks
to get the man freed.

"But that wasn't the worst of it. My grandfather never even
called to explain why he had disowned my mother, and why he
never took phone calls from us, or answered our letters. We of
course stopped calling, and eventually stopped writing. There
were other cases where fathers were afraid to talk to converted
daughters. We accepted it, though it hurt.

"But then, months later, we saw him on the street. Walking,
with his great ivory-handled cane, his great white moustaches,
standing stiff and tall, looking about the crowd as if he were a
king. I was with my mother. 'Grandfather!' I called out. 'Grandfather!' and I ran over to him. There were no Nazis about, only
a crowd of ordinary people. I don't think there was danger. He
could have shaken my hand, he could have kissed his own daughter. He himself had married a Jewish girl, though she was now
dead, and had been a Christian convert."

"He wouldn't talk to you?" said Rachel.

"At first, no. He was with no one—not a friend, not a servant.
I didn't even see his car, his chauffeur. He looked at me, and then
at my mother, and then he said to me—not to her but to me who
was his favorite: 'I am not your grandfather. You are mistaken,
young man. I have no grandchildren.' A week later my mother
killed herself. Exactly a week."

For once, Rachel said nothing. She let her cousin look out
over the hood of the car at the summer day. He seemed to be
calming down after the telling of his story. His breath, which

had become agitated, was now even and easy. The eyes, which had not teared, were not looking in, but were looking at physical objects. She wondered if the lanes and paths through the Kanes' land reminded him of his grandfather's estate. Rachel had no idea of what Germany was like—if its fields were lush and green, if it was hilly, if it was filled with flowers. The only story she could remember that had any intensity to it—something that had remained with her after the telling—had been one about diamonds.

That is not to say that her father had not often filled her with stories out of the Maccabees, or even made-up tales of her own ancestors, the great Cuhenos of Spain, who supposedly gave them the diamond that her father kept in his vault—her present when she would marry. But the story of a courageous Jewess bearing her name as she fought the Grand Inquisitor, or whomever it was she was supposed to have fought, had little meaning for her; she thought he made it up, a legend to teach a moral. But her father's diamond story made sense. Rachel knew that her father and his father had traversed the expanses of southern Africa. She knew that her father was brave, and had fought other men for control of great mineral interests. She had seen at firsthand what the power of diamonds could be; what the possibility of possessing a diamond could mean to men and women otherwise stable and content.

"Wilfred," she said, breaking the long silence against her own will. She didn't want to tell him the story, but her mouth moved, words came out. Some part of her insisted on exhibiting herself to her cousin. "Do you know the story of Shah Shujah?"

"What?" Wilfred turned to look at her. "It's very beautiful here. Perhaps we should go up to the house. You can present me to your parents."

"Do you know the story of Shah Shujah?"

"No."

"The Afghan prince?"

"I've never heard of him," said Wilfred, smiling.

"He was very courageous. I just thought of him as I was listening to you. It's the only story I know where the hero loses, but is courageous right to the end. Do you want to hear it?"

"Very much."

"He owned the Koh-i-Nor diamond. It was given to Queen Victoria. But before that, it was fought over by many men for hundreds of years. One of the men who possessed it was Shah

Shujah. He was captured in battle by Runjeet Singh, the Lion of the Punjab. Runjeet Singh wanted the diamond, but Shah Shujah would not tell him where it was. He was beaten, he was starved, he was whipped, but Shah Shujah would not give up the secret of the diamond.

"His resistance intrigued Runjeet Singh, who was himself a brave man. Eventually, he had Shah Shujah blinded. Only then, when he could no longer see the diamond, when his life was in ruins, did Shah Shujah give up the secret of the diamond's whereabouts. Runjeet Singh asked Shah Shujah why he had resisted so long. Shah Shujah answered that it would have been a sin to give in to Runjeet Singh's demands without resisting with all his might. After all, the diamond was the companion of his life, it rested for years against his heart, and it brought good luck to him wherever he traveled."

It seemed for a moment that Wilfred was looking at Rachel with newfound respect. But his face suddenly went hard. He was not looking at her at all. She did not exist for him, for his world was narrow, as are all the worlds of men of purpose.

"It's a good story," he said finally. "I like a story with a moral." Rachel looked at him, trying to screw up her face into an intelligent mask. She had no idea what the moral of the story was. She wanted him to tell it to her, but she was afraid to ask. It was her story, after all. How stupid could she be? "I like a story where the hero is obsessed. That is the only way to accomplish something, you know? Something big. You have to be obsessed."

The words tumbled out of her mouth: "Are you obsessed? What are you obsessed with?"

But he was not listening to her. He was formulating something new, devising a coherent thought from the fragments of pain he carried in his heart. He was full of hate, a mad, obsessive hate that gave him an unnatural power. But there was love, too—a love not only for the mother who was destroyed by those he hated, but a love for the world of his childhood that was taken from him by men who were mad. Like the diamond carried by Shah Shujah close to his heart, Wilfred had carried his country, his culture, his heritage, and had been unwilling to surrender them.

But his mother's death had not blinded him. It had opened his heart to new pain, but it had also opened his mind to accept the change in his world. He knew that Germany, as it had been for

him, was dead. He had given it up. There was nothing there to
hold on to, to retain. Nothing of the old Germany, of the childhood he'd shared with his grandfather, of the German folk bal-
lads he'd sung with his mother, that he cared to possess. He gave
up the diamond, he saw clearly what had to be done.

His obsession was no longer possession, but revenge.

The murder that he had carried with him in his soul was now
twisting into a finer, more definite shape. It had been there when
his father had asked him to carry a message to England. It had
been there when he had raced the Bentley after the Mercedes.
But now the fact of it was stronger. He had given up the diamond
of his childhood: His mother had killed herself. He was free to
kill, to commit an act of murder against the fabric of the society
that had brought her to that desperate act.

"Wilfred, are you all right? Maybe we should go in. You must
be exhausted. Here I am telling you silly stories when what you
probably need most is a good lunch and a long nap."

This time he heard every word she said. He looked at her
carefully: a pretty girl, with black hair, eager to please. In
Berlin, in the street, he would think her Jewish. This was Rachel,
the girl who would inherit the Cuheno diamond, the most tangible part of his family's legend. Suddenly, because murder had
been decided upon, because he was resigned to live a new, short
life, he was open to a thousand possibilities. Like the man who
discovers he has six months to live, suddenly he wanted to taste
something pleasant, something wonderful that life had to offer.

"Let's walk," he said. "It's been so long since I've walked in
such a pretty place. Do you think you could show me your
gardens?"

"Of course," said Rachel.

When they got out of the car, he took her by the arm, gently,
and they walked under the gentle summer sun, and when they
crossed a little footbridge over a tiny brook, he let go of her arm
and clasped her hand.

Rachel was seventeen, and so much, so suddenly in love that
she could barely see, she could barely breathe.

CHAPTER TWENTY-SIX

Over lunch that same day, Mrs. Kane made remarks about the great age of the solid silver cutlery, about the coat of arms on the two-hundred-year-old plates. She commented on Lord Clayton's healthy appearance, she questioned her son Robert's friend about whether he enjoyed Cambridge, she asked Robert if he had won the tennis match.

Major Kane said little. Lord Clayton had come to discuss the funding of a government-run orphanage for Jewish children in Scotland. This was not a topic for the lunch table, and Lord Clayton was obviously exhausted from his trip. The major could look forward to three days of entertaining the old man before sending him back to London with a large check and a promise of raising funds from the diamond industry. Wilfred was what interested the major. But the handsome young man, sitting with Prussian erectness to the left of his wife, seemed very distant from the conversation. Even Rachel was quiet, a rare event for her family to witness.

Because Major Kane initiated no questions about the state of the Jews in Berlin, the rest of the table was reluctant to question Wilfred. Even Mrs. Kane could sense the impropriety in directing small talk his way. In nearly two hours, she complimented him on his English and asked him if he liked to ride—and that was all.

When lunch was finished, the major was first on his feet. "Rachel, would you like to show Martin the conservatory?" Martin was Robert's Cambridge friend, short, with little blue eyes that sneaked glances, with pale brown hair that covered his forehead like a layer of flax.

"What's in the conservatory?" she started to protest.

"Rachel," said Major Kane, "kindly show Martin the conservatory. I have something to discuss with Wilfred and Robert."

Rachel started to protest again, but caught herself in time. She was resolved to better her ways, to think before speaking whenever possible. Still, it was manifestly unfair. Why should Robert have the privilege of hearing Wilfred's message before she? But Wilfred and Robert had already gotten to their feet and arranged themselves together on the major's right, almost as if they were soldiers following orders to fall into formation. Mrs. Kane took Lord Clayton's arm and walked out with him to the rose garden.

"All right, Martin," said Rachel. "I'll show you the conservatory, since they want nothing to do with us."

Wilfred and Robert followed the major to his study, lined with books on military history and maps of the South African diamond mines.

"Sit down, gentlemen," said the major.

The young men took adjacent leather armchairs, and the major sat himself at his large Louis XIV desk, much too ornate for the simple room.

"Cigar?" asked the major. They declined, and the major lit up his own, looking from Wilfred to his own son as if weighing them on a balance: "You might lend Wilfred some clothes, Robert, until he has a chance to get to London."

"It would be a pleasure," said Robert.

"I was very, very sorry to hear about the death of your mother," said the major.

"Thank you, sir," said Wilfred.

"Is your father well?"

"No, not very well," said Wilfred. "He is often short of breath. He works too hard and suffers from tension."

"Unfortunately, I don't know him very well," said the major. "I'm sorry that he's not well. I'm sure the death of your mother was a tremendous blow to him."

"Permit me, sir," said Wilfred. "I think you want to know why I've come to Sanders House."

"Simply as our guest," said Robert suddenly. "You're a cousin, and we're glad to offer you our hospitality here for as long as you like and help you in any way we can."

"Thank you," said Wilfred. "I am in a position where I am forced to be a burden, and I'm very grateful for your kindness. But I've come here for a specific reason. My father is looking for a man in England who can act as his representative in bargaining for the lives of the Jews left in Germany."

"I don't understand," said the major. "What sort of bargaining?"

"We are convinced that within a year the Germans will allow out only those Jews who pay a ransom. There is already a great deal of talk of the ingratitude of the Jews who leave, having supposedly benefited so much from their country, and not seeing fit to pay for the right to emigrate."

"But they are already forced to leave most of their assets behind," said Robert. "I always understood that to be one of the reasons why so many are still reluctant to go."

"I don't think so," said Wilfred. "You might be right. I can't think of that as a reason, but perhaps there are those who would rather keep their furniture than their lives." He paused, and looked from Robert, whose face was kind but inexperienced, to the major, whose face suggested a greater capacity to understand violence and evil. "They are going to try and kill all the Jews of Germany. Nothing else makes sense."

"I can't believe that," said Robert. "Hitler is mad, but the entire nation of Germany can't be crazy."

"That's not what I've come to discuss," said Wilfred. "If you will forgive me for being blunt. There are things that I know. At night, after the Jewish curfew, I was out on the street. I shouldn't have been there, but I have a special pass. Here, take a look at it."

Wilfred opened his wallet and took out a neatly folded piece of stationery. Robert took the paper and unfolded it. The letterhead was in German, as was the short letter below it.

"You don't read German?" said Wilfred. "This little bit of paper cost five thousand reichsmarks." (At that time, five reichsmarks was the equivalent of two American dollars.) "It's from the office of the legal adviser to the S.A. It says that I am not under any suspicion of subversive activity; and that if anyone wishes to accuse me of such activity, he must first contact the legal adviser of the S.A. That is the way that a lot of Jews get picked up. Suspicion of subversive activity. The Nazis can beat anyone to death in their offices, questioning an old rabbi, or a young child, anyone, about subversive activities.

"Anyway, I have this pass, so sometimes, when I have to get out, I go. And less than a year ago, long before my mother died, I saw an old Jewish woman sitting on the steps of the post office. Either she was drunk or mad or so hungry she didn't know what she was doing. She was of a type that the Nazis particularly want to clean up, and quickly—guilty of being both a beggar and a Jewess. Almost at the same time that I saw her, I saw two storm troopers. They were singing, they were drunk. I knew that the moment they saw the old woman, they would kill her.

"I attacked them. The woman got up from the steps and walked away, very slowly, but she walked away, into the dark. One of the S.A. was able to get out his gun. The other one I'd already knocked to the ground. I would have killed him if I could, but I'm sure I didn't. There was nothing wrong with him. It was just that he was drunk and I surprised him. But the other one hit me with his gun. I think that was an accident too. He probably wanted to fire the gun at me, but I was too close and I tried to grab it, and so it hit me here.

"It was like a knife, the edge of the barrel. It opened my face. I couldn't see, there was so much blood. I just threw myself on the storm trooper and tried to crack his skull on the pavement. As soon as I had gotten him off me, I ran. I got home. Because we are rich and we know many people, a doctor was able to treat me in the house.

"Listen, that is Germany today. Storm troopers in the streets, endless violence, madness. Hitler is not the only one who wants to kill the Jews." Wilfred stood up abruptly and walked the length of the room.

The major said, "I didn't want to interrogate you. I understand that you're under a terrific strain. There's no need to go on with this talk now. Perhaps you'd like to go to your room, rest for a while."

"No," said Wilfred. "I am here for a purpose, let me explain it to you. I will have to explain it again, perhaps, because you might find our fears difficult to believe. But this is the situation.

My father is asking you for his help. You, or perhaps Lord Cohen, who is also our kinsman here. We are not asking for money. We have money in Switzerland, we have diamonds in Geneva and Zürich, we have diamonds in England, the United States, Brazil, and Argentina. But we need you to administer the bargaining when it begins. Because there is every chance that we will be dead."

"Surely if you could get out of Germany, so could your father," said Robert.

"My father will not leave until the Jewish community is safe. He will not abandon four hundred thousand Jews because he was born into the Cohen family. And I am not out of Germany, not permanently. I am going back."

"I thought you would go to school here," said the major. "There is a good chance we could get you a place at Cambridge."

"I don't want to be impolite, sir," said Wilfred, "but I insist that you let me explain what is happening, and what we are hoping for from you."

"Please," said the major.

"We have reliable information," said Wilfred, "that within the next six months the reich will pass a new law sequestering all Jewish moneys over five thousand reichsmarks per person. That law will have little effect on most of the Jews left in Germany, because almost no Jews have been able to retain their jobs, and they have therefore exhausted most of their capital. But it will effect the great Jewish fortunes, the men who could not get their money and valuables out of the country, as we did in nineteen thirty-three. At the same time, the reich will allow no Jews out of the country unless they pay a special relocation tax. Jews who can get out now have to leave most of their money behind. Jews who want to leave in six months will have to leave all their money behind, and then pay a sum that they cannot by law possess."

"But why on earth should the Nazis do that? If they want the Jews out, why make it impossible for them to leave?" said Robert.

"They don't see it as impossible. They think the Jews of the world act in concert. They think that Rothschild of London would give his last penny to help the worst Jew in Berlin. They think of us all as one people, linked together forever," said Wilfred. "They will insist that the Jews of the world pay to free their brothers. Otherwise, we will starve to death. We will be unable to practice any profession, any trade, all our capital will be sequestered, we will be forbidden from selling our property, our clothes, we will have no income, no source of money—and we will starve unless we can get out. My father is asking you, Major, to take charge of his funds, of his diamonds, and bargain with these animals for the lives of the Jews of Germany."

"I just can't imagine any of that taking place," said Robert. "The world wouldn't stand for it. Even if the whole world starts to hate Jews, they still wouldn't stand for it. No civilized country could be silent if a country started to sell the lives of its own citizens."

"We are not citizens," said Wilfred. "May I remind you that, by law, Jews are subjects, not citizens. There is a 'J' on my identity card to prove that. And I am the grandson of a baron, and the nephew of a general."

Wilfred looked at the major, and could see that he was troubled. This satisfied the young man, because it meant that he was being believed.

"It is an enormous responsibility, sir," said Wilfred. "You will be working with the fortune of my father, and with the fortunes of other branches of the family still in Germany. It will involve intrigue, bribery, danger. You will have to meet secretly with representatives of Hitler's government. You will have to work hard, and you will be terrified of failure."

"How much?" said the major. "How much money will the bastards want?"

"We're not sure, said Wilfred. "The only figure we've been told sounds too incredible, even for the Nazi government."

"What figure did you hear?"

"One and one-half billion reichsmarks," said Wilfred.

Major Kane got to his feet. "What are you talking about? Did I hear you correctly? *Billion?* Whose figure is that? That's insane. One and a half billion reichsmarks? I suppose they want it in cash, American dollars, or pounds sterling."

"I don't know how they want it, sir," said Wilfred. "We don't know for certain that they will demand it. It's always possible that the Nazis will be toppled from power. Unlikely, but possible. I'm only telling you what my father has learned, and what he asks of you. He will not be able to negotiate with the Germans, for any moneys that he possesses they will consider their own. You will have access to our diamonds, our funds, and you will be responsible for ransoming the Jews for the best possible price.

"As for that enormous figure, it was suggested by an economist, Hermann Heisler, a long-standing Nazi, a longtime fascist and anti-Semite. He is very close to Hitler, and his study of the Jewish fortunes of England and America lead him to believe that such a sum can be raised."

"But he's crazy," said Robert. "Not even Rothschild has that kind of money."

"I don't know about Rothschild," said Wilfred. "But the money can be raised."

"What are you saying?" said Major Kane. "How much money are you intending to put at my disposal?"

"Let me ask you a question first, sir," said Wilfred. "How much of an interest do you think our family has in the diamond mines of South Africa?"

"That depends on what you mean by 'our family.'"

"Everyone who believes in the possibility of the Cuheno legend."

"Cuheno isn't a legend, Wilfred," said Major Kane. "His diamond is in this room, in a vault behind that painting."

Wilfred was distracted for a moment, as he turned to look at a small Dutch painting, perhaps of Rembrandt's school, of a girl with dark hair and dark eyes. A shudder ran through him, a premonition of how his fate might be related to what was secreted behind that painting of a girl, not unlike Rachel Kane. "What I meant to say, sir," said Wilfred, "was everyone who has an identification with Cuheno, either as a true ancestor or as a legendary figure provides us with a common bond. Robert and I are third cousins, but, speaking for myself, I feel a kinship, a relationship that is quite strong."

"Thank you," said Robert. "I feel the same way."

"We have fourth cousins, we have fifth cousins, we have cousins whose last names have no relationship to Cuheno or Cohen or Kane. What I'm asking you, sir, is how many of these people do you know in the diamond industry, and how many of them feel as I do—that we are a family, that we can act as one?"

"I'm not sure," said Major Kane. "The diamond business is not always conducive to family togetherness."

"What percentage of the South African mines does the family control, either directly or indirectly? Hazard a guess."

Major Kane thought for a bit, shrugged, then finally said, "If I take a guess as to who might identify with our family, and if I take a guess as to how much control these people actually possess, I'd have to say"—Major Kane smiled—"about ninety-five percent."

"What?" said Robert. "That's impossible! What about Cecil Rhodes? What about the big non-Jewish blocs of mine owners?"

"Ninety-five percent," repeated Major Kane. "Wilfred isn't asking for titles of ownership, he wants to know about control. There are plenty of ways to control without owning. The entire family never acted in concert, not all together, but I'm beginning to understand what your father is looking for."

"Stopping production," said Wilfred.

"You've lost me now," said Robert. "Would someone please explain what you're talking about?"

"We want to make the diamonds my family has available for ransom worth one and one-half billion reichsmarks. At their present value, they're worth more than three-quarters of a billion reichsmarks." Wilfred paused. "We have to rely on the family to double their value in the next year."

"That's impossible," said Robert. "Nothing can double in value in such a short period of time."

"Diamonds can," said Major Kane. "Are most of the stones over ten carats?"

"Of course," said Wilfred. "We never use small stones as a reserve."

"If there's war," said the major, "or even the threat of war, and production is stopped, or even slowed, in the diamond mines, the value of existing stocks of diamonds in the world rises incredibly fast. Everyone's currencies change in value, according to the fortunes of war. And I can't conceive of the Nazis asking for money to let their Jews emigrate, unless war was imminent."

"I can conceive of it," said Wilfred. "Nothing is impossible where the Nazis are concerned. What my father is asking of you, and of whatever other relatives you can enlist, is to stop production in the mines. Let the supply dwindle, and the price of diamonds soar. If war comes, diamonds will be more valuable than ever. But we have to be prepared for a ransom demand before any war also. There's no war now, and the Jews in Germany already have no rights. And every day brings us closer to catastrophe."

"I'll write to Lord Cohen today," said Major Kane.

"Perhaps I could go to Kimberley," said Robert. "Or to Amsterdam."

"Yes," said Major Kane, looking sharply at his son. "It would be good for you to take an interest in our business."

"This would be less an interest in diamonds than in helping save lives," said Robert.

Father and son had been slightly at odds, though always with marked reserve, in planning for Robert's future in the family's business. Cambridge had taken Robert a step further toward building a life out of books; business was something he would have others attend to, while he would spend his life with more important matters—scholarship, the world of the mind.

"As you see," said Major Kane, "a business as powerful as ours can become an instrument in saving lives. It need not only exist as a means to make ourselves richer." The major thought for a moment before addressing Wilfred: "I can see why your father couldn't communicate all this to me without sending you here. How does he expect to get an answer?"

"He expected you to give him your support," said Wilfred. "If you had declined, I would have gone to Lord Cohen. If he had declined, I would have returned at once to Germany. Because I'll remain here for a month, my father will assume that all is well, and that you have accepted this responsibility. By the end of a month, we might have a good idea as to whether we can stop production in the diamond mines. That's when I'll go back."

"But you don't have to go back," said Robert. "We could send a courier. Use someone from the Diplomatic Service. Nothing need even be written down."

"I must go back," said Wilfred. He turned to the major. "You understand, don't you?"

Major Kane once again seemed to be weighing the values of the two young men before him. He nodded slowly. "Yes," said the major. "Of course I understand."

Soon after, Robert escorted his cousin up the central stairwell to that section of the first floor reserved for the immediate family's bedrooms. Robert's room was adjacent to Rachel's, and he pointed it out to Wilfred with no special emphasis before leading him to his own room.

"What did my father understand?" said Robert, flopping into a wing chair and gesturing for Wilfred to do the same. "What were you talking about—honor?"

"Do you mean why I must go back?" said Wilfred. He sat down in a straight-backed chair, crossing his right leg over his left, folding his hands together. "Not honor. I don't think so. Not precisely that. More a question of right action. If you weren't very hungry, for example, and you were sitting on a bench in a park and I gave you a great slice of chocolate cake, could you eat it with a hungry child staring at you, begging for a bit of it?"

"They often tell me at school that Jews like to answer a question with a question."

"Your question wasn't simple," said Wilfred. "I thought it easier to answer with an example."

"I just don't see why you should expose yourself to danger without reason. It's a fact that the Jewish community is fleeing Germany. Particularly the children. You should be finishing school, I should think. What good does it do anybody for you to remain uneducated, just to prove a point of honor? Who does it benefit if you get pulled into jail by a couple of storm troopers?"

Robert paused, slouched low enough in his chair so that he could jam his hands into the pockets of his jacket. Wilfred smiled at the sight: His cousin looked so English, so much like an undergraduate ready to discuss abstractions into the wee hours. Robert misinterpreted the smile.

"You think I'm too silly to discuss all this, is that it?" he said, without a trace of pique.

"Not at all," said Wilfred.

"I know you must think me more than a little absurd. I've experienced little, except through books. It's a fault, I know, but correctable. Teach me. Show me where I'm wrong. There's a part of me that says you're right, you know. Without understanding fully what it is that you want to do over there, there's a part of me that insists you're right in going back, and that I'm a rotter. A coward, actually. Staying in my study, safe and warm, when kinsmen are dying. Maybe it's better—I don't know why—to do something that makes no sense."

"It makes sense."

"What does?"

"An action," said Wilfred.

"What action?"

"A rock through a window. A letter tacked to the door of an office of the S.A. A bullet, a bomb, a murder for vengeance, for right. An action. Even if it doesn't succeed. To show that the times are not right. To show that things are not what they should be. That life now isn't normal."

Wilfred got out of his chair and walked to the windows overlooking the formal gardens. In the distance, he could see Rachel walking with Robert's friend.

"I can't go to school now. I can't read a novel, I can't play tennis, I can't fall in love. Things like that take place in an easy world. If I were to fall in love—for example, if I were to fall in love with your sister—it would be wrong. It would be like a reprimand. It would be a proof that Germany no longer existed for me, that Hitler was simply a name in a newspaper, that my mother's death had nothing to do with me; that I was not responsible for anything except my own happiness, where I could find it. I have to go back to Germany, not for honor, not for anything as simple as that. I have to go back because I must. Because life is not smooth. Business is not going on as usual. I cannot simply pretend I am an English boy who wants to read history at Cambridge. No."

Wilfred had tears in his eyes, but Robert quickly averted his gaze so as not to embarrass him. He could not know that his cousin was remembering a tiny moment, a gentle interlude of seconds, when he had clasped Rachel's hand, and felt the delicious elasticity of the thick grass beneath his feet. It was not love that had thrilled him then, not the sunshine, not the clear air, not the vista of flowers and fountains. In the moment that Wilfred had clasped Rachel's hand, there had existed a hope, a distant promise: Life was possible. He might live. The world might right itself, and he might still be young, strong, eager to fall in love. In that moment, anything seemed possible, so full of the sunshine was he, so young and delicious was Rachel's scent at his side.

Wilfred turned from the window, his eyes batted clear of tears. "It's not business as usual," he said. "I must go back."

"I could feel the same way, you know," said Robert.

"Not to the same degree. You are not German. Your mother did not kill herself."

"No," said Robert. "But I could still wish to do something. To show that business was not as usual. That I understood that I must take some action."

"Yes," said Wilfred. He was looking at his cousin so intently that Robert felt impelled to ask why.

"Is there something?" he said. "Perhaps there is something you have in mind?"

"Until nineteen thirty-three I was very much the sportsman. I hunted. I fished. I played tennis. I skied. I swam." Wilfred walked up close to Robert. "I was a good shot with a rifle. A shotgun. Even a bow. But I never learned to use a pistol. I've never fired one. It's a sport I would like to learn. I would like very much to learn to shoot a pistol well."

" I can shoot," said Robert.

"Are there pistols here? At the house?"

"Yes."

"Will you teach me?"

Robert understood what was being asked of him. He was being asked to collaborate in a killing. His cousin stood very close to him, the skin of his face pulled taut with anticipation, his eyes burning with desire. Robert did not know whom Wilfred wanted to murder—Hitler, a storm trooper banging on the door of the Cohen residence in Berlin, a looter running from the ruins of a synagogue. But it did not matter. What mattered was the action, the gesture, the offer of motion in a world static with fear. Wilfred's eyes burned their message at his English cousin: Will you join me in my desire? Will you engage in my madness? Will you stand beside me to howl at the world?

"Of course I'll teach you," said Robert. "I'll be happy to teach you to shoot."

"Thank you," said Wilfred. He was exhausted from his long journey, and a shadow of a dream he'd later explore during sleep touched his consciousness like a single icy finger. Images rushed past: a diamond, a gunshot, a flash of blood.

"Are you all right?" said Robert.

"Of course," said Wilfred. But he was not. His face whitened, and the dream pressed up closer, trying to sweep him from the room, urging him to unconsciousness, where its message would reign. Robert took hold of Wilfred by his shoulders and awkwardly prevented him from falling to the floor.

"Come on, old boy," said Robert, and Wilfred straightened up a bit, remembering where he was, trying to accept the conscious present: This was the young man who would teach him to shoot a gun. "We'll get you to your room, I think. Think you can make it? Just a few steps, all right?"

Wilfred was very accommodating. He nodded his head vigorously and tried to move all on his own. But he could not defeat the layer of fog driving at him from all sides. He hadn't slept in so long, he hadn't done anything but stay awake with nervous anticipation. It had all finally caught up with him: where he was, how safe, how well fed, and this final touch—a gun that would be his, and the knowledge to use it. In the hallway outside his room, he saw Rachel, her eyes wide with terror. Wilfred was not sure if he was already asleep or if this face drifted into his mind as a last flash of consciousness.

"What's wrong? What's happened?" she seemed to be saying, and Robert's calm, Cambridge-accented voice told her that all was well, that she needn't be alarmed, that Wilfred was simply tired.

He slept for twenty-four hours. He had missed one perfect summer's day. It was late afternoon, and he pulled the bell, and a servant brought tea and biscuits, and he swam back slowly, slowly, to a full realization of where he was, where he had been, where he was going.

He was in Sanders House, in Kent. He had been in a dream, where he had held Rachel Kane in his arms and been awarded a diamond, a special diamond, cold with power, warm with the blood of martyrs. He was going to commit a murder. He was going to kill the man who planned to ransom the Jews of Germany for one and one-half billion reichsmarks, and then he was going to return to Berlin. That is what Wilfred Cohen understood, and understanding it all made him content, it made him happy.

He shaved, he bathed, he dressed in one of Robert's white linen suits. Heisler—Herr Hermann Heisler. That was the name of the man who wanted to ransom the Jews of Germany, and he was to be in London in August. Where, what date, what time of day? These things Wilfred didn't know. What thrilled him now was clarity, strength of purpose. It was early July. He had a month. He would learn to shoot a gun. He would play tennis. He would walk with Rachel in the gardens. He would eat muffins and jam. In a month he would kill Herr Heisler, and if the world did not understand that it was not business as usual, that it could not go on with its little enclaves of civilization while nazism debased human lives, that would be all right, too. It was enough that he would act. It was enough at that moment for Wilfred to know what he must do with what was left of his life, one step at a time. This was a godlike advantage, and when he came down from the first floor and saw Rachel looking up at him from her perch on a window seat, saw the anxious, childish look of long-ing in her eyes, he didn't hesitate.

"Hello," he said. "I'm glad you're here. Will you walk with me?"

CHAPTER TWENTY-SEVEN

"This car can go faster than one hundred miles an hour," said Wilfred. Rachel watched the sun dapple his face as he raised his head up from the engine of the Bentley. "The standard four-and-a-half liter Bentleys can't go over thirty-five hundred RPMs, but the supercharged can go as high as thirty-nine hundred. I wouldn't recommend it as a matter of course, but if the car's in tune and you need the power—it's there."

"I don't understand a word you're saying," said Rachel.

"It's tuned," said Wilfred. "It's ready to go is what I'm saying." He washed his hands under the tap in the garage and came out to her in the sunshine, his eyes squinting against the glare.

"I know," said Rachel. "I've brought lunch." She indicated a larger wicker picnic basket, resting under a tree.

"Where do you want to go?"

"Away from here," said Rachel. "I know a place. I want you all to myself for a few minutes." She blushed while saying it, but Wilfred didn't notice. He hung up his dirty overshirt on a peg in the garage, and reached for his jacket.

"Do you want to drive?" he said.

"Yes."

"I don't have to change?"

"No, you're fine. Just get in."

But Wilfred first adjusted his tie, then went around the front of the car, making sure that the leather straps about the hood were fastened tight. He opened the driver's door and gestured for Rachel to get in. Then he ran around the back of the car and stepped over the side, hoisting himself neatly into his seat.

Even this simple motion was admired by Rachel. There was not a thing that Wilfred did that she did not find endearing: his posture, his diction, the way he held a chair for her mother, the way he bowed his head as he shook Lord Clayton's hand. He had been at Sanders House for a week, and every minute with him made her love more pressing, her desire more urgent. He was like a wondrous figure in a fleeting dream; even when she touched his golden wrist, she felt his flesh insubstantial, impermanent. From the moment he'd arrived, he'd talked about leaving. He had come here to taunt her, a symbol of beauty, of moral perfection, of a lover that she could never have except in a dream.

Rachel started the car and threw it in reverse. "It sounds good," she said.

"Thank you."

"Were you on the firing range again this morning?"

"Yes."

"It must have been very early."

"It was. You didn't hear us, did you?"

"No. It's too far. I slept."

Rachel put the car in second and roared out through the open gates, waving to the gatekeeper. She hadn't slept. The first shots had woken her, as they had every morning for the past week. She didn't complain, of course. She knew that she was sleeping lightly, that she was in a state of heightened tension, when anything and everything could send her into a state of fury or panic. It wasn't fair to blame the distant gunshots. She could better blame Robert, who took up Wilfred's time with tennis, with endless philosophizing, and with hours on the firing range.

"No," said Wilfred. "You're letting up the clutch too quickly. That's why the car's lurching. You can only be so fast—up to the friction point. You've got to feel it."

"I can't feel it. I just let it up slowly."

"Of course you can feel it. Downshift to second. Go ahead. Jump on the clutch, then gas it up."

Rachel tried to do as told, but she gassed too little, and when she engaged second gear, the car bucked and stuttered, and finally stalled. "I'm sorry," she said, starting it up again. She pushed in first and accelerated smoothly, engaged second just as easily, then carefully drove to the shoulder of the road and stopped the car.

"I can drive pretty well, really I can. But I can't think now."

"I'm sorry if I said something to upset you."

"It would be better if you drove," said Rachel.

"As you wish," said Wilfred, jumping over the side of the Bentley. When he walked round the back of the car to the driver's side, he found her glumly staring through the low windscreen, and misinterpreted her mood. "Look, if you want to try again, that's fine too. I won't say another word. I've been giving you too much instruction the last few days, and it's not letting you think."

"Too much?" said Rachel, lifting her head. "Don't be ridiculous. I've hardly seen you." With an almost angry gesture, she clambered out of her seat, over the stick shift, and into the passenger seat. "Please drive. I don't want to anymore. We have to go past town. Just go to town, and I'll direct you from there."

It was not fair, she reasoned, almost as soon as he started the car. Everything she said and did where he was concerned came out wrong. She could not blame him. She had wanted to show him her paintings, and he had gone to her studio willingly, and listened to her chatter on about feelings and forms and twisted torsos that were a reflection of the human condition. She liked to watch him work on the Bentley, and he had allowed this, and had shown her what he was doing, though she could not understand it; and he had taken her for drives, explaining how and why she must downshift into curves, how and why she must conquer her fear of losing control of what was only a machine. She had wanted to walk for miles about the estate's gardens and parklands, and this he had agreed to willingly, taking her by the hand and allowing the time to run on without thought.

But none of this had satisfied her. Her paintings had never looked so puerile as when he had looked at them, trying to discover something pleasing to say on their behalf. Her driving had never been as clumsy as when he had sat next to her at the wheel, urging her to excel. Her conversation had never been as pallid and foolish as when she had him all to herself, walking for gentle miles under the shade of trees. She was certain that this young man could love her, would love her, if only she had the key to unlock her own trammeled self. But nothing came out right. He did not know her. He must think her a spoiled child. He would return to Berlin without ever having known how much he could have loved her, she thought.

"I have some news, Rachel," said Wilfred, speaking just loud enough to be heard over the hum of the engine. He had not spoken for ten minutes, allowing her to calm her agitation over, he supposed, her bad driving. They had passed through the tiny town and were traveling up a series of winding hills, without another car in sight. "I might be leaving sooner than I'd planned."

"Leaving?" said Rachel. "Leaving Sanders House?"

"Are we almost there?" said Wilfred. He turned his head to smile at her, and could see that she was trembling. "I'm going to have to be in London in a week."

"London?"

"Then Berlin. I thought it would be three weeks at first, but it turns out that I have to be there sooner. We can discuss it when we get to your picnic grounds."

"Why do you have to be in London in a week?"

"I've got to meet someone there."

"Who?"

"That's not important," said Wilfred. "It's not worth discussing."

"You mean it's not worth discussing with me," said Rachel.

The vehemence with which she said this unnerved him. He had important things he wanted to tell her, but none of them had to do with the man he planned to see in London—the man he planned to murder. Hermann Heisler.

Heisler—whose coming to London in August to attend a meeting of British fascists had been known to Wilfred in Berlin—was arriving early. Robert had brought home a pamphlet published by Sir Andrew Aubrey, denouncing the Jewish capitalists who "controlled" the banking industry of England and urging attendance at a fascist rally in Hyde Park, at which Heisler would speak. The stupidly written pamphlet was a crude imitation of sheets put out in Germany before the Nazis came to power, and afterward, when their absurd libels of the Jewish people became sanctioned by law. Still, the rabid nonsense distilled from *Mein Kampf* would appeal to those who sought a scapegoat to explain their failures and misfortunes in life. Hermann Heisler's economic theories had little basis in fact, but he was an imposing figure, and could excite men to a fury when he told them that they were poor because the Jews manipulated the money markets of the world to keep them that way.

But Rachel was not to have anything to do with this.

She was precisely that part of his life that was free of hate and violence before vengeance and murder would rule him. Wilfred did not see her as the desperate romantic heroine she longed to be, because he wanted to see her as something else—the girl whom he could love in a world that was sane, in a world that did not now exist.

"Take the turn to the right," said Rachel, and Wilfred drove a bit faster, the gear changes effected precisely, his determination to tell her how he felt making the lines of his face firmer, almost grim. "I thought over there," said Rachel, gesturing to a level field overlooking a vista of farmland in the valley below. Wilfred drove off the road, and turned off the engine.

For a moment, neither of them moved. Even from their seats in the car, the valley spread out before them like an advertisement for serenity.

"I would like to live on a farm," said Rachel suddenly.

"And be a painter?"

"Why not? I could milk cows, and still have time to paint."

"Have you ever milked a cow?"

"No," said Rachel. "Of course I haven't. I'm probably not even capable of *that*, if that's what you're wondering. God, I'm such an idiot. I couldn't even milk a cow if you gave me lessons." She opened her door and jumped out, and began to walk very fast away from the car. Her head was down, and she was so absorbed in her own misfortune that she didn't hear his car door slam, and didn't realize that he was chasing her until his hands gripped her shoulders from behind and turned her around with force.

Then he kissed her.

Rachel was astonished. He had kissed her fully on the mouth, and she had accepted the kiss, without returning it. She had

never been kissed before, not by a man, not like that. She thought
he found her laughable, and now, even now when he kissed her,
she was clumsy and inept, looking at him with stupid eyes, eyes
filled with tears. He kissed her again, and she still could not
respond, so hard was she crying. Wilfred kissed the corners of
her eyes, kissed her tears, held her close to his chest, and for the
first time, for the first second, she sensed a vulnerability in him.
He was pressing her close, not out of pity, but out of a need of
his own. Wilfred wanted her.

Rachel stopped her tears and stood on her toes and wrapped
her arms tightly about his lowered neck. She kissed him with shut
lips, her heart leaping for her mouth, the world shaking beneath
her feet. For once, there was no need to talk. She had been
wrong about what he thought about her, because he was holding
her in his arms, he was kissing her, he was needing her. That was
enough for her. She didn't know what she had done, why he
should care for her, but there it was. He did.

Wilfred slowly pulled his face back from hers, and he was as
beautiful as a god, and his eyes were bright with love; a love that
made sense only because it was there, before her eyes, pressed
against her heart. Without a word, he took her hand, and they
walked toward where the view of the valley was best, and they
sat down on the thick grass, their backs sharing a tree. The summer fields of a dozen farmers shimmered in the sunlight—deep
greens, shades of gold, alternating squares of arable land. He held
her hand, and she leaned her head on his shoulder, and slowly the
light of the sun moved over the earth.

"I love you," Rachel said.

"I'm going away," said Wilfred. He didn't look at her.

"Why did you kiss me?"

"Don't talk."

"Did you ever kiss another girl?"

"Please, Rachel."

"I loved you as soon as I saw you. Did you know? You
probably knew that right away. I thought you thought I was
an idiot. I'm not really. It's just that you're so smooth. You know
everything, I think, and you're so brave. How could you possibly like me?"

"I love you."

"That's impossible. There's no reason to. Do you really love me? I hope you love me. Why do you? Why do you love me?"

"Because you're good."

"Good? What is that supposed to mean? I wish you'd think I was pretty, or smart, or an artist. For seventeen, I don't think my paintings are so bad. It takes years to get a real technique. Don't you think I have any talent? I don't think it's fair to judge me on the basis of what you've seen in museums. Seventeen-year-old painters don't get their work into the museums. Did you ever think of painting? You look like a painter. I could see you as a painter, or maybe an architect. An architect, I think. Building great skyscrapers."

"I can't draw a straight line," said Wilfred.

"What will you study?"

"I don't know. There's no need to worry about that now."

"Of course there is. You sound as if you think the whole world's going to just come to an end. Why can't you love me because I'm the most beautiful woman you ever saw? Did you ever see Marlene Dietrich?"

"No. Not in person."

"What does 'good' mean? How am I good? Is it the way I kiss?"

"Rachel," said Wilfred, and he placed his palm against her cheek.

"No," she said. "Tell me. I want to know how you could love me. Why? If I'm good, if that's why you love me, tell me why I am good. Please. I want to hear."

"You have a good heart."

"What is that supposed to mean?"

"When I told you about my mother, I could sense what you felt. You have a good heart. It's not hard. It's open. You're open to the world, in a way that I'm not."

"I don't understand."

"History," said Wilfred.

"What?"

"I'd like to study history, I think. Greek history. I'd like to go to America and teach Greek history to Americans. That's what I would like. We could live together, you and I, in a little house, but very comfortable. After all, we were both spoiled, weren't we?" said Wilfred. "A little house with ten thousand books, a fireplace in every room. Do you like how it sounds? Of course, a studio for you at the top of the house. You can paint, I shall teach at the university. I understand that the American universities are not so very rigorous as ours in Germany. It shouldn't be hard to get a job."

"Do you want to marry me?" said Rachel.

"I like to imagine beautiful things," said Wilfred. "That would be beautiful."

"Yes," said Rachel. "It would be the most beautiful thing in the world."

It had become all of a sudden very cloudy. A storm cloud blew across the face of the sun, dark and threatening, and the wind, which had been gentle and pleasant, picked up a shrill sound, an uneven rhythm. Wilfred held her closer. "You would really marry me," she said. "I can almost believe you."

"You believe me completely," said Wilfred.

"Yes."

"I'm glad for this chance to be with you."

"Me too." Rachel looked at him with a suddenly frightened expression. "When do you have to go?"

"I told you, a week."

"Exactly a week?"

"Yes."

"Why? Can't you tell me whom you have to meet?"

"No."

"You're going to Berlin right afterward?"

"Yes."

"You really would marry me?"

"If I were an English boy, yes," said Wilfred. "Or if my family had left Berlin in nineteen thirty-three. Or if I were a Frenchman, or someone from Mozambique. Or if I found you in India, and I was from Peking."

"You think you might be killed, don't you?"

"I don't talk about that."

"That's what all the gunshots are about, isn't it?"

"Please, Rachel."

"You're taking a gun with you? To London? Or to Berlin? Wouldn't it be difficult to take a gun across the border to Germany?"

"I'm not taking a gun to Germany."

"Then it's to London."

"I haven't said that, have I?"

"Is it to protect you, the gun? Or is it to kill someone? Is that what you're going to do, assassinate a Nazi?" Rachel was looking at him without fear. Her eyes were wide with astonished admiration. "There was a man who killed a Pole in Paris, a man who had killed ten thousand Jews. A leader of pogroms. A Polish Jew murdered him, and the French let him go free. Nothing's going to happen to you. I'm sure of it," said Rachel. "You'll do what you have to do, and one day we'll be together again, one day soon."

Her voice caught as she finished her sentence, because at that moment she believed not a word of what she said. She would never see him again. They would be separated. One or both of them would die. It would be over, what started here today would be over and buried.

"Raindrops," said Wilfred, holding out his hand.

"Maybe it'll pass," said Rachel.

"It's important to me that you—approve of me," said Wilfred. "Robert doesn't think what I'm doing is right. He thinks it extreme. He's a philosopher, your brother, and he understands both sides of every question. Robert thinks I should break a window, or send a letter. He even said that if I refused to go home, my father would come here. That it would be one way to save my father's life. Then, all the same, he teaches me to shoot, he gives me a gun, and says that he's with me in spirit." It was beginning to rain now in earnest. "He's with me in spirit, and thinks himself a coward for not doing the same."

"I approve of you," said Rachel.

"Thank you."

"I don't understand, not everything, but I don't have to. It's enough to know that you're doing what you have to. It's right, it must be right. All the stories I ever heard about Rachel Cuheno were like that. I didn't understand, not the details, so I could never remember what she was fighting. The Inquisitor, the Italians, the Germans, the Poles—it was always confused. The Jews were being persecuted, and there was Rachel. It was right what she was doing, even if I didn't understand. What part I understood was that she was *acting*. Making a *decision*. Even when I didn't appreciate the stories, I appreciated her fighting. Even if I couldn't understand how she had to fight for being Jewish, I understood that she was making a stand.

"You're making a stand. It's their fault that your mother's

dead, and you're going to do something about it. I know. Of course I approve of you. I love you," she said.

By now, the rain was coming down heavily. They had not even had their picnic, but when they ran to the open car, they ran together; more than mutually infatuated lovers, they were conspirators. "You drive," said Wilfred, and Rachel jumped over the side of the car, the way she had seen him do it a dozen times. She started the car as he sat down beside her, and drove off smoothly in first gear, throwing it in second as they turned toward town.

"I never dreamed it would rain," said Rachel. The car top was sitting on a shelf in the garage at Sanders House.

"It's raining," said Wilfred, laughing out loud. The drops had become a steady stream and they were both drenched, head and shoulders soaked with rain as the wind and water blew over the tiny windscreen. Rachel drove faster, throwing in third, the shifting executed with automatic precision. "You did it," said Wilfred. "Kicked it up ten thousand revs before you put in third."

"Oh, quiet," said Rachel. She threw in fourth, and the rain fell faster. At the next curve, she pumped the brake for a moment, then downshifted to third, accelerated about the heart of the twist, and threw fourth back in as they tore out of the straightaway.

"Not too fast," said Wilfred. "It *is* wet."

"I love you!" she shouted over the roar of the car, over the wild weather. As they approached the town, huge puddles splashed muddy water up against the Bentley's sides; rain collected on the precious leather seats, in little pools on the floor.

"Isn't there an overhang?" said Wilfred. "Near the pub?"

"The pub!" said Rachel. "I've always wanted to go into the pub with someone like you!"

"Someone like me?" Wilfred looked at her quizzically.

"Let me drive!" she said, and she tore through the rain, squinting against the water that drove past the windscreen into her face.

In a minute more they were in town, and Rachel parked the car under the ledge jutting out from the landmark pub, so that the car was shielded from the brunt of the wild weather.

"Come on," said Rachel, and she was out of the car first, and he followed her to the inviting door of the little pub.

Inside, they were greeted by the smell of ale, and the sight of polished wood and brass. The man behind the bar looked up at Rachel in surprise; he had never seen her inside the pub before. "Miss Rachel!" he said, voicing his polite enthusiasm at seeing the heiress in his premises, but almost at once his face turned a bright red, as if he had remembered something shameful that was now about to assault them in the tiny enclosed space.

"Hello, Mr. Stewart," Rachel said, looking from the red-faced barman to the lone gentleman at the bar, a stoop-shouldered commercial traveler with his sample case at his feet.

"It's very good to see you, miss," said Mr. Stewart; and as he said this, his hands reached for a stack of pamphlets at the end of the bar and placed them out of reach, and out of sight, behind the counter.

"What's that you're doing, then?" said a deep voice from the back of the dimly lit room. "That's not what I put them there for, to be hidden away from the likes of her."

Rachel froze. She had not noticed Sir Andrew's Mercedes when she parked in front of the pub. But this was his voice. And he was already insulting her.

"Please," said the barman, looking toward the back of the room. But Rachel took a step back from the bar, a step closer to where Wilfred stood, wondering what was taking place. Sir Andrew Aubrey, a heavy-set man of forty, walked up to the bar. He glared at Rachel, glanced at Wilfred, and clapped his hand on the shoulder of the man at the bar.

"Hello, friend," said Sir Andrew. "I'd like to buy you a pint."

"Thank you, sir," said the commercial traveler.

"That's the man who insulted you," said Wilfred, recognizing Sir Andrew in the bad light.

"Let's go, Wilfred."

"No. You don't run," said Wilfred.

The barman pulled out the pint for the salesman, and looked pleadingly at Sir Andrew. "You're not a Jew, are you?" said Sir Andrew to the commercial traveler.

"Me?" laughed the salesman. "If I were a Jew, do you think I'd be wearing these old clothes, eh? If I were a Jew, I'd be selling money instead of these."

"What are you selling?" said Wilfred suddenly.

The salesman whirled about, his pint in his hand. "Sheet

music," he said, looking at Wilfred carefully. "Sheet music, young man. All the latest songs from America."

Sir Andrew was staring at Wilfred now, and Wilfred allowed this. He moved away from Rachel and smiled at the barman. "What was on the counter?"

"Excuse me, sir?"

Wilfred took out a pound note and placed it on the bar. "Show me the pamphlets," he said.

The bar-man looked at the money. "I'd rather not, sir. If you don't mind, sir."

"Show him, Stewart," said Sir Andrew. "I didn't pay you to keep those behind the counter."

"No, sir," said the barman. "Not with Miss Rachel in this room. I won't do it."

Sir Andrew walked around the bar and found the pamphlets. He picked them up, glaring at Mr. Stewart, and then slapped them down on the counter in front of Wilfred. Red letters on a black background blared forth the message: "Jew Bankers Threaten To Pull England Into War."

"What about you, sir?" said Sir Andrew. "Are you a Jew?"

"I'm a Jew," said Wilfred.

"You can't be," said Sir Andrew. "You only say that because of the Jewess."

"I'm a Jew," said Wilfred.

Suddenly, there were two more men getting up from a back-table. They were rougher men than Sir Andrew, and they had none of his sarcastic manner. "He's a foreigner, too," said Sir Andrew to one of them. "A Jew and a foreigner. And he leaves pound notes on the bar the way you would drop a penny."

"Get out of this pub," said one of the two rough men.

"We don't want your kind here," said the other. "We don't want your kind in England, and we don't want it here."

Rachel had taken hold of Wilfred's arm and was urging him to leave. Sir Andrew smiled at this. He had even white teeth and a great shock of red hair. "Take the Jew-girl and get out of here," said Sir Andrew.

"Not until you apologize," said Wilfred. "Apologize for the way you spoke to her last week, and for the way you spoke of her just now."

"He's a brave Jew," said Sir Andrew. "Very rare, I'm told." He took a step closer to Wilfred, and spoke so sharply to him that Wilfred could smell the rush of his beery breath in waves. "You don't understand, Jew. This is an English pub. We're an English town, and this is an English county, and we're in the greatest country in the world, and we don't want you. We don't want you in our banks, we don't want you in our schools, we don't want you in our pubs. We don't want you. We're going to do here what Hitler's doing in Germany, and we're going to do it fast, and we're going to do it even better. We're Englishmen, and we do everything better. Are you leaving, Jew? I'm telling you we don't want your kind in our pub."

"If you're not going to apologize to the young lady," said Wilfred, "I'm going to have to kill you."

"Well, I'm very sorry to hear that, young man," said Sir Andrew, and he turned his head slightly to the side, as if to address one of his men, and then, almost like an afterthought, drew back his right fist and slammed it into Wilfred's face. The young man moved back with the blow, but it connected anyway, and he was knocked away from Rachel and staggered against the side of the bar.

"Stop it," said the barman. "I'll have none of this, not a second longer."

Wilfred was stopped for a moment by Rachel rushing to his side, but he sidestepped her, not even pausing for a gentlemanly explanation. The image of his grandfather ran through his mind: the baron who had taught him to hunt, to fish, to box; and who had disowned him because he was a Jew. In a second, four years of aimless hate welled up in his frame, like a cataclysmic resource. Wilfred kept his chin down and flailed out at the English baronet, hitting him with force in the belly, in the neck, in the chin. He did not hear Rachel scream, nor did he sense the two men trying to hold back his wild arms. Wilfred had only one purpose, and it was very clear: He wanted to punch the baronet's face to pulp. But hardly had he knocked Sir Andrew to the ground than the two men managed to take hold of his arms. Wilfred was riding a wave of fury, but these men were strong, and they held him fast.

Sir Andrew got to his feet, rubbing his chin, spitting up blood. He looked at Wilfred as Rachel screamed to let him go.

"Leave him alone!" she was screaming. "Leave him alone and we'll get out of here!"

But it was the work of a second for Sir Andrew to hit the

young man in the belly, and the work of another second to hit him in the groin, and the work of another second to hit him in the face, and finally Rachel threw herself at the baronet, and Sir Andrew had to divert his attention long enough to throw Rachel against the bar, knocking the wind out of her.

"I'll shoot you, sir," said the barman. "I swear I'll shoot if you don't just get out of here right now." Mr. Stewart was holding a shotgun leveled at Sir Andrew. No one was more angry than the barman.

Sir Andrew motioned to his men to drop Wilfred, and they let him fall to the ground.

"Just get out," said the barman, and Sir Andrew and his men left, and Rachel sank to her knees next to where Wilfred had fallen.

The commercial traveler put his money on the bar. "I'm sorry, miss, but I've got to be going," he said. "I think he's coming to already. Don't worry about it." He followed the others out into the rain.

Mr. Stewart came out from behind the bar with a drop of whiskey. "Here you go, young man," he said, and tried to pour it into Wilfred's gaping mouth. But Wilfred had no need of it; he had opened his eyes, and now he tried to get to his feet. The barman helped him. "I just want to tell you, Miss Rachel," said Mr. Stewart, "and you, too, sir, I just want to tell you that he's a bad man. He's a bad man, and I have nothing against the Kane family, and I certainly have nothing against any Jews. And I'm as English as anybody."

"So am I," said Rachel. She helped Wilfred to stand. "I'm as English as anybody, but I'm also a Jew." And she grabbed the pamphlets on the counter and threw them into the unlit fireplace. "See that you burn those, Mr. Stewart," she said.

"Yes, Miss Rachel," said the barman. "But where are you going? Don't you want a drink? He can't drive like that."

"I'm driving," she said. "Listen—thanks for what you did."

"It's still raining," said Mr. Stewart. He felt that if he could convince her to stay, he would have calmed her fury.

"I like the rain," said Rachel, still furious. Wilfred was standing erect now, and he nodded at Mr. Stewart as he followed Rachel out the door.

The rain was letting up a bit, but the roads were slick and dangerous about the curves. Rachel drove home at high speed, unafraid of the rain, the curves, the dozens of gearshifts. She had seen Wilfred held back by two men, while a third man punched him. It was the closest she had come to Germany. She understood little compared to Wilfred, who had lived under the Nazis for four years; but she understood more than she had before. Rachel understood how he could want to murder, and she understood, too, how easy it was for him to be killed.

CHAPTER TWENTY-EIGHT

"Are you looking for Wilfred?" said Robert Kane to his sister Rachel. She had come up to him on the clay tennis court six days after the rain. The clay was back to its summer best today: slightly damp, smoothly swept, sending up puffs of red dust when Robert kicked out his right leg as he served ball after ball from behind the baseline.

"I was looking for you," said Rachel.

She was in a serious mood, a mood that threatened to degenerate into bad humor; but so was he. Robert glanced at her, picked up a red-stained white ball from a bucket on the court, and bounced it on the baseline, once, twice, three times. Then he straightened up, holding the ball in his left hand. "All right," he said, his attention turned to the net.

On the other side of the court a ten-year-old boy, one of the servants' children, stood impatiently, waiting to chase the ball and add it to the two dozen he'd already collected for Robert. Robert threw the ball high overhead, turning his eyes to follow its path under the bright sun, at the same time bringing his racket back, over his right shoulder; the secret was to match the rhythm of the toss with the rhythm of the racket swing. He waited the extra half-second, when the ball seemed to rest in midair, waiting for the crack of the racket. Then Robert swung with all his force, and he heard the ball slam off the tight-strung catgut, and the sound was enough; he didn't have to look to know that the serve was fine, that it would crash into the clay, and twist and dance like a dervish.

"Just two more, please," he said, without looking at his sister. Quickly, he served two more balls, both of them landing low and fast and in the corner of the opposite service boxes. But the demonstration of his skill seemed to give him no pleasure. He put down his racket and picked up a towel, and turned to his sister. "Sorry to keep you waiting," he said.

"I have a favor to ask," said Rachel.

They had begun to walk toward the broad patio behind the tennis courts, where geraniums, Mrs. Kane's favorite flower, were exhibited in a score of stone urns. Robert stopped walking and placed his right hand, not unkindly, on his sister's wrist. "Look here, Rachel. I don't want him to go either."

"I didn't say I didn't want him to go," she said.

She said this almost angrily, and Robert didn't quite know what to make of her reaction. He mopped his face and walked her over to a table on the patio, under a blue and white awning, and said nothing more till a servant brought them chilled lemonade in a crystal pitcher, and glasses that were cold to the touch. Rachel drank, and Robert said: "I know that you're in love with him."

"*He has to go,*" she said, almost as if she were trying to convince herself.

"I'm surprised to hear you say that," her brother said. His slow delivery threatened the beginning of a speech on philosophical choices. Rachel put up her hands to prevent this.

"*He has to go,*" she said again. "If you know him at all, then you have to know that."

"He loves you," said Robert.

"You think so?"

"Yes." He was about to add something, but Rachel interrupted.

"Is he a good shot?" she said.

"With a pistol, you mean?"

"Of course with a pistol. I'm sure if he's hunted, he's a fine shot with a rifle. He's good at everything he does. It's just that he's had so little practice with a pistol."

"He's all right," said Robert. "Not very good, to be honest. He could be. He could use more time, more practice. There's only so much you can learn in a matter of weeks."

"But he can shoot?"

"Of course he can shoot," said Robert. "He could shoot a pigeon from ten paces, but he might miss at twenty paces. He might miss if the bird was taking off."

"What about a man at ten paces?"

"He would hit a man with no trouble. But to kill a man with a single shot of a revolver is not always so easy. A man is not a stationary target. A guarded man is not so easy to get close to." Robert put down his lemonade. "If I loved a girl, she could influence me. You could speak to him, Rachel."

"I am not going to spoil it, Robert."

"You'd rather see him dead?"

"Stop talking nonsense!" Rachel got out of her seat and walked across the patio, her back to her brother. Robert let her pace. The major knew nothing of Wilfred's plans; Robert and Rachel knew only a little more than nothing: just that tomorrow Wilfred was leaving for London, and sometime after that would attempt to use his gun, and his anger, to assassinate someone. Who, and how, and whether or not he had plans to get away with the crime, were unknown to brother and sister.

Major Kane was in Amsterdam at the moment, conferring with family members about the possibility of stopping production in the diamond mines. When Rachel and Wilfred had returned from their drive in the rain six days before, they had convinced Robert to do nothing about the quarrel between Wilfred and Sir Andrew; Wilfred had more important things on his mind than developing a legal battle between two neighboring squires. Robert wondered what would happen when the major returned to Sanders House. By then Wilfred could be an assassin, or he could be dead.

Rachel turned on her heel and walked back very quickly to where her brother sat drinking his lemonade. "I can't ask him not to go," she said. "Please don't ever ask me again to do that." She sat down across from her brother, sighing wearily. "I need your help," she said.

"Tell me what you want."

"Do you know how to get into Father's vault?"

"What vault?"

"The tiny vault in the study." She was referring to the wall-safe, hidden behind the tiny Dutch painting of a black-haired girl.

"What do you want with that?"

"I'm just asking you for a favor, Robert. If you don't want to do it, just tell me."

"I know how to get into the vault," said Robert.

"Will you open it for me then? Will you open it for me tonight?"

Robert looked at her closely, trying to fathom her motives. Somehow this had to be connected with Wilfred, the young man she was in love with, the cousin who had become like a brother to him in his short stay. But all that was concealed in the tiny safe behind the painting were a tiny leatherbound book containing precise information about the family's holdings in various banks; their father's will; and one diamond. Cash and other valuables—high-quality diamonds between ten and fifty carats—were hidden in a safe secreted in an unused children's nursery on the second floor of Sanders House. The only tangible object of interest in the wall safe in the study was the single diamond that was not in the larger safe.

The Cuheno diamond.

"Why do you want me to open the safe?" he had begun to say, but he shrugged almost at once. "What do you want with the diamond?" he said. They both knew to which diamond he referred.

"It's mine," said Rachel.

"It's yours when you marry," said Robert.

"I know that," said Rachel. "Don't you think I know that?"

Even in the southern part of England, at that time of the summer it wasn't fully dark until past eleven o'clock. Unlike many similar great houses in the Kent countryside, the servants of Sanders House lived in a separate building, hundreds of yards from the main house. Only two maids lived in the basement quarters of the main house, sharing a five-room suite that had twenty-five years before been home to twenty-three servants.

These maids were old, and retired early, but both were light sleepers. They remembered the nights when Rachel woke up, delirious with some childhood fever, looking for someone to hold her hand and place a damp cloth on her forehead. Mrs. Kane never liked to hold vigil on those nights. The maids didn't mind nearly as much.

At eleven-thirty, most of the house was dark. A light burned in Rachel's bedroom where she sat on a chaise longue, in her white silk robe, trying to read Bernard Berenson. Every creak in the old wood of the house, every gust of wind through the gables, every chirp and howl and tweet of every night bird sent a rush of terror through her thin frame. What was she doing? Was it possible that she was to say goodbye to Wilfred tomorrow morning, to willingly send him off to what might prove to be his death?

A light also burned in the large library. It was cold enough for a fire in the marble fireplace, and the glow from this illuminated two-thirds of the great space with a flickering charm. A corner of the room was brightly lit: Here a massive chessboard, bearing hand-carved ivory chessmen, beat back the light of a huge bronze lamp. Wilfred and Robert had been playing the same game for more than three hours. At ten, Rachel had entered the room, kissed her brother's cheek, then touched Wilfred's hand, and, without a word, smiled goodnight at the two of them. At eleven-thirty, Robert dismissed the butler.

"I would like to have you as a brother-in-law," said Robert.

"And I you," said Wilfred. He looked down at the chessboard, taking a sip of Cognac from his enormous snifter, then raised his eyes to smile at Robert. "We're neither of us playing very well tonight."

"How long will you be in London?"

"As long as it takes."

"As long as what takes?" said Robert. "I'm sorry. You don't have to be specific. But I'm an accomplice. I'm providing you with a weapon."

"No, you're not," said Wilfred. "If ever they discover where it's from, I shall say that I stole it. But we mustn't talk about it."

"How do you think I'll feel? What am I supposed to do if you're killed? What then? How am I going to avenge you?"

"You will know," said Wilfred. "You will do what you have

to. What you're driven to do, as a man, as a Jew, as a member of our family."

"The diamond mines will close, you will see," said Robert. "That will be accomplished. Why can't that be your action?"

"We've gone through this," said Wilfred.

Robert sighed, picked up his queen, and moved it diagonally across the board. "Check," said Robert.

"Robert, it's not your move."

"Oh," said Robert, and he laughed out loud, and Wilfred joined him, and finally the two of them knocked over the remaining pieces, their laughter verging on tears. "You'd better get to sleep," said Robert. "You'll need your rest for tomorrow."

"You're not coming up to bed?"

"No," said Robert. He had begun to arrange the chesspieces on the board. "I'm afraid I'm not very sleepy."

"Well, goodnight. Sorry if I wasn't much good tonight."

"Neither was I," said Robert.

Wilfred clapped his hand on Robert's forearm. "Thank you. Thank you for everything," he said.

Robert wanted to thank him too: for friendship, for learning, for making him aware of a world of action; for creating a consciousness of family, of history. His German cousin had taught him that he was a Jew, and that he had better learn to accept the responsibilities that came with this knowledge. Robert wanted to tell him more: that if need be, he *would* avenge him. But he didn't know in what way vengeance would lie. He had none of Wilfred's clear sense of purpose. Robert would have liked to right wrongs, to take action against injustice, but he had not discovered how. He watched Wilfred leave the library, and then remembered, with a guilty pang, what he had conspired with Rachel to do.

Carefully, he finished setting up the chessboard, listening to the silence in the large house. His mother had gone to her room after dinner, bored with her son and her austerely serious relation. He wondered if Rachel was listening, if even now she was starting at the sound of Wilfred's tread on the staircase. Robert drained the Cognac in his snifter; then he drained what was left of Wilfred's. He turned off the light of the brass lamp, and walked out of the library, now lit only by the dying fire.

Robert was one of those people who are completely at ease

in the dark—it held no terrors for him. What he couldn't see, others couldn't see. If others were lurking behind corners, he would be as frightening to them as they would be to him. Besides, this was his house. With his eyes shut, he could cross the expanse of every room, of every hallway on every floor. He found the dark pleasant, tranquilizing. He took little steps in the pitch-black hallways, his shoes passing silently over the Persian rugs, creating a noisy creaking over the sudden stretches of exposed polished-wood floors.

Soon, his eyes grew accustomed to the dark; he could see the polished brass doorknob of the door to the study quite clearly. Robert turned this doorknob and opened the door. He walked directly up to the painting of the black-haired girl and lifted it off its hook over the wallsafe. Then he turned on a single light on his father's desk, sufficient to see the combination lock. In thirty seconds he had opened the safe, extracted a black leather box, closed the safe, and replaced the little painting. Robert turned off the light on his father's desk and walked quickly through the darkness out of the study and into the main hall to find the stairs.

When he got to Rachel's room, he saw the puddle of light on the floor outside her door. She had asked him not to knock, and so he simply opened the door, and found her sitting rigidly on the chaise longue, her unread art book in her lap.

"You've got it," she whispered.

"Yes." Robert approached, his smile very thin, very confused. He didn't quite understand to what ceremony he was contributing his aid. Robert placed the box in her hands.

"No," she said, holding the box out to him. "I want you to put it on."

"I'm not your father," he said, almost crossly. "I'm sorry," he said a moment later. "Of course I'll put it on."

Robert took the box from her and opened it. No matter how many times he saw the old diamond, it thrilled him. Looking into the sixty carats of flawless white stone, he saw first the Rachel of Palestine—the "land of Israel," as she liked to call it—a woman whom his own father had actually met. And beyond this he saw more: centuries of his family in many lands, and always this stone; always this diamond reserved for a heroine bearing his sister's name.

Robert took the diamond out of its box and suspended it from its golden chain. He placed it about Rachel's neck. Then he kissed her cheek, and he took her hands and squeezed them. "I want you to be happy," he said, and then he left her room, closing the door behind him.

Rachel sat for a while longer, resting the diamond in her hands, letting her flesh warm the stone. Then she turned off her light. Barefoot, in her white robe, the diamond about her neck and next to her skin, she walked past her brother's room, past her mother's room, past her father's room, past four unused bedrooms before finding, in the dark, the door to Wilfred's room. There was no light coming from under his door, but when she pushed it open she saw his blond hair, saw his white face immediately, clearly, in the gentle moonlight. He was awake, he saw her at once. She closed the door behind her.

Wilfred did not look surprised.

She was like a vision that he had created out of air. He desired her, and he knew that she desired him. They were nineteen and seventeen. Their bodies had a mutual attraction that was more than youth, more than love; they were light and dark, they were sober and heady, they were the substance of fantasy. When they were apart and they closed their eyes, they saw each other more clearly than if they were together at noontime, under the light of day.

The vision moved closer to him.

"Wilfred," she said, and the vision sat on the edge of his bed, and she smelled of jasmine perfume, and he felt the silk of her robe rub his astonished face. "Wilfred," she said again, and she drove her face to his, and in a moment she was kissing him, and then he was kissing her, he was kissing a vision, he was kissing a shade of night.

She removed her robe, and underneath was a bride's nightgown, white silk and lace, and her young body glowed through the fabric, her hair was smooth to his touch, and he kissed her without thinking, he kissed her neck, he kissed her eyes, he held her dear face in his hands and he kissed her lips, and she moved her body fully into the bed, under the covers, and he was suddenly warm, warm with a power that he had never before known. It was like a radiant heat, rising from the center of his body to every extremity. It was like a fever, running in spasms to his brain. Wilfred wanted her so badly that he felt as if flames were tearing at his heart, burning up his groin.

"No," he said, finally remembering that this was not his wife, and that this was not something he wished her to remember when he was dead. "Rachel, please. Darling, just lie here."

But she was looking at him with a passion that could not be contained. He did not know what she knew: that they would marry. That they would marry right then and there, at that moment, sanctioned by a stone that was holier to her family than any formal ceremony of words.

Rachel didn't argue, she didn't explain. She placed her hand over his lips and she kissed his forehead until he closed his eyes in a pain that was wonderful, in an expectation that was as strong as the nature of life. "I'm your wife," she said. "Tonight, I'm your wife." In the gentle light, he saw the flash of something brilliant. The girl whom he loved was removing her gown; and as he stared in wonder at her white flesh, he saw the stone that was her birthright, hanging over her heart. Wilfred knew what it was, of course. When she came to him, when she brought her chest against his, the diamond was pressed between them, flawless and hard and ancient. "I'm your wife," she said again, and he knew that the stone married them, he knew that their contract of marriage lay between them, he knew that this was their wedding night.

"You're my life," he said. Wilfred loved her so much at that moment that he felt as if his soul, already prepared to fly out of his body, were pressing through his skin, trying to merge directly into her soul. He felt the heat in his body grow yet more intense, but now he was riding it, letting it expand, for it was a fire that was shared, a fire that was as urgent as their love, as beautiful as the gift of life. Wilfred wished that time would stop. He loved the smooth touch of her flat belly, the delicate shape of her calves, the tender throbbing in her temples. He loved to kiss the small of her back, the nipples of her breasts, the inside of her thighs: She was his wife, and this was her body, and he had never imagined anything so blissfully perfect, so awesome, as her flesh. But there was an urgency that he could not deny. Their bodies longed to merge. Her hands reached out for his knees, his thighs, his buttocks, the back of his neck. Rachel wanted to pull him against her, into her; she wanted them to be one. Slowly, he entered her, and if it was clumsy, and if there was pain, their love overshadowed everything. All they were aware of was having become one, of having shared passion, of having married their love.

They fell asleep in each other's arms.

At dawn, they woke, and within an hour she drove him to town, to catch the early train to London. He didn't tell her that he would write, he didn't promise that he would call, he didn't say that he'd be back. And she didn't ask him to do any of those things.

"You're my wife," he said.

"You're my husband," she said.

She said it again as the train pulled out of the station. Once more she touched her fingertips to her lips, to feel where he had kissed her. She was empty. He was gone. Her only direction was to the Bentley, fifty feet away, sitting silently in the deserted town square. But it was a direction without purpose. She imagined his face, framed by the seatback in the first-class compartment. He was alone, and his light eyes were open wide with dreaming. It was easier for him; his direction was rooted in meaning. His fate was coupled with the exigencies of noble action. Rachel walked to the Bentley, got in, and started the engine.

Like a present from heaven, she heard an answering roar.

Sir Andrew Aubrey's Mercedes, tearing across the square from the South. He passed her so quickly that for a second she didn't know if he had seen her. At this hour, he must have driven in from London; he must have been driving through a good part of the night. But he was headed toward home, his home, and hers. It was very simple, what she must do now. He had driven her off the road, he had struck her husband, he had insulted her family and her people.

It was a direction with purpose. She would not be afraid, and she would not be clumsy, because Wilfred had taught her the ways of this machine, because Wilfred had taught her not to be afraid. The supercharged Bentley screamed up to three thousand revs in first gear before she threw it in second, effortlessly, without thought. She hit seventy miles an hour in third gear, and there was more room to go before she had to throw in fourth, and already she had caught the Mercedes, already she was a car length from the slower car.

Rachel leaned on the horn, and she saw Sir Andrew start in his seat. He couldn't turn about, so suddenly busy was he. There she was, a girl, a Jewess, on his roads, rushing him along, and he had nothing to do but slam on the accelerator. The Mercedes twisted slowly up from seventy miles an hour to eighty, but it was a slow, humiliating acceleration; the Bentley remained on its tail, Rachel leaning on her horn, bringing the snout of her car to within inches of Sir Andrew's.

"Bitch," said Sir Andrew, his head clearing from the fury rising in his brain. He had not slept all night; he had been driving for hours, from darkness to light. But he knew these roads, he knew them at faster speeds than that girl could dream of; and he was sure of his car. He downshifted to third, anticipating the curve that was a mile out of town.

Rachel drove the Bentley's shout into the Mercedes' rear. Even at eighty miles an hour, over the rush of the wind and the roar of the engine, she could hear the tap of metal against metal, could hear the tinkle of his taillights as she crushed them to dust. But then she, too, had to slow down. The curve came up so suddenly, and she had so much to think about—the shift down to third, the braking, the tail of the Mercedes, the wrenching wheel—that for a moment a bubble of fear blew up in her throat.

But she revolted against this fear. This man was her enemy, and the enemy of her people.

The shift to third was smooth, and she stepped on the gas pedal in the heart of the curve and blew the horn as she came up again on the Mercedes' rear end, tapping it again. She wanted to drive him off the road. She hated this man, and she wanted to drive him off the road and into a pile of stones, and she wanted his car to burst into flames.

Sir Andrew was rattled by the horn, astonished by her nerve. But even as the Bentley touched his tail, he was coming out of the curve with new power. She had caught him in fourth gear, and he had to get down there, to third, to second, to have the acceleration to leave her standing still, looking at him vanish at a speed faster than she could comprehend. He wanted to drive the Jewess into a frenzy of failure. He would have her going so fast in the straightaway that she would forget the coming of the big S-curve and take the last hairpin in fourth gear, much too fast, and go off the side of the road, careening stupidly through space, falling to her death in a crash of fire and steel.

The Mercedes was fast, in excellent tune, and he took it up in each gear to the limit of its power.

But Rachel, at the wheel of the Bentley, was faster.

He got away for a moment, for two moments, and Rachel allowed this: She was not so crazed that she couldn't think at all. Hate can clear the mind as well as it can befuddle it. She remembered how Wilfred, hating Sir Andrew for what he had done, did nothing to antagonize him in the week before he was to go to London. He had more important things to prepare for; he did not wish to have an incident that would hamper his plans. But Rachel had no other plans than these. She had simply to rattle Sir Andrew, terrify him, wreak vengeance on him; she had only to murder him, and that would be enough.

She let him move away, into the straightaway. She would let him think he was losing her. The Bentley was ready to move, and it needed the room to accelerate. He would not be rattled if all she did was stay glued to his tail. She had to come at him, blowing like a demon from hell, come at him so fast, from so far, that he would see her car in his rearview mirror like an irresistible force, something unearthly, beyond his ken. He would simply freeze. He would see her moving, he would see her pulling, he would see her flying, and he would simply run off the road in despair.

The Mercedes hit sixty-five in third gear and was picking up speed in the straightaway. The Bentley stayed in second, at forty miles an hour, the gearbox shaking, the engine whining at the fast revolutions. When he had gotten a dozen car lengths ahead of her, she slammed the gas pedal to the floor.

The tires screamed, and she kept it in second to the low gear's limit. In third, her eyes squinting at the dust and the wind, she was already catching him, her acceleration a thing of raw power, of perfect control. She was driving on nerve that was the product of hate; and the hate was powerful, for it was connected to Wilfred, and everything that he had taught her. The hate was powerful because it was the obverse of her desire for her husband, it was the opposite end of her love.

Rachel put the car in fourth gear and kept her foot firmly on the gas pedal as the engine whined to its highest power. She could not see the terrible frustration in Sir Andrew's face as he kept his gas pedal pressed to the floorboards, as he watched his speedometer register a slowly creeping acceleration to the very highest speed he could go: to eighty, to eighty-five, to eighty-seven miles

an hour. And just as Rachel had hoped, his frustration was rattling to fear; his fear to terror, as she blew up in his rearview
mirror, as he saw that even at his great speed she was gaining on
him, effortlessly, with such vehemence that it seemed as if she
would not tap him this time but drive directly through him,
smash his beautiful car to a thousand pieces.

Rachel understood at last that she was about to crash.

The speedometer was jumping up in little spurts of astonish-
ment: ninety-six, ninety-nine, one hundred and one. She was a
second away from colliding, and she remembered what Wilfred
had told her about such a smash: "You simply look at it as a
vector problem." Oh, that was funny.

The second was long, very long, and she imagined his face.
He was telling her how to subtract the other car's forward speed
from her forward speed. One hundred miles an hour minus
eighty-five miles an hour—why, that was only fifteen miles an
hour! Like hitting a brick wall at fifteen.

But this problem solving did not take up all her concentration.
Far from it. The moment was longer than that, because she was
certain she was about to die. There was something comforting
about that, something that made her resigned: This was a kind
of relaxation. All the twists in her mind that had ever prevented
her from clear thinking were suddenly gone, relaxed away. She
could see clearly, perfectly. Had her father been there, next to
her in the car, she could have turned to him, answered his questions, been alert and bright and free of mistakes.

The car was hurtling forward deliciously, slowly, twisting
through space at almost two miles a minute. Wilfred might die
that afternoon, that evening. She might die that moment. Sir
Andrew might die at once, and horribly. He was not relaxed, she
knew that. He was suffering for his sins. The car hummed beneath her hands. She understood that she wanted to kill Sir
Andrew, and she wanted this so much that she was willing, she
was glad, she was eager to die for this desire.

In the barest slice of a moment, the moment before the Bentley
was to have plowed apart the back of the Mercedes, she realized
her error.

No, she did not want to die.

No, she did not want to kill this man.

She understood that there were other directions than these: to be with Wilfred, or die with someone he despised. There were other goals. Other worthy things she could achieve.

Rachel turned her wheel slightly to the left. She touched her toe lightly, tentatively, to the brake pedal. Sir Andrew, in the Mercedes, turned his wheel violently to the right. He slammed his foot on the brake, and his wheels locked, and his car skidded on the dry straightaway. Rachel passed him at thirty-seven hundred revs, at one hundred miles an hour, and she let up at once on the gas pedal, she lightly pumped the brake, she waited for the engine to slow enough for the downshift to third. In her rearview mirror, she saw Sir Andrew's car hurtling sideways, skidding all over the road, but still on all four wheels, all tires screaming, as the baronet turned his useless steering wheel away from the trees, away from the stones.

Soon he was out of sight. She braked, she downshifted, her heart was sinking. Everything was clear. She didn't want to kill him. She didn't want to kill anyone. She wanted only to help. She wanted only to be good. She was crying by the time she had stopped the forward motion of her car, and still she had heard no crash.

Rachel turned her car around, and she drove fast, but without maniacal speed, back to where she had passed Sir Andrew. He was alive. The Mercedes was off the road, but it had not crashed. Sir Andrew was standing in front of the car, looking at her as she braked, and stopped the Bentley in front of him.

"You could have killed me," he said.

"I decided against it," said Rachel. Let him think that her tears were a product of the wind.

He never again called her an insulting name.

CHAPTER TWENTY-NINE

Later that day, Wilfred Cohen shot and killed Hermann Heisler, noted Nazi economist and mastermind of the plan to extort one and one half billion reichsmarks as a ransom for the Jews of Germany, while Heisler was addressing a mob of British Fascists in Hyde Park. Nazi bodyguards shot Wilfred in the face and chest, and he died before he arrived at the hospital.

Late in 1938, the Nazi government sent another economist, a banker by the name of Hjalmar Schacht, to London to ransom 150,000 German Jews (although there were still almost 400,000 left) for the figure of one and one half billion reichsmarks, or ten thousand reichsmarks a Jewish head. The Kanes, and other Jews, proceeded to negotiate these demands, trying to insure the safety of as many of the Jews of Germany as was possible. But before the ransom could be effected, Hitler took over Czechoslovakia. By the time the Nazis were marching into Poland, the Kanes had stopped negotiating with Schacht, and had begun to use individual sums, and individual diamonds, to ransom small groups of Jews.

Rachel Kane, at the age of nineteen, and against her parents' wishes, went to Vienna and Berlin to try and ransom out, or at least support, members of her family and any other Jews she could possibly aid. Robert, meanwhile, came down from Cambridge and enlisted in the Royal Air Force.

Major Kane lost contact with Rachel in the spring of 1942. Through English intelligence, he was able to ascertain that she had been taken to Theresienstadt, the Bohemian garrison town turned into an enforced Jewish ghetto. Theresienstadt was not a concentration camp, but people did starve to death there, people were shot to death there, people did succumb to the squalid conditions and die of a hundred contagious diseases. Of the 140,000 Jews sent there, 87,000 were sent to extermination camps in Eastern Europe.

When the Allies liberated Theresienstadt at the end of war, they discovered 17,000 survivors. Rachel Kane was not among them. Wilfred's father, Sigmund Cohen, who had been a major in the German Army during the First World War, had been in Theresienstadt since 1942. He survived. He told Rachel's father and brother, his kinsmen, that he had last seen her in early 1944. It was reported that she'd been sent to Auschwitz. But even with the great resources of the Kane family, no witness of the sufferings of Auschwitz could be found who remembered Rachel Kane. Major Kane consulted rabbis in England, questioning whether he should sit *shivah*, go into mourning, for his daughter, whose death had not yet been proven. He was advised to sit *shivah*—if not for her, then for all the others, the six million Jews who died in the camps, the millions of Jews and Gentiles who died outside of them.

In 1947, Robert Kane, leaving the air force with the rank of major, married a German Jewish refugee. She came from a small family, though her father's family had lived in Berlin for five generations. He had been a surgeon, her mother had been a concert pianist, her brother had been a director of plays. She was the only survivor. She did not want to live in England: It was not Europe, but it was still not far enough away. All during her last year in the concentration camp, she had dreamed of America, of starting a new life there. Robert allowed her this dream. They moved to New York a week after their marriage, and he entered the family's business: diamonds. They had a son in 1949, and another in 1952. In 1955, when his wife was five months pregnant with their third child, his father, by then an old man, called him from London.

"We've found a witness," said Major Kane. "Rachel didn't die in Auschwitz. In a yard, a railroad siding. She was one of five thousand people waiting to be piled into the cattle cars. A soldier pushed an old woman. Rachel spit in his face, and the soldier shot her dead. She didn't die in Auschwitz. She never went to Auschwitz, but she's dead, Rachel is dead."

Mrs. Kane gave birth in August of 1955. It was a girl. She was given the name Rachel. The baby's grandfather flew to New York to see her. He brought with him the Cuheno diamond. It was Rachel's legacy. It was to be hers on the day she married.

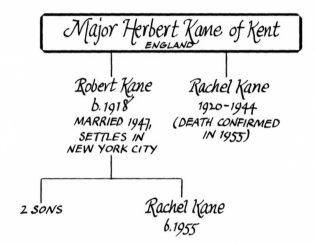

Major Herbert Kane of Kent
ENGLAND

Robert Kane
b. 1918
MARRIED 1947,
SETTLES IN
NEW YORK CITY

Rachel Kane
1920-1944
(DEATH CONFIRMED
IN 1955)

2 SONS

Rachel Kane
b. 1955

EPILOGUE: JUNE 1979

Rachel regained consciousness.

She had fainted, and now she was awake. She had not been unconscious long—perhaps thirty seconds, perhaps less. The diamond remained firmly in her grip. Only her father was in the room. He asked her if she was all right, and she looked at him, her beautiful eyes dull. "Yes," she said. "I think so."

"Brides aren't supposed to faint," said her father. "Not in this century."

"No," said Rachel, speaking automatically. She had no idea what he was referring to. Her vision was still a bit blurry, and she was trying to concentrate on something, some thought that had sped through her brain and that she wished she could remember.

"Shall I put that on for you?"

"What?"

"The diamond," said her father. "It's on a chain. Let me put it on for you."

Rachel looked down at the diamond in her hands. Of course. The diamond. Her father had just given her the diamond, and she

had been so excited it had made her faint. Rachel stood up, surprised to feel how wobbly her legs were.

"You're okay?" her father asked.

"Of course."

"Let me," he said, but for a moment Rachel wouldn't relax her
hold on the stone.

"I'll give it back," said her father.

He took it from her, and slowly, half in a trance, she turned
her back to him. Rachel stared straight ahead, her eyes riveted
on a small Dutch portrait of a black-haired girl. She felt her
father place the golden chain about her neck, and then she
reached out again for the diamond, hanging against her heart.

"It's almost time," said her father.

"Yes," said Rachel.

"You'll be fine," said her father. He was not referring to her
marriage—Rachel understood that, and, for a moment, was surprised that her father could share the strange current of feeling
running through her.

"You think so?" she said.

"Yes," said her father. "That's the tradition, isn't it?"

"I don't know if I'll live up to it."

"Of course you will."

Rachel looked at her father, and felt once again the thrill of
centuries in the diamond against her heart. She smiled. It was
time. She was to be married. She was in love, and the day was
bright, and the world was wide, and there were long years to be
lived. Not exact knowledge, not a true voice, but an echo, a
glimmering, reached her through the shadows of time. She was
Rachel. She was not alone, an accidental entity, but one of a
line of family, of tradition. What she would have to do, she
would one day know. And what she would do, she would do
well.

"Thank you, Daddy," she said.

They joined the wedding party, the old diamond brilliant under
the summer sun.

978-0-595-12820-4
0-595-12820-3